Virgilante

Janet Christian

Plum Creek Publishing
P. O. Box 29
Lockhart, TX 78644
www.PlumCreekPublishing.com

This is a work of fiction. All of the characters and incidents are products of the author's imagination or are used fictitiously. Any resemblance to actual events or people is purely coincidental, unless the person begged to be included, in which case they're stuck with the author's depiction.

ISBN-13: 978-0692611203
ISBN-10: 0692611207

(1)

Virgil Harris hadn't planned to be a vigilante, it just sort of happened. And he was actually more a justice-deliverer or karma-balancer, but those didn't have the elegant ring of *vigilante*. Regardless of what he called it, in the last three years he'd become quite adept at it. Tonight would be no exception.

Virgil sipped his morning tea as he sat at his breakfast table. He stared out the window at the sky, streaked with ever-changing patterns of crimson, orange, and yellow. Even the dirt of his barren backyard seemed to glow.

Red sky in the morning… he thought.

Perhaps any storm would hold off until later. He wanted to spend time during the day working in his antique rose garden, the dominant feature in his front yard. Since his retirement from the Post Office, he loved spending his Monday with his roses instead of delivering mail.

It wouldn't even matter if a spring Texas thunderstorm took the power out tonight. His vigilante abilities didn't need electricity, just great power and concentration from within. His mother called it his *gift of symbols*. She said her family had been gifted that way for as long as anyone could remember. Like many of his ancestors, he could use objects and symbols, and his own mind, to alter the course of events. He could make things happen the way he wanted them to.

In his youth, he'd been more interested in learning chemistry and biology, but his mother had insisted on teaching him about their gift. She showed him how to create a motif, a symbolic representation of a real thing. She also taught him Goidelic, the old tongue they used for their chants. Even his grandmother didn't know how long his family had spoken it. It'd been passed down for generations.

When Virgil balked at the hours of study, his mother put her hands on her hips and scowled. "Some day you'll thank me, and eventually you'll teach your own children."

"Yes, Mama." He'd returned to his notes.

As his skills grew, he started calling his ability *theurgy*, the Egyptian word for those who could do what he did. There was nothing remotely Egyptian about his British-Celtic roots, but he liked the mystical-sounding word better than *gift of symbols*.

He actually didn't often do motifs when he was young, because they took a lot of work and preparation. But during his teens, he occasionally used his theurgical abilities in small ways that didn't require a complicated motif: a nudge toward a better test grade, a blind eye turned by a teacher on a poorly written essay, even getting out of gym on a regular basis because the wood shop teacher had a "sudden need" for his help in the shop.

And with each motif, he never broke his mother's number one lesson, her most-repeated words seared into his memory. "Vee, never let others make you mad enough to use your gift to play God. Always let the heavens sort things out."

"But what if someone deserves it?" he'd asked.

"It isn't worth it. The price is too high."

"What price?" Virgil was confused.

"It's called *karmic backlash*. It's the universe balancing the scales by sending you some of what you've done to others."

"Don't all motifs do something to others?" he'd asked.

"Yes, Vee, they do." His mother had smiled and nodded. "But when you direct one purposely toward another person with the intention to harm them, be prepared for some of that to come back on you."

"But what if it's on accident? What if I just mess up a motif?"

"There's a difference. If you mess up a motif by accident the result is called *diffusion*. You get caught up in the motif and some of the results of the motif also happen to you."

"How's that different from karmic backlash?"

"Only real difference is intention. One was on purpose and the other an accident. But the price you pay can be high in both cases."

"How bad can they be?"

Virgil's mother closed her eyes and shook her head. "Promise me, Vee, that you'll never do motifs to hurt others. Or even to manipulate them to your will. And always take time so you don't make mistakes."

"Does it always happen, Mama? Every time?"

"Just promise, Vee."

"Okay. I promise."

The tea kettle's piercing whistle snapped Virgil back to the present. He'd forgotten about relighting the burner after making his first cup. He crossed from the table, turned off the burner, and poured the boiling water over a raspberry-hibiscus tea bag.

The dark red tea bleeding from the bag reminded him again of the terrible ordeal that had nearly taken his mother's life. He missed her so much. Or he missed who his mother had been.

That incident had led to the first time he'd broken his promise to his mother. To his first attempt at creating a motif to push someone's karma a specific direction. To get even, or at least cause payback. It was the least he could do for his mother.

But she'd been right. He'd paid a price.

He watched his tea steep and thought about that motif. He'd realized after his mother's house was burgled three years ago that the universe, or whatever was out there, sometimes took too long to sort things out.

When the burglars had discovered her hiding in a closet, they beat her nearly to death. His mother, left almost a vegetable, lingered in the absurdly named Oak Creek Estates in Pemberton Heights long-term care facility while the police dragged their feet looking for suspects. All the police managed to determine was that two men were involved. After months of frustration, and the police seemingly uninterested in tracking down her attackers, something in Virgil had snapped, and he took matters into his own hands.

Creating a proper motif was hindered by the fact that no one knew what the burglars looked like. He wasn't sure what to use as the *focalis*, the focal item representing the person or situation, so he improvised.

First, he used a black marker to draw generic male figures on squares of heavy cardboard. He then took broken pieces of his mother's favorite china, which he hoped included traces of body oils from the men who'd broken them, and glued them onto the figures.

He'd squeezed his china men into a dollhouse he'd found at Goodwill and set the whole thing on fire. As he watched it burn, he repeated the Goidelic chant he'd written, then doused the fire, removed the singed male figures, wound them up in chain, and locked them in an old metal ammo box. Then he waited.

He knew it had worked a week later when he saw the headline in the paper:

> Two burglars apprehended trying
> to escape from burning house

The house had been abandoned for years. It was their main hideout and where they'd stored stolen goods until they could fence them.

He'd followed every detail of their case, even sitting in the audience at their trial. They were ultimately found guilty of five burglaries, including his mother's. Battery, with intent to kill, was added to the charges. They each got the maximum of twenty years in prison.

Virgil was pleased, although he'd have preferred an even harsher sentence. He'd attended the sentencing and watched as the men were escorted from the courtroom in chains. He almost wished he'd thrown that locked metal box into the lake, or let the dollhouse burn completely down, but killing the two men would have dishonored his mother. He didn't want to break his promise that severely.

Virgil visited Pearl Harris the next day. As usual, she stared blankly at the ceiling, appearing unaware of his presence. He knew she probably couldn't understand anything he said, but he told her about his motif and its results anyway.

"I hope you understand, Mama," he'd said as he stroked her pale cheek. It was as soft as silk and looked as delicate as tissue paper. "I know I promised, but I still hope you can accept what I did. I love you and miss you."

Her response was too mumbled to understand. He couldn't tell if she was approving or disapproving. He decided not to dwell too much on what she'd tried to say to him. What was done was done.

He barely remembered driving home. The loss of his vibrant, loving mother raised a lump in his throat and burned his eyes. He knew in his heart he'd done right with the motif, but he'd likely never know how his mother felt.

When he turned into his driveway, three bright red cardinals, his mother's favorite bird, were singing from the front porch rail. He smiled. Maybe his mother had found a way to tell him everything was all right.

His karmic backlash had come a week later. A roast in his oven had burned and caught fire. He'd had to repaint the kitchen and replace the stove. *I'll think long and hard before I do another motif directed against a person.*

But it was only a few months before Virgil did his next one. He learned about a man who ran a dog-fighting ring in the woods just outside of Lichen, Texas, where Virgil lived. It was bad enough the man was using the maiming and killing of dogs for profit and entertainment. He was also stealing area pets to use as bait animals during training. Virgil had a soft spot for helpless victims, be they children or animals, so he'd created a motif using a small stuffed dog as the focalis. It seemed the perfect focal point in this case.

He'd carefully crafted the motif and wording of the chant, to ensure no harm came to the animals used in the fights. The end result was that the man was beaten almost senseless by a couple of fight attendees who believed the fights were rigged, that the man was drugging the dog he wanted to lose. The animals were all rescued by a group that specialized in rehabilitating fighting dogs.

The story had been all over the news in San Antonio and Austin, the two cities closest to Lichen. Of course, neither the viewers nor reporters had any idea Virgil had a hand in the man's fate. But Virgil knew. He even toyed with the idea of advertising his vigilante services to those in distress. He'd chuckled to himself about getting a T-shirt made that said `Virgilante`, but he realized he might as well wear a shirt emblazoned with `I'm Guilty, Arrest Me`.

Instead, he made it his private mission in life, and the nickname remained an untold joke. He watched and listened, then took action when he personally deemed it appropriate. Or vital.

Since Lichen was a small town of less than 12,000 souls, there weren't that many instances needing his assistance, but he was pleased that his actions had helped in a number of situations. He believed his town was all the better as a result. Friendlier. Safer. More peaceful.

He'd even come to accept the karmic backlash that inevitably happened, such as breaking several ribs when he'd tripped on the sidewalk a few days after the dog-fighting motif.

In the two and a half years that had passed since the dog-fighting motif, Virgil had done almost a dozen others. Some were simple and focused on the town itself, such as the one to prevent the organizers of their annual Mesquite Bean Festival from relocating to the next town down the road, whose council had been heavily lobbying for the change. Others were directed at a specific individual, some requiring harsh motifs, others getting a karmic boot in the right direction.

Virgil's personal commitment remained the same: when someone did a very bad thing, and heaven, or nature, or the universe, or whatever "it" was, took a long time to balance things out, Virgil stepped in to help hurry things along. Joe Walters was his next project.

(2)

There is no need to go to India or anywhere else to find peace. You will find that deep place of silence right in your room, your garden, or even your bathtub.
~Elisabeth Kubler-Ross

Joe also lived in Lichen. He was a moderately successful local CPA with a small office a couple of blocks from the courthouse square. Even many of his clients called him arrogant and egotistical. They also said he knew how to skirt the tax laws carefully enough that their questionable deductions never got audited.

His tax return ethics weren't the problem.

He drove a flashy red Porsche, which wouldn't have been a problem either, except he drove it with reckless disregard at extreme speeds through the quiet neighborhoods of the otherwise bucolic town. Joe regularly caused problems when driving, including sideswiping cars parked on the streets, blowing his horn in the middle of the night for the hell of it, and, occasionally, hitting a child or family pet. Sometimes he was arrested and fined, and a couple of times he'd hired a lawyer to get charges dropped or dismissed, but more often than not he wasn't caught, although everyone knew it was him. They just couldn't prove it.

A month ago, Joe'd flown down Myrtle Street while texting on his phone. He never noticed he'd run over and killed one of Miss Ellington's beloved cats. It was the third cat he'd hit in as many weeks. Two had been Miss Ellington's. The other had belonged to six-year-old Katy Williams, three blocks east.

Miss Ellington was eighty-three, and all she had left in the world were a dozen cats she'd rescued, now down by two. The first of the three Joe ran over was Miss Ellington's Biggles. No one saw it happen, but there was no doubt around town it'd been Joe. Miss Ellington's neighbor had found the cat's body in the street and buried it in the woman's backyard.

It was only a week later when Joe ran over Fluffles. The Williams family had gotten Fluffles the year Katy turned one. The little girl had never known a single day without her beloved white Persian cat. Fluffles' death devastated the child. She cried non-stop for a week. Her mom even kept her home from school.

The third week, now one month ago, Joe killed Petunia, another of Miss Ellington's cats. The elderly woman was standing in her front yard when Joe shot by, never even slowing when he ran over Petunia with both his front and rear right tires.

Miss Ellington immediately collapsed on the grass in a heap of blue hair and matching polyester housecoat. Her next door neighbor, who'd been washing his car, dropped his tire scrubber and hurried over, while another neighbor dashed from across the street, calling 911 as he ran.

The paramedics determined Miss Ellington had fainted from trauma and agitation, and thankfully had not had a heart attack, although she'd broken her hip and would be laid up for weeks, if she got back on her feet at all.

While the paramedics bundled Miss Ellington into the ambulance, the two neighbors quietly retrieved Petunia and buried her next to Biggles in the elderly woman's backyard. A handful of graves from other cats and dogs that had departed over the years filled the rest of that corner of the yard.

Cat deaths had only been Joe's most recent transgression. Four years earlier he'd hit Betsy O'Hara, a three-year-old toddler who'd darted into the street while chasing a ball. Betsy flew over twenty feet and landed on the sidewalk. She suffered so many broken bones she spent six weeks in a full body cast.

It was the worst tragedy that had happened in Lichen in several years and was the talk of the town for weeks. Everyone expected that this time Joe would finally go to jail, but that was sadly not the case.

Joe hired a lawyer from nearby San Antonio whose billboard ads expounded his ability to get anyone out of traffic accident charges. In court, the lawyer wove a series of random events into a tapestry of tragedy that ensnared his poor, innocent client.

By the time the lawyer was finished, the position of the sun coming and going from behind clouds, blowing leaves creating a confusing swirl in the air, Betsy's long hair blowing across her field of vision, the mesmerizing pattern of the spinning ball, and even a stray dog that happened by at that exact moment, were all at fault, but not Joe.

The nonplussed jury couldn't help but rule the case an accident, and Betsy's family did not pursue it any further. They'd instead chosen to move to San Antonio, forty miles up the highway from Lichen.

Joe gloated all over town that it was really *that brat's fault*. It hadn't occurred to Virgil at the time to do a motif on Joe, since Virgil's mother was still vibrant and healthy, and Virgil had yet to entertain thoughts about motifs against people, to sort things out himself instead of waiting for God to do it.

But the times had changed Virgil's mind. The demise of the three cats wasn't as serious an infraction as Betsy's injury, but this time Virgil was ready for action. He didn't witness any of the recent incidents with cats, but that didn't matter. He overheard every detail of all three the day after the third cat death. He'd been sitting in his favorite booth in Harold's Cafe, where he ate breakfast almost every morning.

Harold's served the best food in town, but Virgil also viewed it as Vigilante Central Headquarters. If someone in town did something bad, it was all over the cafe the next morning. Virgil didn't have to find people's transgressions on his own. All he had to do was eat breakfast at Harold's.

It'd taken a month to prepare for Joe's motif. First, Virgil had to select the right focalis. He decided on a scale-model car that matched Joe's beloved Porsche.

Next, he had to collect something that belonged to Joe. Virgil lucked out on the personal item two weeks earlier, when he found himself eating lunch at the table beside Joe at the local Mexican restaurant.

Virgil ate slowly so Joe would finish first, then Virgil scurried to Joe's table to retrieve the man's dirty napkin before it was cleared. The model car, hard-won on eBay, had been delivered Friday.

A distant car horn snapped Virgil back to the present. He'd been so lost in thought he'd let his tea grow cold. He poured it down the drain and rinsed the cup.

Tonight's the night. In the meantime, I'll keep myself occupied with more mundane things.

Virgil spent the rest of the cool Monday morning puttering in his lush rose garden, which occupied over half of his front yard. He often spent hours clipping off dead blooms on his twenty-three antique rose bushes. Over the years he'd amassed an impressive collection of the old varieties. This morning he was focused on his six-foot Alba rose, originally associated with the Middle Ages and castle gardens.

His grandmother had traced their family line to northern England. Although she hadn't made it as far as the Middle Ages—

the trail had petered out around 1400, the heart of the Inquisition—no one doubted their heritage continued much farther back in that same region.

The Inquisition had been a time when their family's ability with the Goidelic language and manipulating events would have been a death sentence if discovered. Many people, probably including family members, had gone into hiding or changed their names. Some day Virgil hoped to discover his family's *missing link* and continue the path of research his grandmother had begun.

Virgil paused in his clipping of the Alba's pale pink blossoms and leaned forward to inhale their heady fragrance. He smiled, remembering how much his mother loved his roses.

He glanced at the Apothecary Rose in the back corner of his garden. It was his first one, a gift from his mother that had fired his passion for the heirloom plants. He'd learned it was one of the oldest in the world, dating from 7th century ancient Persia. The Apothecary Rose remained his most prized specimen. There were currently only three dark pink blooms on the small bush.

I'll take her a nice mixed bouquet next time I visit.

Maybe seeing and smelling a bouquet of his Albas mixed with white Floribunda, and scarlet Portland would awaken some awareness in her damaged mind. He'd even sacrifice a couple of his Apothecary Rose's blooms for her.

Would the roses reach a part of her damaged mind? I'd love to see my real mother again, if only briefly.

Virgil shook his head to clear away the pain rising like hot tar and moved to the next rose bush. He continued his trimming, keeping his mind a smooth, blank slate, for the next two hours.

A short toot from a car horn snapped Virgil's attention to the street. It was Marshall, his UPS driver, pulling up to the curb in his brown van.

"Good morning, Mr. Harris," Marshall called as he clambered down the steps of the van, a bread-loaf sized box in his left hand.

"Another delivery?" Virgil set his clippers at the base of the Polyantha, snicking his hand on a large thorn. "Ouch!"

"Everything okay?" Marshall stopped at the edge of the rose garden.

"I'm fine." Virgil wove delicately through the rose bushes toward the grey-haired delivery man.

The brown cardboard box Marshall handed over was clearly stamped with CORROSIVE in large, red letters.

"You sure get some strange stuff." Marshall held out the electronic pad for Virgil's signature.

"I've developed a lot of odd hobbies since I retired." Virgil shrugged, then laughed. "Guess I can't decide what I want to be when I grow up."

Marshall guffawed. "Have any of us? Well, you have a great day." He turned to go, then paused, "Your roses are gorgeous. Mom would be jealous. Maybe I'll plant one in her yard one of these days. Or mine. I like them, too."

Virgil watched the brown van disappear around the corner, wondering what would happen if Marshall left or transferred. In spite of occasional jokes about packages, it seemed he'd always been reliable and discreet. Some of Virgil's packages would definitely raise eyebrows and uncomfortable questions if word got around. It hadn't yet, as far as he could tell.

(3)

It is the nature of ambition to make men liars and cheats,
to hide the truth in their breasts, and show, like jugglers,
another thing in their mouths. ~Sallust (86 BC-34 BC)

Virgil shook his head then glanced at the box in his hand. It was from Flexel Scientific, specialists in chemicals and lab supplies. Virgil rarely needed the type of product they sold, but when he did, he did, so he always replenished the supply in his chancel as soon as any quantity got low.

Chancel. Virgil stared across his small field of roses, remembering the first time he'd heard that word. It was a couple of weeks after the most complicated motif he'd ever done resulted in his winning the blue ribbon in his Junior High's science fair.

His project was to show how plants grew with and without fertilizer. But as the days passed, both plants continued to look exactly alike. A week before the actual fair, he'd resorted to a motif. He'd individually crushed leaves from each plant, then mixed the oily residue from one plant's leaves with a sickly yellow-brown watercolor paint. The other he'd mixed with a rich green.

He'd drawn sketches of both plants on cardboard, then painted the leaves on one with the yellow and the other with the green. He placed the two paintings behind their respective real plants, and placed small standing mirrors opposite, so the plants would be exposed to the paintings from both sides.

Four days later, one plant yellowed and wilted. The other filled out with healthy green leaves. He'd won a blue ribbon at the fair and received praise from the science teacher.

Virgil was confused and disappointed by his mother's reaction.

His mother smiled. "Vee, I'm proud of how well your motif worked. But you must be mindful of how you use your gift. It is not to be used to cheat at life or to beat others. Hard work, dedication, and honesty are still the most important part of learning."

"But I won the blue ribbon!" His lips pushed into a pout. "My motif was great. I spent so much time on it. And it worked so fast."

"Yes, your motif was clearly wonderful. But it was the motif that won the ribbon, not you."

That last sentence had been a slap of insight that caused him to drop his head and blink back tears.

His mother reached out and stroked his light brown hair. "Vee, there are many ways to use your gift. You don't need it to get ahead in life. You have all the ability you need on your own. I'm so very proud of you."

"Thanks, Mama. I won't let you down again."

Both plants he'd entered in the science fair had withered and died five days later. He'd shoved them deep into his mother's compost bin. He shouldn't have underestimated her attentiveness.

"Vee, where are your plants? They aren't in your room."

Virgil hung his head and whispered. "They died. I threw them away." He looked up to see his mother nodding slowly.

"Of course," his mother said.

"Why, Mama? What did I do wrong?"

"Where did you do your motif?"

"On the desk in my room."

His mother nodded again. "Our gift of symbols is powerful but also capricious. You need a chancel for your motifs."

"What's a...chancel?" Virgil's tongue stumbled over the unfamiliar word.

"It's a sacred space around an altar that no one else enters. It becomes a part of you and your energy."

"But you don't have a chancel."

"Ah, but I do. I've had one since long before you were born." Virgil's mother smiled. "I don't use it much these past couple of years. I let my life plod along as it will and don't worry about motifs."

"I've never seen it."

"And that's how it is supposed to be. No one must ever see or enter your chancel. You must remember that."

"Your storage room!" Virgil's eyes flashed wide.

"Yes, the room off the hall."

"You always keep it locked." Virgil laughed. "You said it's filled with boxes of old tax papers and family records, and that you didn't want me messing them up."

His mother nodded. "When you grow up and have your own place, you must create your own chancel."

And he had. His mother would be proud of it, although he knew she wouldn't have entered his chancel even if she were still physically capable.

A dog's bark caused Virgil to jump. How long had he been standing in his garden, the UPS box still in his gloved hand? He retrieved the clippers, setting the box in their place, this time minding the thorns, and returned to his trimming. He finished the roses then pulled weeds, leaving the milkweed for the butterflies. When he finally stood, a sharp spasm crossed his lower back. That pain, and the heat of the late morning, told him it was time to stop. He gathered his things and went inside.

Virgil rested for nearly an hour in the cool comfort of his living room. He shifted on the heavily-padded sofa, seeking a better position to ease his aching back.

Living room. Quite the misnomer in his case. He no longer did much living there. His mother's ordeal and confinement in the long-term care facility, *permanent-term* in her case, meant she'd never again join him on Sundays for lunch, or evenings for tea and conversation. So the large room with the soft grey walls had become his place to study and think. And to plan his next motif.

His latest needed no more planning. All was ready and waiting for dark. Tension coiled through Virgil's stomach. He always felt that way the day of a motif unless he kept himself fully occupied: restless and anxious.

Enough sitting around.

Virgil headed to his wood shop in what had once been half of his oversized, two-car garage. A single nightlight glowed in the otherwise dark space.

Virgil flipped every switch, turning on five banks of overhead halogen lights. He crossed the room and raised the single-wide garage door, filling the room with even more light, as well as warm air. A large fan in one corner of the room helped to compensate for the afternoon heat.

The rhythmic sound of the belt sander along the left end of a bench he was making calmed Virgil's nerves and eased his mind. The heavy oak bench was for the Penningtons, who lived over off Mayview Circle. It would sit grandly in their large, formal foyer and would rarely, if ever, actually function as a place for someone to sit. But it was still a beautiful ornament and testament to his skill.

Virgil had worked for the Post Office until his mother's beating; woodworking was only a casual hobby back then. He'd retired two months after his mother was settled into Oak Creek.

It's nothing but a nursing home. Why can't they just say so?

Still, Virgil knew he was lucky to have such a fine facility in his small town, and that it hadn't been necessary to move his mother to San Antonio.

Virgil had taken advantage of his post-retirement free time to turn woodworking into a new full-time career. He now made a comfortable income from his beautiful, hand-crafted pieces of furniture. This latest commission would bring him four figures.

Good money and no co-workers. Just the way I like it.

Virgil smiled and switched to sanding the right end of the bench.

"Heya, Virg, how's things doin'?"

Virgil looked up to see Stan Walker yelling at him over the noise of the sander. Virgil shut down the belt sander. "Not bad, Stan. What's up?"

Stan was the closest person Virgil had to a friend. Stan was a likable fellow, although a little dim-witted and clumsy. Still, Virgil enjoyed his company enough to invite him fishing now and then.

"Wanted to tell ya they're restocking Lake Segler next week." Stan grinned. "'Bout time for some more fishing?" Stan had the eager, innocent look of a small child, even though he was in his mid twenties. Virgil knew he had the intellect to match.

"Sounds good." Virgil patted Stan on the shoulder, causing the younger man to briefly bounce on his toes. "The new stock of bass and trout will be too small, of course, but there's probably still some good size ones in there worth casting for."

"Let's catch us some of them bigguns!" Stan nodded enthusiastically, and grinned from ear to ear. His childlike brown eyes filled most of the space above a nose too small for his face. The nose also now bent left as a result of a street beating by a bully who thought Stan's simple phrases and mannerisms had been a conscious attempt to belittle the bully's Neanderthal looks.

"Let's keep an eye on the weather. Maybe we can go next week." Virgil gestured at the bench. "I'll have delivered this to the Penningtons by then."

"Can I help with sumthin? Ya know I'm always glad to help."

Last time Virgil had let Stan help he'd almost cut off three fingers with the band saw. But Stan was like a lonely puppy, hard to ignore and impossible to be mean to.

"Tell you what. I'll be ready to stain soon. You can help me then. Maybe Thursday, day after tomorrow." Virgil smiled at the eager young man.

"All right! You can count on me. You know that!"

"I sure do," Virgil said. "You're about the only person around here I do count on."

"Aw." Stan shuffled his feet. "There's lots of townsfolk you can count on. Most of 'em ain't bad. Didja hear that the Lichen Animal Shelter gave two new kittens to Katy? They even let her pick 'em out from all the kittens they have."

"The little girl whose kitten was run over? That was awfully nice of them. Although it was a pity about her other cat. I heard she'd had it since she was barely a toddler." Virgil shook his head. *And these two can't replace the one Joe ran over. But Joe will pay for that soon enough.*

Stan frowned. "Yeah, sure was a shame. I hate when bad things happen to little critters."

Stan looked ready to cry, so Virgil changed the subject. "How's your mother doing?" Stan still lived at home, both because of his own limited development, and because his mother had cerebral palsy and needed care.

"She's great!" Stan beamed, switching emotions with the speed of a child. "Got new cuff-style crutches last week. Sure easier for her to walk on than her old ones. She complained about those a lot. Said they made her, um…boobies hurt." Stan blushed bright red.

"I'm glad the new ones are more comfortable." *I need to be done with this conversation now.* Virgil waved toward the bench. "Guess I better get back to work, Stan, or I won't be ready for us to stain on Thursday. You be sure to tell your mother I said hello."

"I'll sure do that!" Stan nodded and grinned. "And I'll see ya in a couple days."

As soon as Stan was gone, Virgil returned his focus to the Penningtons' bench. He quickly finished sanding, then spent the rest of the afternoon etching the elaborate bas relief of bluebonnets that filled the bench's inside back. His furrowed brow conveyed his deep concentration, his clicking carving tools the only sound, as he worked on the most complex carving he'd ever done.

The bank of overhead lights kept the room bright even as the outside light faded, but the setting sun brought cooler air, which Virgil felt across his damp neck. He looked up and blinked toward the garage door.

Finally dark.

Virgil cleaned and put away his tools and swept the sawdust off the floor. Chores done, he closed and locked the garage door and flipped off all the lights as he returned to the kitchen.

Time for Joe. Thanks to years of Joe's abusive and thoughtless behavior, Virgil was especially looking forward to this motif.

(4)

Before anything else, preparation is the key to success.
~Alexander Graham Bell (1847-1922)

As Virgil crossed toward his bathroom, and a much-needed shower, his stomach rumbled loudly in the quiet room. He'd been so focused on his various tasks in an attempt to keep his mind occupied that food hadn't occurred to him since an early morning bagel.

He briefly debated eating now or after his shower, but decided that waiting would be counter-productive. He'd use his shower time to cleanse his mind of the day's activities and prepare for the evening. He wanted to go from his ablutions directly into the chancel.

He turned to the refrigerator and studied the contents. The chilled space was well-stocked with the makings for salad, grilled chicken, a diner-style breakfast, or even a steak and baked potato. His mouth watered for the steak, but the evening ahead called for a light meal. After some consideration he fried an egg and constructed an egg, deli ham, and cheese sandwich on rye bread.

While he ate, he thought about the first time he'd done a motif against someone for how they behaved when behind the wheel of a car. It was a few months after he'd used his ability to end the dog-fighting ring.

A neighbor's little boy was badly maimed by a drunk driver with the ironic name of Adam Smirnoff. The five-year-old had been riding his new bicycle on the sidewalk in front of his house when the drunk's car jumped the curb and plowed directly over him. The boy suffered permanent brain damage and would need round-the-clock care for the rest of his life.

Smirnoff, a very rich man thanks to oil discovered beneath his ranch, had immediately hired the biggest cutthroat lawyer in the state. The lawyer was ruthless. He claimed the child's parents were at fault for the severity of the accident, because the boy wasn't wearing a helmet and was riding erratically since he was just learning to ride. The fact that the child was on the sidewalk was incidental.

Virgil doubted a helmet would have made much difference. He'd seen photos of the bike, mangled into a pretzel, as if it had suffered a spin in the heart of a tornado. Regardless, Virgil couldn't let the guilty man walk, especially not after learning this was Smirnoff's fifth arrest for drunk driving. He'd gotten off each time.

Virgil's biggest challenge was acquiring a personal item to use as a focalis from a man who was in jail. Virgil fretted through five sleepless nights before the solution came to him. He'd sat bolt upright, grinning.

Of course!

He'd worn his best suit and appeared at the local police department headquarters, claiming to be an underling with the Dallas lawyer's office.

"I'm to take photos of the liquor bottle that was found in the car." Virgil held up an expensive camera he'd rented from a large shop in San Antonio.

"Why?" The sluggish-eyed officer who asked was slouched in a rolling chair, his shirt wrinkled and dingy. His beer-belly drooped over his belt.

Virgil shrugged. "Because that's what they told me to do."

The officer barked out a laugh and stood, sending the chair rolling into the desk behind him. "Yeah, I get that. Come on."

Virgil took half a dozen photos of the half-empty Black Jack bottle before the officer yawned, turned away, and started a quiet conversation on his cell phone. Knowing he'd only have a minute or two, Virgil quickly pulled a small bottle from the camera case on the table near the square glass bottle.

He silently uncapped the bourbon and tipped a few drops into the bottle. The officer glanced up as Virgil slipped the precious cargo into a side pocket of the case.

"You still not done?" The officer shoved his phone into his pocket.

"Yes, just now." Virgil stood, wrestled the camera into its case and closed the zipper. "Thank you for your time. I'm sure at least one of these will be satisfactory."

The rest of the symbolic items were simple. Thanks to the bit of bourbon, though, Virgil's motif was a masterpiece of creativity. It had, ironically, sent Smirnoff, newly-vegetative from an accident involving a tree, to the same long-term care facility as Virgil's mother.

The karmic backlash for that motif hadn't been too severe. The fan belt on his SUV had broken while he was driving home from San Antonio. By the time he'd safely pulled over, the car was seriously overheated. The engine repair had been expensive, but Virgil considered it a small price to pay to eliminate a dangerous drunk driver.

As he cleaned up the kitchen, Virgil wondered what karmic backlash he'd suffer from his upcoming motif against Joe. He'd accept whatever came his way, as long as the motif was successful.

Before leaving the kitchen, he opened the UPS box and removed the small, opaque, white plastic bottle of hydrofluoric acid. The pint would last him a long time. His previous supply had lasted over two years. But he'd be using the last of his current bottle tonight. This one would take its place.

Virgil headed to his shower, carrying the bottle of acid, which he set on the floor outside his bedroom door. He dropped his dirty clothes into the hamper and stepped into the steaming torrent of his shower. It was his one true luxury. The five-by-six granite tile space was fitted with four high-powered shower heads, one on each wall, and one large rain shower head in the ceiling.

He viewed the space as his private purification room. The expansive flow pounded him from every direction, washing away not only the day's grime and sweat, but also his stress and worries. As the steaming jets worked their magic, his muscles unwound, his face and neck relaxed, and his breathing slowed to near-meditation levels.

When Virgil stepped from the shower his skin was bright pink, but his countenance was sublime. He walked naked to his closet, where he retrieved a black cotton cassock he wore only for his motifs. As soon as he slipped the vestment over his head his entire ethos changed. He wondered if priests felt the same shift, as if the garment itself informed the brain that powerful and mystical things were coming.

He padded barefoot down the hall, grabbing the bottle of acid without pausing, and unlocked the door to the back room of his house, a small room another owner might have used for guests.

Instead of a guest bed however, Virgil had outfitted the room with a rectangular, heavy, golden oak table in the center. It had belonged to his mother. She'd inherited it from her mother, and so on as far back as any family member could remember.

Virgil remembered when he'd acquired the unique family heirloom. After her beating, his mother became nearly comatose, hardly aware of people or activities around her, except for one time.

On Virgil's visit the day after she was transferred from the hospital to Oak Creek, she'd been agitated. He'd assumed the stress of her being relocated upset her. He'd leaned in, stroking her hair in comfort, and trying to understand her mumbling.

She'd grabbed his arm in a death grip and managed three clear sentences, "You must get the table from my chancel. Use it in yours. The key is behind the bridge."

Virgil went to his mother's house that afternoon. It wasn't hard to find the key. It was on a hook taped to the back of a print of Monet's bridge and lilies painting, which hung in the hall across from the bathroom door. What was harder was unlocking her chancel and entering.

For years as a child he'd ached to enter that room, even though he believed it held nothing but paperwork. It was still a Forbidden Space, something irresistible to most kids. Now, as an adult, he truly understood the power and significance of this room, and he hesitated in the doorway. He could feel his mother's presence, her energy. It made him cry, knowing those things were gone.

He'd approached the antique oak table with reverence and slowly circled it. It had thick legs, ornately carved with a dizzying mix of animal heads, twisting vines, and runic symbols. The top of the four-by-seven table was glass-smooth. Except for a couple of small nicks, and a few black spots that were probably singe marks, it was in remarkable shape for its age. It had never been protected with varnish, only oiled with linseed oil for a century or more.

He'd spent almost an hour in his mother's chancel, feeling her energy like a lost hug, running his hands along the tabletop while imagining the motifs she'd done. He'd bothered nothing else in the room. It felt too intrusive so soon after his mother's ordeal.

Transferring the table to his own home took some doing. Virgil didn't want anyone else to enter his mother's chancel, and he certainly didn't want to answer awkward questions. He managed to wrestle the heavy table into the hall. He then hired Stan, knowing the simple-minded young man would be more trusting and more likely to accept a less-than-detailed explanation.

Virgil didn't want Stan's energy permeating the table, so he'd taped moving blankets around the entire thing and told Stan it was to protect the old wood from damage. Stan helped load it into the rental van and unload it into Virgil's own hallway.

"Ain't we gonna move this into your dining room?" Stan asked.

"I need to unwrap it."

"I can help!" Stan reached for a blanket.

"NO!" Virgil had lunged at Stan and grabbed his arm, causing the young man to jump, startled.

"Whoa!" Stan rubbed his arm, where bright red marks already bloomed.

"I'm sorry, Stan," Virgil said. "Guess I'm overly sensitive. This was Mama's favorite table. I'm so afraid of damaging it. And I'm a little sentimental. It'll be okay. I can get it from here."

Stan had grinned like an innocent child. "That's okay, buddy. I gotcha. Call me again, though, if'n ya need more help."

"I'll do that."

It had again been an ordeal to get the table down the hall and through the door, but he'd managed. Sliding it on the moving blankets helped. Now it dominated his chancel. Virgil smiled as he entered the room.

There was a scattering of other furnishings in his chancel. A simple wooden chair was pushed into the corner to the left of the door. A row of four black metal cabinets spanned the length of the opposite wall.

The doorless closet on the right was all shelves, on which were dozens of boxes of taper candles in a rainbow of colors. Heavy black plastic and black-out curtains covered the one window beside the chair.

The room was slightly stuffy, since the ceiling air vent was tightly closed, but Virgil barely noticed. This wasn't a room for comfort; it was a room for purpose.

Virgil retrieved a box of long fireplace matches from a closet shelf and moved slowly around the room, lighting thick, white pillar candles, mounted in a large brass sconce in each of the four corners. Smoke from the candles spiraled straight up, joining the dark smudges already on the ceiling.

Virgil turned off the overhead light, leaving nothing but the flickering candles' illumination. He could hear thunder in the distance. The storms predicted in the morning's weather report were arriving. Virgil could ignore the thunder, and lightning wouldn't penetrate the blackened window.

Crossing to the table, he stood quietly staring at its center, feeling the energy from the thousands of motifs it had featured. He closed his eyes and slowed his breathing, purging any remaining thoughts of the outside world with every exhalation.

It is time.

(5)

Virgil placed his hands on the thick wood table top, closed his eyes, and focused on the task ahead. Everything had to be done exactly right or the motif would not work as planned. He'd come to accept that there would always be karmic backlash when he did a motif against someone, but he didn't want diffusion on top of that because of a stupid mistake. Besides, even a simple mistake could cause it to fail. A serious mistake could have deadly consequences for the target individual. Or perhaps even for himself.

Only once had one of his motifs diffused its energy. Virgil created it for a local man who was cyber-stalking young women in town. Because the man wasn't making direct, physical threats, the authorities weren't taking it seriously. They probably would today, but not back then.

Virgil had used an old desktop computer he'd stuck on a shelf in the garage as the focalis of the motif. He carelessly hadn't erased his personal files from the hard drive. The day after he completed the symbolic diorama, his laptop's hard drive crashed beyond repair. Thankfully he had backed up his files a week earlier, but he learned a valuable lesson: do not use personal items in a motif. He hoped never to repeat such a mistake.

I know what to do. Everything is fine. I'm ready.

Virgil breathed deeply one last time and crossed to the left-most cabinet, reserved for the specific symbolic items currently awaiting use. First, he retrieved the 1:12 scale model Porsche that matched Joe's prized possession. He removed it from its display box and placed the nearly fifteen-inch car on the table.

The flickering candlelight glinted off the car's glass windows. Virgil had winced when he saw the price of the serious collector car, but it was the only scale model that didn't have plastic windows. The symbolic items used had to be as authentic a representation of the real thing as possible, so he'd paid the exorbitant price, knowing the ultimate result was what mattered more than anything.

Virgil grabbed the soiled napkin Joe had left on the table at the Mexican restaurant, and selected a small Ken doll from a box filled with naked Barbies and Kens. He kept them in stock for whenever he needed to represent a specific person. Soon the Ken doll would represent Joe. Depositing the objects near the car, Virgil moved among the remaining cabinets, selecting the tools and other items for the motif.

Once he was in creation mode he wanted to remain there. He wanted all tools and supplies at the ready. It took two trips between various cabinets and the table before Virgil had the necessary items. His last trip was to the closet for black candles.

Virgil placed everything into a neat row, arranged from left to right in the order he'd use them. Except for the hydrofluoric acid and candles, Virgil could be preparing for a bit of scrapbooking or craft work.

He began by tearing the napkin into small squares, then used multi-purpose glue to create a patchwork set of clothes on the doll. When he'd covered the doll's body with the entirety of Joe's napkin, Virgil nodded with satisfaction.

Hello there, Joe.

Virgil used a red felt marker to draw a dollar sign on the doll's napkin-covered chest, then added a circle and slash over it. He smiled.

No money for you.

Joe would not profit from his upcoming accident, no matter how much insurance he had.

Virgil bent the Ken doll's left leg at a severe angle until he heard the distinct snap of the knee's plastic ball joint, then he used pliers to mangle the doll's right foot.

It will do.

Placing the doll on the table, he turned his attention to the car. It took more preparation. First, he used a razor knife to carefully slice deep cuts into the car's rubber tires. But his anger at Joe's callousness grew with each slash of the knife. Soon he was gouging and gashing with little regard to consistency.

Slashing into a tire and missing his thumb by a hair's breadth jerked Virgil back to the present. He drew a long, ragged breath to calm himself and placed the knife on the table with a shaking hand.

Keep your feelings out of this. Focus.

With deliberate effort, Virgil slowly uncapped the glass-etching acid, dipped the watercolor brush, and returned to work.

With the skill and patience of an artist, he painted the thick, white acid in swirls and waves over the car's glass windows and headlights. Breathing in and out in slow motion, his movements became almost Zen-like. Once done, he counted to three minutes then used a shop rag to wipe the acid off the car. The windows would be obscured but not dissolved. He set the car aside.

Using scissors and tape, he cut black construction paper into angled sections to create a five foot long, winding black "road" across the table. He adjusted several paper sections, carefully peeling off and retaping them to the wood surface, until the road flowed in an S-curve along the entire length of the table. He nodded with satisfaction, but didn't smile.

He placed the five black candles along the road, starting a foot and a half in from the near side of the table and ending where the road met the far side. Several times, he stood back to evaluate the candles and shift their positions until they looked evenly spaced.

Time for the final step.

Virgil had saved the potent hydrofluoric acid for last. After donning goggles, gloves, and a filter mask, he opened the bottle. Even through the protective gear he could still smell its acrid odor. He adjusted his mask even tighter across his nose and mouth, reducing the smell to barely noticeable.

Flipping the car upside down, Virgil briefly marveled at the detailing in its chassis. The model's undercarriage included wiring, tiny rubber belts, and even a drive train. He shook his head to return his focus to the task at hand. Using a second paintbrush, Virgil carefully applied the clear acid to one-inch sections of every wire and rubber belt.

I hate to destroy such a beautiful creation. But I have no choice.

His anger again climbed toward distraction. He'd always had trouble controlling anger when creating a motif for an especially cold-hearted individual. He didn't notice his hand was shaking when he dipped the brush into the bottle of acid. Instead of the next drop landing on the car, it landed on his left wrist, just above the glove, which had slipped down as he worked.

Pain shot through Virgil like lightning. His eyes teared inside the goggles and he hissed through clenched teeth. He gasped in short, ragged breaths. Between blurred vision and a shaking hand, it took three tries to balance the brush on the bottle cap so it wouldn't mar the table. He squeezed his eyes against the pain. He could hear his heart pounding.

Must get control.

Virgil willfully forced his breathing to slow and blinked rapidly to clear the tears. He squeezed and released his grip to increase the circulation in his left hand. The acid was already eating a hole in his wrist. It would need treating soon.

Not now. Must finish.

Virgil breathed deeply several times, then returned to work. With shaking hands, he put a drop of acid on the tiny metal brake on the inside of each wheel. As a final step, he added a small drop of the metal-eating acid on the model car's gas tank.

He wanted the gas to drip slowly, so Joe didn't run out before he reached the curve. This motif mustn't cause Joe's car to catch fire from the rupturing of a full gas tank during the crash. Virgil's goal was an accident, not fiery death.

Placing the car at the beginning of the paper road, Virgil unfastened and removed the convertible top. He stuffed the Joe-doll into the driver's seat and snapped the car's top in place.

After one final adjustment of the car's position on the road, Virgil stepped back and removed his protective gear, dropping the gloves into a small trash bin beneath the table. The hole in his wrist was deeper now, the acid eating into the dermis. There was no blood; the acid ate it, too. The perimeter of the hole was dead-skin white, the center an oozing raw-meat red.

Virgil wasn't finished, so the wound, and the pain, would have to wait. The still air reeked with the potent smell of acid and he coughed several times to clear his lungs and blinked fresh tears from his eyes. He replaced the safety goggles and mask. The air would have to clear before he could finish. He couldn't chant while wearing the mask or coughing.

I'll treat my burn while I wait.

Virgil opened the middle cabinet and shuffled through a dozen small bottles, looking for the Hexafluorine. Before he'd first used hydrofluoric acid, he'd researched what to do for potential burns. The best treatment, without visiting an emergency room and answering too many questions, was either calcium gluconate gel or Hexafluorine solution. He'd chosen the latter because it could even be used in the eyes, although tonight was his first time to need it at all.

The intensity of the burn's pain caused his hands to shake again. When he removed the solution's cap and tried to pour some over his wrist, the bottle slipped, shattering on the floor. The neutralizing liquid disappeared under the cabinets and between the small cracks of the laminate wood.

Oh. Oh. Oh. Damn!

Virgil would need an alternate treatment, but he couldn't leave the chancel until he was finished. He moved to the wooden chair, where he sat and closed his eyes. From inside the mask came the muffled whispers of the meditation mantra he'd learned years earlier while taking yoga classes at a Buddhist temple in San Antonio.

Virgil's mind cleared to a flat, gray pallet. The pain in his wrist didn't go away, but moved to his subconsciousness. His heart rate and breathing slowed to levels that would have alarmed some doctors.

When he opened his eyes, he wondered how much time had passed, not that it mattered. There was no clock in the room, and the blocked window allowed no clues from the outside.

But is the room safe now?

Virgil removed his protective gear for the second time. The air was still vaguely acrid, but his eyes and throat didn't start to burn again, so he set the gear on the chair and returned to the task at hand.

He began chanting as he lit the candle nearest the car. The Goidelic words he'd chosen were, first, an invocation to the universe to send Joe the karmic payment he deserved for his past actions. Virgil followed this with a second chant, beseeching protection from repercussions for anyone even tangentially involved in the motif.

He'd been diligent in writing the second chant. It wasn't just about protecting himself. His mother had fiercely taught him that the most important lesson to learn was to always keep his gift contained so as not to hurt the innocent. Even in the deep concentration of his chanting, Virgil heard his mother's words like a whisper blending with his own voice.

"Vee, once you interfere with the universe's energies you stir up much more than you realize. It's like a rock thrown into the water. You see the ripples on the surface, but the water is disturbed all the way down."

Virgil nodded unconsciously, but never broke the rhythm of the chants. He spoke each one five times, once for each candle. When he lit the last candle, he shook out the match and uttered the closing maxim.

So mote it be.

As these last words left his lips, Virgil's shoulders slumped with exhaustion. The pain in his wrist returned full force. He must have been in the chancel for hours.

He quickly returned the tools and supplies to their proper cabinets and tossed the used brushes and scraps of black paper into the trash. He picked up the larger pieces of the broken bottle, but would have to bring the broom and dustpan later, after the motif had finished. When he blew out the corner candles, the room's light barely changed, thanks to the five candles that burned along the curved paper road.

At the door, Virgil turned one last time to view his work before passing into the hall and locking the door. He returned to the kitchen and did some quick searches on his laptop. He laughed out loud, in spite of his pain, at the alternative treatment for his burn.

It took some rooting around in the bathroom cabinet, but he found his target: magnesium hydroxide, in a pretty turquoise bottle labeled *Mylanta Antacid*. He returned with the bottle to the kitchen. After coating the burn with the antacid, Virgil used plastic wrap and packing tape to seal the area and hold the treatment in place.

The pain diminished, but didn't stop. Virgil poured himself a generous serving of Scotch and sat at the table. He shook his head. He hoped the accident and his bursts of anger hadn't damaged the integrity of the motif.

Time will tell. All I can do now is wait.

As soon as he'd taken the last swallow of liquor, his eyes drooped. Glancing at the clock on the microwave, he was unsurprised it was 4:30 in the morning. He headed to bed, hanging his cassock on the door hook before slipping under the covers and drifting into dreamless oblivion.

(6)

Virgil checked on the motif Tuesday morning. It only took eleven hours for the "twelve hour" candle at the edge of the table, the last one he'd lit, to go out. He knew it would not be long now, perhaps a day or two, for the motif to do its work.

He gathered the remains of the motif, placed them in a boot-sized cardboard box, and sealed it with tape. He carried it into his backyard and set it on the patio table while he retrieved a shovel from a storage cabinet against the wall.

He'd never tried to save any parts of his motifs, not even the chants. He'd never kept a journal. He'd always sealed all the remnants of each motif item in a box, which he buried so no one could tamper with the contents.

It took half an hour to dig a big enough hole in the corner of his yard. He put the box in the hole and covered it, packing the dirt down. *One more motif securely buried. Don't want anyone to ever mess with the remains. No telling what would happen.*

After stowing the shovel, Virgil returned to the chancel. He got a white candle and simple holder from the closet and placed them in the center of the table. As he lit the candle, he repeated a short chant he'd said after every motif. The candle and chant would purify the room and purge any energies remaining from Joe's motif. Virgil wanted to ensure no motif would ever pick up the remains from the previous one.

The white candle would burn down in a day. If any wax remained, he'd throw it away. He saw no need to bury the wax, since the white candle's job was to purify, not send out energy to make changes in the world.

Chancel duties done, Virgil spent a few minutes replacing the bandage on his acid burn and treating the wound with an antibiotic gel.

I wonder if this is my karmic backlash, or if there's more to come?

There was nothing else to do now but wait. Virgil busied himself in his wood shop for the rest of the day.

࿆࿆࿆࿆࿆࿆

Wednesday morning Virgil dressed in khaki slacks and a navy pullover knit shirt. Glancing at his reflection as he brushed his teeth, he noticed his hair was past his collar.

Gotta get a haircut soon.

He took the short drive to Harold's Cafe. It quickly became obvious to Virgil that Joe's accident had occurred, and that no one was surprised he'd crashed his car. What captivated everyone at the small cafe was the unusual condition of his Porsche. He heard snippets of conversation about it from every table as soon as he walked in.

"What happened to Joe?" Virgil asked as he slipped into an empty booth.

Harold's had five booths down one wall and a 1950s-vintage soda fountain counter down the other. Half a dozen tables were scattered in the center of the space.

"The police found him." Tammy Carter approached Virgil's booth, coffee pot in one hand, menu in the other. "He was in a mangled heap off that bad curve on Highway 699. You know the one, about a mile east of town."

"Morning, Tammy," Virgil said to the assistant manager/head server. "Busy this morning!"

She glanced around, looking first through, then over, her glasses. "Yeah, I guess a little more than usual."

"I like your new glasses." Virgil smiled. "Those purple frames go with your blonde hair."

"Still getting use to the new prescription." Tammy laughed then sashayed her plump hips and hooted. "But the purple makes me feel like a perky teenager again!"

"Sounds like there's only one topic among everyone here this morning." He opened the menu and pretended to look it over. He was too interested in what others were saying to focus on the menu.

"Yep. Tragedy is always an interesting topic." Tammy shrugged.

"How 'bout Joe, Virgil," Dan Baxter spun on his booth at the counter to face Virgil. He waved his fork for emphasis before returning to his food.

"They say it took paramedics using a Jaws of Life to extricate Joe from what was left of his car." Tammy shook her head. "Guess his speeding finally caught up with him."

"And guess I won't be getting calls from him at 3 am demanding I come to Mesquite Hall cuz he just discovered after drinking all night that he lost his keys," Dan called over his shoulder.

"Life of a Locksmith, Dan." Tammy laughed. She poured Virgil's coffee. "Anyway, real shame about Joe."

A brief second of guilt washed through Virgil then was gone. *Joe is getting what he deserves. I don't send people more than they deserve.*

"Yes, damn shame." Virgil tried to sound like he meant it. "But Joe was alway speeding and being reckless." He shrugged. "Make it pancakes and sausage today, Tammy."

Tammy nodded and headed for the kitchen window. She added Virgil's ticket to the two pending orders. "Yeah, but this accident was weird," she called over her shoulder.

"Oh? How so?" Virgil asked.

"EMT was in here earlier. Said the cops reported all four of Joe's tires was blown," Lisa said as she entered through the kitchen's swinging door and began clearing dirty tables. She wiped the top off one and motioned for Marshall, who'd just come in.

"Morning, Marshall." Virgil waved.

"No packages for you today." The UPS driver nodded at Virgil as he sat at the table. "Heard about that accident when I was loading my truck this morning. One of the other drivers passed it on his way in. Stopped to see if he could help. Said it looked like Joe lost control just as he reached the curve."

"Hope they cleared the road up good. I gotta work on a barbed wire fence out that way later today." Bernie, a local ranch hand shook his head. He sat at the counter near Dan. "Don't got time to circle around the long way." He returned to wolfing down the Harold's Ranch Hand's Breakfast Special dominating the counter space in front of him.

Virgil couldn't imagine eating that huge platter of food, probably why his girth would never match Bernie's.

"Someone said the police reported the windshield, windows, and even the headlights were cloudy, almost whited out," Dan said.

"That'd sure make it hard to see." Bernie slid off the stool and tossed a fistful of ones on the counter. He drained the last drop from his coffee cup then added. "Musta been quite a ride. I heard Joe's left knee is shattered and his right foot got crushed."

"If Joe walks again at all, he's gonna have a big limp." Dan frowned.

"Guess we won't be seeing him on the dance floor at Mesquite Hall anymore, showin' off his *mooooves*." Bernie barked out a laugh as he headed for the door.

"Sounds like pretty extensive injuries," Virgil said. "Where'd they take him?"

"Where all of the bad accidents get taken." Dan shrugged. "The Robert B. Green Hospital in San Antonio."

"Heard they had to call the LifeFlight helicopter." Lisa lifted the bin full of dirty dishes and headed for the kitchen. "Some day I want to ride in a helicopter. For fun, though, not like Joe just did."

"He's probably gonna be holed up recuperating for a while." Tammy held the swinging door for Lisa, then crossed to Marshall's table, coffee pot in hand.

"He'll probably sue Porsche and get filthy rich from it." Marshall held up his steaming coffee in a toast. "Like he did McDonald's that time."

Virgil looked up, startled. Had his motif all been for nothing? He thought back to the McDonald's incident. The young cashier had messed up Joe's order. Even though she tried to apologize and correct the error, Joe had screamed a stream of profanities at her and thrown his tray on the floor. When he turned to storm out he'd slipped on his own garbage. He'd broken a tooth and cracked his wrist in the fall. Joe sued McDonald's, which settled out of court for $100,000.

Virgil couldn't let that happen again! Joe could NOT come out of this rich and satisfied. Then Virgil remembered the dollar sign and *NO* symbol he'd drawn on the Joe-doll's chest. He smiled and sipped his coffee.

"Not likely gonna sue." Tammy crossed the room with Virgil's order. "Didn't ya hear? Joe wasn't wearing his seat belt. Probably too arrogant. Anyway, he got some pretty bad brain damage. Bet he'll have the IQ of a turnip from now on."

Virgil suppressed a smile. "I'd say his karma caught up with him."

"Don't know about no karma crapola," Lisa said as she cleared Bernie's breakfast dishes, "but Joe got what he deserved. He's nothing but bad news. Poor Miss Ellington and Katy. Joe's legs may heal but their kitties are gone for good."

"Not to mention little Betsy Williams, the toddler Joe hit four years ago." Dan waved his fork in the air.

"Ya know, he never used his brain anyway." Tammy grinned. "Don't know how anyone trusted him as their CPA."

Everyone laughed and nodded agreement.

"Still." Dan cocked his head. "Seems like a lot happened to that car all at once. Tammy's right. Pretty weird accident."

"One of those things would've been bad." Tammy shrugged. "But four blown tires AND fogged windows AND fogged headlights at the same time? That's just too much."

"Even that's not all. I heard both the drive belt and brake lines were sticky and half-melted. Like he ran over acid or something." Lisa headed to the kitchen with the bin full of dirty dishes. "But how'd acid get on the road?"

Virgil looked up to see Marshall staring straight at him. Tammy was glancing between Marshall and Virgil. Virgil lowered his left arm and hid his wrist beneath the table, unaware he'd done so.

(7)

We do not have to visit a madhouse to find disordered
minds; our planet is the mental institution of the universe.
~Johann Wolfgang von Goethe (1749-1832)

Even into the early afternoon Virgil was still shaken by the morning's events at Harold's Cafe.

Does Marshall suspect something? But he doesn't know what's in the packages he delivers to me. How could he know I got acid?

Then Virgil remembered that the latest package, the one Marshall delivered the day Virgil did Joe's motif, had been clearly printed with CORROSIVE on the outside. Marshall may not have known the exact contents, but perhaps he remembered that word.

Virgil paced through his house, deep in thought, wiping beads of sweat from his forehead every few minutes.

Should I say something to deter suspicion? Or would that only make things worse? Should I ignore the incident and never mention it? Would ignoring it look like I'm hiding something?

The more Virgil thought about Marshall's stare, the more worried he became.

I need to see the results of my motif. To know I did the right thing.

He grabbed his keys from the table by the door and immediately dropped them on the floor.

Calm down! Marshall doesn't know anything. No one does.

He snagged the keys from the floor and headed for the hospital where Joe was recovering. The Robert B. Green Hospital was a perfectly fine facility near downtown San Antonio. Virgil couldn't help but smirk. The RBG was also the location the county used for indigent patients. If Joe knew where he was, he was probably mad as a hornet at being treated in the *poor people's hospital*.

Virgil stopped at the Information desk to inquire about Joe's room number, then proceeded to the fourth floor. The cream-colored vinyl floor glistened in its almost mirror-shiny sterility. The soft beige walls had few gurney-scratches on them. Pictures of generic nature scenes added a touch of color and robust cheer.

This may be the indigents' hospital but it still looks top notch.

Room 412 was near the nurse's station and stood open, the sound of the television drifting into the hallway. Virgil nodded at the three nurses occupying the station, before poking his head into Joe's room. "Joe? May I come in?"

"Who's that?"

"Virgil Harris, from Lichen."

"Who? Yeah, sure, whatever. Why not?"

Joe looked drawn and pale, probably from pain. His left leg was encased in a thigh-to-toe cast. His right foot was heavily bandaged with only the toes exposed. They were eggplant purple. Both legs were elevated several inches above the mattress

"Sit on down for a bit." Joe waved to the room's only chair.

"Thought I'd see how you're doing since your accident." Virgil sat in the molded plastic chair. He didn't want to lie, so he didn't add anything about being sorry.

Virgil watched the man in the bed. There was no visible evidence of any brain damage. It didn't look like Tammy's gossip was even true. Joe wasn't lolling or twitching or anything obvious. Gauze bandages did liberally encase his head, neck, and the section of exposed shoulder Virgil could see. One bandage spanned from the top of Joe's head to behind his right ear. Bare, shaved skin showed at the edges of the gauze.

"Doc says I'm prolly gonna lose my right foot, but they're whuppin' their butts to save it. Left knee's all tore up, too." Joe adjusted the bed so he could sit up straighter. "Hey, you gotta bandage too!" Joe pointed to Virgil's wrist.

"Yes." Virgil fought the urge to cover the gauze square with his right hand. "Burned myself cooking."

"Bummer. I ain't had ta cook in a couple days! Nurses bring me whatever I want." Joe laughed and slapped the bed.

Virgil assumed the slang-filled speech was due to the drugs. Joe might be a callous jerk, but he was also an educated, intelligent CPA. Or had been.

"I'm sure you're upset about your foot." Virgil waved toward it. "How else are you doing?"

"Right good. Them nurses are real nice. And purty too," Joe grinned and waggled his eyebrows.

This isn't just the drugs.

Virgil studied the injured man. Something about Joe's crooked smile and unexpected use of southern slang and grammar gave Virgil pause.

Is Joe no longer his arrogant self? Is he really as simple-minded as he sounds? Of is he faking it for some reason?

Virgil decided to test the situation.

"Too bad about your Porsche. Did everything fail at once? What are you going to do about it?"

Joe shrugged and grinned again. "Nuthin. Cain't drive noways. Least not without a foot." He wiggled the swollen, purple toes of his right foot. Joe winced then clicked the pain-medicine release button. He closed his eyes and lay still for a full minute. Virgil said nothing.

Joe opened his eyes and smiled. "Maybe I'll get me one a them scooters. They have little foot platforms instead of pedals. Drive 'em with your hands." He held up both hands and wiggled his fingers. "Hands both work." He mimicked twisting the controls on handlebars and made *vroom, vroom* noises.

Joe definitely wasn't his old self, but he clearly wasn't as dumb as a turnip like Tammy had said. Still, Virgil doubted Joe would be returning to his former CPA career.

I wonder what his clients will do? Oh well. I know I did the right thing. He won't be hurting anyone again.

The uncertainty and stress coiled inside Virgil unwound as he stared at the man he'd sent to this bed. Joe no longer seemed to be a danger to anyone. Or their pets. Or to the Porsche Corporation for that matter. There would be no lawsuit. The motif had worked as intended, in spite of the glitches. Virgil hated when he had to do a follow-up motif. He wondered what Joe would do for money from now on, but quickly shook it off.

He got what he deserved. I don't send people more than they deserve.

"I need to head home." Virgil stood. "How long will you be here?"

"Dunno. One nurse told me I'll prolly go home next week, but I gotta see what the doc says. Guess'n it depends on my foot." Joe pointed at his toes, but didn't try to wiggle them again.

Virgil nodded. "You do what the doctor and nurses say and you'll be fine."

"Not much choice." Joe laughed then winced again. "I'm their prisoner."

Virgil left the hospital and headed down the highway to Lichen. He moved over to take the exit to his neighborhood, then changed his mind and continued to the far side of town, where Oak Creek was located. Oak Creek wasn't as stark as the RBG Hospital, but it didn't elicit any more cheer, either. It was the best he could do for his mother without taking her to a facility in San Antonio.

Instead of generic nature prints on beige walls, the hall leading to his mother's room was painted sky blue, and the walls were covered with real oil and watercolor paintings by a well-known local artist.

Virgil wondered how they'd managed to acquire such a collection for the facility. *I'll bet the artist's mother or grandmother was here. Or maybe still is.*

Virgil reached the far end of the hall and turned to the last door on the left. He'd insisted on this specific room, because it had an extra window, which made the space brighter and more welcoming. He'd mentioned the window once, but his mother hadn't even responded.

"Hello, Mama. How are you today?" Virgil kissed her forehead then pulled the simple wood chair to the side of her bed and sat.

I need to bring a more comfortable chair. Next time I'm at Mama's house I'll get her favorite chintz chair. The one she used to sit in to read.

Virgil's mother was dressed in the pink flowered gown he'd bought for her last birthday. It smelled of lavender. She must have recently received her bath as her curly brown hair was damp on the ends and her cheeks were rosy pink against her delicate, pale skin.

"Just came from seeing Joe. He won't hurt anyone else." Virgil stroked her cheek and tucked a loose lock of hair behind her ear. "I did a very good motif."

Virgil told his mother about it, leaving out the part about dripping acid on his wrist. He kept his left arm low, so she wouldn't see the bandage, if she even still had that much awareness in her.

Pearl Harris blinked and mumbled. Virgil wished he knew if she understood. He leaned in closer to see if any of the mumbling made sense. He would have sworn he heard her say *proud.*

He was happy at his mother's reaction as he started his car and pulled out of Oak Creek's parking lot. He hadn't gone three blocks, however, when he heard the distinct sound of a blowing tire. His car shuddered and he held tight to the wheel to keep the car from lurching to the side and hitting a parked car.

Pulling into a shopping center's parking lot, Virgil exited the vehicle and walked around it. The right rear tire was flat. A large flap of torn rubber hung loose.

Damn, I guess the acid burn wasn't my only retribution for Joe's motif.

Virgil spent the next fifteen minutes changing the flat, grunting from the pain in his burned wrist. Virgil's stomach growled as he was putting away the jack and blown tire, reminding him he hadn't eaten lunch.

He checked his phone. *Wow, already after four.* Instead of heading home, he crossed through town for a bite at Harold's.

(8)

The key to good eavesdropping is not getting caught.
~Lemony Snicket, The Blank Book

Virgil was almost to Harold's when he changed his mind.

No. Not today. I need something different.

He made a U-turn and headed instead to Domingo's for some Mexican food. And a margarita. Or two.

The usually-packed restaurant was nearly empty. Less than half a dozen of the thirty-plus tables held customers. Virgil sighed with relief. He wasn't in the mood for local chatter and gossip. He wanted a quiet meal and a little alcohol. He crossed to the far wall and sat at a table by a window.

Virgil chose to visit Harold's when it was busy so he could keep up with local goings on, but he didn't enjoy that atmosphere. He viewed the crowded cafe as his office and his time there as work. He usually avoided Harold's after a long night in his chancel.

Eating there this morning had been a mistake, and not just because of Marshall's reaction. It took Virgil a few days after a motif to regain his equilibrium and sense of peace, and Joe's had not only been intense, it was barely two days ago. Visiting both Joe and his mother had drained Virgil even further.

Emotionally exhausted, he found it hard to concentrate on the menu he'd been handed. He stared at the Pepto Bismol-pink walls painted with colorful scenes from life in a Mexican village.

His brain felt like oatmeal. He couldn't even remember if his waitperson was male or female. It didn't help that the burn on his left wrist was stinging again, probably because he'd been so active today. At least it was healing and showed no signs of infection.

"What can I get you this afternoon?"

The female voice at Virgil's right shoulder caused him to jump.

The waitress laughed. "Sorry, didn't mean to startle you."

"It's okay." Virgil forced a smile. "Hmmm, can't decide. Do you have a special today?"

"Sure do!" The waitress grinned as if the special was her own creation. "Grilled tilapia with mushroom and onion cream sauce. Served with refried beans, rice, and guacamole salad."

"That sounds fine. And please bring me a large frozen margarita, with salt."

"You betcha." The waitress stopped at the kitchen window to deposit Virgil's order slip, then headed for the bar. She returned within a couple of minutes and set the frosty mug on a coaster in front of him.

A young man came up beside her and set a large basket of tortilla chips and a bowl of fresh salsa on the table. They moved off together, giggling as they walked. Virgil heard the words *Mustang* and *ugliest paint job ever*, right before they turned toward the kitchen.

He shook his head, glad they weren't talking about Joe's accident. Lichen was a funny town. Or maybe it was exactly like every other small town. Certain locations were rife with the latest gossip and news. In Lichen, that place was Harold's.

The regulars knew what had happened, who it had happened to, and where it had taken place. They knew which businesses were closing and what was opening soon. They knew who was currently fighting and what the fight was about. And they knew who was doing *Bad Things*. Virgil was amazed even thinking about the amount of local knowledge some people managed to possess. Still, they made his job as *Virgilante* all the easier.

Virgil sipped the cold margarita, licking some of the salt off the rim of the glass. He glanced out the window and couldn't help but laugh. In the parking lot sat a Mustang painted a dismal color of purple. Poorly painted lime green and putrid yellow flames ran the length of the side he could see. Was this the *ugliest paint job ever* the employees were laughing about?

He glanced around the restaurant, wondering who owned such a hideous car, and if they realized how bad it was, or if they had a misplaced sense of pride in it. Virgil's eyes landed on a young man, perhaps twenty, at a nearby table. He had stringy blond hair and a sad excuse for a goatee. His plaid shirt was rumpled. He slouched unattractively in his chair.

Across the table sat a girl who looked a little older. She was a knockout. Long, flowing auburn hair and porcelain skin. Even from the distance Virgil could see her eyes were emerald green. How such a pitiful excuse for a male landed such a beautiful young woman boggled Virgil's mind.

The two were clearly in an earnest conversation. Virgil's curiosity took over and he turned his attention toward them. His eyes widened as he listened.

"Booger, you can't DO that." The young woman's voice was plaintive and firm.

"Can TOO, Donna, you just watch me."

"Do you know how much that'll hurt Mom?"

"Don't care anymore. She ran Dad off. I'll never forgive her for that."

"SHE DID NOT!" Donna's voice rose then dropped. She blushed and glanced quickly around. "Don't ever say that. She caught Dad with that no-good hairdresser. You want to hate someone, you should hate Dad for hurting Mom. Or hate that bitch for stealing him away. If he'd stuck with Raymond, none of this would've happened." She took a big gulp of her margarita.

"Raymond was old. He was butchering Dad's hair. Made him look like a circus freak. I don't blame him for switching to Bonnie-Mae."

"Yeah, well, look what that caused." Donna wiped her eyes. "Mom cries every day. And how's she gonna keep the house now? Dad won't even help with the payment."

"Course not. He's too busy fuc—"

"Booger! That's enough!" Donna reached across the table and punched the young man.

Virgil guessed he was listening to brother and sister. But what was Booger planning that had so upset Donna? He closed his eyes to concentrate.

"Anyway," Donna continued, "promise me you won't."

"Can't do that, Donna. I need the money."

"For what? You live at home. You eat food Mom cooks. You have a car. You dropped out of school and got fired from your part-time job. What's so damned important that you need to steal from Mom?"

"I need guns. For protection." Booger slumped even deeper on his chair.

"From what? Are you in more trouble?"

"None of your business."

"It's that stupid group you joined. They're no good I tell you. Candice said the city has the member names they've identified on a watch list. I don't want you on it. They're all crazy."

"They are not! We're doing a lot of important good. You just don't get it. And if Candice is right, then her city manager boss doesn't get it, either. There's bad things happening around here. Evil stuff."

"You mean like the doorway to hell they said would open if the city approved that girl's drumming circle in City Park?"

"She got her drumming permit. Nothing happened."

"But those people claimed something would. They believed it. They also claimed at a City Council meeting that the fluoride in our water was turning local cattle into slug-like monsters."

"Quit it." Booger leaned in and pointed at his sister. "Fluoride's a real danger."

"Yeah, if you drink it straight. You can't seriously believe this stuff."

"You don't understand. You believe the official bullshit stories."

"Come on, Booger. Do you really think their new claim is true? The one about the county leasing a bunch of land to the Feds for an internment camp for dissenters when the U.S. joins the New World Order?" Donna laughed so hard she snorted.

"You stop making fun." Booger's voice was low and hard. "If you'd come to a meeting you'd learn the truth."

"Do NOT sell Mom's things for anything to do with that bunch of nuts. Don't you dare! It's bad enough that you joined them."

"I'll do what I have to. I swore to help protect the righteous. Besides, it's not like Mom's using 'em anyway." Booger shrugged.

"But those are the only things she got from her own Mom. Been in the family even longer than that. Mom said Grandma had inherited them from her mother."

"So what?"

"So those diamonds aren't only valuable, they've been in our family lots longer than YOU have. You have no right to take them."

"Mom's probably gonna sell 'em anyway. To pay for the house, or the divorce, or somethin' else like that."

"You really are stupid if you think Mom would sell something so precious to the family because of a temporary problem. No wonder Dad nicknamed you Booger."

"He called me Boogerman because I used to hide and jump out and scare everyone. He told me so."

"That would have been *Boogey*man!" Donna sat back so fast her napkin slid to the floor. She bent to retrieve it and held it over her mouth to stifle the giggles. "Of course he'd tell you something like that. You think he'd admit he thought you had boogers for brains?"

"That's not true!"

"Whatever you say, *Boogerman*, but you leave Mom's diamonds alone." She drained the last of her margarita then waggled the glass toward the waiter, who quickly brought her another.

"Gotta go. Gotta be somewhere." Booger stood and jerked his chair to the side, almost tipping it over. He grabbed it at the last second and shoved it under the table. He left without a second glance at his sister.

"You hear me? Don't you dare!" she called, but he was already gone.

Virgil turned to look out the window again and, sure enough, Booger climbed into the Mustang. When he started the motor it chugged like an old farm tractor.

Sounds like a bad cylinder head, Virgil thought automatically, thanks to years of tinkering on cars as a teen.

Virgil wasn't surprised, even with the little he'd learned about this young man. He didn't seem very responsible.

What's this about some group? Sounds like a weird conspiracy-theory bunch.

Virgil watched Booger drive away then returned his attention to Donna. She sat, quietly sipping her margarita and eating chips. He didn't know if she was done eating and just finishing her drink or was waiting for her food.

Virgil debated what to do. He needed to know what kind of group Booger was a member of, but he hated talking to strangers. It made his hands sweat and his stomach quiver.

The folks those two were talking about sound like trouble. I try to deal with people who are trouble. What should I do?

He was still debating when Donna's food arrived at the same time as his. He swallowed hard, picked up his plate and margarita, and walked to her table.

"Hi, Donna. May I join you?"

(9)

Memories of our lives, of our works, and our deeds will continue in others. ~Rosa Parks (1913-2005)

Donna jumped, but then smiled. "Oh, um…of course. It's always nice not to eat alone."

"It certainly is." Virgil set his plate and mug on the table then took the seat opposite the young woman. It was still warm from Booger's rear.

"Do I know you?" Donna cocked her head.

"Don't think so. My name's Virgil. I heard your brother call you Donna."

"Ohhhh." Donna's voice was wary, cautious.

Virgil didn't blame her. He was an older, strange man who'd just sat at her table and admitted he already knew her name. And his own nervousness was probably radiating from his body.

"I'm sorry. I couldn't help but overhear part of your conversation and was concerned. Wanted to see if you were okay, or if I could help in some way. I'm caring for my own mother who is ill, so guess I have a soft spot for mamas."

"Mom isn't ill, at least not physically, but she's definitely hurting." Donna took a big swallow of her margarita. Her posture visibly relaxed, although she remained leaning back in her chair.

"I gathered that. Has your dad been gone long?"

"Two months. Short enough that Mom's wounds are still fresh, but long enough for the money to start running out."

"That's a rough thing in any family, especially when it's sudden. Although I guess in every case it comes as a surprise for at least one family member. Did your mom take it pretty hard?"

"Shook Mom up real bad." Donna frowned. "Us kids, too. If Mom and Dad were having problems we sure never saw it. Mom never talked about it. Dad didn't talk much about anything." She paused. "Maybe that was the problem."

"Does your mother work?"

"Used to, but that was before Booger and I were born. She was a landscape designer. She loved designing gardens, planting them, then watching them grow and thrive."

"Did she work around Lichen?"

"You know the big green house on the corner by the courthouse? The one with the spiky iron fence?"

"Yeah. Did your mother design that garden?"

"Yep. It was the last one she did before I was born. She was already pregnant with me, but still managed to do most of the work herself."

"It's lovely, and it's really held up over the years. That's the sign of a good designer. They can see the long-term effects of what they plant."

"I'll tell her you said that. It'll make her smile."

"Would she ever return to doing that?"

"Maybe. I don't know." Donna shrugged.

Without thinking about it, Virgil blurted, "Would she design a garden for me? I'd like to hire her. My front yard is well-planted with roses, but my backyard is a complete mess." *What did I just do? Why did I say that?*

Donna's mouth dropped open. She quickly snapped it shut. "But you don't even know her!"

"You're right, but I've admired that house's garden for years. That's enough reference for me." *Am I crazy? No, I've got to trust my gut.*

"That was over twenty years ago! She may have lost her touch."

Virgil shook his head. "I doubt that. Love of plants doesn't go away. Neither does true talent. Perhaps working on my garden would help her get back into business full time."

"I don't know what to say," Donna dropped her eyes. "That's so very nice of you."

"Look, I know I sound a little crazy, but I've watched my own mother fade to almost nothing. I can't save her, but maybe I can help someone else's mother."

"I'm sorry. What happened, if you don't mind my asking."

"She has a brain injury. Beaten by burglars when they found her hiding in a closet."

"You're Virgil *Harris*!"

"Yes," Virgil's eyes grew big. "You know the story?"

"It was horrible. Your mother's story scared Mom so bad. She made Booger install bars on all the windows." Donna shook her head. "I heard both your names over and over from Mom for weeks. I'm so sorry."

"Thank you. I'm doing better. Mostly. It's still hard when I visit her."

"I can understand that. And I see why you're offering to help my Mom." Donna smiled and reached over to pat Virgil's hand. "Thank you."

"I'd like to arrange to meet her. You can talk to her first. I'll give you my phone number." Virgil pulled one of his custom wood-working cards from his wallet and handed it to the young woman.

"I'll give it to her. And I'll try to talk her into taking you up on your offer. Or at least calling."

"I'll look forward to hearing from her. To change the subject, is your brother in trouble? What's this group he was talking about? Hope you don't mind my asking."

"I don't know a lot about the group." Donna shrugged. "But what I've learned scares me. They believe pretty much every conspiracy theory out there. And they claim those crazy things are happening right here in our little town."

"How'd he get involved?"

"The group looks for people who aren't...people who are less..." Donna sighed. "They attract losers. I'm sorry to say that my brother's made to order for them."

"I heard you talking about some of the conspiracies they say took place around here. Were you serious?"

"Oh, yeah, those and more. They're even convinced our utility meters are reading our minds."

"They...what?"

Donna laughed. "They actually filed a petition with the city to make the utility service stop using smart meters. You know, the ones that can be remotely read. They claim they cause brain tumors."

"But that's crazy."

"I know. Sure wish my brother did."

"I get why you're worried." Virgil set his fork on his plate and leaned back.

"Not only worried. I'm scared. People like that can turn on you in a heartbeat if they decide you're *in on* some conspiracy, or that you're a spy."

"I'm stunned." Virgil shook his head. "Had no idea such a group existed."

"They think they're preparing for war. But why Lichen? Seems big cities would have way more stuff to worry about."

"Good question. And a war with who?"

Donna shrugged. "The New World Order, or alien lizard people secretly running the government, or maybe the zombie apocalypse. Who knows? Even my own brother won't tell me much, and I'm afraid to go to one of the meetings."

"Can't say I blame you."

"Want to hear one of their latest theories?"

"Sure." Virgil leaned forward and took a sip of his margarita.

"They think there's a secret group of sorcerers in town." Donna leaned in and lowered her voice. "They use spells and ancient chants to wreak havoc on others. To destroy lives. To dispense their own version of justice. Whatever."

The blood drained from Virgil's head and he choked on his drink. He coughed and patted his chest. *Are they talking about me? Are they talking about other people like me?*

"Are you okay? You sure got pale all of a sudden." Donna grabbed Virgil's hand and squeezed. "You know those folks are crazy. This is just another of their wacky beliefs."

Virgil got himself under control through sheer force of will. And fear. "Yeah, I just got a bit of brain freeze from the margarita, although I admit I'm a little surprised by these nutty conspiracies."

For the rest of lunch, Virgil fought his desire to get away. Every moment he had to remain was a strain. He kept the conversation focused on safe topics – Donna's childhood interest in rocks and recent Masters of Geology, his wood-working projects and roses, and his pre-retirement life as a postal worker.

"Donna, it was really nice to meet you," he said when they'd finally finished eating and walked to the cashier. "Thank you for letting me join you."

"I'm glad you did. And I won't forget to talk to Mom about your backyard. And give her your card."

"I'll look forward to hearing from her."

Once he was safely in his car, Virgil shuddered and leaned his head on the steering wheel.

What is going on? Who is this group? What do they know about me? What about other people like me? How many other people are there like me?

He doubted the conspiracy group was after him specifically, but he couldn't be sure. Was he safe at home? *Don't get paranoid. Of course you're safe.*

Still, he wondered. He thought about it as he drove. He thought about it for the next four days while he finished etching the bluebonnets on the Penningtons' bench. He left the garage door down while he worked. He didn't even go to Harold's, or any other local restaurant. He didn't leave his house at all.

Neither Donna nor her mother called, which was fine. He wasn't ready to deal with that yet. Too many uncomfortable questions whirled through is brain like a tornado.

How can I find out more about this group?

How many members are there?

Does the local chapter suspect one of these "sorcerers" lives here?

Am I the only one in Lichen?

Where do others like me live?

How can I find them?

What would I say if I did?

He had no idea where to begin finding the answers, but his gut told him it was vital.

(10)

Suspicion always haunts the guilty mind.
~William Shakespeare (1564-1616)

Monday morning Virgil was again in his wood shop, doing final touch-up sanding. He couldn't take the dust the sander was stirring up, so opened the garage door. Within minutes, Stan strolled in. Virgil wondered if the simple-minded man watched his house.

"Heya Virgil! Ready to stain that puppy?" Stan waved toward the bench.

No. I want to be alone. "Sure Stan. Let me get the stain and a couple of brushes."

Virgil put Stan to work on the back of the bench, in case Stan's work was less than best quality.

"Remember," Virgil said in a kindergarten teacher's tone, "you have to paint on a thick coat of stain, then wipe it completely off with a shop rag after a few minutes."

"Sure thing. How long is a few minutes?"

"You paint one section and I'll set a timer. You can paint another section until the timer goes off. How's that?"

"Great idea!"

The two men worked together for the next two hours. Stan chattered like a mockingbird while Virgil remained silent except for an occasional noncommittal response when Stan asked a question.

Virgil kept a close eye on Stan's progress as he repeatedly painted and wiped. They were nearly finished when Stan's next question hit Virgil like a hammer.

"You heard about the Truth Seekers?" Stan stood up and stretched. "They asked me to join! I'm gonna be a part of a real, serious group!"

Virgil froze mid-wipe. "Truth Seekers?"

"Cool name, ain't it!"

"Yes, quite...*cool*. Who are they? What do they do? Do they actually seek the truth?"

"Yeah. They find out about all the bad stuff going on and they expose it and stop it. They said I'd be a..." Stan paused, his forehead wrinkled in concentration. "...a *valuable and useful asset to their cause*. Me!"

"That's great, Stan. Congratulations. When are their meetings? Maybe I'll look into them." *Is this the group Donna was talking about? The group Booger joined?*

"Really? That'd be awesome. I can tell 'em all about you, and you can come to a meeting with me!"

"NO!" Virgil forced his voice to normal. "No, that's all right. Please don't mention me to them. I may not be interested at all, and I wouldn't want to let them down."

"Yeah, sure, okay." Stan's face sagged and he bent back to work.

Virgil spent the next few minutes wondering if he'd ever said or done anything potentially revealing around Stan. As an enthusiastic new member seeking acceptance, Stan would want to pass on anything he could to the others.

No. I haven't confided anything to him. He's not that good a friend.

"Let's go wash up, and I'll make us both a ham sandwich." Virgil took Stan's brush and dropped both their brushes into a can of solvent.

"Wow! Sounds great!"

Stan followed Virgil into the kitchen and scrubbed the copious amount of stain off his hands. Virgil gathered items from the refrigerator onto the counter then waited for his turn at the sink.

Virgil was busy scrubbing off the stain on his hands, carefully avoiding the bandage over the acid burn, and didn't notice Stan wander into the next room. When he looked up and saw the man was gone, a quick sizzle of panic crossed his stomach.

Stop worrying. The chancel is locked. Stan has the mind of a child. He'll believe whatever I tell him is stored in there.

Stan re-entered the kitchen with a frown on his face. "Where's your table? Ya know, the one I helped move. Figured it was gonna be your new dining table."

Virgil dropped the towel and quickly bent to pick it up, using the moment to think. "It had a damaged leg so it's being repaired."

"The people repairing it have had it for three years?"

"No, no, no. I recently damaged it with the, um…vacuum cleaner."

"But you work on wood. How come you ain't repairing it?"

Dammit. Good question. "I can work on other people's furniture, but was so upset that I'd damaged my mother's precious table I just couldn't work on it. Made me nervous even thinking about it. The man who taught me woodworking is repairing it."

"Huh. Okay. When ya gonna get it back? I can help move it again."

"Oh, I'm not sure. I moved my old table back to the dining room, so I told him to take his time." Virgil thrust the sandwich toward Stan. "Here's your sandwich. Want a Coke?"

Stan grinned and grabbed the large sandwich. "You bet! I love Coke."

Virgil waved toward the vintage chrome and formica kitchen table and sat with Stan. He ate quicker than usual, but couldn't keep up with Stan, who wolfed his food like a starving man.

Good. I want him out of here.

"All done?" Virgil stood. "I'm beat. Hate to rush you out, but I'm getting a headache. Think I need a nap." Virgil ushered Stan to the door.

"You ain't that old. But you have a good nap." Stan laughed. "Hope it helps your headache." He added as he headed down the sidewalk.

Virgil locked the door behind Stan and tossed his own half-eaten sandwich in the trash. He paced the house as he thought, unconsciously jiggling the locked door handle to his chancel every time he passed it.

I'm probably safe.

Virgil realized Stan never told him when the Truth Seekers met. At least Stan didn't seem suspicious about the table, but Virgil couldn't be sure.

When will Stan next see the Truth Seekers? When will he have a chance to mention me?

Virgil didn't for a minute believe Stan wouldn't say anything about him. Stan was like a small child who knows what a sibling is getting as a birthday gift – simply unable to contain such precious information inside.

I need to get away.

He didn't want to go far. His mother's house would do. It was still in town, but was in an older area with lots of sprawling homes on large, heavily-treed lots. He could put his car in the garage and remain incognito for several days. He might not *be* safer, but he'd *feel* safer, and Stan wouldn't be able to wander up unannounced.

Before he could leave, he needed to deliver the Penningtons' bench, and it wouldn't be dry for twenty-four hours. It was going to be a long Monday.

Virgil spent the time gathering personal items, reading material, and groceries he'd need at his mother's. He didn't want his neighbors to see him lugging a big suitcase out to his car, so instead he folded everything into paper grocery bags, wrote DONATION on the side of each bag, and shoved them into the backseat of his SUV.

You're being paranoid, you know that. But better safe than sorry, as they say.

ই০৯ ই০৯ ই০৯

On Tuesday morning Virgil loaded the bench into the back of his SUV.

The Penningtons were thrilled, and paid Virgil full price plus a little extra "for your outstanding quality work." He tucked the check into his shirt pocket to deposit later. He didn't want to go to the bank right now.

It took less than ten minutes to reach his mother's home. He turned up the long driveway while shuffling through his glove box for the garage door remote. The door opened smoothly and closed behind him just as easily.

He breathed a sigh of relief as the door opener's timed light blinked out, engulfing him in protective darkness. Still, he was glad when he opened his car door that the dome light provided enough visibility to cross to the switches on the wall and flip on the garage's overhead fluorescent light.

Virgil unloaded his car, then sat in his mother's chintz chair and studied the room. Nothing had changed in his childhood home. He hadn't stepped foot in her house in three months. He came only often enough to dust and make sure there were no maintenance issues.

He knew he should sell it, but couldn't. A part of him still wanted to believe his mother would return someday. Although his logical mind knew that wasn't true, hope always won out.

Virgil retrieved the key hidden behind the bridge painting in the hallway. He'd only been in his mother's chancel the one time to retrieve the table. And he'd purposely not looked around or touched anything else. He'd already felt like he was violating her privacy even being in the room to retrieve the table. Now it was different. Things had changed.

It's time to see what else Mama has in her room. What did she use for her motifs?

(11)

The beginning of knowledge is the discovery of something we do not understand. ~Frank Herbert (1920-1986)

Without its central table, the chancel looked sad and forlorn. Except for a large antique wardrobe on the far wall, the room was empty. It had the stale smell of dust and disuse mixed with the subtle smells of incense, candle smoke, and sage.

Sage? What did Mama use sage for in here?

Virgil cooked with sage, but he also knew that Native Americans and European Pagans had used its smoke for smudging, to drive away everything from mosquitos to evil spirits. But neither of those things should be in her chancel.

He crossed to the closet and opened the bi-fold doors. Much like his, the shelves were filled with colored, twelve-inch taper candles in neat rows of nearly-full boxes. She must have restocked at one point, then not done many motifs afterward.

Most of the candles were stuck together. Some were visibly distorted. He'd kept the house thermostat off, except for running the heater on the coldest nights in winter. He hadn't thought to worry about the heat of summer. He touched a dark purple candle.

The surface was oily and slick. Probably all the candles would end up in the trash, too mangled for motifs, and too ugly to burn at a dining table.

Sorry, Mama. I didn't even think about your candles. I was being frugal when I switched off the AC.

He turned to the monstrous wardrobe. He'd never seen it anywhere in the house. His mother must have purchased it specifically for her chancel. He reached for the knob and pulled. It didn't budge.

Why did she lock up her supplies when they're already in a locked room? First the sage, now this. What was wrong Mama? What had you so worried?

Virgil needed to find the key to see what was in that wardrobe. He leaned against the wall and closed his eyes, trying to think like his mother. She'd hidden the key to the chancel's door behind a picture in the hallway. Did she follow the same pattern with the wardrobe key?

She'd have put the key somewhere within the same vicinity. Her knees were bad, so she'd have minimized the walking distance required simply to gather two keys.

Virgil left the chancel and studied the hallway. The picture of the bridge was a few feet to the left of the chancel's door. There were a dozen family portraits farther down on the opposite wall. He didn't think she'd use one of those. They were too personal.

To the right of the chancel door, near the opening to the living room, was a hall table. It stood on spindly legs and had no drawer. A vase of dusty silk flowers sat in the center. Above the table was a gold-framed mirror.

Virgil tipped the mirror away from the wall but no key fell out. He felt around behind it, but his hand found only smooth backing paper. He lifted the heavy ceramic vase. There was no key hidden beneath it. He removed the flowers and flipped the vase upside down. No key was inside.

He was about to move on when he decided to check the table itself. He ran his hand beneath the top and hit an obstacle tucked against one leg. He knelt to look. His mother had glued a magnetic key holder to the underside of the table. Virgil slid it open and smiled as a small brass key dropped to the carpet. He grabbed the key and hurried to the wardrobe.

He hesitated before inserting the key in the keyhole. He needed to know what was going on, but still felt he was violating his mother's privacy. He drew the double doors wide and stared. Inside were shelves covered with his mother's tools and supplies.

These look like regular motif supplies. Why the extra concern?

The top shelf was packed with small bottles, all hand labeled in his mother's handwriting. He shuffled through a few. Most were what he'd expect: salt, alcohol, bleach, oil, various dried herbs – including sage. Two bottles raised his eyebrow: sugar and insecticide powder. He couldn't begin to picture a motif that would use either of those.

I guess insecticide would work as a symbol to repel a person away from you. But sugar? To make someone sweet on you?

But they weren't supposed to use their gift for things like love spells. They weren't supposed to use it at all to manipulate others. His mother had been adamant during his lessons. Was she guilty of that old saying, "Do as I say, not as I do"?

Except Virgil knew he was now doing it too. *Only to those who deserve it. I don't pick people at random.*

The middle and lower shelves held the usual items like scissors, glue, and tape. There were scraps of fabric and felt in a rainbow of colors, plus black and white construction paper. A heavy mallet on the lower shelf, however, gave Virgil pause. That seemed an odd motif tool.

Why would his mother have a tool designed to smash things? Usually you didn't smash motifs. You carefully assembled and arranged them.

Virgil closed his eyes and imagined his mother looking among the shelves for just the right items for a motif. He sensed her presence more than he had since the day she'd gripped his arm and told him to get the table from this very room.

He wished he could have seen her do an actual motif. They'd done many practice ones together when she was teaching him, but none were meant to actually work. They weren't done in a chancel, just on the dining room table. And none ended in a chant. They were dismantled and everything put away after the lesson.

Virgil scanned the shelves again. The few unusual items didn't seem dangerous or particularly malevolent. There was nothing for a specific motif or individual. He shook his head. He didn't see anything in the wardrobe worth locking up.

He was closing the wardrobe when the edge of something sticking out from under the stack of fabric caught his eye. He lifted the scraps and found a book hidden beneath.

The three-ring binder's vinyl black cover was covered with different colors of felt, cut and glued into the shape of a tree. He sat on the floor and stroked the tree before slowly opening the two-inch thick book.

It was his mother's motif journal!

He felt both guilty and excited looking at something of his mother's that was so personal. He'd never even thought of keeping a journal, although a vague memory stirred of his mother suggesting it back when she was teaching him about their ways.

Inside her journal was page after page recording motifs she'd done over the years. Flipping through the book Virgil could see lists of tools and symbolic items, drawings, and chants carefully recorded in the Goidelic language.

Each motif was dated at the top of the page. The oldest, in the back, was from almost sixty years earlier, over a decade before he was born. The pages were yellowed, and his mother had glued those little reinforcement donuts around the frayed and torn holes.

Virgil touched one of the reinforcements and smiled at the conscientiousness of its being there. His mother would have wanted to be sure to preserve her journal pages, so she could pass them on to him.

He scanned the first motif his mother had logged. It was right after she and his dad had married. The motif was to protect their new home from harm and to fill the space with joy and happiness.

Virgil smiled. It definitely skirted the edges of manipulating another, namely his dad, but was vague enough to avoid that danger zone.

Glancing at the bandaged acid burn on his wrist, he thought again of his mother's lecture about karmic backlash and diffusion. He definitely knew all too well the repercussions of both.

He flipped to the front page. The most recent motif was only one week before the burglary. At least the burglars hadn't made it into this room. What would they have done to the magical items? What else would they have done to his mother if they'd thought she was a witch, or something worse?

Virgil turned to random pages, scanning a few of the motifs. Most were what he'd expect from his mother – friendly and gentle nudges on people she knew, including himself, to remember important things, to be more responsible, to be willing to try new things, to be adventurous while staying safe. One motif was to help him get well when he was so sick with mononucleosis.

I never felt your hand on me, Mama, but I can see now that it was there many times.

He wiped a tear from his cheek, flipped again to the front of the book, and froze. He stared in disbelief at the last motif she'd done. A chill ran through him like an ice storm and the hair on the back of his neck stood on end. The title of the motif was easy to read in his mother's precise handwriting.

Stop the Truth Seekers

Virgil clambered to his feet, the book sliding to the floor. What had he just read? His mind reeled. Wasn't that what Stan had called the group he'd recently joined?

Mama, what was going on? Were you in danger? Why?

He circled through the room, rubbing his arms against a chill that came from deep inside. He stopped where he'd been sitting and stared down at the book. He took a deep breath, exhaling slowly as he sat on the floor and retrieved the book.

The motif looked complicated – it filled three pages in the binder. He quickly scanned them. She must have gone to a meeting, because she'd used an agenda page as the focalis. She'd torn it into strips, woven them into a ball, coated it with insecticide, and shoved it into a small box. She'd then beat the whole thing nearly flat with the mallet.

Virgil made a rueful smile.

She used insecticide powder to stop them. That's why it's in her supply closet.

He turned the page. The note she'd scribbled on the bottom caused him to utter a loud, "What?"

> *Paper cut left blood on bits of the ball*
> *Hope that doesn't hurt the motif*
> *Hope there's no diffusion*

She'd sealed some of herself up in that ball, and gotten some of the symbolism—the insecticide—on herself, yet she'd finished the motif anyway. He slammed the book closed, causing it to flip off his lap and fall to the floor.

Oh Mama. You knew better. You warned me over and over. You even made me promise. Why didn't you dismantle and abandon that motif?

He stared at the book. His mind worked feverishly, trying to understand his mother's decision. Had she been so desperate that she was willing to take such a dangerous chance? Virgil froze as realization dawned on him. His mouth tightened into a grim, straight line.

You only had the one symbolic item. You were afraid to attempt getting another agenda page. But why did you do the motif at all?

Virgil reached for the book, and this time he read the motif slowly, absorbing every detail. Her words filled him with horror.

She'd heard about the group from a neighbor, then followed the same neighbor to a meeting. She sat outside the community center's free meeting room, huddled low in her car, watching the door.

When everyone had left, she went in and stole the agenda from the trash. Although the door was still unlocked, she entered the space without permission. She'd essentially broken into the room. And when someone unexpectedly returned, she briefly hid in a closet.

The burglary. The closet. Her beating. The motif had diffused full force onto her.

Virgil's howl was feral. Haunted.

He threw the binder across the room. It hit the opposite wall and fell like a broken doll. The stress of his own last week, and the realization of what he'd read, tore through him like lightning. Sobs erupted from deep inside. At first he tried to stop them, but gave in and let go.

He cried from all the pain and grief he'd held in for three years. His body shuddered. Tears rolled in a river down his cheeks. He slumped to his side in a fetal position, eyes squeezed shut against the truth. He held his legs tight until the anguish finally drained away. It took great effort to push his weary body to a sitting position.

Virgil wiped his nose and eyes on his shirt. He didn't care. He hiccuped out the last of his tears, fighting to calm down. He needed to know more. He needed to know her exact intention for the motif.

He didn't think he had the strength yet to stand so he crawled to the book and turned again to the first page. This time he focused entirely on the chant. He knew most of the words at a glance, but some took effort. He squinted at the page, puzzling out the entire chant.

These people shall turn their attentions elsewhere

They shall harm no one with what they do

Their own anger and fear shall turn back on them

They shall reap what they are sowing

No power from these people shall harm my child

He shall be invisible and untouchable to them

My son is safe - my son is safe - my son is safe

Virgil stared at the chant. The Goidelic writing looked like scribbles, but the translated meaning was crystal clear.

Me? Mama, they were after me? What did you find out? You must have been sure of the information to do such a dangerous motif.

Another wave of pain engulfed Virgil when he realized that he was ultimately the cause of his mother's current condition. She'd done the motif for him. She'd sacrificed her safety, and taken a chance on diffusion, for him. He roughly wiped his eyes with the back of his hand. He felt a sting in his right eye but ignored it.

I will find out what you learned. I will find out who these people are and what they planned for me that upset you so much. I will avenge you. I promise.

Virgil stood with the book, his back straight, his chin raised, his jaw set tight. His cold, hard eyes stared straight ahead, his mind fixated on his promise. He left the chancel without locking the door. No motifs would ever be done in there again. It was time to let the energy dissipate. He wanted it to be nothing but another room when potential buyers arrived.

(12)

It's never too late. Don't focus on what was taken away.
Find something to replace it, and acknowledge the blessing
you have. ~Drew Barrymore

Virgil slept little Wednesday night, restless from dreams of being pursued by vague monster shapes. He awoke feeling drained and shaky. He shuffled into the bathroom and grimaced when he caught his own face in the mirror.

"Damn."

His right eye was a dark red mess. Virgil frowned, trying to think how he'd hurt his eye, then remembered it stinging when he'd rubbed it after crying about his mother's compromised motif. He wet a washrag in the cool tap water and pressed it to his eye.

He hadn't broken a capillary since his high school sports years, but he still remembered there wasn't much to be done except give it time.

Oh well, best get this done.

Virgil spent the day mindlessly working on the contents of his mother's house. He sorted and boxed paperwork, folded clothes and shoes into bags for donation, carefully packed the few mementos he wanted to keep. He'd finally accepted the permanence of his mother's condition, but he needed to keep busy so the pain of that reality wouldn't wash over him again.

He'd kept his mind carefully blank while he worked, but a paper cut's sting raced through him like fire. Emotions flooded in.

Mostly he was angry. Angry at his mother for finishing a motif she had contaminated with her own blood. Angry that she'd done such a powerful motif to protect him without ever mentioning anything. Angry at himself for being angry at her.

He sagged into her chintz chair. She'd done it all out of love. He knew she'd do it again. And he'd have done the same for her.

Mama, I knew you loved me but this…this is beyond my imaginings.

He took a deep breath and stood, quickly wiping his tears. Nothing could be reversed now. He'd plow ahead. No matter what. He'd do whatever it took to make sure his mother's motif meant something, that it hadn't all been for naught.

Virgil was entering the kitchen after carrying another load to his car when he saw his cell phone skittering across the table.

Who's calling me? Not in the mood. Too much going on here.

He'd put the phone on vibrate when he'd left his own home two days ago. He glanced at the display. It wasn't a number he recognized but the Caller ID indicated a local Lichen number.

Sorry. You'll have to leave a message.

Within seconds his phone bounced one final time, indicating the caller had, indeed, left a message. Without picking up the phone Virgil pressed to hear it.

"Mr. Harris? My name is Sylvia Parker. You met my daughter Donna at Domingo's several days ago. She came home quite excited about your offer of landscape design work. I must admit I was a little shocked, but having slept on it, I'm also now touched. And excited at the opportunity. If you were serious, I'd love to talk with you more. Please give me a call."

Damn I'd forgotten all about that offer.

He poured a glass of red wine and sipped it while he thought about what to do. He wasn't looking forward to happy chat with someone about the possibilities for his back yard. His mood was as dead and barren as that fenced space.

But she may know something about the Truth Seekers. Or maybe through her, I can get more information from Donna, or maybe even specific details from Booger.

Virgil picked up the phone and returned the woman's call. She answered on the first ring.

"Ms. Parker, this is Virgil Harris."

"Mr. Harris! Thank you, and please call me Sylvia."

"All right, Sylvia. Let's plan to meet and discuss my garden. We can meet at a restaurant first if you like, or you can come and see the backyard for yourself. And please call me Virgil."

"How about a restaurant for a bite of lunch? I can tell you more about my experience and skills. If you're still interested, I can follow you to your place. And thank you again for the opportunity... Virgil."

They made plans to meet at Botticelli's Italian Cafe on the south side of Lichen at 12:30 the next day.

It's time to go home anyway. I can't hide here forever.

He realized now that his mother's was probably less safe than his own home, considering she was the one who did the motif. The diffusion had happened there.

Virgil packed his personal items and cleaned up the house. He wrestled his mother's chintz chair into the back seat. The last thing he grabbed as he left was his mother's journal.

The drive across Lichen to his own home was uneventful. Traffic was even lighter than usual, and he saw no one he knew. His mood was lifting until he turned into his driveway. Someone had taped a large folded note to the garage door.

Virgil sat for five minutes after turning off the car, staring at the folded piece of paper. No matter what was inside, he was sure he wouldn't like it. He sighed and climbed out of the car.

He shuffled toward the garage, making the trip last as long as possible. Before he could think of another way to postpone, he'd reached the door. He grabbed the paper and yanked it off.

Hey Virgil, since you still ain't home I left this note. I told the Truth Seekers about you and they can't wait to meet you! Next meeting is Thursday night. You can go with me. Or maybe you can drive so we don't have to walk. See ya! Stan

He'd been right. Stan had the mind and maturity of a child. He simply couldn't keep a secret. Well, it was done. Virgil had until the next night to decide whether or not to go. In the meantime, he'd ask Stan what he'd told the Truth Seekers.

He didn't have to wait long to find out. The younger man came loping up the driveway while Virgil was still unloading boxes and bags.

"Virg! You're back! Didn't know you was gonna leave for a few days."

"It was unplanned."

"What's wrong with your eye? Looks creepy."

"My eye will be fine. Smacked it when I was packing Mama's things."

"Glad your eye's okay. Hey, didja get my note? Can't wait!" Stan rocked back and forth. A wide grin stretched across his face.

"Yes, I got your note." Virgil wanted to yell at Stan that he'd promised to say nothing to the Truth Seekers, then realized it would do nothing but hurt the kind-hearted man's feelings. "What did you tell them about me?"

"About how bad stuff happened to your mama, and that you quit workin' after it happened cuz you was so upset. And how the police didn't do much to find the bad guys and you didn't like it."

Virgil froze. What had he told Stan back then about the police investigation? He may have casually mentioned he was not happy, but surely he'd said nothing to raise suspicion in Stan.

"Anything else?" *I sure hope not.*

"Nah, just that you know about not trusting authori…auth…the guys in charge."

Virgil relaxed. On that, Stan was correct. Perhaps he should attend a meeting to see what the group was about. He wouldn't commit to Stan yet, though.

Stan reached for a bag of clothes. "Can I help you carry this stuff? What is it?"

"No thanks, Stan, that's fine." Virgil managed to keep his voice calm. There was nothing Stan shouldn't see except his mother's journal and he'd already taken that inside.

I don't want him touching her things.

"Most of this stuff is going to Goodwill." Virgil waved at the items. "But I'm sentimental, even if they are things Mama won't ever use again."

"Oh, okay. I get it. Still sorry about your Mama."

"Thank you, Stan. That's very kind. I need to go inside now. It's been a busy couple of days."

"You gonna take another nap?" Stan hooted with laughter.

"Maybe. Anyway, see you later." Virgil slammed the SUV's door closed and headed in, leaving a dejected-looking Stan on the driveway.

Virgil hid inside the rest of the day. He didn't even check on his roses. He needed to think about Thursday night's Truth Seekers meeting. Was it safe to go? They knew about people *like* him, but that didn't mean they knew about *him* specifically. Had his mother known they were after Virgil, or did she just worry they might go after him?

He poured himself a Scotch and sat in the chintz chair he would soon take to Oak Creek. He could have left it in the SUV but wanted a chance to enjoy it himself for a while. His mother had loved it so much. Perhaps its being in his mother's room at Oak Creek might stir a memory from deep inside her damaged brain.

(13)

Never refuse any advance of friendship, for if nine
out of ten bring you nothing, one alone may repay you.
~Madame de Tencin

Thursday morning was gorgeous. Virgil sat at his breakfast table and stared out the window at his barren backyard.

Today's the day I meet Sylvia for lunch.

He thought about postponing because of his eye, which was still angry red, but now his motivation to see her was even stronger. He wanted to question her before the Truth Seekers meeting. He decided she'd understand about his eye. If he explained it happened while getting his mother's home ready for the market, she might even feel sorry for him. And if she noticed his bandaged wrist, he could say that happened at his mother's, too. Sympathy could make her more willing to talk about Booger.

By the time Virgil was dressed and ready to go, he found himself looking forward to lunch. Not usually one to worry about style or fashion, he'd stressed over what to wear. He'd finally settled on grey slacks and a Virgin Mary-blue button-down shirt.

He was normally shy, and found it hard to meet new people, but this felt different. Since he had a couple of specific topics already planned, namely his backyard and the Truth Seekers, he hoped he could avoid awkward silences and fumbled words.

As Virgil pulled into the parking lot at Botticelli's, he realized he had no idea what Sylvia looked like. A shot of panic pinched his stomach, but he took a deep breath and briefly closed his eyes.

Donna probably described me to Sylvia. Stop worrying.

He was a few minutes early, so he took the opportunity for a restroom stop to check his hair and make sure he didn't have anything stuck in his teeth. His eye was still a bright red mess.

Oh well. Nothing I can do about that.

When he exited and re-entered the restaurant's foyer, a woman was just coming in from outside.

"Mr. Harris? Virgil?" The woman smiled brightly when Virgil nodded. She crossed the room and extended her hand. "I'm Sylvia Parker. It's so nice to meet you."

Virgil instantly found her attractive. She was nearly as tall as him, with shoulder length auburn hair. She wore a tailored navy dress with a white collar and round white buttons to the waist.

He shook her hand and found her grip firm and confident. "Hello, Sylvia. It's nice to meet you."

They followed the waiter, remaining silent until seated and holding menus. The waiter retreated to fetch drinks.

"I wondered if you'd recognize..." Virgil began.

"Donna described you perfectly..." Sylvia said at precisely the same time.

Both abruptly stopped and laughed.

Virgil smiled. "Please, you first."

Sylvia smiled in return. "I knew you wouldn't know what I looked like, and I forgot to tell you a cryptic description such as *I'll be carrying a book and wearing a purple orchid in my hair*, so I made Donna give me a detailed description. She did quite well. Although she said nothing about your eye. Are you okay?"

Virgil's nervousness and stress drained away, as if someone had pulled a plug from the bottom of his foot. Her manner was comforting and easygoing.

"Oh this." He waved toward his eye and repeated the excuse he'd thought up that morning, about packing his mother's things.

"At least it was for a good cause. Terrible when something like that happens for a totally stupid reason. I used to be covered in cuts and bruises because I was a clumsy tomboy as a kid."

The more they made small talk, the more he liked Sylvia. Her quick sense of humor flowed through their conversation. He enjoyed listening to everything she said. They were finishing their salads when Sylvia's expression turned serious.

"I can't tell you how much your offer to Donna means to me. I've been a mess since Oscar left with…that woman. Thought about returning to work, but didn't know how to get started. I can give you a résumé, but I don't have any current references."

"I see it as a win-win. My backyard is a wasteland. I told Donna I'd long admired the garden at the house by the courthouse. When I learned it was yours, that was all the reference I needed."

"She mentioned that. She was surprised, considering I installed that landscape while pregnant with her, and that was twenty-three years ago!"

"Exactly! And look how well it's held up and how beautifully it filled out. That's the mark of a true artist."

Sylvia blushed.

"That's settled. After lunch you can follow me to my house. I have a survey somewhere that shows the dimensions of the yard and the size and location of the patio. I can dig it out while you walk around and look things over."

"Sounds like a plan."

They grew silent while their entrees were served. Virgil took the opportunity to change the subject. It was time to see what he could learn from her about the Truth Seekers.

"Hope you don't mind my asking, but is everything okay? The reason I approached Donna in the first place was because of how upset she was at her brother."

"Oh. Yes. Ignatius." Sylvia shook her head. "He's in some kind of trouble."

Ignatius?

He must have had a look because Sylvia laughed. "I know. It's a terrible name, and if I had it to do over again I'd fight more. Oscar insisted on naming our son after his grandfather. That's probably why my son thinks *Booger* is an improvement."

Virgil smiled and shrugged. "Mama named me after her favorite great uncle. I thought of changing it when I was younger, but I've come to accept it over the years. At least your son and I have unique names by today's standards."

"That you do. But I find Virgil a perfectly fine name."

"Thanks. You said Booger...Ignatius, was in some type of trouble. Do you know what it is?"

Sylvia repeated most everything Donna had already told him.

"This an official group or just a bunch of angry people? Does it have a name?"

"He called it, let me think...Truthers? No. Truth Hunters? No. Oh! Truth Seekers!"

Virgil already knew what she was going to say, but the confirmation still shot through him. His stomach lurched. Then Sylvia added one additional statement that made Virgil sit up straight and raise his eyebrows.

"He's been going to those meetings for a couple of months now." She frowned. "Guess they just elected a new president and he's recruiting hard. I don't know why, but Iggy said they're preparing for some type of confrontation. They've apparently been creating a *target list*, people they want to go after first. It scares me to death that he's involved with these people."

"Target list?" Virgil had to work hard to keep his voice calm. "Who's on the list?" *And what put them on it?*

"Iggy won't say much and believe me, I've asked. Repeatedly. The best I can get from him is that there are what they're calling *sorcerers* in this area. They believe these sorcerers are evil and are messing with the natural order of things. I have no idea what made them think someone is a sorcerer. I don't believe any of that nonsense."

"Sorcerers." Virgil forced a laugh, hoping it sounded natural. "Imagine that. Donna said the group was full of nuts. Oh, I'm sorry."

"Don't apologize. I'm worried about my boy. It's like he's lost his common sense. Or maybe he's going crazy. I don't know." Sylvia shook her head and dabbed her napkin at the corner of her eye. "We raised him better than this."

Virgil decided not to pursue it. Sylvia sounded like she didn't know more, anyway, and he didn't want to appear pushy or anxious.

"Let's go look at some barren dirt." Virgil dropped his napkin on his plate and grabbed the check.

"That sounds perfect. Working outside always improves my outlook on things." Sylvia reached for her purse. "What's my share?"

"This is on me."

"Isn't the sales person supposed to pick up the check?"

"You can make it up to me later."

"That's really sweet. Thank you."

It only took a few minutes for them to reach Virgil's home. He pulled into his driveway while Sylvia parked at the curb. Virgil fervently hoped Stan wouldn't come running over.

"Let's go this way." Virgil pointed to a pebble path leading from the front sidewalk around the right side of the house. "We can walk past my roses on the way to the side gate."

"They're lovely!" Sylvia paused to sniff several blooms.

Virgil fidgeted behind her, glancing around warily.

"I've never seen such a fine collection of heirloom specimens." She waved her hand across the garden. "Your Gallica is exquisite, and this Rugosa is unbelievably prolific."

"Thank you. Most people don't even know they're heirloom, let alone recognize any specific class." He pointed right and stepped around her. "Shall we?"

The two proceeded through the heavy wooden gate to the backyard. Virgil discreetly locked the gate behind them so Stan couldn't follow.

"My goodness, you weren't lying!" Sylvia lifted her hand to her mouth as she stared at the barren yard.

"Help!" Virgil gently took her elbow and steered her deeper into the yard.

"Have you lived here long?"

Virgil tried not to bristle at the implication of his neglect. "Certainly long enough to have done something back here."

Sylvia whirled. "I'm so sorry! I didn't mean to imply anything. Honest."

"It's okay. You're right. I should have addressed this long before now. Guess I have enough ego to want to show off my roses, so I planted them in the front yard. I don't throw patio parties, and don't have pets, so my backyard rarely even crosses my mind."

Sylvia patted Virgil's arm. "Please don't apologize. Most people don't put the love and attention you have into their front yards, let alone the space few people see."

"Thank you. Feel free to walk around. I'll go hunt down the paperwork. Won't take a minute."

He hated abandoning his guest, but wanted to take a quick look around before inviting her inside. Sure enough, he'd left his mother's motif journal on the kitchen table, where he'd set it the night before. He should have locked it in the chancel. He'd do so as soon as Sylvia left.

He temporarily tucked the journal into the pantry with his cookbooks, then quickly hurried to the closet in his home office. He'd known all along where the original survey was - in a cardboard tube tucked in the corner behind some file boxes.

Virgil poked his head out the back door and waved the tube. "Seen enough? Would you like some tea? We can look at this in more comfort than out here on the patio."

"I'd like that."

Sylvia sat at the breakfast table and watched Virgil brew mint tea.

"So is it hopeless?" Virgil carried two cups of tea to the table and sat across from Sylvia.

"Not at all, although most of the yard is hard-packed and barren and will need tilling and amending before we can plant anything."

"More like concrete, you mean."

Sylvia laughed. "It's our heavy clay soil. And with the recent drought really drying things out, concrete isn't that far off the mark.

"What can you plant there?"

"I'll plant shade-tolerant ferns and flowers under the large sycamore in the one corner. The other corner is heavily overgrown with weeds. Looks like that soil is more disturbed. It'll still need amending, after we kill the weeds, but it won't need as much tilling."

"You're the expert. I trust your judgement on what needs to be done."

The two chatted about landscape ideas for another hour.

"I've occupied your time long enough." She waved at the large paper in front of them. "May I borrow this so I can work on a plan for you?"

"Of course, but I have one request."

"What's that?"

"No more roses!" Virgil laughed. "I love my roses, but I want something different back here."

"Deal." Sylvia stood. "Give me a week."

"Wait. We haven't discussed your fee."

"I can't charge you for this! I'm too out of practice."

"Nonsense. You're a professional. You don't forget how to do something you love and have done for years. Tell me what you used to charge."

"I asked $100 for an initial design, then $50 an hour for the installation, plus the cost of plants and other materials."

"Since that was over twenty years ago, you need to update your rates. How about $175 for your design and $75 an hour?"

"I… I don't know what to say. Thank you. That's very generous."

"No, it's logical. Prices have changed since the nineties."

As Virgil walked Sylvia out, he found he wanted to kiss her. It'd been a long time since he'd dated or been in a relationship. Since right after his mother's ordeal.

Don't rush things. There's time.

He paused at the door, then held out his hand. She shook it with a firm grip then gave him a quick hug.

"You've renewed my faith that everything will work out," she whispered in his ear before turning and hurrying down the sidewalk.

With a long, ragged sigh, Virgil closed the door and leaned on it. He'd enjoyed the afternoon immensely, but was distressed by the additional news Sylvia told him about the Truth Seekers.

She said sorcerers. I'm not a sorcerer, but are they talking about people like me?

She'd said the Truth Seekers were after people who were "messing with the natural order of things." From their perspective that could be him.

Are there others like me in Lichen? Do the Truth Seekers possibly know of me specifically?

Virgil sat in his mother's chair and buried his face in his hands.

Mama, I wish you'd told me what you knew, or at least suspected.

When Virgil raised his head he was determined. He'd go to the meeting. He needed to see who these people were and how many were involved.

I just hope no one calls me a sorcerer.

(14)

Man can learn nothing unless he proceeds from the known to the unknown. ~Claude Bernard (1813-1878)

Virgil opened the door to Stan's banging at 6 that evening.

"Hello, Stan." Virgil didn't extend an invitation to come inside. He dodged as Stan's hand swung forward to knock one last time. "I have a doorbell, you know."

Stan ignored the comment. "Heya Virg! Ready to go? Your eye sure still looks bad."

It occurred to Virgil he'd never actually confirmed to Stan he was going. The young man had clearly jumped to that conclusion.

"It'll take a few more days before my eye is all better. And you're an hour early, Stan."

"I know it's early." Stan shuffled his feet. "But I can't wait to bring you as my guest. And anyways, some people show up early."

Virgil sighed, then considered. Perhaps going early was a good idea. He could scope out the place and meet members. If he felt uncomfortable, he could slip out before the meeting began.

"Okay, let's go." Virgil grabbed his keys from the foyer table and locked the door.

"Yeah!" Stan loped to the passenger side of Virgil's SUV and jerked on the handle. "Hey, it's locked." Stan jerked on the handle again.

"Stop doing that." Virgil unlocked the vehicle from the porch, then followed the young man. "Where are they meeting?" Virgil asked as he backed his SUV out of the driveway.

"The Community Center by the bank."

Virgil nodded and turned that direction. While Stan babbled, Virgil turned his thoughts inward. They were going to the same location where his mother had gotten the agenda she used in her last motif.

This is going to be hard.

There was still plenty of parking since they were early. Virgil pulled into a spot near the parking lot entrance, so it would be easy if he chose to leave.

Stan bounded from the car and headed for the door. He paused, tapping his foot as he waited for Virgil to catch up.

Virgil ducked his head to hide a smile.

I guess I'm his show-and-tell trophy tonight.

Thirty or so folding metal chairs were arranged in several rows facing a folding plastic table that was set in the front of the room. On the table was a short stack of paper with a half brick on top.

Virgil wanted to see what was on the papers, but the minute he and Stan entered the room, all eyes turned toward him. Instead, he stopped just inside the door and smiled and nodded toward the small group of men by a coffee pot on a shelf in the back of the room.

All men? I wonder if there are female members, too?

"Come on." Stan crossed the room and joined the men, pouring himself a half a cup of coffee, then filling the rest of the cup with milk from a gallon jug.

Before he could follow Stan, a man with fluffy white hair and wearing a wrinkled grey suit said something to the other men, then headed Virgil's direction. Halfway there a smile appeared on his face, but it didn't reach his eyes.

"Hello, there." He extended his hand and shook Virgil's in a crushing grip. "Stan said he was bringing a friend. I'm Cotton."

Of course you are. Virgil noted the lack of a last name and followed suit. "My name's Virgil." *Is this the white-haired man Mama followed here that night?*

"Sorry about your eye. Stan said you hurt it helping your mother." Cotton's tone didn't match the sincerity of the words.

"Thanks." Virgil nodded. He studied the man before him. In spite of his snow-white hair, he didn't look that old. Perhaps late-fifties. But his expression was cold, hard, that of a man who's spent many years angry or bitter. *Wonder what his problem is?*

"Stan told us all about you," another man, wearing a faded plaid work shirt and baggy jeans, said as he approached. His handshake was less aggressive. "My name's Warren."

"Nice to meet you, Warren." Virgil smiled. "Probably some of what he said is true."

The two men laughed, but Virgil caught a quick unspoken exchange between them.

One by one, the other men ambled over and introduced themselves. Virgil couldn't remember all the names but got the same impression of each — slightly disheveled, wary, brash.

After a brief introduction, generally including an appraisal from Virgil's head to his toes, each man moved away, back to the coffee pot or a chair in one of the rows. Virgil noticed most of the men sat near the front.

Eager beavers.

It was still twenty minutes until the meeting would begin. Before more members arrived, Virgil moved away from the door. He headed toward the coffee, then decided he was jittery enough. Instead, he checked out the books on the shelves along the far wall.

Most were old non-fiction about Lichen and Texas, including a dozen about various battles that had occurred over the years. He didn't find them particularly interesting, but they kept him occupied and his back to the door, so the new arrivals to the meeting left him alone.

He felt uncomfortable, but not worried, at least not yet, so when Cotton moved to the front of the room and called for everyone to be seated, Virgil did so. But caution prevailed, and he chose a chair on the end of the back row.

"Great bunch, ain't it!" Stan whispered as he sat beside Virgil, slurping on his pale coffee.

Virgil waggled his head toward the front as an indication of why he wasn't answering. In truth, he had no answer.

As the last of the people settled down, squeaking chairs and clearing throats, Virgil looked around the space. *Where did Mama hide?*

He saw a door in the wall behind Cotton. *Is that the closet?*

It must be. He saw no other doors. A chill ran through him. He was looking at the door that influenced how the motif diffused onto her. When the burglars broke in, she'd been compelled to hide in her closet. It was her near fatal mistake.

Cotton cleared his throat and the last of the shuffling and noise stopped. "Let's start with a prayer. Bubba, why don't you do the honors this week."

Virgil took the opportunity to check out the other people. There were now perhaps twenty in the room. Only three were women.

There was no way to know if the women were there alone or accompanying their husbands.

Twenty! Bigger than I expected for such a small town.

When the prayer was over, Virgil raised his head and quickly scanned the room again. Booger was on the far end of the front row. He was surprised to see one member of the Lichen Police Department in the second row. *Is he undercover or is he a member?*

Virgil vaguely recognized two other men from around town, although he couldn't place from where. A blonde woman wearing large purple-framed glasses turned just as he glanced her direction. She caught his eye and smiled.

He automatically returned the smile, then quickly looked away. She looked familiar. A second later, recognition slammed into his brain. Those purple glasses! It was Tammy from Harold's Cafe!

Should I slip out? Stay? What's Tammy doing here? Is she one of these loonies?

She'd never seemed like a conspiracy nut. Every time he saw her at Harold's she came across as perfectly normal. Then he realized he'd never seen her anywhere but Harold's. *I don't really know her at all.*

That realization drew him up short. He stared down at the bandage on his wrist as Cotton droned on about who was responsible for next week's coffee and asked someone to pass out the agenda.

When an agenda was waved below his face he glanced up to see Tammy standing beside him. She winked, but said nothing. Instead she moved on, handing out more agendas.

Virgil's mind raced.

What was the wink about? Does she think I'm a Truth Seeker? Is she one? Or is she here spying, and the wink is conspiratorial?

He'd best be careful and jump to no conclusions. There were just too many unknowns.

"Everyone have an agenda?" Cotton held one up. "Good. Let's get started."

Virgil glanced at the agenda to see what was planned. The items were about what he'd expected: fluoride update, death meter update, FEMA camp status. The last item caught his eye: sorcerer names collection update.

He broke out in a cold sweat. When he saw Stan staring at him he grinned and fanned his face with the agenda. Stan nodded and mouthed "hot" in response.

Virgil closed his free hand into a fist, digging nails into palm, to divert his attention back to reality. He focused entirely on Cotton. The first few agenda items were so ludicrous they were almost boring, but he listened anyway, hoping to gain more insight into the group and its members.

Warren gave the report on fluoride. He and a small committee were preparing a petition they'd have area residents sign before presenting it to the city. The petition would demand an official end to fluoridation in the city's water supply. Warren quoted statistics about fluoride causing everything from low IQ to defective thyroid and pineal glands. Virgil had to stifle a laugh a couple of times. His choking cough caused Stan to poke him in the arm.

A man Virgil hadn't met reported on the *death meters*, which Virgil realized were the utility company's Smart meters Donna had mentioned. The man claimed two people had recently been hospitalized with meter-induced brain tumors. "One of them is now dumb as a bucket of rocks. Probably going to die soon." The quoted source studies sounded less than reliable to Virgil.

How does anyone believe this crap? He glanced around the room and saw many heads nodding. He suddenly felt like an injured bird surrounded by cats. Donna was right. So was Sylvia. These people were nuts. He had to be cautious and alert.

Another man stood to give the FEMA report, but he didn't have much to say. He mostly repeated sound bites from certain news channels and claimed to know "for a fact" what he said was true.

At last they came to the final agenda item. Virgil shifted nervously in his seat, eliciting glances from a couple of nearby members. He froze and sat stock still, barely breathing.

Do not attract attention. Be careful!

"Now to our most important task." Cotton picked a sheet off the stack of papers from the table. "As many of you know, our small town is under attack. Most people aren't even aware of the danger, but we've been given the ability to see and know the truth."

Murmurs of support, and even a few "Amens!" swept the room.

"So far we've identified four sorcerers." He waved the paper in the air. "Their actions have been subtle to this point but we know they're planning a major assault on the innocent people of Lichen. They must be stopped."

Another round of support forced Cotton to raise his hand for silence. "Now I'm not one to condone violence, but we're going to have to get aggressive if we want to save our town. I'm going to assign teams of three to each sorcerer. Your job will be to follow them for the next week or so to get a feel for their habits."

"What if we see 'em doing something bad?" a woman in the third row called.

"Bring it to my attention immediately." Cotton slapped the table. "Do NOT do anything on your own. Does everyone understand? These people are evil. We must protect ourselves. We must protect our families. Confronting them could be dangerous for everyone in this organization."

"Yeah," Stan yelled, causing Virgil to jump. "Just look at ol' Joe."

Tammy nodded. "Stan's right. Joe's accident was no such thing. Did you read the condition of his car? That's not normal failure."

"Maybe it was vandalized," Virgil said before he could stop himself. *What the hell am I doing?*

"Maybe." Cotton shrugged. "But Tammy's right. We need to be careful. We must assume Joe knew something and was taken out, at least mentally. He's lucky they didn't kill him."

Virgil glanced toward Tammy and caught her eye. This time she didn't wink. She glared. He turned away, his face burning.

Now I know. She's one of them. This complicated everything. Could he still use Harold's as his research point? He hoped so, but he'd have to be wary from now on how he reacted and what he said. *What am I going to tell her about my being here tonight?*

Virgil would have to worry about that later. Cotton yelled for quiet and returned to the topic of sorcerers. He called twelve of the attendees, including Tammy, Warren, and Booger, to the front and handed each a single sheet of paper from the stack Virgil had wanted to see when he'd first arrived.

"Here's the list of confirmed sorcerers." Then, pointing down the line, he assigned one name off the list to each team of three.

What makes Cotton and the others believe they have "proof" these people are sorcerers? What did these people do?

Virgil badly wanted to know the names on that list. He assumed his wasn't, since he was still safely sitting in the room. He was afraid to ask Tammy about it. Same for Booger, who'd struck him as being on the volatile side. Perhaps Virgil could speak to Warren at the end of the meeting. He'd only just met him, but he'd been friendly enough.

As the group returned to their seats, Cotton continued, "The addresses we've provided are residences. We added work locations and addresses where known. Follow your targets. Always be in teams of two. That's why there are three of you — even with busy schedules, two of you should be able to make time on a regular basis. Take turns. And make notes of everything you see and hear.

Do not try to just remember. Report only to me. I'll put together an update for next week's meeting."

Virgil knew in his gut it was vital he find out everything he could. He didn't want to raise any flags like the four people on the list had apparently done.

Are they really like me, or are they innocent victims of a witch hunt?

He let his mind wander as the meeting wound down. He jumped when those around him, including Stan, shuffled and squeaked chairs as they stood and moved down the rows. He stood, too, and moved quickly away from Stan before the young man said anything.

Scanning the room, Virgil spotted Warren near the coffee pot. Someone had placed a box of grocery store cookies next to the coffee. Members were clustered in twos and threes, munching cookies and talking softly. Some stopped talking as he walked by.

"Warren, I'm glad I came. Sounds like important stuff in the works." Virgil smiled and nodded toward the paper still in Warren's hand.

"We're doing our best for Lichen."

"I can see that. What's it take to become a member?" Virgil didn't really want to be a member, but he wanted to keep Warren talking and alleviate any concerns the man might have.

"I'll get you a form. You turn it in to me or Cotton, along with your membership fee."

"That's it?" Virgil was surprised. It probably showed on his face.

"Cotton interviews you, then presents his opinion to the board members, who vote before the next meeting. If you're accepted, we call you."

Virgil nodded. "That makes sense." He decided to take a chance and waved toward the paper. "Four people, huh? Wow. That's pretty scary. We're not a big town. Wonder why so many are here? Think the big cities have this problem?"

"Who cares?" Warren shrugged. "We only worry about Lichen."

"Sure. I must admit, I'm curious if I know any of them. Would you let me look?"

Warren stuffed the paper in his pants pocket. "Sorry, no. Even non-committee members don't know. We don't want any vigilantes before we're ready to make a move."

"I understand." *Damn. I'm going to have to try Tammy.* He'd need to be careful how he asked.

Warren excused himself and brushed roughly past Virgil. He turned to look for Stan and almost bumped into Tammy.

"Fancy seein' you here, Virgil!" Her grin was toothy, almost menacing.

"You, too. I didn't expect to know anyone but Stan." Virgil wasn't sure how to take her expression. He was definitely seeing a side of her he'd never noticed at the cafe.

Tammy shrugged. "I keep up with things in this town. The Truth Seekers found me. Figured I could help them learn about stuff."

That could be trouble. "I'm sure they're happy to have you. Harold's Cafe seems like THE local source for all the latest gossip and inside information around town."

"And I hear it all!" Tammy laughed, then leveled her gaze at Virgil. "Of course, I haven't decided if I'm going to share everything with Cotton and the others. There's value in keeping a few secrets to myself."

Ice ran up Virgil's spine. *Is she telling me something? Does SHE suspect me?*

"Nothing wrong with that. Secrets can be powerful tools."

"Ya got that right." Tammy hrmphed. "I'll decide when it's time to pull out my best ones."

Virgil wanted to probe for more details, but Stan came hurrying up. Tammy took that opportunity to slip away without another word.

"Ready, Virg?"

Virgil sighed. He'd learn nothing else tonight. Maybe he'd find out something if he went to Harold's Cafe for breakfast. Tammy may not say anything else, especially in a public place, but he had to try.

Who was on that list? His gut told him his life depended on finding out.

(15)

Trapped, like a trap in a trap. ~Dorothy Parker (1893-1967)

Virgil arrived at Harold's on Friday morning at his usual time of 8:30. He'd been up since 5, but didn't want to break his pattern. It might raise suspicion in Tammy.

"Morning Virgil, long time no see." Tammy hooted with laughter.

Virgil chose to ignore the remark. "Morning, Tammy."

"Hi, Virgil!" Lisa waved, then returned to clearing the table next to where he sat. "Haven't seen you in here for days."

"Had to take care of some things for Mama." He wasn't lying, although the things likely weren't what Lisa would have guessed. "How've you been?"

"I'm awesome!" Lisa grinned from ear to ear. "Got a new boyfriend. He's totally amazing."

"That's great." Virgil nodded. "Everyone deserves to be happy."

"How's your mama?"

Virgil turned to see who'd asked and saw Marshall, his UPS delivery man.

"She's good, Marshall. Saw her a few days ago. I picked up some things from her house to make her room more personal. Even got her favorite chair. Going to deliver it later today."

"That's mighty nice," Marshall said.

Tammy grinned. "Always nice to do special things for people we care about. Better than doing crummy things to people we don't like."

"Huh?" Lisa cocked her head.

Huh is right. What the heck did Tammy mean by that weird statement?

"Never mind." Tammy shook her head.

"No delivery for you today, Virgil," Marshall said. "Haven't had any for a week now. Not since whatever that dangerous package was." Marshall laughed.

"Dangerous package?" Tammy raised her eyebrows and stared at Virgil.

Virgil shrugged. He hoped it looked casual and disinterested. "I use solvents with my woodworking. When I can't find them locally, I have to order them online. Anything that falls into the category of solvents has to be labelled on the outside as corrosive."

"Hmmm." Tammy frowned. "What do you need scary chemicals for with wood? It's *wood*, for cryin' out loud. Not metal, like, I dunno, car parts or something."

"Daddy used solvents to clean his varnish brushes." Lisa lifted the heavy bin of dirty dishes. "He hated having to buy new brushes." She laughed as she shuffled toward the kitchen. "Although in Daddy's case it was usually gasoline he'd siphoned from his truck."

Virgil sighed. Lisa had innocently saved him having to respond to what seemed more than idle curiosity on Tammy's part. He was now more convinced than ever that she was an actual member of the Truth Seekers and potentially dangerous to him.

I better not ask her anything today about the list of alleged sorcerer names.

Tammy approached his table and poured coffee. "Surprised to see you last night."

Her tone on the surface was casual, but Virgil detected an edge he couldn't quite pin down. Was she suspicious? Was she being conspiratorial? Maybe he was being paranoid and she was just tired. *I don't believe that for a minute.*

He shrugged. "Stan told me about the group. After what happened to Mama, I figured maybe they were folks I'd have things in common with."

"Maybe so. Still, wolves and sheep don't mix well."

Virgil flinched. *Does she think I'm the wolf or the sheep?*

He took a chance. "They didn't strike me as wolves. A bit confused, maybe." *And dangerous.*

Her expression turned piercing and cold. "You never know about people, do you?" She stared for a beat, then added, "I'll have Harold make your usual breakfast." She turned and walked away, leaving Virgil shaken and confused.

Tammy didn't come near his table again. Lisa delivered his food, even though her job was bussing tables. When he walked to the register, Lisa hurried over.

"Can you run the register?" Virgil asked.

"Tammy said…um…she's…uh, she's busy in the back. I'll manage."

He paid his $6.23 breakfast with a $10 bill. Lisa was clearly flummoxed and frustrated, so after several minutes Virgil told her to keep the change.

"Thanks!"

His attempt to learn more from Tammy had failed.

What the hell am I going to do?

He sat behind the wheel of his car, but didn't start it. His heart pounded. Beads of sweat formed on his forehead. He closed his eyes and rubbed his temples. After several minutes, the idea hit him like a lightning bolt. He'd try Booger, Ignatius, Iggy, whatever name he needed to use to get the young man to talk to him.

He called Sylvia as he drove toward home.

"Hello? Sylvia speaking."

Virgil smiled at the sound of her voice and the formal way she answered her own cell phone. "Hi, Sylvia, it's Virgil. I hope I'm not disturbing you."

"Not at all! I was just looking over your survey. I don't have anything for you yet."

"I'm not calling for that. I don't expect anything for a week or more. Take your time. I wanted to pass an offer by you."

"Oh?" Sylvia's voice sounded both excited and wary.

"Nothing sinister. I thought it might be nice to reassure your son and daughter I'm serious about hiring you, and not some stalker or nutcase."

"That's very sweet! Iggy asked what happened at your house. He was the epitome of the concerned son."

"Then how about dinner for four tomorrow night, if your kids are available. I know it's Saturday, but it's a small town. Maybe they don't have plans."

"I'll ask them. Donna is stopping by on her way home. Iggy… well, I'll text him. Who knows where he is or what he's up to."

Indeed.

"Where did you have in mind?"

"The new steak and seafood bistro that opened last month?"

"Oh! I'm not sure I can swing that at the moment."

"No, no, no! My treat. I insist."

"You already paid for lunch. I can't take advantage of you again."

"You can discount me a half hour of labor if it makes you feel better."

"Make it an hour and you've got a deal. I'll call you back soon."

Virgil clicked off his phone and smiled. *It's a start.*

He was tending his roses when Sylvia called two hours later.

"Donna is thrilled at your offer and immediately said yes. In spite of his previous concern, I had to talk Iggy into changing his plans but he said yes, too. He said he'd tell someone else they had to help set up the kegs for the party. I didn't pursue it. I'm not sure I want to know."

"Wonderful! I'll call the bistro. How does 7:30 sound?"

"That's fine. Should we meet you there?"

Virgil wanted to see where Booger lived. It might come in handy. Since he still lived with Sylvia, it should be easy to do.

"No, parking is pretty tight there. How about I pick you three up at 7:15?"

After a brief pause Sylvia said, "Sure. That'll be fine. Iggy and I live at 303 Sattler. Donna can meet us here."

I won't get anything out of him over dinner, but I can at least set the trap for later.

"Great! See you then." Virgil nodded as he disconnected the call.

He spent the evening sitting in his mother's chair and staring out at the street. A few neighbors walked by with their dogs, and an occasional car passed, but even the town seemed to be on hold.

Virgil was wary and concerned. He knew he couldn't wait long to do something to protect himself, although he didn't yet know what to do. There were Tammy's suspicions, and the Truth Seekers in general. Then there was Booger, who might grow more curious about Virgil if his mother began showing interest.

Too many unanswered questions hung in the air. He knew he'd made statements at Harold's he'd intended as deflectors, but maybe that wasn't how they came across. Maybe instead, he'd shined a light on himself.

Virgil again thought of the conversation the morning after Joe's car accident. What had he said at breakfast? He'd feigned surprise about Joe, pretty convincingly he thought. He'd commented about how Joe'd always been reckless. That shouldn't have aroused suspicion.

"Oh hell." His eyes grew big and he nearly dropped his teacup when he remembered he'd specifically made a crack about Joe's karma catching up with him. And Marshall had turned to stare at him after Lisa mentioned Joe's car looked like he'd run over acid. Virgil closed his eyes and shuddered. Tammy'd noticed Marshall's stare.

And it had come up again this morning at the restaurant.

Not good.

Had he made offhand comments after past motifs, too? It was too long ago to remember that level of detail. Maybe Tammy's suspicions had grown over time, not just because of the recent comments about Joe's accident.

I wish I could talk to Mama. Maybe she could help. Maybe she could tell me what to do.

(16)

What greater thing is there for two human souls than to
feel that they are joined…to strengthen each other…
to be one with each other in silent unspeakable
memories. ~George Eliot (1819-1880)

Saturday morning, Virgil avoided Harold's and instead strapped his mother's beloved chair to his dolly, loaded it into his SUV, and drove to Oak Creek. He used his furniture dolly to transfer it from his car down the long hallway to his mother's room at the far end.

"Morning Mr. Harris." Nancy Williams, the director of nursing, nodded as he passed the central station. "Beautiful chair."

Virgil stopped. "Thank you, Nancy. It was Mama's favorite. I'm hoping its presence makes her happy."

"That's mighty nice of you," another nurse said.

Virgil didn't remember the name of the second nurse who'd spoken. She'd only been there a month. "Thank you."

Virgil wheeled the dolly into his mother's room. "Good morning, Mama. I brought something today."

Although his mother turned her head toward him, her expression was blank.

"Remember your chintz chair? I brought it here."

His mother mumbled something but Virgil couldn't tell what from across the room. He stopped the dolly inside the door and moved to sit on the side of his mother's bed.

"What did you say? Did you see the chair?"

"Chair." His mother's voice was clear and smooth. She followed that one word with more mumbling, but Virgil still took heart. She'd said one specific word that actually fit the situation! It wasn't exactly a conversation, but it was as close as they'd come in weeks.

"Yes, Mama, I brought your chair. Would you like to try sitting in it?"

When his mother nodded, albeit barely detectable, Virgil leaped up. "I'll get Nancy to help move you." He hurried to the nurse's station.

"Might be pretty hard to have her sit up," Nancy said as she and another nurse followed Virgil back to Pearl Harris's room. "She has no muscle strength anymore."

"I'll hold her if I have to, but seeing that chair elicited a spark of awareness I've not seen in a long time. It may go nowhere, but even if it lasts only a few minutes, I want to give it a try. Miracles happen now and then."

Nancy pursed her lips and said nothing.

Virgil dollied the chair to near the bed, then angled it toward the window.

"Please step aside while we move her." Nancy waved toward the corner.

Virgil stood to the side and watched the nurses move various tubes and collection bags around. They struggled with the slight but dead weight of the elder woman to lift her from the bed and shift her into the chair. Pearl slumped first one way then the other until they finally got her reasonably upright.

"Please don't leave her unattended for even a moment." Nancy frowned. "She's pretty unstable."

"Promise." Virgil pulled the nursing home chair next to his mother and sat.

Once Virgil had hold of his mother's arm, the second nurse let go. She adjusted the bags again so they were tucked beneath the edge of the upholstered chair, away from where Virgil might accidentally trip over or kick them.

"I'll check on you in a few minutes." Nancy pointed to the call button. "You press that if anything happens and you need help."

Virgil nodded then turned to his mother. He held her gently but firmly by one arm to help keep her from slumping again. Her skin felt as delicate as a flower petal. He hoped his fingers wouldn't leave bruises.

"Do you like your chair? Are you happy to be sitting in it?"

"Chair."

"Yes, Mama, this is your favorite chair. I brought it from your home."

"Home."

"Yes, Mama, your home. I've been taking care of it for you."

"Care."

"That's right. I go to your house to take care of your things. To keep them all clean and ready for you." He knew she'd never return there, but perhaps part of her still thought it possible. He doubted that, too, but the pretense eased his heart.

"Chancel."

Virgil started; for a brief moment he let go of his mother's arm. She immediately slumped to the right. He rose enough to shift her back upright and again gripped her arm. She was the most cognizant and aware he'd seen her in many months. It didn't matter that she was saying only one word at a time.

"I entered your chancel, Mama. I'd only been in there the one other time, when you told me to get your table."

"Tuble."

"Yes, your table. It's now safely in my chancel. I'm very proud of it. But I haven't removed anything else. Your wardrobe is still there."

"Keys."

He noted that she specifically said "keys" and not "key" so he assumed she remembered she'd locked the wardrobe that held her supplies.

"I found both keys. The one to the chancel door and the one to your wardrobe. I went through your supplies. Everything was still there and undisturbed, and just as organized as you left them."

"Warbole."

"Warbole?" Virgil frowned. "Do you mean wardrobe?"

Pearl nodded.

"Yes, Mama, I opened your wardrobe. I found your motif journal."

"Journal. JOURNAL. JOURNAL! JOURNAL!! J-O-U-R-N-A-L!!!!!"

With each repetition of the word, his mother grew louder. Her body tensed. He didn't want the nurse to return yet, so he gently covered his mother's mouth.

"Shhh, Mama, it's all right. Your journal is safe. I have it at home."

"Safe."

"Yes, it's safe."

The muscles in his mother's arm softened and relaxed. Her breathing slowed. He wasn't sure if it was wise to pursue the journal's contents, but he needed to see if he could learn anything while she had even a tiny spark of awareness.

"I read your journal, Mama. Read about your last motif."

"Moftit."

"Yes. The *motif* you did to protect me."

"'tect."

"Yes. The motif was against the Truth Seekers. The one with the ball of paper you made from one of their meeting agendas."

His mother's scream pierced his ears. He lurched away. She immediately slumped so far she almost fell out of the chair, but she continued to scream.

"Mama, it's okay. Mama, please. Please be quiet." Virgil grabbed and tugged on both her arms, but he couldn't get her upright from her awkward and precarious position.

The two nurses came charging into the room and shoved Virgil to the side.

"Please move, Mr. Harris." Nancy elbowed past him.

"Let us get her back into bed," said the other.

Virgil shrank into the corner, as far out of the way as possible, while the nurses lifted the now quiet and limp woman onto her bed. Nancy took a syringe from her pocket.

"I'm giving her a sedative. This amount of stress is very hard on her weakened system."

Virgil didn't even ask what it was. It didn't matter. It would put his mother to sleep. At least she'd be calm, but he'd now learn nothing of value from her. All he'd learned was that she probably knew her final motif was why she was there. That her blood on the motif had diffused onto her and caused the series of events that led to her permanent residence in the Oak Creek Estate in Pemberton Heights.

He sighed, garnering a glare from Nancy.

"What did you say to her? What happened?" Virgil flinched at the sharpness in her voice.

"I'm sorry. Didn't mean to upset her. I thought sitting in the chair might make her happy. I was telling her I'd been taking care of her house and that I'd decided to bring her chair from there."

"And that's all? That's what caused her to scream?" The other nurse put her hands on her hips.

He struggled to think how to respond. "Yes. I told her I'd been looking at one of her favorite books. Maybe she was reading it the night her house was burgled. I don't know." He hated to outright lie, because he wasn't good at it, but he didn't know what else to say.

"I'd avoid inflammatory topics from now on." Nancy scowled, then dropped the empty syringe into her pocket.

"It wasn't... I didn't..." Virgil stopped. He HAD been talking about a potentially upsetting topic with his mother. That wasn't what he'd just claimed to Nancy, but it was still the truth. "Of course. You're right."

Both nurses nodded and left. Virgil turned to his mother, who was now snoring softly, and kissed her forehead.

"I'm sorry, Mama. I didn't mean to upset you. But we'll have to try again soon. I need to know anything you can tell me, even if only one word at a time."

"Thank you again." Virgil paused at the nursing station.

Nancy nodded. "Probably not a good idea to try the chair again."

Virgil blushed and nodded, then hurried out to his car.

(17)

*Some things you do because you want to. Some things
you do because of the needs of others in your family.*
~Gordon Atkinson

Instead of heading home, Virgil turned toward the highway and
pulled into Bobby's Hauls-All Rental. He rented a medium-sized
trailer, which he hooked behind his SUV, then drove straight to his
mother's house.

He spent the rest of the day cleaning. He emptied her chancel of
every motif-related item and loaded everything into the trailer,
along with her remaining clothes and personal items, the few items
left in her pantry, and assorted mementos he wanted to keep and
hadn't already retrieved. He stuffed all of the partially melted
candles in a garbage bag.

Once the third bedroom was no longer a chancel, he shifted
furniture from around the house—a bookcase from the guest room,
another from the corner of the breakfast nook, armchairs from the
living room, and the table from the hallway that had hidden the
wardrobe key—until the space was a reasonable-looking library/
reading room.

He raided the upper shelves of the pantry and various closets for vases, centerpieces, and decorations to indicate the wardrobe and closet were simply storage for seasonal and specialty items. His mother had so many books, it was easy to transfer some of them into the bookcase he'd moved into the former chancel without leaving other bookcases looking too empty.

He stood in the doorway when he was done and nodded. No one would think anything was unusual about the room, and only those who were extremely sensitive would ever detect any odd energy about the space.

Virgil sighed. He hated to destroy his mother's chancel. It'd existed here since before he was born. But especially after his mother's agitation this morning at even the mention of this space and her last motif, he knew it was time to let it go and get the house on the market.

Things change. Sometimes not for the better, but they still change.

His last action before locking the front door and driving away was to turn the thermostat off.

No candles to melt anymore. I'll call a realtor on Monday.

Virgil unloaded the trailer as soon as he got home, stacking things in his guest room and on his dining room table. He'd sort everything later. Perhaps he could ask Sylvia for recommendations on what to do with his mother's clothes. She'd probably like to help.

He returned the trailer and spent the rest of the afternoon absentmindedly puttering around his own house. He took a break and headed for his mother's chair by the window, but remembered it was now at Oak Creek. His shoulders slumped, and he sat among the items heaped on the dining room table.

Touching one of his mother's favorite crocheted afghans, he thought about what he'd done. He'd closed a chapter in his mother's life without being able to ask her about it. Tears brimmed in his eyes.

I'm sorry, Mama.

His thoughts turned to his own life. He'd fathered no children and never expected to, since he was already 48, even if he did eventually marry. So who'd be there to deal with his personal items? Would anyone care at all? And what of his chancel?

He especially worried about his chancel. What would happen when he died? What if he ended up in a nursing home like his mother? He had no one he trusted to enter his chancel and dispense with its contents. *I wish I could talk to Mama. Or at least to another relative.*

Who were his relatives? Where might they be? His mother never spoke of anyone. He didn't even know if she had siblings. He'd met his grandmother once, but the memory was vague, almost ephemeral. He'd only been five or six, and all he remembered was being frightened of her stern and imposing nature.

His father'd died in some type of industrial accident when Virgil was eight, so he had even less of an idea about that part of his family tree. He recalled his dad had a younger sister, but he hadn't seen or heard of her since his father's funeral. His mother never mentioned her again.

Virgil had never before cared about any extended family. But as he got older, he felt ever more isolated from his mother, and the desire to know his roots grew stronger. Someday, he'd pursue it.

He drained his teacup and glanced at the clock on the wall. It was already after 6. *Time to get ready for dinner!*

Virgil pulled up to Sylvia's house at 7:12. He was nervous, both at seeing her again and at his opportunity to start building a bridge to Booger. He had no idea how long it might take to get any information from the young man, but he had to try.

He was walking up the sidewalk when the door opened and Donna stepped out. "Hi, Virgil. It's nice to see you again. Mom will be ready in a couple of minutes. Come on in."

"Thank you, Donna. Nice to see you again, too."

"Mom's not used to getting dressed up anymore," Donna whispered when Virgil reached the porch. She blushed deep red and added, "I didn't mean to imply… I'm not trying to say…"

Virgil smiled. "No need to apologize. Consider this a date with the whole family. I hate to work with someone I don't know personally, at least not a little."

Donna smiled in return. "Thanks. I'm glad you feel that way."

"That him?"

Virgil assumed the insolent voice yelling from inside the house belonged to Sylvia's son.

"Yeah, that's Booger." Donna shrugged and rolled her eyes.

"What should I call him?" Virgil whispered. "You call him Booger. Sylvia calls him Iggy. His real name is Ignatius."

"Whatever you do, don't call him Ignatius! How about Iggy?"

Virgil nodded and went into the house. His target was sprawled in an overstuffed chair, one leg dangling across a padded arm. He wore faded jeans with a tear on the left knee and a ragged T-shirt with an image of a rapper making an obscene gesture.

Virgil was instantly repulsed by the crude young man, even more than when he'd first spotted him at Domingo's Restaurant. But Virgil had a goal, and the goal was always paramount. He crossed the room and held out his hand.

"It's nice to meet you, Iggy. I'm so pleased your mother will be working on converting my Death Valley of a backyard into Eden."

Iggy slouched even deeper in the chair and purposely pulled his arms back, tucking them down at his sides. This action was not lost on his mother, who entered the room at that moment.

"Ignatius Parker! How dare you be so rude to our guest. Get your bottom out of that chair and show some manners. And change clothes. We are not going to a nice restaurant with you dressed like a homeless drug addict."

Iggy made a great show of pushing himself from the chair and shuffling down the hall. He never acknowledged Virgil's still-extended hand.

As soon as Iggy left, the room Virgil dropped his hand to his side.

"I'm so sorry." Sylvia pursed her lips. "I don't know what's happened to him. He used to be such a sweet boy."

"It's all right. Kids can be pretty obnoxious at his age."

"He's an adult! He's twenty-one. He knows better. And he certainly knows how to behave. I raised him better than that."

"Sometimes he's very much the *baby* brother." Donna shook her head. "I'll never call him anything but Booger as long as he behaves like a little snot."

"Donna!"

"Sorry, Mom. You know he is."

Virgil despised ill-behaved, rude people, no matter their age. It would be a challenge to be civil enough to get him to open up, if that was even possible. *Eyes on the prize, Virgil, eyes on the prize.*

Iggy returned, wearing clean black slacks and a red polo shirt. It appeared he'd even combed his hair.

Sylvia beamed. "You look so handsome. Please say hello to Virgil."

Virgil dutifully again extended his hand. This time Iggy took it in a bone-crushing squeeze. Virgil had no intention of taking the bait, so he subtly but quickly twisted his wrist to the left, forcing Iggy to let go.

"Nice to meet you, Iggy." Virgil wanted to get everyone out of the house, where Iggy obviously felt totally in control. He gestured toward the door. "Shall we? I made reservations for 7:30."

Let's hope this is all worth it. Iggy's a tough nut to crack.

(18)

A dinner lubricates business. ~Lord William Stowell

Dinner was a combination of awkward and pleasant, at least for Virgil. He focused his conversation on endearing himself to Sylvia and her children, especially to Iggy. Iggy, on the other hand, mostly ignored everyone else at the table and refused to look at Virgil at all.

"I'm looking forward to seeing your design for my backyard." Virgil sipped his wine and smiled at Sylvia.

"I'm so excited at a chance to get back to work. I'm even considering taking an extension course through the University of Texas in San Antonio." Sylvia buttered a roll and nibbled on it.

"But you already have a degree in landscape design, Mom," Donna said.

"I've been out of landscaping a long time." Sylvia shrugged. "People are into natives these days, and there are hybrid versions of native and adapted plants that I'd never even heard of."

"Great idea." Virgil nodded as he chewed a bite of steak. "Nothing like a refresher course to kickstart things." He turned to Iggy. "What are your interests? What drives you?"

"What drives me?" Iggy smirked and rolled his eyes.

"Iggy!" Sylvia frowned. "You used to love working on electrical things. I thought you wanted to be an electrician."

Iggy shook his head. "Yeah, well, I guess you thought wrong."

Sylvia stared at her son, her cheeks flushed red.

Virgil had to bite his tongue to keep from making a retort about the value of a good skill. *Now's not the time. Get on his good side.*

He turned to Donna. "How are things going with you? Didn't you tell me you recently finished your master's in geology?"

"Sure did!" Donna nodded, grinning from ear to ear. She lifted her wine glass in a toast, then took a big swallow of wine. "And I just got offered the chance to join an expedition to a newly discovered cave in the Amazon jungle. I'd be working side by side with the lead geologist! Well, probably more like gophering for him, but still, it'd be—"

"When were you going to tell me about this?" Sylvia's sharp voice cut her daughter off.

"I only got the call a couple hours ago. Figured I'd tell you after dinner. But I'm so excited, I couldn't help blurting it out when Virgil asked what I was up to."

"Yeah, you go play with your rocks." Iggy dropped his fork with a clatter onto his plate.

All heads turned to stare at him.

"Better than the rocks in your head." Donna gave her brother a toothy grin.

Sylvia sighed loudly. "I'm so sorry, Virgil. You'd think my ADULT children would know how to behave themselves."

Virgil hated this, but believed it might pay off in the long run. He could wiggle into the gaps in the awkward family dynamic.

He patted Sylvia's arm. "It's fine. I probably wasn't much different when I was their age." *I need to try a different angle.*

He cut a piece of steak and popped it into his mouth while he thought of how to word his next question. "Iggy, Sylvia tells me you're involved with that new group in town. The Truth Searchers? I attended a meeting the other night."

"Truth SEEKERS." Iggy rolled his eyes, but said nothing else.

"Sorry. Sounds like they're doing important things. Wasn't that you they called up front? They must know they can count on you."

"Yeah." The word came reluctantly, but Iggy followed with a little more enthusiasm. "They need lots of good people. There's bad shi…" he glanced at his mother, "…stuff going on."

"That's certainly the impression I got. Good for you!" Virgil looked briefly at Donna and Sylvia. Both gaped at him. *I'll have to deal with their shock as soon as I can.*

"'Scuse me." Iggy stood, dropped his napkin on his chair, and headed toward the door. "Gotta go smoke a cig."

As soon as the young man was out of earshot, both Donna and Sylvia accosted Virgil.

"What are you doing in that group of freaks?" Donna asked

"Please don't tell me you're involved," Sylvia pleaded.

Virgil waved his fork in the air. "No ladies, please don't worry. My neighbor Stan, who is mentally disabled, was invited to join. I went with him to check them out. For whatever reason, I feel a certain paternal affection for the young man. I didn't want him getting into something dangerous."

"But they ARE dangerous!" Sylvia's eyes grew big.

"I certainly believe that after the other night." Virgil nodded and took a sip of wine. "Haven't figured out how to ease Stan out yet. For now, I'll monitor things and make sure he's okay."

"Thank goodness you aren't really joining them!" The relief was evident in Donna's voice. "Maybe you can keep an eye on Booger, too."

"What did you mean about seeing Iggy get called up front?" Sylvia put her hand to her chest. "Is he in trouble?"

"Don't think so." Virgil shook his head. "He was picked for a... committee doing surveillance on people they have concerns about."

"That sounds dangerous." Donna frowned.

Virgil shrugged. "It really is hard to say, but for now I'd guess he's fine. The leader of the group, a man named Cotton, made it clear no one was to do anything but watch and make notes."

"I just hope he—" Donna cut off as Iggy returned to the table.

"Y'all done talking about me?"

"We weren't talking about you, actually." Sylvia smiled. "We were talking about Stan, Virgil's friend, and the reason he attended the meeting."

So, Sylvia isn't above tinkering a bit with facts. Good to know.

"Stan's your friend?" Iggy laughed. "He's mentally slow as a slug." He paused, then added, "But he's okay, I guess."

Virgil bristled at the insult to Stan, even though he knew it was true. He took a breath to calm himself before speaking. "Yes, he's my friend. I went with him to be sure he was okay, but then I got interested myself in what was being said."

"Don't want to talk about it anymore." Iggy pulled his phone from his pocket.

"Iggy, stop it." Sylvia scowled. "And put that phone away."

"No, it's all right." Virgil waved his fork. "Not much more to say anyway. Donna, why don't you tell us about this expedition?"

For the remainder of the meal, Sylvia and Virgil listened to Donna explain the plans for the Amazon trip. "I'll probably be gone three months. We leave one month from now."

"But you don't have a passport," Sylvia said.

"The foundation funding the expedition is paying for expedited passport processing."

"Sounds like they really want you." Virgil smiled and pushed his empty plate toward the center of the table.

"I know! I still can't believe it." Donna went on to talk about all the things she hoped to learn. "Gonna be a challenge, though, squeezing three months' worth of clothes and toiletries into a single suitcase."

"Guess you'll have to learn to live without makeup." Sylvia laughed.

"And lotion, and curlers, and pretty much everything else." Donna grinned. "But that's okay."

Virgil feigned interest while keeping a furtive eye on Iggy, who slouched in his chair the same as he'd done at Domingo's.

As Donna droned on, Virgil let his mind wander. *This isn't working. How can I worm my way into Iggy's world? What's it going to take to get my hands on that list? I need to see those four names.*

In a flash of inspiration, Virgil knew he had it. Iggy'd clearly demonstrated laziness. The paper was probably laying around in his room. Virgil didn't have to befriend Iggy. He needed to encourage a closer relationship with Sylvia, so he could get access to Iggy's room when the young man wasn't home.

Virgil smiled at Sylvia, eliciting a smile in return. The fact that he liked Sylvia would make it both easy and pleasant. He stifled a flash of guilt for using her. *This is important.*

The waiter quietly delivered the check to the table just as Donna wrapped up her explanation of the shots she'd have to get.

"Everyone ready to go?" Virgil dropped his credit card on the small plastic tray and caught the waiter's eye. "I'm sure the restaurant would like their table for someone else. We've occupied it for over two hours."

When Virgil stopped in front of Sylvia's house, he put his hand on her arm as a signal to wait. Donna and Iggy piled out of the back.

"You coming, Mom?" Donna asked.

"In a minute," Sylvia replied.

"Beware of strangers in cars," Iggy mumbled as he slammed his door and slouched up the sidewalk.

Donna laughed, gently closed her own door, and hurried after her brother.

"What's up?" Sylvia asked.

"Was hoping you'd like to go get a quiet cup of coffee or a drink."

"I'd like that. I'm a little frazzled after the behavior of my progeny."

Virgil laughed. "No worries."

"Let me tell Donna. Give me a sec."

As soon as Sylvia returned, Virgil pulled away from the curb. "So, coffee or alcohol?"

"After tonight's spectacle, I could use a drink."

"I know just the place." He drove to a wine bar near the courthouse square. Tony's was a quiet, small place with an impressive selection of regional wines and a few craft beers. It wasn't the most romantic spot, but it was the only bar in town that didn't feature loud music and cigarette smoke.

"I've never been here, although I've been meaning to," Sylvia said as Virgil pulled up to the curb.

"I've been here only one other time, right after Tony's opened. It's nice, but I honestly think he chose the furniture to ensure quick turnover."

"What?"

"You'll see."

"Oh!" Sylvia stopped in the doorway and stared at the decor. Tall, wooden, backless stools circled large, rough-wood construction cable spool tables. "This doesn't look like furniture designed for middle-aged backs and bottoms."

"Certainly not mine." He touched her elbow and pointed across the room, where two real tables with padded chairs were tucked in a corner. "Let's grab one of those while the getting's good."

Once seated, they perused the menu and ordered a bottle of merlot. Virgil nodded approval as the waitress opened the bottle and poured a taste into a stemless glass. After she left, Virgil filled his and Sylvia's glasses.

"I truly enjoyed this evening." Virgil smiled. When Sylvia rolled her eyes at his comment he added, "Your kids' antics made it more homey."

"Thank you. It was quite embarrassing."

"Don't be embarrassed. I know families are complicated, even though I never had much of one."

"What do you mean?" Sylvia asked.

Virgil shrugged. "I don't have siblings, and my mother's no longer really with me. I only saw my grandmother, Mama's mom, a couple times. I never got to know Dad's parents. They lived up north somewhere. And they've been dead a dozen years. Dad had one sister, but I haven't seen her since Dad died, and that's when I was eight. She may be dead, too, for all I know. If I had other relatives, I never heard about them or met them."

"That's so sad. We had many family gatherings when I was growing up. And we still see each other on holidays."

"That sounds nice. Tell me more about it." Virgil spent the next hour encouraging Sylvia to talk about herself. He occasionally touched her arm and made sure to always keep his expression interested and attentive.

It seemed to be working. Sylvia's body language gradually altered, until she was leaning into him. She shifted once, causing her knee to touch his. She left it that way, although she occasionally moved enough to cause her knee to brush his leg.

Virgil carefully calculated every word, touch, and expression. But he also found he was genuinely attracted to her. Another flash of guilt crossed through him, but he mentally beat it down. He was protecting his own life and avenging his mother's attack.

Got to keep my eyes on the goal. If things go somewhere with Sylvia, that's fine, but I must get that paper.

When he dropped her off at the end of the evening, he got out and circled the car. As she exited the passenger side he took her hand and pulled her into a gentle embrace.

"I'd like to see you again. Just the two of us."

"I'd like that."

Virgil kissed her lightly, then pulled back. "What are you doing tomorrow afternoon? How about a picnic?"

"Oh, that sounds fun!"

"Great! I'll pick you up at two. Wear something comfy."

With that, he gave her a longer kiss, then headed home.

Things were moving along as planned. By the end of the weekend he hoped to get into Iggy's room. Maybe Sylvia's, too.

(19)

As you journey through life take a minute every now and then to give a thought for the other fellow. He could be plotting something. ~Hagar the Horrible

Virgil headed to Harold's at 9:30 Sunday morning. He was surprised to find Tammy working. She usually took weekends off.

The restaurant was empty. The before-church breakfast crowd was gone, and the after-church lunch crowd wouldn't arrive for a couple of hours. *A good opportunity to chat.*

Even though he'd decided not to pursue the list of names with her, he still wanted to know the waitress's motivation for joining the Truth Seekers, and what she meant by the cryptic comment she'd made to him Friday morning about wolves and sheep not mixing.

"Morning, Tammy, how are you this beautiful day?"

"Morning, Virgil. I'm doing pretty good. Coffee?"

She was friendlier today. Had something changed? Or was she just in a better mood?

Virgil ordered a waffle and side of fresh fruit. He sipped his coffee and watched Tammy putter around, wiping tables and arranging salt and pepper shakers.

"How long have you worked here now?" he asked.

"Hmm, I guess two years. A long time for a waitress job."

Virgil laughed. "Yeah, guess that's true. Did you know Lisa before she came here? About six months ago if memory serves."

"Nope. Met her on her first day. She's really nice. I've become something of a big sister to her."

"Always great to work with someone you really like. Makes all the difference."

"Sure does."

He was already out of small talk. He furrowed his brow in concentration. Before he could think of something else to say, Tammy headed to the kitchen. She returned shortly with his food, which she set on the table, then slipped into the opposite side of the booth.

"I like you, Virgil. But I also worry about you."

What's this all about? "Oh? How so?"

"I think you're into something over your head." Tammy stared at her hands.

"Over my head?" Virgil raised an eyebrow.

"I think you had something to do with Joe's accident."

"Oh come on, Tammy." Virgil uttered a forced laugh. "What could I possibly have done?"

She shrugged. "Dunno. But I trust my gut. And there are little clues. You say things and make jokes that are just...off. Marshall commented about some of the weird places you get shipments from."

Virgil bristled. *I thought delivery drivers were supposed to be discreet.* "Marshall has no idea what I get. All the boxes are sealed. Whatever he's told you, he's made up."

"True, but he does see where the boxes come from. Doll manufacturers. Model car collectors. Candle companies. Marshall even made it a point to mention how big the box from the doll company was. And don't forget about that box of acid."

How do I answer this? Virgil knew the longer he sat in silence the worse it would look. He shrugged. "I have weird hobbies." He cringed inwardly, knowing just how lame that sounded.

"I'd say so." Tammy slid from the booth and stood. "But are you hurting others in the process? Don't want to see you end up on that Truth Seekers list. I'll have Lisa ring you up. She's taking inventory for tomorrow's order." She turned and walked away.

Virgil's heart pounded. Tammy was suspicious. He'd have to do something. Tammy didn't necessarily deserve a motif, but he had to protect himself.

He hurried to the register counter before Lisa came from the kitchen. On the floor behind the counter was a brown leather purse. Sticking out the top was a pack of cigarettes. He knew Tammy smoked. *Her purse! Perfect.*

He glanced over his shoulder, then dropped his wallet. He stooped and reached into the purse, grabbing the first thing he saw, a lipstick.

"Drop something?"

He jumped as Lisa came up behind him. "My wallet." He stood and held it up for her to see. "It's really bulky. Dropped it when I pulled it from my pocket. Guess I need to clean it out."

Lisa laughed. "I've seen fatter ones but, yeah, you need to thin that puppy up."

Virgil was sweating by the time he paid his check and left. He knew Lisa hadn't seen him steal Tammy's lipstick, but he wasn't used to collecting a motif's focalis in such a potentially compromising manner.

While driving home, Virgil thought about what the motif's goal should be. He didn't want to harm Tammy in any way, but needed to deflect her attention away from the Truth Seekers and himself.

He rummaged through his inventory of supplies as soon as he got home. Nothing inspired the right type of motif. Then he remembered his mother's dried sage. *That's it! Sage repels evil.*

If he worded the chant correctly, it would drive away Tammy's suspicions, or at least cloud her mind from related thoughts. The lipstick wasn't only a personal item, it was a perfect representation of the mouth. He could use the motif to stop Tammy from talking about him to the Truth Seekers, too.

Virgil hurried to the dining room where the boxes of his mother's things were piled. He wished he'd labelled them, but had been too distracted. The bottle of sage was in the fourth box he opened.

He spent the rest of the morning working on the chant. It had to be just right, with no unintended consequences. He sat at his breakfast table, writing the chant on notepaper, wadding up rejected versions and tossing them on the floor. When he was satisfied, he transcribed the final chant onto a piece of parchment.

When he sat up, he realized how tired he was. And his back ached from leaning over in concentration. He glanced at the clock.

Twelve thirty! I'm supposed to pick up Sylvia for a picnic at two!

There would be no nap in his immediate future. He collected the discarded chant drafts and tossed them in a metal trash can, followed by a match. He needed to be careful with motif remnants and rejects from now on. Marshall was noticing what was arriving at his home. Was anyone paying attention to what he was leaving in his garbage can?

Virgil hit shower, then dressed in khaki shorts and a white polo shirt.

I have no food.

When he'd made the date last night, he hadn't even thought about needing to prepare food. He'd have just enough time to stop at Laura's Lunch Box for fresh sandwiches and chips. He filled a cloth shopping bag with napkins, two wine glasses, and a couple of bottles of shiraz from the kitchen. He grabbed his cooler from the garage on the way to his car.

He was shoving supplies into the SUV when he remembered he had nothing for them to sit on. He hurried back to his guest room closet and grabbed a quilt.

At the Lunch Box he ordered four sandwiches, since he had no idea what Sylvia liked: turkey, ham and Swiss, tuna salad, and a Reuben. He had them add half a dozen bags of chips and a handful of assorted cookies to the bag.

"Can you pack me up some sweet tea?" he asked.

"Sure thing, Hon." The woman grinned. "Gallon be enough?"

Virgil stowed the food in the cooler and headed to Sylvia's. He hoped the picnic would go well. He'd break into Sylvia's house if he had to; he needed that list. He truly hoped extreme measures wouldn't be necessary. It'd be a shame to spoil any potential relationship before it even began.

(20)

*You may be deceived if you trust too much, but you will live
in torment if you do not trust enough. ~Frank Crane*

Sylvia opened the door on Virgil's first knock. She beamed a bright smile from ear to ear. Her yellow flowered sundress showed her fine figure. A yellow ribbon held her hair in a stubby ponytail.

"You look beautiful!" Virgil meant it too. What had begun as his plan to use Sylvia to gain access to Iggy's room was quickly blossoming into attraction and affection.

"Thank you." Sylvia slung her purse over her shoulder. "Where are we headed?"

"It's a surprise."

It was a short drive to the city park. When Virgil drove past the entrance, he heard Sylvia utter, "Hmmm." Fifteen minutes later, he turned into the Everett Ranch Nature Preserve.

"Oh! I heard about this place. I didn't know it was open yet."

"Opened last week." Virgil stopped at the park headquarters. "Be right back." He left the car running while he went inside to pay the day pass fee and pick up a trail guide and preserve map.

Sylvia scanned the brochure as Virgil pulled away from the park office. "Says the Everett heirs donated the entire ranch to the state when their father passed away. Their mother passed years ago."

"Let's hope it isn't crowded," Virgil said. "It's almost twelve hundred acres, so should be plenty of room for just us two."

Virgil briefly glanced at the map, then took the right fork through the preserve. He pulled into a small lot and parked.

"How's this?" He pointed toward a scattering of picnic tables at the entrance to a nature trail. Only one table was occupied by a family with a couple of kids.

"Looks perfect." Sylvia grinned. "I'll help unload the car."

"Guess we won't need to sit on the quilt I brought." Virgil opened the SUV and moved the quilt to the side.

"Can I help?"

"Sure. Thanks. Between the two of us, we should be able to get everything to the table in one trip."

They spent the next two hours nibbling Laura's Lunch Box goodies, drinking wine, and talking.

"I'm sorry I forgot all about ice for the tea."

"Don't apologize." Sylvia patted his arm. "This wine is lovely." Her words slurred slightly.

Good. She'll be more malleable if she's tipsy. He felt bad for manipulating her, but nothing right now was more important than that list. "I'm sorry Iggy doesn't like me. I thought telling him I'd also attended the Truth Seekers meeting would soften him up."

Sylvia shook her head. "Don't worry about it. These days he's angry most of the time. There are very few things he likes."

"I have to be honest, I'm more worried than I let on last night."

"About what?"

"The committee Iggy was selected for. What they're doing might be dangerous."

"Oh no! Dangerous how?" Sylvia almost tipped her wine glass over, barely catching it. Her hand shook as she gripped the stem.

"They're supposed to be following and watching people the Truth Seekers think are menaces. I don't know who's on the list, since I was just a visitor, so I can't tell how the Truth Seekers' targets might react if they feel threatened."

"I don't want Iggy to get hurt. Can you help? What can I do?"

Perfect response. "If I could see the list they gave Iggy, I could tell you more. And maybe do something to help keep Iggy safe."

"Who has this list? You're sure Iggy has one?"

"I saw Cotton give one to Iggy. He probably brought it home."

"Cotton?"

"The head of the Truth Seekers."

"And he told my son and the others to spy on these people?"

"He sure did."

"I'll get that list for you. I promise."

"And I'll do what I can to help Iggy. I promise." *And to help myself.*

They chatted for a few more minutes, but it was clear to Virgil that the mood had changed. Sylvia's thoughts had turned inward, to her son…and that critical piece of paper.

"Tell you what. Let's go back to your place. If Iggy's not there, perhaps we can find the paper together. The sooner the better."

"Yes. Let's. I was thinking of asking you, but hated to ruin your picnic plans. I'm sorry."

"No need to apologize at all. I understand why you're worried. I am, too." Virgil reached over and took Sylvia's hands. "It's been a great afternoon. Ending it now doesn't ruin the picnic at all."

They packed their supplies and loaded the SUV. Virgil was already tense by the time they reached Sylvia's house. When she opened the door, his apprehension skyrocketed. Iggy was not only at home, he had three friends with him. All four were sprawled around the family room. The television blared an action movie.

Sylvia turned to Virgil and frowned. She motioned him back outside and closed the door. "Looks like we failed."

He put his hands on her upper arms. "Don't worry. We haven't failed. It's just postponed for a bit. I'll bet they go out later. Tell them you don't have anything to eat. You can look after they leave."

Sylvia laughed. "And I won't be lying. I don't have much food right now. I'll search as soon as he's gone."

"You can call me if you like, and I'll come help."

"Thanks, but I know his room, since I do my best to keep it from being a biohazard zone. I'll call you as soon as I find it."

He pulled her to him and kissed her. "I trust you." *I hope this works. I need that list in the next couple of days.* "Call me later." Virgil waved as he climbed into his car.

Virgil reflected on the afternoon as he drove home. Sylvia seemed more than willing to help him, but of course her motives were directed at her son. That was okay. As long as he got the Truth Seekers list, he didn't care what her personal motives were.

And what about Sylvia? Virgil had only known her a short time, and his original reason for getting closer had been selfish. But he was growing fond of her. She was attractive, smart, and funny. She was the type of woman he'd like to date. Or more.

Could he balance getting the results he needed with his attraction to her? Did that make him a bad man? He hoped not. He was being pragmatic. He wasn't trying to hurt her.

Shortly after Virgil arrived home, he headed to his bedroom, where he stretched out on his bed without bothering to turn down the covers or remove his clothes. Within minutes, he was asleep. He woke some time later. The room was dim. The sun had set.

Time for the motif.

He showered, donned his cassock and headed for his chancel. He didn't spend as long on this motif as he'd spent on Joe's. It wasn't as complicated. The power of this motif was in the chant.

He selected one of the Barbie dolls from the supply box. He'd almost grabbed a clean napkin from Harold's to use as a waitress dress, but didn't want the motif to inadvertently affect the cafe, so he opted instead to leave the doll naked.

He painted the doll's lips with Tammy's bright red lipstick. As an afterthought, he used the lipstick to draw a circle around the doll's neck and add a small cross in the front. It was crude at best, since the end of the lipstick was fat, but he hoped it was a reasonable representation of the cross necklace Tammy always wore.

He set the doll and makeup in the center of the table and sprinkled a ring of sage around both. Outside of the sage, he placed a circle of six candles, alternating yellow and black. The black candles would dissipate negative energy. The yellow candles would affect memory, concentration, and other mind-related energies.

As Virgil lit each candle, he repeated the short chant.

Suspicion is abolished. Negativity is dispersed.

Her eyes divert away from me.

Her thoughts do not include me.

Her mind focuses elsewhere.

Other things occupy her thoughts and actions.

She turns from the Truth Seekers.

She has no interest in my activities.

She pursues nothing about my life.

When all candles were lit, he closed his eyes for a moment, then nodded and left the room, locking the door behind him.

ॐॐॐॐ

He didn't check on the motif Monday morning. He did call all three realtors in town. None answered. He left each the same message about wanting to list his mother's home.

Why hadn't he heard from Sylvia? It was almost ten. Maybe Iggy stayed home last night. He and his friends could have ordered a pizza instead of going out.

Virgil sorted more of his mother's things. He'd forgotten to ask Sylvia for help. It was a good excuse to call. He dialed her number. She didn't answer. When he got her voicemail, he left a short message, "Hi, Sylvia, it's Virgil. I have a question for you about Mama's clothes. Give me a call when you have a minute."

He wanted to ask if she'd had any luck, but even an obtuse message might raise Iggy's suspicion if he overheard it.

His phone finally rang at nearly four in the afternoon. He tripped over his coffee table lunging for the phone. "Ouch! Hello?"

"Are you okay?" Sylvia asked.

"Yeah, I'm fine, just stubbed my toe."

"I got your message. You had questions about your mother's clothes? How can I help you?"

Was her formality signaling that Iggy was within earshot? "Yes. I don't know what to do with them. I hoped you might have suggestions or be able to help." He strained to hear any background noises that might give away what was going on at Sylvia's house, but he heard nothing.

"I'd really have to see the clothes. It depends on if they're still in style. How about if I pop over and have a look?"

"That'd be great. I'd like my dining room back." *Does she have any other reasons for coming so quickly? Please have the list.*

"Give me half an hour. I have some landscape plant options to go over with you. I do have one question first, though. Iggy, dear, would you grab the binder that's on my desk?" Sylvia's voice dropped to a whisper. "I have it. I'll bring it with me. See you soon."

(21)

The greatest obstacle to discovery is not ignorance –
it is the illusion of knowledge. ~Daniel J. Boorstin

Sylvia arrived within thirty minutes, but it felt like hours to Virgil. He opened the door as soon as he heard her car pull into the driveway.

"I hope you're as glad to see me as you are to get the piece of paper that's in my purse." She laughed as she walked up the sidewalk.

As soon as she was within reach, Virgil pulled her to him and kissed her. "I'm anxious about that paper, but that doesn't mean I wasn't looking forward to seeing you."

Sylvia smiled. "Glad to hear that. I'm happy to be here."

They settled side by side on the sofa and Sylvia handed the paper to Virgil.

"Did you look at it already?" His hands trembled as he took it. He couldn't bring himself to open it. He held it on his lap and stared at it.

Sylvia shrugged. "I scanned it, but none of those names mean a thing to me. Why is this so important to you? What's the big deal? What are you afraid of?"

"I…um… I'm worried about the people on this list. After attending the meeting, I don't trust what some of the members might do. Not Iggy, of course."

"I'm not even sure about Iggy." Sylvia frowned. "He's not the same anymore. He's darker. Angrier. Sometimes I worry having him in the house."

Virgil turned to her and took her hands. "If you ever become afraid, get in your car and head here. You'll always be welcome. My home can be your sanctuary."

"Thank you. That's sweet. And comforting." She leaned in and kissed his cheek. "Let's see if you recognize any of the names."

Virgil unfolded the paper. Sylvia leaned in for a better look. "Oh no." He closed his eyes and sighed.

"What? Who do you recognize?"

Virgil opened his eyes and pointed to the first name on the list.

"Who is Marshall Welker?"

"He's my UPS delivery man."

"Oh." Sylvia put her hand over her mouth. "At least he's not someone you know intimately."

"No." *How can I tell her how important this is? How dangerous?* He couldn't, of course. He wasn't even sure himself. But his gut told him this was a big problem. Maybe that was why Marshall was so suspicious of the wide variation and frequency of packages Virgil received.

But why had Marshall violated company policy to mention Virgil's packages to Tammy? She had a copy of the same list. Was Marshall now in danger? Whose name had Tammy's team been assigned to watch? Beads of sweat formed on Virgil's forehead and he suddenly felt cold and clammy.

"You look like you're about to pass out." Sylvia gently pushed on Virgil's neck. "Here, lean over to get some blood flow to your head."

"I'll be all right." But Virgil did as she suggested. After a minute he felt better and sat up. "Thanks. It's just a shock to see someone I know. And I get a lot of packages, so I know Marshall pretty well. We've talked lots of times about my roses."

"What kinds of packages?"

Virgil knew it was likely idle curiosity, but his defenses jumped to attention nonetheless. He stifled his fear and shrugged, to make it look like he was unconcerned.

"Stuff for my hobbies, mostly. Wood-working and roses. And I write a little. Plus I hate shopping, so I even get clothes and sometimes food delivered."

Sylvia's laugh was clear and gentle. "Spoken like a consummate bachelor." She pointed to the list. "Recognize anyone else?"

The next two names were unfamiliar. Their addresses were on the other side of town. Although one was in his mother's neighborhood, it was half a dozen blocks from her house.

The fourth name was familiar, but Virgil wasn't sure why. A vague memory placed the man as an employee at the local hardware store. He stood and turned. "Let me make a copy of this. You should put the original back where you found it, so Iggy doesn't grow suspicious."

"Good idea. How about I brew us some tea?"

"Also a good idea. The tea's in the pantry. Find one you like while I go make the copy. Whatever you pick is fine with me."

He only took a couple of minutes, but it was long enough. When Virgil entered the kitchen he found Sylvia standing at the pantry. In her hands was his mother's motif journal.

Virgil froze. Then, before he could stop himself, he lunged and jerked the book from Sylvia's hands. "GIVE ME THAT!"

"Virgil! I'm sorry!" Sylvia backed into the corner and crossed her arms, hands on her shoulders. "Please. You're scaring me."

He clutched the book tightly to his chest and forced his breathing to slow. "I'm sorry. This was very personal to my mother. Please don't be afraid of me. I'm sorry I yelled. I'm okay now. I promise. Please, come sit down." He pointed to the breakfast table.

Sylvia looked down at her hands. "I… I was looking for the tea. I saw this book with the pretty felt tree on the cover. I thought it was a homemade cookbook, since it was stacked with the others. I didn't know it was anything private."

He only had himself to blame. He'd intended to move the journal to his chancel and hadn't followed through. "It's not bad. And it's okay. Really. But…did you read it?"

"Yes. Some." Sylvia nodded without looking up. "It's very confusing." She raised her head and looked directly at him. "What is it, Virgil? What does it mean?"

His mind raced, unsure what to do. What had his mother done about his dad? Had he known before they married? How did members of his family deal with sharing their secret?

He was attracted to Sylvia. A lot. The potential for a serious relationship was definitely there. Was it too early to share his family's secret? How much should he share? What would happen if she never wanted to see him again?

He sighed and set the journal on the table, then moved past Sylvia, who flinched. He turned off the stove, quieting the kettle, which had begun to whistle. He prepared two cups of tea and moved to the table, setting one cup on the side of the table where Sylvia stood.

"Please, sit. I'll tell you what I can." He sat and waited. After almost a minute she joined him, although she kept her chair backed away from the table.

"Thank you." He smiled, hoping to ease her discomfort. "Please tell me what you read, so I'll know where to begin."

Sylvia hesitated. "At first I though it was a diary. Then I thought it was a book of poetry. But it isn't, is it? What looked like poems aren't in English. What was your mother? What are you? Is this why you're so worried about the Truth Seekers? Are you a sorcerer like they said they're after?"

Virgil flinched at the word. "No. We aren't sorcerers. At least that's not what we'd call ourselves. Always called myself a theurgist. Mama called it our gift of symbols."

Sylvia frowned, but said nothing.

Virgil continued. "Everyone on my mother's side of the family has always been able to…nudge destiny in the right direction when it wasn't happening on its own. To change the course of events."

"I don't understand."

"What you thought were poems are actually chants in a very ancient language. They have an effect on the universe. Think of it like tossing a pebble in water. It sends out ripples of change. But it doesn't affect everyone, only the person it's directed to."

"That doesn't really explain anything."

"Let me show you one my mother did." He opened the journal and flipped through the pages. "Here." *This is a safe motif to show her. It stays in the family. It's goal is healing, not karmic retribution.*

He turned the book so she could see. "This is one she did for me when he I was really sick with mononucleosis. She didn't believe the medicine was working. She didn't think the doctors were taking it seriously enough. So she sent healing energies my way."

"I can't read the…chant." Sylvia touched the page.

Virgil stifled an urge to jerk the book from her hand. *It doesn't matter now. Mama won't be using her journal again. A stranger's energy won't hurt it.*

"You can see the items she used. One of my cotton handkerchiefs, herbs, candles. I'll read you the chant." He angled the book enough to translate the words his mother had written.

Healing energies surround my boy
Fill his lungs, ease his pain
Renew his energy, give him strength
Remove this terrible disease
Bring life, light, joy and health back to him
Be well! Be well! Be well!

"How is that different from a prayer?"

"I guess it's not that much different, except we aren't religious. We aren't appealing to some god or deity to effect the changes. Our own energies do that."

"So she did magic?"

"We've never thought of it as magic." Virgil shrugged. "I guess some would. And this is our family's only ability. I'd think sorcerers would have lots of powers. We only have one. Tweaking the energies around us."

"That's why you fear the Truth Seekers?"

Virgil nodded. "Yeah. I don't know about their opinion of anyone on the list, but I'll bet the Truth Seekers wouldn't care that I have only one ability. Or that my mother raised me with stern lessons about not using our gift to harm others." *Please don't ask me if I've ever made exceptions.*

"I see." Sylvia shifted in her chair. "I'm not sure what to think about all this. It makes me very uncomfortable."

"I'm harmless. Honest." *Mostly.*

"What have you used your...powers for? What's in your journal?"

Damn. She had to ask. "I don't have a journal. If I did, I'd show you. But I've never been that organized. I can tell you I did one to save dogs from a dog-fighting ring. All the dogs were rescued by a group dedicated to rehabilitating fighting dogs so they could be adopted."

"I remember seeing that story on the news. You did that?"

Virgil nodded. "I focused on bringing justice to the man who ran the dog fights, while preventing any harm coming to the dogs." *I hope she doesn't remember that the man who ran the fights was almost killed by two angry attendees.*

"That's very compassionate." Sylvia nodded. "But what about the past few days? Have you manipulated me? Or Ignatius? Have you just been using me to get to him?"

(22)

Throw your dreams into space like a kite, and you do not know what it will bring back; a new life, a new friend, a new love, a new country. ~Anais Nin (1903-1977)

The use of her son's full name didn't escape Virgil's notice. He had to proceed carefully. A little honesty was his best bet at this point. He didn't want to lose her already.

"No! I admit at first I approached Donna in the restaurant because of what Iggy was saying. But I didn't make the offer to her about landscaping my yard with any ulterior motives in mind. I honestly didn't mean anything sneaky."

Sylvia uttered a dismissive, "Hmmph."

"It's true. I can't help my own mother. Her situation is permanent, at least until she passes on. But I was inspired to help you get through a temporary setback. Frankly, I kind of surprised myself. The landscaping offer sort of popped out."

Sylvia raised an eyebrow.

"I'm honestly pretty shy and reserved. It took a lot for me to even approach Donna after I overheard her and Iggy, but it didn't take much to make my offer. It just felt right. Please believe me."

Sylvia's shoulders relaxed and she smiled, although it was a small smile. "Thank you. That's nice to hear."

Virgil leaned forward and placed his hand over hers. He was pleased she didn't pull away. "I realize it's been less than a week, but I've grown fond of you."

"I was attracted to you, too."

"Was? Please. I truly hope my family's quirk doesn't scare you or drive you away. I don't want to lose what I hope is a good thing between us." *And I mean it. I really do!*

Sylvia spent several seconds staring into Virgil's eyes. He knew what she was searching for. The truth of how he felt. He may have started out with no qualms about using her to get that list from Iggy, but things had changed. He had true feelings for her. That had to show.

She closed her eyes. "Learning about your mother—and you—certainly took me by surprise." She opened her eyes again and smiled. "It seems a little creepy and weird, but I guess it's not much different than folks who heal by laying on of hands."

"That's as good an analogy as any." It was very different, but she didn't need to know that. *I don't want you to be scared of me. I'm not a bad person.*

"Can you do anything to help Iggy? To bring him back to me?"

Uh-oh. She's asking me to manipulate someone for her.

"I don't like manipulating people. And it can cause karmic backlash. Kind of a *what goes around comes around* payback. Our own energies can get affected, and not in a good way."

"I understand." Sylvia withdrew her hand from beneath Virgil's. "It's late. I should go."

"Please don't. Can we move into the living room and talk a while longer? It would mean a lot to me. I want you to be comfortable with me."

Sylvia hesitated. "All right."

Virgil poured them each a glass of red wine and the couple relocated to the comfort of the sofa. He left the journal on the breakfast table.

"Will you tell me more about your family?" Sylvia asked. "About your gift?"

Virgil nodded. He spent the next hour telling her about growing up with only him and his mom, and all the theurgy lessons she taught him. He told her about the first motif he'd ever done. The one to help him win the science fair. And his mother's stern words afterward.

"She sounds like any other mother." Sylvia laughed. "Even when the transgression is in some other realm, the lecture is the same. What about your dad?"

"He died when I was eight. My mom didn't talk about it much, but it was some kind of industrial accident. He was a machinist. When I was younger I didn't want to know. As I got older, it became less important. He'd become a vague memory."

"That's sad. To lose your father so young, I mean. Not that you didn't care."

"That's sad, too, actually. I wish I'd cared more. Now it's too late to ask Mama."

"I remember the story about your mother from the news reports. It scared me to death at the time. What happened? Were the stories true?"

"Yes, for the most part. She'd hidden in the closet when burglars broke in. When they found her, they beat her so badly, she almost died. She was in intensive care for weeks. When doctors said she was as whole as she would ever be again, I moved her into the Oak Creek Estate in Pemberton Heights. She'll die there, I guess."

"I'm so sorry. I can't imagine how difficult that's been. My own mother passed away two years ago, but we knew it was coming. We were able to say our goodbyes."

"I think that's the hardest part. All the unspoken words and loose ends. It's really made me rethink my life. To appreciate everything. To take nothing for granted." He leaned over and gave Sylvia a gentle kiss.

When they parted, she sat back and smiled. "What was that for?"

"Like I said, I try not to take life for granted anymore. You never know what might happen."

"I can understand that. Changes in my life these last couple of years have really shaken me, made me realize that the firm footing I thought I had over my life wasn't firm at all. I was standing on a rug, and fate yanked it out from under me."

"What happened?" He refilled their wine glasses. "Your mother died two years ago. You've had more?"

Sylvia hesitated, then nodded. "I went through a health scare. They found breast cancer. They said they got it all, but it was a scary year. And I won't really know it's all gone for a decade or more."

"I'm so sorry. That would be scary."

"Sure was. Then Iggy decided to quit school and move back home. Then he was fired and got lazy. I was dealing with chemo while taking care of an adult child."

"Damn." Virgil shook his head. "He should have been helping you."

"I know. I just didn't have the energy to push for it. I think my illness, and Iggy's moving back in, both contributed to Oscar's... wandering eyes. And why he left."

"You definitely had a couple of bad years." He moved closer to her on the sofa and stroked her auburn hair. "I wish there was something I could do to make all that go away."

"You've helped already." Sylvia smiled. "You're giving me a chance to return to a career I loved. And you've been so nice. I guess that's why I didn't get more upset when I found out that your mother and you are sor...about your and your mother's ability."

Virgil divided the last of the wine between their glasses. "I never thought of it as anything but normal, although I was forbidden to talk to any of the other kids about it. It's just who we were. And I've never met anyone else like me. Or if I have, I don't know, since it's not something people are going to talk about with strangers."

"I can understand." Sylvia nodded. "Finding that book creeped me out, and you're not a stranger. Mostly. I know we just met less than a week ago, but I already feel comfortable with you."

"I'm glad." Virgil kissed her again, then glanced at the clock on the fireplace mantle. It was after midnight. "Please stay."

One fear crossed his mind. If she stayed, it might encourage her to get even more curious. What if she asked about the locked door in his hall, behind which his chancel still held his latest motif? How would he explain a naked, lipstick-adorned Barbie in a circle of sage and candles?

I'll manage. The chancel is at the end of the hall. I can keep her away from it. And I don't want her around Iggy yet. That could be dangerous. for me, and maybe even for her.

"Tonight? I… I'm… I'm still married."

Virgil dropped his gaze then again met her eyes. He leaned forward and kissed her for the third time, much more passionately. "It's up to you, of course, but I don't care. When a man abandons his wife, he loses his rights in my book."

Sylvia said nothing for a full two minutes. She swirled the remainder of the wine in her glass then downed it in one deep swallow. Finally, she reached out and rested her hand on his cheek. He leaned into her touch.

"Yes. I'll stay." Her voice was barely above a whisper.

Virgil stood and took Sylvia's hand. He pulled her up, embraced her tightly, and gave her a deep kiss. She responded, leaning into him with her whole body.

He turned and led her to his bedroom, but paused inside the door, suddenly awkward and shy. It had been three years since he'd been with a woman. Before his mother's beating.

Sylvia smiled. She put her arms around him and kissed him. Without a word, and without breaking their kiss, she unbuttoned his shirt and slipped it off. Her breathing quickened. So did his.

Virgil pulled her sweater over her head, interrupting their kisses barely long enough for the garment to pass their lips. He fumbled for her bra strap, causing her to giggle against his mouth. She reached behind her back and within seconds the lacy bra joined their shirts on the floor.

They moved apart and quickly shed the rest of their clothes. He stared at her naked body. "You're beautiful."

Sylvia's eyes shone. "Not too bad for a middle-aged woman who's had two kids."

"You look perfect to me." Virgil's voice was husky. He thought briefly about picking her up and carrying her, but he wasn't sure he could manage, and dropping her would definitely ruin the mood. Instead, he circled her waist and guided her to the bed. He swept the covers aside, then eased her onto the soft, white sheets.

Their lovemaking was slow and tender, their moves as compatible as if they'd been lovers for years. Sylvia's soft sigh as she came pushed Virgil over his own edge. He moaned, then eased down beside her.

"I haven't felt like this in a long time." Sylvia rolled to face Virgil and kissed him on the nose.

"Neither have I." Virgil smiled. "I stopped dating after Mom went to the nursing home. I focused on her. And I didn't have the heart for it. I've almost become a hermit."

"What about your other relatives?"

"Other relatives?"

"At Tony's, you talked about having a few other relatives. You really lost touch with everyone?"

Virgil shook his head. "I have no idea where any relatives from my childhood might be now. Mama never kept in touch. I haven't even seen my grandmother in years."

"Your mother didn't keep in touch with her own mother?"

"No, but I can understand why." Virgil laughed. "She was scary. Very formidable."

Sylvia laughed, too. "My dad's mother was also like that. Nothing like Mom's mom. Now SHE was a kid's ideal grandmother."

"People are people, I guess. Some are good. Others not so much." Virgil paused. "A few are downright evil."

"Like the men who beat your mother. What happened to them?"

"Locked up for twenty years, if they don't get out early. Not that that does any good. Certainly not for Mama."

"Did you…do anything to them?"

Virgil hesitated. He didn't want to lie again, but he also couldn't be totally open. He took the middle ground. "Did one for Mama. For justice. Shortly after, they were caught and convicted."

"I can understand that. If I had your ability, I'd certainly use it to help others, even if that meant I'd face karmic…what was it?"

"Karmic backlash. Yes, exactly. Sometimes, it's worth it. Thanks for understanding, and for not freaking out."

"I WAS pretty freaked out when I saw your reaction. But you eased my mind, especially when you showed me the…what do you call it? Not spell."

"No. We've always called them motifs."

"Hmmm. Odd word, but okay. Anyway, when you showed me the motif your Mom did when you were sick, it made me feel better."

"Mom did a lot of motifs on me, although I never knew at the time. Most were for better grades, success on tests, that kind of thing."

"A mother's love." Sylvia smiled. "We do what we can. We use whatever skills we have."

Virgil sighed. "I really miss her sometimes. I was finally old enough, and no longer a stupid kid. We were really starting to enjoy each other's company. She got me started with heirloom roses. Gave me my first one. We planted and tended the garden together."

"I'm so sorry."

"Thanks. Whether we like it or not, life moves on. I visit her two or three times a week. I keep myself busy with my roses, which also makes me feel close to the memory of who she was. And I began my wood-working business. For the most part, I'm happy. Or at least content. Happier now that I've met you."

Sylvia sat up, the sheet slipping off her breasts. She pulled the covers up and turned to Virgil. "What about the Truth Seekers? Now you have to worry about them. Are you going to do something to them?"

Virgil sat up, too, and brushed a lock of hair from Sylvia's cheek. "No. I have no idea what they're really about. I want to find out, though. Who knows. Maybe we have common ground."

"Are you kidding! Do you really believe that?"

"Honestly have no clue." Virgil gazed into the distance. "They supposedly seek and expose evils. I may disagree with what they consider evil, but I can't argue with their desire to expose the information to others."

"And what about Iggy?"

Virgil tuned to Sylvia. "Iggy? What about him?"

"Will you help him?"

Virgil hesitated. "I'll see what I can come up with, but give me some time. Let me learn more about the Truth Seekers. What they're really up to. Their methods. Other members. I would never do a motif on someone, or a group of people, without solid knowledge of who they were and what they were doing."

"Fair enough. You haven't done a love spell on me, have you?" Sylvia winked and lay back down.

"Some things just come naturally." Virgil slid down and rolled onto her. Was he falling in love? He wasn't sure but he was willing to explore that possibility.

(23)

Some think it's holding on that makes one strong;
sometimes it's letting go. ~Sylvia Robinson

Virgil woke Tuesday morning to find the bed empty. He quickly pulled on pajama pants and hurried to the kitchen. He found Sylvia sipping tea at the breakfast table and staring into his backyard. She wore one of his plaid button down shirts, buttoned only once.

"Good morning!" She jumped up and gave him a hug. "Hope you don't mind. I snuck into your closet and borrowed a shirt."

Virgil kissed her, looked her up and down, and grinned. "I'd say it looks better on you."

"Tea? I pulled out the Earl Grey."

"Earl Grey is perfect. But you don't have to get it."

"Sit. I don't mind. I like bustling about a kitchen."

Virgil sat at the table while Sylvia poured the still steaming water into a cup and dropped in a tea bag. She carried it to the table and sat down.

"I've been staring at your yard. Taking time to study your view from the house has given me some great ideas on plant selection and layout."

"Glad to hear that. It's a pretty gloomy view right now."

Sylvia laughed. "Not for long. I'll have a design for you in a couple of days. If you like it, I'll start later this week. Is that okay?"

"No time like the present." Virgil drained his cup. "I'll get us some more." He moved to the stove and lit the burner under the kettle. "How much was a typical complete landscape when you were doing them full time?"

"Hmmm." Sylvia tapped her finger on her chin. "I'd say the average was around $3000, if we used native plants. More for exotics."

"Tell you what. I know a great deal about roses and little to nothing about anything else. Keep the budget under $4000 and do whatever you want. I trust you."

Sylvia blushed. "But...are you sure?" She dropped her eyes. "You don't want to see the plan?"

She thinks I don't care about her design. "Of course, I'd love to see the plan! But don't wait on me. Go ahead and start. Use the plan to show me what you're doing, not what you want to do after I approve. I'll enjoy watching how your design becomes reality right before my eyes."

He returned to the table with a ceramic teapot shaped like a chicken.

"Now that's adorable." Sylvia laughed.

Virgil blushed and sat down. "It was one of the last gifts I got from my mother. Doesn't exactly fit my decor, but it reminds me of her."

"That's a good reason to use it."

Virgil was glad the morning wasn't awkward. A few overnight stays in the past had been painful the next morning. *Maybe Sylvia is the one.*

"You know, we never did finish talking about that name you recognized on the Truth Seeker's list. We ended up…distracted."

"Marshall Welker, my UPS driver."

"That's right. You reacted pretty strongly. Is it because of your family's special ability?"

"Yes." Virgil sighed. "Remember I said that a motif only affected the person it targeted?"

Sylvia nodded.

"To do that takes a token to represent the person. I order a lot of strange items online. Dolls, for one thing, which I use to represent a specific person."

"Like Voodoo?"

"Not really. The doll is simply a focal point. We even call it the focalis. It's a place to concentrate energies. I don't stick pins in it." *I just break their plastic legs or put lipstick on them.* He chuckled.

"What's so funny?" Sylvia cocked her head.

Virgil blanched. "Sorry. I was just thinking of what Mama would have said if someone asked her about Voodoo dolls."

"Oh! I hope I didn't offend you."

"Nope. Not at all." Virgil gave a dismissive wave. "I get the confusion. Think of the doll like a votive candle a Catholic lights in church. It represents their prayer. The candle doesn't *make* the prayer, it just lets the petitioner have something to focus on."

"Okay. That's very helpful." Sylvia paused and stared out the window for a moment, then turned to face Virgil. "I know you're withholding, and I understand why. But do those who become part of your family join in on these motifs? How does that work?"

Is she falling for me? Is she growing serious? "They definitely learn more about our family's history and abilities, but they don't really get involved. It's a gift you either have or don't have. It can't be taught. Well, that's not true, I guess. My mother taught me how to use an ability I already had, not how to create an ability where none existed."

Sylvia nodded. "I had to ask. I wasn't trying to be forward."

"I'm glad you asked. I like the implications." Virgil reached over and stroked Sylvia's arm.

"Good. Me, too." Sylvia smiled and stared into Virgil's eyes for a few seconds before looking down. "But back to your UPS driver. Tell me more about what you're thinking. Do you believe he has the same ability, or that the Truth Seekers are after an *innocent* man?"

"Good question. I've never met anyone outside my family who can do motifs. That'd be pretty exciting, actually. Shocking, but exciting."

"I'll bet. But aren't you worried for yourself, about your own safety, if you approach him? You said the Truth Seekers were spying on the four people on that list."

"At least one of them is already suspicious. I know Marshall told Tammy, the waitress at Harold's Cafe, about some of my odd shipments. Tammy mentioned it to me. She has a copy of the list. She's seen his name on it."

Sylvia's hand flew to her mouth. "Oh hell! Why would he do that?"

"I have no idea." Virgil shook his head. "But now she's suspicious. She said so."

"Sounds like you need to have a chat with Marshall."

"I'm afraid you're right. It's going to be awkward, for sure."

"Is there any way I can help?"

"Not yet, but I appreciate your offer." Virgil leaned over and kissed Sylvia. His body responded to the intimacy. Hers did, too. Her breathing grew heavy.

"Come on." Virgil pulled her to her feet and they retreated again to his bedroom.

Two hours later Sylvia was showered and wearing the clothes she'd arrived in. Her hair was damp, curling around her cheeks and along her neck. Her face was scrubbed clean of makeup.

"You look gorgeous." Virgil hugged her from behind and looked over her shoulder into the bathroom mirror.

"You're a good liar." Sylvia laughed. "I look my age without makeup."

"Nothing wrong with that." He turned her around and kissed her. "You sure you don't want to go to Harold's with me?" He knew it would be easier if she didn't go, but he was still enjoying her company. *But I need to get back to the task at hand.*

"I've got to get home. By now Iggy knows I wasn't there last night. Their father is a piece of work, but I'm still married to him." She kissed Virgil on the cheek. "Besides, I want to return that paper to his room. At least his desk was a wreck. He probably hasn't missed it yet."

Virgil nodded and followed Sylvia out of the bedroom.

"Oh, before I leave, show me your mother's clothes. You wanted some suggestions where to take them."

They spent an hour looking through the boxes and bags of clothes, dividing them into several piles."

Sylvia pointed to each pile. "Remember, those are for Goodwill, those over there would be great donations to the local women's shelter, and these should go to a resale shop. I'll text you the address of the one I recommend."

"Thanks. I'll get them delivered today. I'd like my dining room back. And they're too depressing to look at."

Sylvia hugged him tight. "I understand. I had a tough time going through my mother's things."

"It's like I'm giving up on her."

"No, you're not! You're just accepting the current reality of her situation."

"Thanks." He kissed her.

Her breathing quickened then she pulled back. "I'm sorry I have to go. I wish I could stay." She waved at the remaining boxes in the dining room. "And I wish I could be more help."

"You've helped a lot. Go on now, and reassure your son I haven't kidnapped you."

"No, just ruined my honor." Sylvia laughed at Virgil's shocked expression. "I'm kidding! No regrets." She gave him a quick kiss. "Call me later. I want to hear if you learn anything."

"I will." *As much as I can tell you.*

As soon as Sylvia was gone, Virgil headed to Harold's. It was 9:45. The breakfast rush would be over. No chance of seeing Marshall. He'd already be out making deliveries. Maybe he could find out more from Tammy.

He was halfway to Harold's when he remembered the motif he'd done to divert Tammy away from him. How could he have forgotten something so important? *Well, I was distracted.*

He assumed the candles were burned out, but he hadn't looked. It would be interesting to see if there was any difference in her behavior toward him.

"Morning, Tammy," he called as soon as he opened the door. Tammy was across the room, taking an order from a couple he didn't recognize. She didn't even look his way.

He did a quick scan. There were no clean tables in the place. The only other diner was Bernie, the ranch hand, who sat at the counter.

"Hey, Bernie." Virgil moved the dishes from his favorite booth to another one, then slid in. "How are things going? Staying busy?"

"Can't complain. Got a good job late yesterday that's gonna take me at least a week. Running barbed wire around the old Jackson place."

"Isn't that one of the biggest ranches around here? Something like three-thousand acres?"

"That's it." Bernie nodded. "Hot, hard work, but it's good pay. Not many folks these days want to learn how to string barbed wire. And they don't have the stretcher and other tools."

"I can believe that."

"Gonna head over there from here, see how many fenceposts I need to replace. By the way, didja hear about Dan?" Bernie waved his fork in the air.

"Dan who?" Virgil asked.

"Dan Baxter!"

"The locksmith? No. Haven't seen him lately, either. What's up?"

"Dead."

"WHAT?" Virgil's mouth dropped open.

Bernie nodded. "Was swapping out the front lock at some house for one of those newfangled digital fingerprint scanner things. Owners found him dead on their porch when they got home. Heard he was electrocuted. Musta hit a hot wire or something."

"Wow. I hadn't heard that." Virgil shook his head. "When did this happen?"

"This past weekend. Saturday I think."

"Well, you just never know when bad luck is going to strike."

"No, siree. Ya sure don't. I might get scratched and poked up bad by barbed wire, but it ain't gonna kill me." Bernie stood and tossed cash on the counter. "I'm good, Tammy. Don't worry about change."

"Thanks, Bernie." Tammy nodded and headed to Virgil's table.

"You have a good day, Bernie." Virgil waved as the other man left.

"Sorry for the mess." Tammy shrugged. "I'm alone here this morning."

"Where's Lisa?" Virgil asked.

Tammy's expression was tight and harried. Her hair was a tangled mess. Her glasses were smudged, the purple frames sat crooked on her nose. Was it Lisa's absence or his motif?

"Sick I guess. Or with her new boyfriend." Tammy poured coffee, splashing it onto the table. "Sorry. I'll get a cloth." She hurried off before Virgil could say anything.

When she returned Virgil asked, "You okay?"

"Yeah. Pretty pissed at Lisa. She didn't call in. That was probably a mistake. Harold doesn't like it when employees don't show up and don't call."

"Oh. Sorry. I'll make it easy for both you and Harold today. Bring me the Ranch Wife's breakfast."

"Yes, *ma'am*. Guess you aren't up to bein' a Ranch *Hand*." She hooted with laughter as she walked off.

She seems her old self. Does that mean she's forgotten her suspicions of me? Did the motif work?

He needed to test her more specifically. When she delivered his breakfast of one egg, hash browns, sausage patty, and toast, he asked, "Seen Marshall lately? I wonder what he does with his spare time. I only ever see him here or when he's bringing me packages."

"Nope." Tammy pointed toward his cup. "I'll get more coffee."

Her answer hadn't been helpful. He'd have to try bigger bait.

"I hear through the grapevine that he's on that list," Virgil said when she returned with the coffee pot.

This time Tammy splashed coffee onto Virgil's wrist.

"Ouch!"

"Sorry. And so what if he is? None of your business. Unless you know more about all that than you're telling. You and Marshall in something together?"

"NO!"

The unfamiliar couple from two tables over briefly turned to stare.

Virgil lowered his voice. "No. I'm not *into something* with Marshall. I was curious, that's all."

"Curiosity killed the cat. Remember that."

Tammy avoided him for the rest of breakfast. He didn't get his check until he walked to the register. She was all business, handing him his check, taking his money, handing him change.

"Thanks for coming," she said without smiling.

He sat in his car for a few minutes, rehashing what he'd just experienced. He was confused. What was going on with Tammy? At first, it'd seemed that perhaps she was changed, distracted and absent-minded. Then she'd still acted angry and suspicious. His motif either wasn't finished or it hadn't worked.

I've never had a motif fail to work.

It was possible not all of the candles were burned out yet. Sometimes one of the tapers burned freakishly long. Probably something to do with the density of the wax. Or the oil content. Or whatever. He'd check on the candles the minute he got home.

He was backing out when his phone rang. "Hello?"

"Mr. Harris, this is Lyn Reagan from Bluebonnet Properties. You left a message about your mother's house."

"Yes. Thanks for calling me back. I'd like to get it on the market as soon as possible."

"I need to see it, of course. I have time now, if you're available."

"Now is good." He gave her the address. "I'll head straight over. I'll be there in less than ten minutes."

"See you soon."

(24)

If you have made mistakes, even serious ones, there
is always another chance for you. What we call failure
is not the falling down but the staying down.
~Mary Pickford (1893-1979)

Virgil had just flipped on the air conditioner in his mother's house when the doorbell rang and the door opened.

"Mr. Harris? Are you in here?" A head poked around the corner.

"Come on in." He hurried to the door, his hand extended. Her handshake was firm and confident. "And please, call me Virgil."

Lyn looked all business in her grey linen suit and low-heel pumps.

"I'll show you around. Let's start in the back." Virgil headed to the hall, then paused at the door of the former chancel and let Lyn enter first.

"What a nice use for a spare bedroom. It could use more light, seeing as it's set up as a library, but it'll show fine."

Virgil exhaled. He hadn't noticed he was holding his breath. They moved through the remainder of the house, Lyn making minor suggestions on some rooms and complimenting others.

When they returned to the dining room, Lyn sat at the table to complete the listing agreement. "The furniture is fine for showing, but what about when it sells? Will you be taking it?"

"I actually hadn't thought about that." Virgil paused. "No. I have no place for it. My mother's in a nursing home and won't be needing it anymore. Can it sell with the house?"

"Unlikely. I can arrange for an estate sale."

"That'd be fine."

"I also need a key." Lyn indicated where Virgil should sign on the agreement. "I'll make a couple of copies of the key so I have one for the lockbox and a spare in case I need to loan one to a maintenance man. And the photographer will want to come by later this afternoon to take pictures."

"Here's my mother's key." Virgil sighed as he retrieved it from a small table by the front door. "I've finally come to terms that she won't ever use it again."

"I'm sorry about your mother." Lyn pocketed the key. "It's never easy making that decision. Had she lived here a long time?"

"Since shortly after my father died, so almost fifty years."

"It's obvious she loved the home. I find it nicely decorated and well maintained."

"My mother would appreciate that. It was a great place to grow up."

Lyn smiled. "I bet it was. Well, I'll be off. I'll put a FOR SALE sign in the yard; I have one in my car. The listing will be online sometime tonight, once I get the pictures to upload."

"Thank you."

Lyn paused at the door. "Oh, I should have mentioned sooner. I'll need a copy of your power of attorney for your mother. I assume you have one."

"Of course. I'll drop a copy by your office."

Lyn nodded and left. Virgil wandered around the house, running his hand over the backs of chairs, studying each picture on the wall. The ones he'd left were nondescript. He'd packed the family pictures. They were in a box in his dining room.

His heart ached for the loss and pain of the past three years. If only he could go back. If only he'd known about his mother's plans for the motif to protect him.

Could I have stopped things from happening? Would my mother still be whole and healthy?

He shook his head and wiped a tear from the corner of his eye. It was pointless to ask such questions. Nothing could be changed. He needed to keep moving forward and do everything he could to stop the Truth Seekers. It wasn't specifically their fault what happened to his mother, but he still blamed them. If they didn't exist, his mother would never have done the motif that diffused on her in the first place.

He paused in the hall, stared at the painting of the bridge, then grabbed it off the wall. The painting probably hid the key to his mother's chancel all through his childhood, and he'd had no clue.

Mama would want me to have it. I'll use it to hide my own chancel key from now on.

Right now his key was in the desk drawer in his home office.

He took one last look around then turned off the thermostat and left. He stopped at home long enough to load his mother's clothes into his SUV, then made the rounds: Goodwill, the South Central Women's Shelter donation center, and Upscale Resale.

At the resale shop, he accepted the printout showing listed price and their commission. He glanced at the numbers and shook his head. *Used clothes sure aren't worth much.*

He started to say he didn't want his percentage, then changed his mind. He'd give it to Sylvia. It was her idea to bring the clothes here.

It was just after noon, but he wasn't hungry. *Wish I had Marshall's address. That's right, I do! It's on the Truth Seeker's list Sylvia brought.* He'd made a copy, which was safely tucked in his desk drawer. *Damn. Too bad I didn't grab it when I loaded Mama's clothes.* He swung by home for the second time to retrieve it.

Marshall's street was on the west side of town, in one of the older areas that featured ancient pecan trees and a spring-fed creek. Half the houses were mansions, the other half were former servants cottages, with some of those cottages being close to shacks.

I wonder which he lives in? No time like the present to find out.

Virgil drove to the once-elite neighborhood, now mostly populated by tenants, the restored homes converted to apartments. Cottages that weren't in disrepair were occupied by small families or converted to boutiques, cafes, and coffee shops.

Virgil slowed to a crawl as drove past Marshall's large home. It was a two-story Colonial beauty with tall cream columns flanking a wide front porch. The clapboard siding was smokey-grey. The window trim and shutters were the same cream as the columns.

The house didn't look like apartments. It looked like a private home. There were no multiple mailboxes, no mismatched curtains in the windows on opposite sides of the central, leaded glass door.

Virgil whistled. *Nice digs. Must have been his mother's home. Can't see him buying this on a UPS deliveryman's salary.*

The yard was well maintained but sparsely planted. A rose next to the wide entry steps would stand out. The large live oak on the left side of the yard would provide a touch of shade from the brutal August heat. Other than that, the rose would get the sun it needed.

There was also no sign of life. The long driveway was empty, and the open carport at the end of the driveway held no vehicle. Virgil debated whether to leave a note and decided against it. *I have to plant that rose.* He U-turned his car and headed home.

Carla would likely ask Marshall the next time he delivered a package to the tax office. She'd be upset and suspicious if Marshall didn't report on his new rose. Plus, he needed to talk to Marshall, and this was how he'd initiate a friendship more personal than "Here's your package."

When he stepped out of his car at home, Virgil frowned. It was the wrong time of day to be digging up an expensive rose. Neither he nor the plant would appreciate the heat. But it had to be done now, while Marshall wasn't home and his Truth Seeker spies were elsewhere.

He selected one of his smaller roses, a three-foot Brenda Burg in full bloom. The yellow-orange blossoms would look good in front of Marshall's smokey-grey house.

By the time Virgil dug up the rosebush, wrapped the roots in a wet towel, and stowed it in a mop bucket in the SUV, he was a sweaty mess with half a dozen thorn pricks on his hands and arms. Instead of cleaning up, he headed straight for Marshall's.

Virgil pulled into the man's driveway until he was parallel with the porch, lugged the heavy bucket to the open area left of the front steps, and began digging. He shouldn't have been surprised when a voice called from behind him.

"Hey! Who are you? What are you doing?"

Virgil jumped, then straightened, grimacing at a sudden kink in his back. As he rubbed his lower back, he turned to see an elderly, blue-haired woman wearing a purple-flowered housecoat, her hands on her hips.

He gave her his most disarming smile. "Good afternoon, ma'am. My name's Virgil Harris. Marshall is my UPS driver. He's been very kind since my mother became ill. I'm planting this rose as a surprise."

The woman waved toward the plant. "What is it you're planting? What's wrong with your mother?"

"It's an heirloom rose. And my mother was…in an accident. She's in a long-term care facility now."

"You mean one a them damn nursing homes. Bless her heart. Heirloom rose, huh? Love those. Used to grow 'em myself. Can't bend over anymore."

"Thank you for your kind words."

The woman's posture relaxed and she smiled. "That's mighty nice of you. What color are those blooms? My eyes aren't what they used to be."

"Yellow-orange. I thought they'd look pretty next to his grey house."

She nodded. "Yep. Yep. I'd say so. You go on then."

"Thank you." As if she needed to give him permission. "I want him to be surprised when he gets home. He's always admired my roses. Please don't tell him you saw me. He'll probably figure it out, but if he doesn't, that's okay."

"You betcha." She turned and hobbled across the street.

Virgil returned to the hard, hot work. It was after 2 when he finally finished. He had no idea what time Marshall might get home, but he wanted to be gone. He wanted to follow up with Marshall AFTER the man had seen the new rosebush.

Virgil loaded his supplies into the SUV. He hunted around the edge of the house for a hose and gave the rose a generous watering. Hopefully it would do the trick and open Marshall up for an unusual conversation.

(25)

I always tried to turn every disaster into an opportunity.
~John D. Rockefeller (1839-1937)

As soon as he got home, Virgil took a quick shower, then dressed in khaki slacks and a yellow polo. There was little food in the house, and he didn't feel like cooking. He also wasn't in the mood for the store, so he decided to return to Harold's, curious to see if young Lisa had shown up and if Harold had forgiven her or fired her for her thoughtlessness.

Virgil smiled. It was easy when you're young to get caught up in fun and forget all about the responsibilities of a job. He'd only been fired once – for falling asleep in the local grocery store's stockroom after attending an all-night science fiction movie marathon at a friend's house.

Before leaving the house, he walked down the hall and unlocked the door to his chancel. The motif was finished. All the candles were out. He had no way of knowing if that had happened before or after breakfast. Perhaps the motif hadn't worked yet. That's why Tammy was no different this morning.

She may still be the same. It might take a day or two.

He gathered the remnants of the motif, put everything into a small box, and taped it securely with packing tape. He'd bury it later in the corner of his yard with all his other motif leavings.

Oh hell.

Virgil hadn't thought about all the boxes buried in his yard. Once he buried a motif's remnants, he didn't think about it again. It was one of his mother's lessons to *send the energies into the universe and let it go.*

But now they weren't likely to remain buried. It was a good bet that Sylvia would find some of the boxes. She knew now that he did motifs, but finding their remains would be a different story. If she opened any of the boxes, she'd see details he didn't want her to see.

He paced the room. Could he move all of them? Not likely. He wasn't even sure at this point how many were there.

I've got it!

He'd stop at the statuary and fountain place on the highway and have a large, terraced concrete fountain delivered and installed in that corner. Sylvia wouldn't be happy he was jumping the gun on her design, but he'd deal with that later. He HAD to protect those boxes.

I'll tell her how inspired I was and that I wanted to surprise her. That my enthusiasm got the better of me.

Concrete Heaven was on the highway a few miles outside San Antonio. Since his choice would be based on footprint size and not overall design, it only took him five minutes to decide. He chose a large, Italian-style monstrosity with four tiers and an eight-foot basin. As an afterthought, he selected a curved bench to go next to it.

Both would cover enough of the corner that his boxes should be safe. He arranged for the fountain to be delivered the next morning and paid the extra fee for the workers to run a water line from his faucet to the fountain's autofill. He didn't want anyone digging around looking for a sprinkler system mainline.

He'd bury Tammy's motif box tonight. It would be the last to ever go in his yard. It'd be a challenge to find someplace that wouldn't be disturbed for new boxes, but he'd deal with that later.

Smiling with satisfaction, he headed for Harold's. His stomach growled audibly. He glanced at the dashboard clock. It was after 4. He hadn't eaten since breakfast, and his day had included some hard labor. No wonder he was hungry.

He pulled up to Harold's and saw only a local police car out front. It was late for the lunch crowd and early for the dinner crowd, but cops ate when they could.

"Hmm." The OPEN light was out. He hadn't noticed this morning. He'd tell Tammy, so she could turn it on before the dinner crowd arrived. Most, like him, wouldn't even notice, but a few would go home or go elsewhere.

No reason to lose business over an ON switch.

He knew something was wrong the moment he opened the door. Harold was pacing around the room instead of cooking in the kitchen. He was mumbling and waving his arms. And he was smoking inside his own non-smoking restaurant. A stinky cloud hung in the air above where he circled.

Dirty tables filled the room. It smelled like something greasy had burned in the kitchen. Tammy sat at a table, crying into a napkin. A woman in police uniform patted Tammy on the shoulder. A stack of papers and a pen were on the table beside Tammy's elbow.

Virgil took the seat across from Tammy. "What's wrong? What's happened? Are you okay?"

Tammy raised her head and stared at Virgil. Her face was streaked black with eye makeup. Her purple-framed glasses were pushed up onto her head like a headband. "No. I'm not okay. I've never been worse. But I'm better than Lisa. Oh, God. Poor Lisa."

Virgil's stomach lurched. "Lisa? What's happened?"

He glanced at Harold. Had he fired her? No. This was more than firing. Why was a police woman here?

"She… She…" Tammy burst into tears and lay her head in the crook of her arm on the table. Her shoulders shook. Her sobs tore at Virgil's heart. The officer glared at him, but said nothing.

"I'll tell you what happened!" Harold whirled on Virgil. "This town's going to hell. She was raped. Bernie found her naked and almost dead on the side of Ranch Road 27."

Virgil's eyes grew big. Before he could speak, Harold slammed his fist on the table and continued. "It was lucky Bernie was out there checkin' on a new barbed wire fence job. She was in a ditch surrounded by weeds. He wouldn't have seen her if he hadn't pulled over to look over the old fence posts."

Tammy looked up. "She's such a sweet girl. Innocent and trusting. And whoever did it meant to kill her. She had a big red ring around her neck. Cops said she'd been strangled. Lucky to be alive at all."

It was then that he noticed the purse at Tammy's feet. It was not the one he'd reached into the other day. He hadn't used Tammy's lipstick in the motif. He'd used Lisa's.

Virgil closed his eyes in horror. His groan escaped before he could stop himself.

"Sir, are you all right?" the police woman asked. "You're awfully pale. Just how well did you know Miss Anderson?"

Virgil fought to get himself under control. "Only from here. At Harold's. I'd never even heard her last name until you just now said it."

"You seem extremely upset for a casual acquaintance." The officer narrowed her eyes, then shoved the notepad and pen across the table so they were in front of Virgil. "We'll need your personal information, sir. In case we have additional questions for you."

"Of course." He wrote his full name, address, and phone number on the pad, then handed it back to the police woman.

"Thank you. Now if you'll excuse us, the restaurant is closed. I have additional questions for these two."

"I understand." He dared a glance at Tammy as he stood. She was glaring at him, her mouth a grim line.

Does she suspect me of being involved?

There was nothing she could actually know that tied him to Lisa's assault. It might simply be bad timing. Only this morning Tammy was insinuating she knew he was up to something. She was probably jumping to conclusions now, with no actual facts to go on. Still, he was in a dangerous and precarious situation.

He was terrible at lying. If brought in for questioning and asked if he'd been involved, he'd of course say no, but that wasn't true. His motif HAD involved him. Not only had he used a focalis from the wrong person, he'd totally blown the motif. He'd never meant for anyone, not even Tammy as his intended target, to get raped. What had gone wrong?

(26)

If we knew each other's secrets, what comforts we should find. ~John Churton Collins

As soon as Virgil got home he made a beeline for his chancel. He cut open the box, spread the contents on the table and grabbed the chant. His eyes widened in horror as he read what he'd written.

He hadn't included Tammy's name. Why not? *How could I be so stupid.*

If he had added her name, what would've happened? The lipstick was Lisa's. Would the motif simply not have worked if a chant about Tammy hadn't matched a focalis from Lisa?

I'll never know now. Virgil shook his head, disgusted with himself.

He picked up the doll, then dropped it as if it were on fire. Lisa had been naked. So was the doll. Lisa had been strangled. Virgil stared at the red ring he'd drawn around the doll's neck. It was supposed to be Tammy's necklace. But it didn't look like that, not even to him.

The line was fat because he'd used lipstick instead of a pen. And it was red. Blood red. The mark that was supposed to be her cross pendant was an indistinct blob. It could've been oozing blood for all the universe knew.

Virgil broke out in a cold sweat. His heart raced and his temples pounded. He took several deep breaths to clear his head.

I screwed up bad, Mama. Very bad.

It was the first time he'd ever rushed to do a motif. It would absolutely be the last. He'd always spent days, sometimes weeks, preparing. He'd spent less than a day preparing for this one. He frowned.

How could I have been so stupid, he thought again.

There were few options. He couldn't fix Lisa, or reverse what'd happened. It would be nuts to try another motif on Tammy. At the moment, just the thought of doing another motif on a specific person made his stomach lurch.

The pounding returned in Virgil's temples. He felt like a trapped animal. He needed help. His mother wouldn't understand, let alone be able to offer any help.

Marshall! I can't wait for him to call me. I need to talk to him now. I just hope he's on that Truth Seeker's list because he's like me. I hope he can help.

Virgil grabbed his car keys and headed to the UPS driver's house. *What am I going to say? Will he even talk to me? Doesn't matter. I have to give it a try.* It might be his demise, but confronting Marshall felt like his only place to go.

Two blocks from Marshall's house, Virgil slowed to a crawl and banged his hands on the steering wheel. *Dammit. This whole thing sucks. I can't just pull up in front of Marshall's house. The Truth Seekers might be watching. I don't want them to see me.*

Even at 9:30 at night, he didn't feel safe. A house with a For Sale sign in the yard seemed as good a place as any to park. From there, he walked to Marshall's.

To avoid the glow from a nearby streetlight, Virgil skipped the sidewalk and cut across Marshall's yard at an angle. Maybe anyone watching would think he was only a neighbor. At least it'd be hard to recognize him from the back.

Climbing the porch steps, he glanced at the rose. A few blooms had fallen off from shock, but otherwise it looked healthy in the dim light. When he reached the porch, he resisted the urge to glance over his shoulder.

The doorbell chimed *The Eyes of Texas*. Virgil couldn't help but chuckle. *Perfect. I sure hope it isn't too late to be here.*

Marshall answered the door wearing gym shorts and a faded, ancient-looking Beatles T-shirt. "Virgil! What brings you here? I was gonna stop by tomorrow." He made a sheepish grin and ran a hand through his grey hair. "Thanks for the rosebush but, um...you know I'm straight, right?"

"Oh! No, no." Virgil was glad Marshall probably couldn't see him blush. "It's not like that. I'm straight, too. I thought—"

"Hey, it's cool. I appreciate the plant. Just wanted to get that out there. No hard feelings, I hope."

"No. No hard feelings. And I didn't mean anything like that. I wanted to...it was just that..." How could he explain what he wanted without sounding like a weirdo or stalker? That the rose was almost a bribe so he could ask awkward questions? No matter what he'd told the elderly woman across the street, Virgil knew it wasn't a thank you for any special favors for his mother.

"Come on in. You look ragged. How about a beer?"

Virgil wasn't big on beer but a cold alcoholic drink sounded good. "Sure. Thanks." He followed Marshall into a large living room paneled with polished oak.

"Have a seat. I'll be right back." Marshall waved toward two overstuffed leather chairs and headed for the kitchen.

Virgil eased into one of the chairs and glanced around. The room was masculine in its burgundy and brown tones. Everything also looked expensive and high-quality.

How's he afford these digs on a UPS delivery driver's salary?

Here and there were feminine touches: a crocheted doily on the back of a velvet-upholstered chair by the window, a few porcelain figurines scattered on the shelves of a bookcase, a needlepoint wall hanging depicting flowers in a basket. It occurred to Virgil that they all looked old-fashioned. Perhaps Marshall's mother or grandmother had added them.

How long has his family lived in this house?

Marshall returned with two bottles of beer from a local microbrewery. He handed one to Virgil, then sat in the identical chair opposite a central, marble-top table.

"So tell me what's up? Why the rosebush? Why the late visit?"

Virgil grinned sheepishly. "Thanks for getting right to the point. I wasn't sure how I should bring things up." He set his beer on the table and leaned toward the other man. "You're in danger, Marshall."

Marshall laughed, but Virgil's glare shut him up. "You're serious. I deliver packages. Some are weird, and I sometimes make comments that I wonder what I'm delivering, but that's as controversial as I get."

Virgil pulled the copy of the Truth Seekers list from his pocket and handed it to Marshall. "You're on this list."

"What list?" Marshall scanned the paper. "I don't even know any of these other people. Wait, I recognize this first name. I deliver packages to her. But I don't *know* her. And these other two are complete strangers. What is this?"

"Have you heard of the Truth Seekers?"

"No. Should I?"

"For your own safety? Yes." Virgil told Marshall everything he knew, including his attending a meeting.

"They think I'm a WHAT?"

"A sorcerer. Someone who does magic. They're following you. They probably saw me on your porch. I'm hoping it's dark enough they didn't recognize me. I parked around the corner and walked."

"You really are worried. Or crazy."

"Maybe I'm crazy, but I don't think so." Virgil leaned back and took a long swig of beer. "I need to ask you a question and please, for both our safety, answer me honestly."

"Sure, whatever you need," Marshall said.

Virgil saw the *you've got to be kidding* expression on the other man's face. "Does your family have...abilities? Could one of your parents do things to change the course of events? To control what happened? Can you?"

"Do what? Of course not."

Virgil didn't say a word, just stared hard at Marshall.

After a minute, Marshall sighed and turned to the dark window. "How'd you know?"

"Because so can mine. So can I."

Marshall's head snapped around and his mouth gaped open. "I thought my family were the only ones."

"I used to think the same about mine. But some freaky coincidences led me to believe you have the same ability."

Marshall's voice dropped to a whisper. "It was from my father's side of the family. He taught me about our talent and what I could do. About how to use it. It's been a financial blessing for us for generations."

"Financial blessing?" Virgil cocked his head.

"It's how our family got this house four generations ago, and how I'm able to keep it today."

"I was curious about that," Virgil said. "How do you use your ability financially?"

Marshall grinned. "I'm very good at winning weekly lottery tickets for moderate amounts."

"I'll bet that's what caught their eye. It's not normal to win a lottery every week, even the small scratch-off amounts."

"Caught whose eye?"

"The Truth Seekers." Virgil shrugged. "I wondered what caused people to be put on that list. They're probably watching for anomalies anywhere they can. Things that raise eyebrows."

"Like winning the lottery every week."

"Well...yeah. In our family, at least, we always made sure we stayed under the radar. I was taught not to draw attention to myself. That's probably why I'm NOT on the list. At least, not yet." Virgil glanced toward the window.

"We've always been cautious, but I guess not cautious enough." Marshall frowned and looked down at the list he still held. "Who'd you get your ability from? Your Mom or your Dad?"

"My mother." Virgil smiled. "And her grandmother before her."

"Dad got the ability from his Mom. So did my aunt."

"Do you have siblings? Do they have the same skill?"

"Three. Two brothers and a sister. One brother has it. My sister does, too. The other brother hasn't a shred of our talent in his body. We teased him when we were kids, even though Dad told us not to. These days, we leave him alone. How about you?"

"I'm an only child. So was my mother. Not only did I not know anyone outside the family could alter events, the only ones *inside* the family I knew were my mother and grandmother."

"This calls for another beer." Marshall carried their bottles with him and returned moments later with two cold ones. "Looks like we have a lot to talk about."

(27)

*No one is normal. There are just a lot of weird
people with things in common. ~Unknown*

Virgil sighed a long ragged breath and downed half his beer in one
swig. "I can't believe I'm finally talking to someone else who
understands."

Marshall smiled. "I always wondered about you, based on the
packages you got. No way I ever would've asked, though."

"But you mentioned it to Tammy." Virgil's voice turned harsh
and he slapped the marble table. "You told her all about my
packages. She's a Truth Seeker. She has a copy of that list. Why the
hell did you do that?"

"Yeah, I did." Marshall hung his head. "I'm sorry. I wasn't trying
to start anything. I was joking." At Virgil's glare, Marshall added, "I
know I'm not supposed to talk about packages I deliver. You'd be
surprised at some of the funky things people get around here."

"But my packages were okay to talk about?"

"No. Again, I'm sorry. I was flirting with Tammy. I wanted to
sound cool and clever. You'd just received a big box from a doll

manufacturer. I found it funny. Had no idea she'd take it as something sinister."

"Yeah, okay. I guess. At least you didn't do it on purpose."

"Good grief, no!" Marshall set his beer down and leaned toward Virgil. "Believe me. I'd never have said a word to anyone if I'd had a clue my suspicions were really true. I know how important anonymity is. That's why I've never gone for a big lottery win. One of my great, great, great, whatever, aunts was burned at the stake in England. I shouldn't have even joked about something that made me wonder. It was stupid. Sorry."

"Thanks. That helps, actually."

"I'm glad." Marshall leaned back and smiled. "By the way, what do you call it? When you do something to change the way things are? Tell me you don't call them spells."

Virgil shook his head. "Of course not. We call them motifs."

"Our family calls them dioramas. They've always reminded me of a science fair exhibit. Little objects and candles arranged just so."

"We use lots of candles, too."

"Yep, I've delivered a fair number of boxes from Candle Country to you." Marshall laughed.

"Your dioramas sound like our motifs. Besides candles, we also use objects. We call the main object a focalis, since it's the focal point and the most important part of a motif."

"Like a doll." Marshall drained his beer. "That's why you got a whole case of them."

"Yeah, I use a doll to represent a specific person. I personalize it with an item that belongs to them."

"What personal item did you use for Joe's doll?"

The question shocked Virgil so much he almost dropped his bottle, barely catching it at the last second.

What does he know about my involvement with Joe's accident? Or is he just guessing? "What do you mean?" Virgil raised his eyebrows.

"Don't bullshit me, Virgil. I know you had something to do with it. I wondered at the time."

Virgil turned his face away from Marshall, who remained silent.

What do I tell him? The truth? Am I setting myself up? Or can I trust a fellow theurgist? I have to. I have no one else to help me.

He turned to face the man he still barely knew. "I dressed a Ken doll in a suit made from one of Joe's used napkins, then put the doll in a toy car like Joe's."

Marshall nodded. "I remember now. I delivered a big box from a model car company. I collected Matchbox cars when I was a kid. Sure wanted to see what you'd gotten."

"It was a work of art. Hated to bury it."

"Bury it?" Marshall cocked his head.

"What do you do with the remnants of your motifs...dioramas?" Virgil asked.

"Oh. Of course. We sink ours. I'll bet the bottom of every lake and pond we've ever lived near is littered with our family's secrets."

Virgil laughed, then grew serious. "Joe got what he deserved. I don't do motifs on people who don't deserve them."

"Never said you did." Marshall stood. "I'm getting us another beer."

"I'm not sure I need one."

"Yes, you do. You should see your face."

Marshall returned, his bottle already half empty. "I'd thought about doing a diorama on Joe. Glad you stepped up to the plate, so to speak."

Virgil shrugged. "It seemed the right thing to do."

"Can't argue with that." Marshall raised his eyebrows. "How'd you use that acid?"

Virgil started. "Acid? Oh never mind. I painted it on the undercarriage wiring of the model car."

"Makes sense." Marshall nodded. "Whatever else you did, you did a good job."

"Thanks!" Virgil blushed. "Wow. I've actually never been complimented for a motif before. At least not by anyone but my mother."

"It's not like we can advertise them."

"Virgilante for hire."

"Huh?"

Virgil laughed. "Once upon a time, I fancied advertising my motif services under the name *Virgilante*. Obviously a stupid idea."

"You'd for sure be on the Truth Seekers list if you had!" Marshall grinned.

"I can't get over how weird this feels. You're the first person, aside from my mother, I've ever talked to who shares our talent."

"That must have been rough." Marshall frowned. "At least I had my brother and sister, plus my mom and grandmother."

"Don't even have Mama anymore. Not really."

"You ever been married?"

"No." Virgil's face softened. "Dated lots of women over the years. Came close to marrying a couple of times. The most recent... I'd given her a ring, and we were talking about wedding dates. Then Mama's...incident happened."

"Did she know about you? I mean your girl, not your mother."

"Not until I talked about going after the burglars who attacked Mama. Maybe I scared her. I was so angry. Anyway, it fell apart pretty quickly after that. She moved away. Phoenix."

"That sucks."

"Yeah, it does. Or did. I'm okay now. You're not married?"

"Was. Twice, in fact. First time for almost twenty years. The second for less than ten. Had a son by the first marriage, two kids by the second."

"What happened?"

"First marriage was great. Sheila never had issues with me, or our son, who turned out to have strong abilities himself. He and I did some great dioramas together. Sheila died of cancer when Brandon was fifteen.

"Sorry," Virgil said.

Marshall smiled. "Thanks. It was a long time ago."

"You said you were married twice."

"Married Betty Lou the year Brandon went away to college. He'd gotten a little radical after Sheila died, but we still kept in touch, even after he moved away. College seemed to straighten him out and get him back on a good path." Marshall shook his head. "Time sure flies. He's married with kids of his own now."

"What about your second wife and kids?"

"Betty Lou always said my abilities didn't bother her." Marshall's expression hardened. "That sure as hell turned out to be a lie."

"What happened? Your wife had to know about you before you married."

"Sure she did. Everything was just fine for a while. Aaron, our first, had no abilities, so Betty Lou didn't have to deal with it. But Cindy, our youngest, started showing abilities at three. When I wanted to start training her, the shit hit the fan. Betty Lou wanted no part of it. Wasn't going to have me turn her daughter into a *freak*." His voice dropped to a whisper. "You can guess how it went from there."

"I'm sorry. Do you still see those two kids?"

"Once a year." Marshall almost spat the words. "She moved 'em to upstate Maine. Probably trying to get as far away from me as possible."

"Sorry, man. I always wondered how outsiders joining the family would accept our theurgical abilities."

"Our what?"

"I call myself a theurgist."

"What the hell is a theurgist? Sounds made up."

"It was actually used by the Egyptians to describe those who could do magic."

"So that's not a word your northern England ancestors used." Marshall smirked.

Virgil grinned in response. "My mother called it our *gift of symbols*. I remember hearing my grandmother call it that one time, too. Guess I wanted something less clunky. More elegant. Whatever."

"I like it. Think I'll use it to. My sister calls herself a witch, but there's too much bullshit attached to that word for me."

"My mother hated that word. Said Hollywood ruined it."

"Anyway, back to your mother." Marshall drained his beer. "Tell me that you did a diorama on the burglars. They deserved one."

"First motif I ever did against specific people. What about you?"

"I avoid dioramas on individuals. Too risky. What if something goes wrong?"

"Like lipstick." Virgil mumbled.

"Huh?"

"You realize I'm taking a big chance, talking to you. I could be setting myself up if the police ever start asking questions."

"Would it help if I showed you my chantry? Would that make you more comfortable?"

"Chantry?"

"The room where I do my dioramas. What do you call yours?"

"Chancel. Never heard the word chantry before, but they sound similar."

"From the same Latin or French or Celtic or whatever word, no doubt," Marshall stood. "Come on. It's down the hall."

(28)

*It takes a wonderful brain and exquisite senses to produce
a few stupid ideas. ~George Santayana (1863-1952)*

Virgil followed Marshall to the back of his house. The chantry was at the end of the hall. Marshall unlocked and opened the door, but Virgil remained outside.

"It's okay. You can go in."

"Thanks." Virgil stepped slowly into the room. In the center was a wooden oval table of oak or pecan. It was clean, except for a few spots of melted wax near the center.

As in Virgil's own chancel, Marshall had a row of cabinets along one wall. Virgil touched the table. He felt its energy, like the vibration caused when loud music played. Marshall was a theurgist, too. Virgil had no doubt.

He turned. "You said your relatives came from England. It's quite a coincidence that your family and mine have the same abilities. Maybe they lived in the same area. Maybe they knew each other."

"Wouldn't be surprised." Marshall pointed at Virgil. "We could even be related. That wouldn't surprise me, either."

That gave Virgil pause. Could they be? Was there one bloodline out there where these abilities existed? Were all theurgists ultimately related? Or were there different families that all evolved with the same gift?

Or curse.

"What did you mean when you said *lipstick* earlier?"

Virgil cocked his head. "Lipstick?"

"Nuh-uh. Don't even try playing dumb. After I said I worried about a diorama going wrong, and that's why I avoid doing them on specific people, you mumbled *lipstick*. Did something go wrong? What happened?"

Virgil closed his eyes and sighed. He'd have a hard time confessing to his mother, let alone a man he barely knew, even if he did have the same ability.

He spoke without opening his eyes. "I screwed up. Bad." He told Marshall about his motif on Tammy. And what happened with Lisa. "I was prepared for the karmic backlash, but now there'll be diffusion on top of it. Can't imagine what's going to happen."

"Karmic backlash? Diffusion? What the hell are you talking about?"

"I was taught long ago to always expect to pay a price when doing a motif against another person. That's karmic backlash. But when you screw up a motif can get sucked into the mistake and some of the motif can happen to you. That's diffusion."

"I had the same lessons. Just didn't call them that. So what are you thinking?"

"No idea." Virgil shook his head. "I'm afraid it's going to be bad."

Marshall whistled. "I need something stronger than beer. Want a bourbon?"

"Hell yes." Virgil nodded and followed Marshall to the kitchen.

Virgil stared out the kitchen window into the dark backyard while Marshall poured their drinks. His heart was heavy with guilt over Lisa. Confession was supposed to be good for the soul, but telling Marshall had only made him feel worse.

"Here." Marshall handed Virgil a highball glass filled to the brim with half-moon ice cubes and golden-brown liquid. "Let's go sit down."

"Let's check outside first. See if we spot anyone."

"Why not." Marshall headed up the stairs. Virgil took a large gulp and followed. He immediately began coughing, causing Marshall to look over his shoulder and laugh.

"Didn't expect it to be straight." Virgil wiped his watery eyes. "Good, though. Hits the spot."

"Seemed we needed the fortification." Marshall raised his glass as if in a toast.

The two men entered the dark guest room. Marshall closed the door to eliminate light from the stairwell, then they crossed to the window.

"See anything?" Marshall asked as he leaned into the window. "I sure don't."

Virgil squinted into the darkness. "Maybe. Look one house down on the right. Next to that big bush."

"You're right. Those're definitely people-shaped shadows. Looks like two of them."

After a minute, one of the shadows shifted.

"Well, now we know. They really are spying on you." Virgil rubbed his eyes and took another swallow of bourbon.

Marshall shook his head. "Damn. Who'd have thought all this shit would be going on in Lichen. Why couldn't they just let me play my lottery and deliver my packages? I wasn't hurting anyone."

"Good question." Virgil frowned. "But they've got themselves convinced we're out to destroy the town. Or at least Cotton does."

"Cotton?"

"The head of the Truth Seekers. I didn't like him the minute I met him."

"But he's wrong," Marshall said. "We aren't out to do anything. None of us even had any idea others like us existed."

"True, although if you'd heard all the crazy conspiracy theories they actually believe, you'd realize our being part of some evil gang pales by comparison."

"Let's go downstairs. I'm topping off our drinks."

"I'm going to regret this, but okay."

Armed with full glasses of bourbon, the two settled again into the living room chairs they'd occupied earlier.

"So what now?" Marshall asked.

"No idea. Lay low, I guess. I'm not doing any more motifs, at least for the time being."

Marshall nodded. "I think your decision to do nothing else is smart. Especially considering Lisa. Let's hope Tammy doesn't get suspicious or find anything out."

"Don't know why she would. I hope no one else ever finds out. It was a stupid mistake." Virgil swirled the ice in his glass for a minute. "Have you ever totally screwed up a motif?"

A shadow crossed Marshall's face. "Once. A decade ago. He died." He shook his head and he flexed the fingers of his right hand. "Please don't ask me for details. I paid the price for it."

It was then that Virgil noticed Marshall was missing half the pinkie finger of that hand. Whatever had happened must have been bad.

The pair sat in silence, sipping their drinks. Minutes ticked by.

Marshall spoke first. "Who was at that Truth Seekers meeting? How many were there? And how many did you recognize?"

"Around thirty there." Virgil shrugged. "I went with Stan, my dim-witted neighbor who got sucked into joining. Didn't recognize most of the others. Tammy, of course. And a couple of faces were vaguely familiar, but can't place 'em. A kid named Iggy, the son of the woman I just hired to landscape my backyard."

"That a coincidence?" Marshall raised his eyebrows.

"Let's just say it's convenient."

"Right."

Virgil changed the subject. "So do you think the other three names on the Truth Seekers' list are like us? Do you think we're that common?"

"I wouldn't call five people common."

"In a town of only 12,000, five is a lot."

"Okay, that may be true." Marshall nodded. "But we have no idea about the others."

"How would we go about finding out?" Virgil asked.

"We could talk to them." Marshall took a healthy swallow of bourbon.

Virgil turned to Marshall. "I'd be hesitant to approach them."

"You approached me."

"Yeah, but I knew you. Somewhat. Sort of. These are complete strangers. At least to me. What about that name you recognized?"

"Emma Short? I know her less than I knew you just a couple of hours ago. Most of the time I leave her packages on her porch. She's rarely home. Or let's say she rarely answers her door."

"I recognize one name as an employee at the hardware store, but that's it. Most I've ever spoken to him was to ask where the duct tape was."

Marshall pursed his lips. "So where does that leave us? What do we do?"

"Well, it seems the big issue is that the Truth Seekers are going after folks who haven't done anything illegal or wrong." When Marshall smirked, Virgil quickly added, "Yeah, my screw up with Lisa was wrong, but doing a motif, or diorama, isn't actually illegal. Except maybe winning the lottery every week."

"Yeah, okay. So I'll ask again. What do we do?"

"I have only one idea. And it's a doozy."

"Okay, I'll bite." Marshall drained the last of his bourbon. "What do you have in mind?"

"Bhfuil a fhios agat an teanga ársa?"

"Yes! I do know the old tongue!" Marshall's eyebrows shot up. "Our families must have lived in the same region to both speak Goidelic. But what does that have to do with your idea?"

"I want us to do a joint motif. Diorama. Whatever. Not only for protection for ourselves, but to bathe the town in protection from the Truth Seekers, and others who might bring harm from the outside. To not just protect us and the others on that list, but everyone in town."

"You don't want much."

"Yeah, it's big." Virgil turned and stared at Marshall. "But hear me out. We have a gift few people have."

"A little while ago you called us *common*."

Virgil rolled his eyes. "I still think five is a lot for a small town. But ultimately I'll bet there are only a few of us. Maybe more than we're aware of, but you know as well as I do that we're still a seriously insignificant minority."

"Fair enough. But I'm not sure how I feel about such an all-encompassing diorama. We're begging for, what did you call it?"

"Karmic backlash."

"Yeah, that," Marshall said. "Could be pretty bad."

"Maybe. But things are getting worse. Don't tell me you don't feel it." Virgil waved toward the door. "Hell, you've got spies out there right now, even this late. Watching every move you make. Remember what I said earlier, when I told you about the Truth Seekers? Their plan is to stop the people on that list any way they can. They believe they're trying to save the town."

"Isn't that what you're proposing we do? What's the difference."

Virgil sat back. *He has me there. Are we no better?* "Not much difference, I guess." Virgil shrugged. "Except I want to protect us from danger, without harming anyone."

"I'm not sure that's possible. A big, broad diorama covering a lot of people is bound to hurt someone."

"Yeah, you're probably right." Virgil drained his own glass. "But I still want to try. I want to protect me. And you." *And Sylvia.* "And the rest of the innocent people in this town. Groups like the Truth Seekers can turn dangerous, even deadly."

"Can't argue with that." Marshall stood and stretched. "We need more bourbon."

"If I drink more, I won't be able to drive."

"I think you need to stay here. If they're watching, you shouldn't be seen leaving. They'll follow you."

"I have to leave some time. And you have to work tomorrow."

"Don't remind me. I'm going to pay for all the booze."

"And you still want more?"

"Don't you?"

Virgil sighed. "Yeah. I do."

While Marshall was out of the room, Virgil thought again about Lisa and Tammy. *What a total mess. And there's just no good solution.* Then his thoughts turned to Sylvia. They'd barely begun a relationship. Was it destined for success or doomed from the start because of who he was and what he could do? Had done? Before he could delve any deeper, Marshall returned with the bottle.

"What say we change the subject until we're sober and rested?" Marshall asked as he refilled their glasses.

"Sounds like a smart idea."

The two men spent the next hour finishing the bourbon and talking about their childhoods. Both were amazed at how similar their upbringing had been. In spite of the terminology differences, they'd been taught almost identical styles and methods.

"Oh hell, it's after three. I have to be up at six." Marshall rubbed his eyes and sighed.

"I should go."

"Not a chance. Remember I said you should stay here. I'm not being responsible for you crashing, or getting arrested on a DWI." Marshall stood. "Follow me."

At the door to the guest room, Marshall turned to Virgil. "I can't miss work tomorrow, but I want to continue this conversation. Wednesdays are usually light delivery days. I'll call as soon as I get home. We can pick up our conversation then."

"Sure. There's lots more to talk about."

"And I have an idea. Stay for a while in the morning. At least until I've been gone a couple hours. If nothing else, the spies will have followed me, so they won't see you leave."

Virgil nodded. "Sure. Makes sense."

"Thanks. See you tomorrow."

(29)

Everything we see hides another thing, we always want to see what is hidden by what we see. ~Rene Magritte

Virgil woke thick-headed and queasy. It took him a minute to remember where he was. He sat up and grabbed his phone from the nightstand. It was 7:45. The house was deathly quiet.

Ugh. I cannot drink like that. His mouth was dry and tasted like he'd licked the floor. His eyes burned, and his stomach flopped around in his gut. He eased out of bed and cleaned up in the guest bathroom. A long, hot shower would have to make up for not being able to shave or brush his teeth.

He found a note on the kitchen table:

I made coffee. Hope it's still warm when you get up. There's cereal in the pantry. Best I got. Talk more later.

Virgil touched the pot. "It'll do," he mumbled as he filled the large mug on the counter. He sat at the table and stared at the note. *Now what? How long should I stay? Did both spies leave or is one still out there?*

He spent the next two hours dozing and watching TV. He avoided the news and instead tuned to a channel specializing in home remodeling and house hunting.

His phone rang shortly before noon.

"Mr. Harris? This is Jorge from Concrete Heaven. We're at your house. Your gate is locked. Where do you want this fountain?"

Oh hell. "I'll be right there!" *Guess it doesn't matter if a spy is still out there. Gotta go.*

He scrawled his phone number on the bottom of the note Marshall had left him and locked the door on his way out.

In case the house was still being watched, he angled across the yard the same way he had the night before. If they'd thought he was a neighbor, he wanted to maintain the illusion. Once he was around the corner he ran to his car. His heart pounded as he climbed in, and not from the short jog. *I hate being nervous in my own town.*

Half a dozen Hispanic men were wandering around his front yard when he pulled up. Two were messing with his roses. He opened his mouth to yell, then changed his mind when he saw they were carefully snipping off dead blooms.

"Thanks fellas," he called to them, then approached the only man not wearing a company uniform shirt. "You must be Jorge."

The men shook hands. Virgil noted Jorge's hands were rough and calloused. He might be the supervisor, but he was also a worker. Virgil liked that. He distrusted managers who didn't do anything but boss others.

"Let me go through the house and unlock the gate." Moments later Virgil met the men at the side yard and led them to the motif burial corner. "What does it take to install this? You don't have to do any excavating do you?"

"Installation is included in the price." Jorge cocked his head in confusion.

"I wasn't worried about that. It's just…" What could he say? *I don't want you digging up remnants of my motifs?* He continued, "just that I have a landscaper coming, and I don't want big piles of dirt for her to deal with."

"Ah, sí, sí. We pound the ground level and then use our Bobcat to install. Very little or no dirt moved."

Virgil nodded. "Great. I'll be in the house. Knock on the door if you need me." His head felt like a volcano. He needed aspirin. And a very large glass of water.

⤞⤞⤞⤞⤞⤞

The pounding on the door jolted him awake. It seemed he'd sat on the sofa only minutes earlier. He blinked and shook his head to clear it, then checked the time. He'd slept three hours. "Coming!"

"We finish. Want to see?" One of the men pointed. Jorge was bent over the fountain, fiddling with something.

Virgil heard the sound of the water as soon as he stepped outside. He briefly closed his eyes and smiled. "Nice."

"Sí, sí. Nothing like falling water. Comforting as a mama's heartbeat."

"That it is." Virgil approached the fountain. Jorge was adjusting the autofill. "You and your men did a great job. This is beautiful."

Jorge straightened. "Thank you, señor. Glad you like it. It's our biggest fountain. We like installing them but not many sell. Mostly businesses buy them."

Virgil stepped back. It was monstrous in his yard. Sylvia was probably going to flip. He'd have to think of a good reason why he'd stepped on her plans.

"Thank you, gentlemen. Can I get you a cold drink for the road?"

Every man nodded and grinned. When Virgil returned with cans of Coke, the men's faces fell, but they took the cans and nodded.

"Sorry, I didn't have any beer. Best I could do."

Jorge shot the men a dirty look. "This is great. We go to another job from here. No drinking yet."

Virgil thanked the men again and returned to the house. He peeked through the window, watching the men gather their tools. When they'd gone he sat at the breakfast table.

I have to call Sylvia. The longer I put it off, the worse it'll be.

He'd use the same tactic his boss used to use on the post office employees — he'd meet her in public. If she got upset, she'd have to contain it. He pulled his phone from his pocket.

"Hello?" Sylvia's voice was light and relaxed.

"Hi, there. Want to meet for a late lunch?"

"Virgil! I was making myself a sandwich, but I can stick it in a baggie. Want to meet at Harold's?"

"NO! Um…I'm just kind of burned out on the place. How about Domingo's. Seems fitting. That's where I met your daughter."

"Sounds great! See you soon."

(30)

Twenty minutes later, Virgil and Sylvia sat just two tables from where Virgil had intruded on Donna.

"This was a surprise." Sylvia leaned over and kissed Virgil on the cheek. "By the way, I'm almost done with your plan."

"About that."

Sylvia sat back, her face fell. "What? Are you changing your mind? Did the other night upset you?"

"Of course not. I invited you to lunch!"

"I'm sorry." Sylvia blushed. "I sound like a paranoid teenager."

Virgil squeezed her hand. "Don't apologize. New relationships are like riding Space Mountain at Disneyland. The fun of a roller coaster ride, but you're riding it through pitch-black uncertainty, with only occasional flashes of insight."

"Oh my!" Sylvia laughed until she had to wipe away tears. "That's about the most perfect analogy of a new relationship I've ever heard."

"Thanks. I'll have to remember it myself."

"Now what about my plan?"

"I did something potentially stupid, but it's too late now. Made an impulse purchase. I'm afraid you'll have to work around it. I'm more afraid you're going to hate me."

"Not more roses!"

"Good grief, no. I bought a concrete fountain. One of those terraced, wedding-cake monstrosities. The men installed it this morning. Wanted to break the news to you before you saw it. Didn't look that big at the store."

Sylvia smiled. "I had a fountain in my design. I'll simply shuffle things around. How big is it?"

"It's got four tiers."

"Okay. So it's tall. But how big is the footprint?"

Virgil paused. "Eight feet?"

"Eight FEET! Wow, that's...big. Sounds like the kind you see outside Italian restaurants."

"Actually, Jorge said they usually installed them at businesses."

"He probably meant restaurants." Sylvia raised an eyebrow. "That all?"

"I bought a bench, too. It can be moved, but right now it's beside the fountain."

"Well...your backyard is good-sized. I'm sure I can manage to make everything work around it. Where'd they install it?"

"In the back right corner."

"That's the one with all the weeds, right?"

"Yes, the other corner has the large sycamore."

"What were you covering up? What's buried there?"

"What?" Virgil choked on a tortilla chip. Sylvia said nothing while he gulped water.

"You heard me. I haven't forgotten what you told me the other night. So what's buried in that corner? I wondered about that before I found your mother's...book. The rest of your yard is rock hard and barren. That corner is thick with weeds. Weeds grow in disturbed soil."

Virgil looked down at the table and fidgeted with his water glass. *What can I tell her? I have to tell her the truth. I want us to work out.*

"Remember, I told you about motifs? That we use symbolic items to help us focus our energies?"

"Yes. Is that what's buried there?"

Virgil nodded. "I can't just throw them away. They represent real people and situations. They've absorbed energies. I bury them in that corner of my yard." *So much for buying an expensive fountain so Sylvia wouldn't find the boxes.* Virgil laughed.

"What's so funny?"

"All that money I just spent. And now you know what's buried there anyway."

Sylvia smiled. "You could have just told me."

"You're right. I should have trusted you'd understand. It's just that..."

"I get it." Sylvia nodded. "You aren't used to telling anyone anything."

"Yes." Virgil sighed in relief. "Until recently I've never talked to anyone but my mother. I never even spoke to my grandmother about it. Now it suddenly seems that's all I talk about anymore."

Sylvia started. "All you talk about? Are you talking to others besides me? Wait...did you talk to Marshall?"

Virgil shifted in his chair. "Last night. In fact, MOST of last night."

"Isn't he on that list I brought you? Who is he again?"

"Yes. Marshall Welker. My UPS driver."

"That's right. You told him about your family? Your...abilities? That's pretty chancy. Are you nuts?"

Virgil leaned forward and lowered his voice. "Maybe. But I don't think so."

Sylvia's huffed and shook her head.

"Yeah, I took a chance, but it didn't simply pop out. I went to his place. I showed him the list. Turns out Marshall's like me." Virgil relayed as much of the night's conversation as he could remember, leaving out a description of how much they drank.

Sylvia sat back. "Okay, I get that you felt you had to talk to him. How'd he react?"

"He was as shocked as me to find out there are others like us. But he was also glad to find out he's not alone. Same as me. He even showed me his chantry. The room where he works."

"You didn't show me yours."

Ouch! "I'm sorry. I was already pretty freaked out just telling you about my family." He looked down and frowned.

"I guess I can accept that. I know I shouldn't sound bitchy." Sylvia sighed and reached across the table to squeeze Virgil's hand. "It really is okay. I can't imagine how big a step telling someone outside the family must be. I'm sure it's scary."

Virgil looked up and smiled. "Thanks. Scary is a good word. It was harder than I expected telling you, and I know you better than Marshall. Telling either of you is also risky. Even these days. It was really dangerous in the past. Marshall said he'd had an ancestor burned at the stake. Doesn't matter it was several hundred years ago in England."

"Oh my." Sylvia bit her lip. "Thank you. Thank you from the bottom of my heart."

"For what? For hiding secrets from you?"

"No. For trusting me, at least some."

Virgil met her eyes. "You're welcome. I'm glad I did."

They spent the rest of lunch discussing how the fountain would alter Sylvia's landscape design.

Virgil paid the check then turned to Sylvia and grinned. "Follow me home? You can see the now pointless monstrosity in all its glory."

"I'd like that. Was going to ask you."

⚜ ⚜ ⚜

Sylvia's first reaction upon walking out Virgil's kitchen onto his patio was, "Wow! That's a big fountain."

"On the upside, you can hear it from inside the house."

"Probably so can the neighbors!" Sylvia laughed, then crossed the yard to sit on the bench. "The bench is nice by the fountain. I'll modify the plan to add some brickwork or gravel here to create a weed-free seating area."

"That sounds great." Virgil sat beside Sylvia and put his arm around her waist. "You aren't mad?"

She shook her head. "No. Well, maybe a little. At first I was angry and hurt. But I really do understand why you didn't want to tell me."

"I'm falling in love with you, you know."

Sylvia turned to him, her eyes wide.

"Didn't mean to scare you!" Virgil met her gaze.

"No, no, you didn't." She leaned on his shoulder. "The same thing is happening to me. I was afraid you'd think I was rushing. Or crazy."

"What I think is that adults of a certain age no longer want to play games. We've lived enough to know what we want."

"And what we don't want."

"Huh?" Virgil frowned.

"Not you! Oscar has apparently had second thoughts. He wants to come back."

"Oscar?"

"My wayward husband. I guess Bonnie-Mae, the hairdresser he ran off with, wasn't all he'd hoped she'd be. Or maybe she dumped him and he doesn't want to admit that."

Virgil removed his arm. "Oh."

Sylvia put her arm around Virgil. "I told him no. I know I DON'T want that. Not anymore. I did at first. But once love is betrayed, it's hard to fix. Our marriage hadn't been good for a while. A long while."

Virgil turned and gave her a passionate kiss. "Are you in a hurry?"

"Not especially." She winked. "What did you have in mind?"

"Follow me." Virgil grinned and waggled his eyebrows.

An hour later, they snuggled under the covers. Virgil ran his fingertips across her forehead. "Should have asked earlier. What are your plans now? With Oscar."

Sylvia grabbed his hand and kissed his palm. "Haven't thought very far ahead. He's not welcome back. If he gets ugly about the house, I'll sell it and give him half."

"What about Iggy? Would you take him with you to a new place?"

"That's the one thing I have thought about. A lot." Sylvia frowned. "No. I don't think so. I honestly believe one of the reasons he's gotten sucked into the Truth Seekers is because he doesn't have to worry about anything else."

"I don't understand." Virgil cocked his head.

"I do his laundry and cook his meals. I probably should have booted him out long ago. He used to have a job. He was going to school. He was more responsible. When his roommate moved away, I let him move back home. Then he quit school and got fired.

Instead of making him get another job, I let him get lazy. Not very good parenting, I'm afraid."

"You love him. You wanted to be supportive."

"And look where that got me! But I'm not going to worry about that today. I may stay in that house indefinitely." Sylvia shook her head.

Unless we end up together. "Sounds like a good idea." Virgil smiled and nodded.

"Speaking of Truth Seekers, so you told Marshall about them?"

"Yeah. I had to. When I showed him he was on their list he said he'd never heard of them. That's what led to our long conversation. We still have a lot to talk about. He's supposed to call when he gets home from work. He's worried."

"I'd be worried, too." Sylvia nodded. "But what is there to talk about?"

"He's being watched. Saw them through the upstairs window. Not surprised. That was the assignment given to the teams chosen at the Truth Seekers' meeting."

"I understand that. And I'm sure it's scary. But what's that have to do with more talking?"

Virgil nodded. "We need to come up with a plan to stop them. Or at least to protect Marshall and the others."

"That's not your job. And you barely know the man! It could put you in danger."

"I don't think so. Right now the Truth Seekers don't seem aware of me. I have to help if I can."

"Are you sure they don't know about you? How do you know you're safe?"

"Well, at least I'm not on their current list, the one you borrowed from Iggy. So I'm safe for now. That's why I hid my car around the corner and walked the rest of the way last night. I hated having to walk to my car this morning."

"This morning? You stayed there last night? Were you that worried?"

"Noooo." Virgil hesitated, then sighed. "To be honest, we had a little booze, and Marshall didn't want me driving."

Sylvia laughed until tears rolled down her cheeks.

"What's so funny?"

"Sorry." She sniffled and wiped her eyes. "You sound like Iggy admitting something he doesn't want me to know. *A little booze*, indeed. What you mean is you got shit-faced."

Virgil grinned. "Okay, I'll admit it was more than I'm used to."

"And that's a good thing. So you're supposed to go back when Marshall gets home?"

"Yeah. When I got up, Marshall was gone, but he'd left a note saying he'd call."

"Do you think the Truth Seekers followed him around as he made his deliveries?"

"Probably, but if they watched me arrive last night and never saw me leave, they may have split up so at least one could watch the house, too."

"This whole thing is too much. I'm worried about our little town."

Should I tell her about my idea to protect the town? No, not yet. She already thinks doing something isn't my job. "Anyway, I was still there when the fountain installers called." Virgil shrugged.

"So he showed you his secret room? And you have one too?"

"Yes."

Should I show her mine? Am I moving too fast? It didn't feel too fast. It felt just right. "Come on. I'll show you my chancel."

Virgil opened the door and stepped aside, the same as Marshall had done for him. It felt incredibly strange to let Sylvia see what really was a sacred space.

Did Daddy ever see inside Mama's chancel? She never said. Oh well. I wish I could ask her, but it's too late now.

Sylvia stood at the door, but made no move to enter.

"You can go in. It's all right."

She turned to him. "No, I think I won't."

Virgil's eyes widened.

"No, no! It's not that I think anything is wrong with your chancel! Or that it's evil. Nothing like that." She placed her hand on Virgil's arm. "I honestly don't want to violate it. I can't tell you how much it means that you're showing it to me, but I don't need to enter it. It's yours. It's your family and your history. I'm okay just looking from here."

Virgil gathered her into his arms and kissed her. "That means the world to me." He closed and locked the door. "Come on. Let's go rustle up some breakfast."

"Love some."

They were sipping tea and eating stale muffins Virgil had tossed into the microwave for a few seconds when his cell phone chimed.

Virgil glanced at the display. "It's a local number, but I don't recognize it." He shrugged and put it to his ear. "Hello?"

After a short conversation, he disconnected and turned to Sylvia.

"I gather that was Marshall." She stood. "You need to go back over there. Finish your conversation with him."

Virgil hugged her and pressed his cheek to hers. "Thanks. Thanks for understanding. I'll call you later. At least this time Marshall and I'll be sober while we're talking."

Silvia raised an eyebrow. "I hope you get the answers you want." She pecked him on the cheek before leaving with a final wave.

(31)

One person can have a profound effect on another.
And two people...well, two people can work miracles.
They can change a whole town. They can change the world.
~Diane Frolov and Andrew Schneider,
Northern Exposure, 1992

Virgil showered and changed in record time. The last thing Marshall said before hanging up whirled through his mind.

"Delivered a package to Emma Short, the name on the list I recognized. She was home. We talked. I'll fill you in when you come over."

Virgil headed to Marshall's house a half hour after Sylvia left. This time he parked in the driveway behind Marshall's car.

Virgil did his best not to dart his head left and right as he climbed the stairs to Marshall's front door. *I'm probably being watched.*

Marshall must have thought they were being watched, too. When he opened the door he loudly proclaimed. "Virgil! Come on in. I'm ready to order those roses we talked about."

"Nice." Virgil laughed as soon as the door closed behind him.

Marshall shrugged. "Part of me cares. Part doesn't."

"I know what you mean."

"Are they even out there?"

"Thought I saw someone earlier, lurking behind the big pecan tree near the corner. But I'm not sure."

"Guess it's better to be safe."

"We could meet somewhere else."

"Hell no." Marshall shook his head. "I'm not going to let them get to me that much."

"Agreed. Besides, they'd probably find us anyway, unless we leave town."

"Yeah." Marshall shrugged. "Beer?"

"Not a chance. I want to stay clear-headed today."

"That sounds like a better plan."

The two men sat in the same chairs as the previous night. Virgil shook his head. "A lot sure has happened in less than twenty-four hours."

"There's more, too." Marshall leaned forward. "Told Emma about the list. About that group. Couldn't remember their name, but she already knew it."

"How'd she hear about them?" Virgil raised an eyebrow.

"Said she used to date one of the members. She didn't mind when they were talking about fluoride and smart meters. Thought they were nuts, but she laughed it off."

"Anything for love?" Virgil grinned.

"Probably some of that." Marshall laughed. "I'd have a hard time going to the meetings and pretending I cared. Anyway, when they shifted to going after people, she quit. Shortly after that, her boyfriend dumped her."

"So I'll bet he put her on the list."

Marshall shrugged. "Maybe. She didn't know who did. She caught a couple of them following her. Not her boyfriend, of course."

"Of course."

"She didn't actually confront them, but still made it clear she knew they were there."

"How'd she do that?"

"Forgot to ask." Marshall shrugged again. "We can find out when she gets here."

"Wait...you invited her here? Tonight? Is that smart?"

"Trust me on this. You'll be glad I did."

"So do you think she was really on the list out of boyfriend revenge, or is she—"

"Like us?" Marshall nodded. "She is. That's one reason she rarely opened the door when I delivered a package. She never wanted to answer questions. But now she wants in."

"I understand not wanting to answer questions." Virgil smiled. "So why the change? Why does she suddenly want to hang out with two middle-aged guys and talk about our secret lives?"

"She..." Marshall pursed his lips. "I'll let you ask her."

Virgil stared at Marshall for a moment, but it was clear Marshall would say no more. "Did her boyfriend know about her?"

"She said she was always careful, kept everything hidden when he came over, never talked about anything funky, as she put it. But she thinks that still might be what happened."

"So what now?"

"Like I said, she wants in. She wants to help with a town-wide diorama. Only she called it a charm."

"There's nothing charming about a few of the ones I've done."

"Same here." Marshall barked out a hoarse laugh. "But I don't think that's what she meant."

"I know. Couldn't resist."

"Anyway, she'll be here soon."

Virgil closed his eyes. One day ago he thought he was all alone. Now he was sitting with one person like him, and getting ready to meet another. "I never imagined—" The doorbell interrupted.

The two men exchanged a glance as Marshall rose. Virgil could hear the front door open.

"Hi, Emma. Virgil's already here. Come on in."

When the two entered the room, Virgil stood and extended his hand. He blinked several times to clear the surprised look off his face. Emma was perhaps twenty, with short, spiky, watermelon-pink hair and piercings in her nose, eyebrow, and lip. A dozen more rings and studs circled the outside of both ears.

"Heya." She shook Virgil's extended hand.

Virgil noted her nails were painted alternating black and hot pink. "Hi, Emma." He couldn't help but stare.

"She's not what I expected either." Marshall laughed. "But she knows her stuff."

Emma grinned. "Been doing charms since I was two. Daddy taught me."

"That's great." Virgil nodded. "Three heads are better than two."

Emma wiggled her fingers in the air. "Can I use your bathroom? I always feel grimy after riding my scooter."

"Scooter?" Virgil asked. "You rode a kick scooter all the way here?"

Emma laughed. "You're funny. I have a Vespa."

Marshall pointed toward the hall. "Second door down, on the left."

"Are you crazy?" Virgil turned on Marshall as soon as Emma was out of the room.

"Like I said, trust me. I spent two hours talking with her this morning. Otherwise I'd have been done much sooner with my deliveries."

"Where's she work, looking like that?" Virgil waved toward the hall.

"She works for a florist. She's smart. And she knows a lot. She didn't say if she's studied on her own, or if her dad taught her that well, but she'll be an asset to us."

Virgil smirked and opened his mouth to speak, but Emma re-entered. He snapped his jaw shut.

"Better. Okay, let's get this party started." She curled up on the sofa opposite the two men and grinned.

"Before we start, I've got to ask, well…" Virgil shifted nervously. "Marshall said something happened that caused you to open up to him. To ask about joining us."

Emma stared out the window for a moment, then turned toward Virgil. "Oh. That. Okay. After I broke up with my boyfriend, weird shit started happening. I wasn't stupid. I'd changed my locks the day after he left, but stuff was happening around my place. Just… stuff."

"Tell him what you told me." Marshall tipped his head toward Virgil.

Emma bit her lip. "First, I found clean spots on the outside of my windows, like someone wiped them off so they could peek inside. Then my car was broken into. Nothing was stolen, but everything was messed with. Two days ago, my puppy got really sick and died. Vet said he was poisoned."

"Maybe that was just your boyfriend coming back. Getting even. It happens. And sorry about your puppy."

"Thanks. Yeah, maybe him, but then the Truth Seekers started hanging around. I'd heard Marshall's name mentioned in the past. At a meeting several months ago. That's one reason I avoided him.

But after Bailey was poisoned, I decided to see if what the Truth Seekers said was true. So today I opened the door."

Virgil glanced from Emma to Marshall and back to Emma. "What had they said? Who said it?"

"Old guy with white hair. Can't remember his name."

"Cotton," Virgil said.

"Yeah, that's it. Cotton was worried about Marshall. Thought he was a threat to the town. Cotton never gave any details at the meetings. It was all pretty vague. But Marshall's the reason they started that list. His was the first name on it."

"Wow. I'm glad you decided to open your door for him today." Virgil shook his head. "Welcome, I guess."

Emma shrugged. "I'm not good at blowing off bullshit. And no one hurts someone I love and gets away with it. So, Virgil, start by telling me about your experience at the Truth Seekers meeting. Then let's plan how we're going to deal with them."

(32)

When evil men plot, good men must plan.
~Martin Luther King, Jr.

Virgil told Emma about his attendance at the meeting and his conversation the next day with Tammy. He debated not telling her about Lisa, but decided if they were going to trust each other enough to do a joint motif, she needed to know everything.

"Holy shit!" At the revelation about Lisa, Emma sat up and her eyes grew wide. "That's messed up. Poor Lisa."

Virgil sighed. "Yes. And I can see no way to fix it."

"And you want us to do a charm on the whole town with you?"

"Look, I get that I screwed up. Bad. But that's not how I operate. That was a fluke."

"How can I be sure?" Emma frowned.

"He can't prove it, and you know that," Marshall said. "I've messed up bad, too. Once. Haven't you ever messed up one of your charms?"

Emma turned and stared out the window for a couple of minutes. When she turned back, her face was pale. "Yeah. Twice.

But I was pretty young. I wasn't taking it serious enough yet. You're old. You should know better."

Virgil winced. "I admit I'm older than you, but geez, don't call me old."

"Fine." Emma made a face. "But you still should have known better."

"You're right." Virgil nodded. "I do know better. I panicked when I found out Tammy was a Truth Seeker. I do all my research, and pick my motif targets, from things I learn from Tammy and other folks at Harold's. So I rushed to protect myself. But that's not like me. I've always taken plenty of time to get every detail right. And you can bet I won't rush again."

"We'll fix the whole town," Marshall said. "Lisa and Tammy included."

Emma looked from Marshall to Virgil. "Okay. Let's do this."

"We'll make sure it's right. And as perfect as possible," Virgil said.

"Sounds cool." Emma grinned from ear to ear. "It'll be the biggest charm I've ever done."

"How do we even get started with this?" Virgil asked.

"Doesn't matter what the charm is," Emma said. "It won't work without the right jewel."

"Jewel?" Marshall asked.

"You know, the thing that'll represent the town." Emma rolled her eyes.

"Ah, the centerpiece." Marshall nodded.

"Oh, the focalis," Virgil said at the same time.

Emma laughed. "How can we all have the same gift, and speak the same ancient Goidelic language, but can't even agree on the basic words that describe what we do?"

"The language comes from the region in northern England where our families are all from." Virgil shrugged. "But it wasn't safe to talk to each other, especially back then, so—"

"So each family chose its own words to describe what they did." Marshall finished Virgil's comment.

"But these are modern words, not part of the ancient language." Emma frowned.

"Hadn't thought of that." Virgil tapped his chin. "Some may be modern translations. Then again, I use new words I picked for myself. My mother called what we do our *gift of symbols*. I call it theurgy, a term that actually has Egyptian roots. I like it better than Mama's term."

Marshall cocked his head. "This all makes me wonder…how'd a small town like Lichen end up with three of us? If our families really did all come from the same rural region of northern England, how'd we descendants end up here? Even if every family in the original village had the gift, there can't be that many of us."

"He's right." Emma nodded. "This isn't just coincidence. It's kinda freaky, actually."

"Destiny?" Virgil shrugged.

"But why?" Marshall asked. "Even if it was about the Truth Seekers being here, they didn't exist when my family settled here in the 1800s. What about y'all? You didn't just arrive, either."

"I've been here since I was eight, so over forty years." Virgil leaned forward and put his elbows on his knees. "But yeah, I'm not exactly a straight line from northern England, either. My family lived all over. My Mom and I moved from Alpine in West Texas. I have no idea why she chose Lichen. We didn't know anyone here. My grandparents moved to West Texas from Oklahoma. And I think my great grandparents started out in Ohio."

"Well, I'm new." Emma grinned. "I only moved here a year ago."

"Okay, still…why?" Marshall asked. "You're not exactly what I think of as a small-town-in-Texas girl. What brought you here?"

"Good question, and I'm still not sure. I had a pretty good gig going in Austin. But one morning I woke up with this feeling. I can't describe it other than to say it was a nagging, pulling sense that I needed to be here. I even gave up a lot to make it happen."

"Maybe your ancestors and my mother were the same." Virgil waved toward Marshall. "Maybe there was a reason we all ended up here. Might be the same reason the Truth Seekers formed here."

Marshall shrugged. "No idea. Maybe Lichen is on a Ley line or surrounded by some weird energy vortex."

Virgil laughed. "Maybe the Truth Seekers are right. There *is* something in the water."

Marshall laughed, then turned serious. "Looks like whatever got us here is finally coming to a head. It's becoming us versus the Truth Seekers. I just hope we're successful at what we decide to do."

"What we're doing is saving our town." Emma untucked her legs and retucked them in the opposite direction. "But first things first, what do we use for our jewel-centerpiece-focalis?"

"Great question," Marshall said.

"How about a phone book?" Virgil asked.

"None of my friends are in that ancient thing." Emma laughed. "Cell phones aren't listed there."

"Good point." Marshall nodded. "I Might be able to help with this."

"Of course!" Virgil sat up and grinned. "You're a UPS driver. You probably have a detailed list of addresses and names."

"I don't have everyone." Marshall winked. "But there are only two other drivers in this zip code. I'll see if I can get their lists, too."

"Great!" Emma said. "So now what? What do we do for the actual charm?"

"We focus strictly on creating a barrier or energy field against evil hurting the town." Virgil frowned. "We don't want to mention any specific names or groups. We know about the Truth Seekers, but not all members may realize what's going on."

"And they may not be the only group," Marshall said.

"I hate to think there's more than one group like that!" Virgil shook his head.

"Got a pad and pencil?" Emma uncurled and sat up. "I'll make notes. Let's get started on writing the chant."

Three hours later Emma had one page of notes and half a dozen crumpled papers around her feet. "Let me read this back. Once we agree on the wording we can transcribe it into Goidelic."

"Sounds good," Virgil said after Emma was done.

"I agree." Marshall nodded. "It hits the highlights we want without being too specific."

"Awesomesauce." Emma grinned. "You two want to tackle the transcribing or want me to do it?"

Marshall and Virgil exchanged a glance. "Go for it." Virgil pointed at Emma. "I think we both agree you have the energy. After all, we're *old*."

"Aw, I didn't mean that the way it came out. But okay. Give me until Friday. Either of you have any parchment? I just ran out."

"Have some in my chantry. Be right back." Marshall headed for the hall.

"That's a funny word." Emma giggled. "What do you call yours?"

"A chancel. How about you?"

"It's my chapel." Emma shrugged. "That's what Daddy called his. He said it was a sacred space."

Marshall returned and handed Emma a manilla envelope. "Didn't want my Truth Seeker spy seeing you walk out with a wad of parchment paper."

Emma nodded. "Right. Anything could be in the envelope." She walked toward the foyer then paused and turned. "Where do we meet? When are we doing the charm?"

"How about my place," Virgil said. "Mama already did one motif against the Truth Seekers, and she used the table I now have. Seems like a good place to continue." He handed Emma one of the wood-working business card from his wallet.

"Why not?" Marshall grinned. "How about 8 Friday night?"

"Coolio," Emma said. "I love this plan. Anything I should bring besides the chant?"

Virgil chewed his lip. "Not that I can think of. Bring what you usually wear in your sacred space. I have plenty of candles and supplies."

"I can vouch for that." Marshall grinned. "I'll bring the lists of residents, of course. And a map of the area."

"Friday it is." Emma nodded at the men. "Guess I'll go wave at the spies, if I can spot 'em."

After Emma left, Marshall stood. "Now I DO need a beer. You?"

"One. Just one."

The two men deliberately avoided any more talk about their plans. Instead, they rambled for a while about local politics, new shops and restaurants, and other mundane topics.

It was almost eleven when Virgil stood and stretched. "I'm heading home. I guess it's my turn to give the spies something to do. I'll see you Friday night."

"No deliveries due from me before then?" Marshall asked. "You all stocked up?"

Virgil laughed. "Nope. No deliveries. I brought home all of my mother's supplies. I'm hoping my house doesn't look like a flea market by Friday. It's full of boxes and bags from Mama's house. I put the house on the market."

"That's sad, but I'm sure it's the right thing."

"Yeah, she'll never go back there." Virgil sighed. "Not going to tell her. She got really agitated the other day when I mentioned finding her journal. She doesn't need any more pain."

Virgil called Sylvia on his way home and got her voicemail. "I realize it's late. I just left Marshall's. Have even more to tell you. Call me in the morning."

(33)

Shy and unready men are great betrayers of secrets;
for there are few wants more urgent for the moment
than the want of something to say. ~Sir Henry Taylor

Virgil's phone rang at 6:30 Thursday morning, waking him from a disturbing dream about being tortured and locked in a cage. After arriving home from Marshall's, he'd sat up for another hour, staring at his mother's belongings. Debating what to do.

He scrambled for the phone. "Hello?"

"Oh, Virgil did I wake you? I'm so sorry!" Sylvia said.

Virgil sat up and rubbed his eyes. "You did, but it's high time I got up. I didn't mean to sleep in. Will you come join me for breakfast? I have updates to tell you about."

"Be there in half an hour."

Virgil was barely finished showering and dressing when his doorbell rang. *That was fast!* He opened his door and the grin on his face instantly vanished. "Stan! What brings you over so early?"

Stan shuffled his feet. "I'm scared. Please, can I talk to you?"

Virgil hesitated then stepped aside. "Sure, come on in."

Stan sat at Virgil's table, chewing his lip and wringing his hands.

Virgil sat across from the clearly distraught younger man. "Well? What's up? Tell me what's wrong."

Stan cleared his throat. "It's the Truth Seekers. I'm scared of what they asked me to do about you."

Blood rushed from Virgil's head and he had to take several slow, deep breaths to keep from passing out. He eased into his chair. "What did they ask you to do? What happened? It's okay, Stan. Tell me and let's see what we can do."

Stan nodded. "They been watching those folks on that list. They saw you was with two of 'em. Cotton added you to the list. He wants me to spy on you."

A hot flush of anger replaced Virgil's shock. "That bastard. Marshall and Emma are no more threats than I am. Than my mother is. Do you think I'm a threat, Stan? DO YOU?"

Stan recoiled at Virgil's harsh words and said nothing. He frowned and looked at his hands in his lap.

Virgil took a long, deep breath. "I'm sorry, Stan. It's not your fault. Marshall is a friend. I transplanted one of my roses for him. Emma is a new friend. She's interested in the same stuff, too." *I'm stretching my almost-truth telling to the breaking point, but I can't let Stan suspect anything.*

"I don't think you're a threat, Virg." Stan didn't look up and his voice was so soft Virgil had to lean in to hear. "But you are sorta… weird sometimes."

How do I answer that? "We all can seem weird to each other sometimes, Stan. What about me do you think is weird?"

"You got pretty freaky about your Mama's table and stuff. A couple times."

"You're right. I'm just sensitive about Mama's things. I feel responsible for them now, since she's in the nursing center. You can understand that, can't you? She's my Mama!"

Stan looked up and smiled. "Yeah, I sure can." He frowned. "But what do I do now? Should I quit? I'm scared of Cotton. He might put me on that list. Or do something worse. I heard he poisoned some woman's puppy."

You're probably right about getting added to the list. "I heard about the puppy, too, Stan. I understand why you're afraid. Tell you what. How about if we come up with some things you can report to Cotton. Things that are true, but won't put me in danger and won't make him suspicious of you. Would that be okay with you?"

"That sounds great!" Stan bobbed his head with enthusiasm. "What can I tell them?"

"Let me show you my new fountain. And I'll give you a reason you can tell them I got it." *It'll be close to the truth.* The doorbell rang again as they were standing.

"Who's that?" Stan backed into the wall and shifted his gaze back and forth.

"It's my new lady friend, Sylvia. It's okay, Stan. Stay here and I'll go let her in."

Stan nodded, but otherwise didn't move.

Virgil hurried to the door. As soon as he opened it he put his fingers to his lips, then whispered. "Stan's here. He's freaked out. No time to fill you in right now. Just play along. I'll tell you everything after he leaves." At full volume he added, "Morning Sylvia. Come on in. I was getting ready to show Stan my new fountain."

"Morning!" Sylvia echoed Virgil's volume.

The two exchanged a short kiss then headed for the kitchen.

"Virgil tells me you're Stan. I'm Sylvia. It's nice to meet you." She extended her hand.

After a hesitation, Stan shook her hand. "Hi, Sylvia. You're new."

Sylvia laughed. "That's true. I'm going to be landscaping Virgil's backyard. He already added a fountain. He said he was about to show it to you when I got here."

Virgil opened the back door. "Shall we?" He kissed Sylvia's cheek as she passed.

"Yowza! That's a big 'un!" Stan's eyes grew wide as he stared at the fountain.

"Yes, it is. That's why I wanted to show it to you. I can give you the reason I bought it. You can tell it to Cotton."

Stan's eyes didn't leave the fountain. "Okay."

Virgil glanced at Sylvia. She smiled and winked. "I've spent years burying stuff in that corner, but—"

"Bad stuff?" Stan yelped.

Virgil laughed. "No, Stan, not bad stuff. But personal things. Poems, trinkets, mementos. Childhood things of mine that Mama had kept. Stuff I was too sentimental to throw away, but that I knew it was time to let go of. If you wrote a bad poem when you were seven, would you want someone else to find and read it?"

Stan made a face. "No. But why not burn it? Or keep it in a box in the attic?"

"Guess I could have. But burning is so final. Part of me thought maybe someday I'd want the items again. And hiding them in a box meant someone could find them. Burying them felt temporary, even if they're buried under a giant fountain, but still safe from others." *Bless Stan's heart for being so gullible and simple-minded. Otherwise this wouldn't work.*

"Yeah, okay, but what about the fountain?" Stan frowned.

"He didn't want to be embarrassed by having me find his treasures." Sylvia smiled. "That's all. We'd talked about a fountain, so he got that one and had it installed before I began digging holes for plants."

"Oh." Stan still looked confused. "Why will Cotton care? How's this going to make him think I did what he asked?"

"It may not." Virgil shrugged. "But it gives you something to tell him. It'll show you're following through on your assignment."

Stan nodded and smiled. "Yeah, it will. Thanks. Tell me again, so I can tell him just right."

Virgil repeated his re-imagined reason for installing the fountain. *It's not a complete lie. My chants are like bad poetry, and my motif remains are mementos of a sort.*

"You need to head on now, Stan. I have some landscape plans and other things to discuss with Sylvia."

"Sure, Virg." Stan opened the back door then turned. "You coming to the meeting tonight?"

Oh great, that's tonight. "You think that'd be a good idea, now that I'm on their list?"

Stan shuffled his feet. "Nah, guess not. I'm really sorry."

Virgil smiled. "It's okay Stan. I know you're a good man. I'm sure everything'll be fine."

Stan gave them an awkward smile, then was gone.

As soon as Virgil heard his front door slam, he gathered Sylvia into his arms and held her tight.

Sylvia stroked his hair. "Come on. Let's go inside. Tell me everything that's happened."

(34)

When you make a mistake, there are only three things you should ever do about it: admit it, learn from it, and don't repeat it. ~Paul "Bear" Bryant, I Ain't Never Been Nothing but a Winner

Sylvia ushered Virgil to the breakfast table "Sit! I will get the tea."

Instead of protesting, Virgil nodded and sat. He fiddled with a crumb on the table, his lips pursed.

Sylvia ignited the burner under the kettle, then sat. "First, what did you mean when you told Stan you were on their list? I thought Marshall and that young woman were on the list. Not you."

"The spies must have reported back fast. That's why Stan came so early. The Truth Seekers now know I've been with Marshall and Emma. I've been added to the list. Stan's been assigned to spy on me."

"Tell me everything."

When Virgil was done, Sylvia stared wide-eyed for several seconds before speaking. "Oh my. It's a lot for me to take in. I can't imagine what it's like going from feeling you're only one of something to suddenly meeting TWO others. And are you sure it's safe to do a motif so…big?"

Maybe. I hope so. I just managed to totally screw up a small motif. "The chant is quite gentle. Nothing intense. No group names. No peoples' names. It'll be fine."

The kettle whistled, startling both Sylvia and Virgil. She hurried to the stove and turned off the heat, then made tea in the chicken-shaped teapot, which she carried to the table, along with two cups.

"You're sure I don't need to worry? Nothing…unusual will happen to me?"

"I promise. We're going over every word of the chant Friday night. I'll make sure nothing will happen to you." *I hope that's possible.*

"Thank you. How long will it take to work? I mean, for things to happen? For the protection to take effect? I don't even know how to ask the question!"

Virgil smiled and took Sylvia's hands in his. "Shortly after the last candle goes out. The town shouldn't change much. There may be lots of subtle, small changes. Maybe a few big ones."

"Such as?"

"Lichen might feel more peaceful. People may be nicer. The Truth Seekers could disband."

"Isn't that awfully optimistic? Are you sure that's what'll happen?"

"No, I'm not really sure. But I'm hoping for the best. Regardless of how much change we bring, it's something we have to do. We can't simply sit by while we're all targets. While they poison our town with their hate and fear."

"I do understand that. I wish I could do something. Anything. To help."

"You have no idea how much your being here helps. I love you. I really know that now. I'm not falling in love anymore. I'm IN love."

Sylvia blushed. "I love you, too. You may be weirder than I'd bargained for, but that's okay."

"Can't ask for more than that." Virgil grinned and winked. "I'm done with my tea. You?"

Sylvia dumped the last half of her cup in Virgil's. "Why, yes. Look here. My cup's empty."

❧∼❦∼❧∼❦∼❧∼❦

The lovers didn't shower and dress until almost noon.

"I just realized I never ate. I'm starving." Virgil slipped on his loafers. "How about let's go get a bite?"

"I'd like that." Sylvia zipped her jeans and tucked in her tank top. "Where'd you have in mind.?"

"Harold's."

Sylvia paused mid-tuck. "Are you sure? Is that safe? Or smart?"

Virgil shrugged and stood. "Maybe. Maybe not. But if we're going to blanket the town with protection tomorrow night, I'd like one last confirmation it's the right thing to do. And I want to see how Lisa's doing." He winced, realizing he'd not told Sylvia about Lisa.

"Who's Lisa?" Sylvia frowned. "And what about her?"

Conflicting thoughts slammed rapid-fire in Virgil's brain. Tell her? Don't tell her? Tell her some? All? Nothing? He wasn't aware that he started swaying, but suddenly Sylvia had his elbow.

"Here, sit on the bed." She sat beside him. "You obviously haven't told me something. And it must be a doozy."

Virgil's face crumbled and his voice shook. "I screwed up bad." He told her about his latest motif. About the wrong lipstick. About Lisa's rape.

"Oh, Virgil." Sylvia's voice was soft. "I'm so sorry. For everyone. Has that happened before? I thought you did motifs to heal and bring justice. Not hurt someone."

❧ 228 ❦

"I never meant to hurt anyone! I only wanted to divert Tammy's attention away from me. But I rushed. Didn't take the time to really clarify every word in the chant. I was stupid."

"I'd agree with that. And you're sure nothing will happen tomorrow night?"

"I'm sure." Virgil wiped his eyes. "First, there are three of us combing over every word in the chant. Second, this isn't specifically to stop anyone from doing anything, it's about protection for everyone."

Sylvia nodded, but said nothing.

"I'm sorry I disappointed you. I'm sorry if I scared you. I've never done anything that stupid before. I'll never do that again. You have my promise."

Finally, in slow motion, Sylvia leaned over and kissed Virgil's cheek. "Thank you. But I'll ask again. Are you sure you want to eat at Harold's? To see Tammy?"

"Yes." Virgil nodded. "I'll take my chances with Tammy. There's nothing I can do to make things right, but I want to know how things are going with Lisa. If I could take it back, I would in a heartbeat."

Sylvia smiled. "I believe you would."

They spoke little on the drive to the cafe. Virgil pondered how to get Sylvia to trust him again, if that was even possible. *I don't want to lose her.*

Sylvia stared out her side window. When she sighed, Virgil reached for her hand. "I really am sorry," he said.

Sylvia turned to look at him and smiled. "I know. And I'll be okay. But I have to admit, it's not what I wanted to learn about you."

"Yeah, I know. But please realize that's not me. That's not how I was raised. And it certainly isn't how I'll behave in the future."

It was 12:20 when they walked through the door. The place was hopping. Tammy was rushing around the room. A young boy Virgil didn't recognize was clearing dirty dishes, but he moved slow. Most of the tables were still cluttered.

Virgil pointed to a booth against the far wall. "That one has fewer dishes on it. We can stack them on another table."

They waited almost ten minutes before Tammy made it to them, menus and water glasses in hand. "Sorry. It's crazy here with Lisa gone. Travis is doing his best, but he's not used to this. He's Harold's fourteen-year-old nephew. Pitching in until Lisa's better." She handed them their menus, then looked Virgil up and down. "You're looking bright eyed and bushy tailed this time."

"Huh?" Virgil raised his eyebrows.

"Nothing."

"I heard about Lisa." Sylvia shook her head. "I'm so sorry. How is she doing?"

Tammy narrowed her eyes at Virgil, then turned to Sylvia. "She's out of ICU. Her mama got here from Dallas this morning. She'll stay until a few days after Lisa gets home."

"Guess I always thought Lisa's family was from here," Virgil said. "She's so young to be on her own."

"She is from here. She lived with her Dad after her parents divorced. Her Mom moved to Dallas. But Lisa didn't want to change schools. Now she shares an apartment with another girl. I never can remember her name. She rarely comes in here."

"Such a tragic accident." Sylvia frowned.

"Yeah, if that's what you call it." Tammy glanced again at Virgil. "Y'all ready to order? I got lots of tables to cover."

They both ordered burgers and fries. Tammy nodded, collected the menus, and walked away without a word.

"That was weird. Does she suspect you were involved?" Sylvia asked.

"Wouldn't be surprised. She made several cracks like that the other morning, too. I think she's trying to get a reaction, see if she can push the right button."

"Didn't you say she's a Truth Seeker?"

Virgil nodded. "And assigned to watch someone on that list, although I don't know who. But based on her comment when we first sat down, I'm betting it's Marshall. I think she saw me hungover."

"I can see why you feel like a protection motif is in order."

"Thought that before I was on the list. Who else will be added? Are the two others already on the list like me and Marshall and Emma? And what about folks they add in the future. Are there more of us, or will just plain folks accidentally be included?"

"Just plain folks? Like me?"

"Aw, I'm sorry. Honey, you're anything but plain."

Sylvia laughed. "I'm glad you noticed."

"Oh, I have." Virgil grinned. "You couldn't be plain if you tried. You sure brighten my world."

When Tammy brought their food, they abruptly stopped talking, which didn't escape her notice. She glanced from one to the other and frowned. "Here. Need anything else?"

"No, thank you, this looks great. Not plain at all." Sylvia produced her most charming smile and winked at Virgil.

"Hmmmph." Tammy turned and walked away.

"This place is starting to give me the creeps." Virgil frowned. "I've always loved Harold's, but—"

"It may be time to find a new favorite place."

"Yeah. I'm afraid so." *I'm not doing any more local motifs after Friday, anyway. No need for the daily gossip.*

They chatted about the landscape plans while they ate, both seeming to agree it was a safe topic for a public area. Tammy never returned to their table.

When he was done, Virgil pushed his plate to the side. "Do you still have some time? I'd like to go see Mama. I haven't been since I took her chair by. Would you go with me?"

"I'd like that. Thanks."

"She won't know you. Most of the time she doesn't even recognize me."

"That's all right. She's your mother. I'd still like to meet her. However that works out."

(35)

A mother's love for her child is like nothing else
in the world. ~Agatha Christie (1890-1976)

"Tell me about your mother. What was it like growing up?" Sylvia asked as they drove to Oak Creek.

"She was strong. But she was also soft." Virgil smiled. "After Dad died, she picked up the pieces and moved on with her life. With our lives. The factory gave Mom a cash settlement, but it wasn't enough to live on. She had to work."

"That factory should have taken care of her for life."

"I agree, but that didn't happen back then. She got a job at a fabric store. She took over all the household responsibilities, learning skills like wiring and installing floor tiles as she went."

"Is that when you moved to Lichen?"

"Yeah. She couldn't bear moving to a big city, but Lichen was close enough to San Antonio she was able to get a job on the outskirts of the city and still live up the road in a small town."

"Maybe she wanted to get away from the memories, too."

"Probably. I never saw her cry, but I heard what I'm sure was crying more than once from behind her bedroom door."

"The only cure for grief is action."

"What's that?"

Sylvia shrugged. "A quote by English philosopher George Henry Lewes I read a long time ago in English Lit class. It stuck with me because that was right after my grandmother died. My grandfather was like your mother. He dove head first into finishing every chore and honey-do my grandmother had always asked for. In his case, it was probably a combination of grief and guilt."

"Here we are. Home sweet home." Virgil pulled in and parked. "This way," He motioned toward the entrance as they walked across the lot.

When they passed the nursing station, Nancy, the head nurse, looked up. "Afternoon, Mr. Harris. Ma'am."

"Afternoon, Nancy," Virgil said without pausing, but Sylvia stopped, so he did a quick double step and stopped, too.

"Good afternoon." Sylvia smiled at the nurses. "You have a lovely facility. And Virgil has told me how caring and thoughtful the nursing staff is here."

Nancy nodded and the nurse behind her stood up straighter. "Thank you!" Both beamed with wide smiles.

"You're quite welcome. If I ever need a place like this for a parent, I'll absolutely bring them here."

Both nurses nodded and again said, "Thank you."

"What was that about?" Virgil whispered as they moved down the hall.

"Never forget that it's the worker bees who make the world turn and keep the wheels greased. Take care of them, or just be nice, and they'll always do right by you."

"I'll remember that." Virgil nodded. "I've probably not paid attention to them like I should. I did bring them roses once."

"And I'll bet they still talk about that."

Virgil stopped at his mother's door. The soft murmurs of the television drifted out.

"You okay?" Sylvia gently grabbed Virgil's arm.

"Yeah. Mama had a…spell last time I was here. No pun intended. She got really agitated when I told her I'd found her motif journal. Nancy had to sedate her. It kind of freaked me out."

"I'm sorry."

"Thanks. Guess I shouldn't have brought it up. Had no one else to talk to. This was before I went to see Marshall. It's kind of what pushed me into going, in fact."

"It's hard when there's no one else with the same issues."

"Yeah, it is. I'm glad you're here."

"Is that why I'm here? But I'm not like you, so I can't really understand what you go through."

"You may not really get it, but you're my moral support." Virgil gave Sylvia a quick kiss. "I'm glad you're in my life."

"I'm glad, too. Since that bastard Oscar left me, I've felt pretty isolated."

"Not anymore." Virgil turned to her and smiled. "I like having you around. Far as I'm concerned, this is only the beginning. I mean that. That's why I want to introduce you to Mama."

Sylvia kissed Virgil. "Aw, that's sweet."

They entered the room. "Mama?" Virgil called. "I'm here. And I brought someone."

"Hello, Mrs. Harris." Sylvia approached the foot of the bed and stopped. "I'm Sylvia Parker. It's so nice to meet you."

Pearl Harris opened her eyes. For a few seconds her expression remained blank. She glanced at Virgil, then turned to Sylvia.

"No. No. No. No. NO! NO! NO!" Pearl Harris shook her head and twisted the sheet in a tight fist.

Virgil hurried to Pearl's side. Sylvia stepped back toward the door.

"Mama, what's wrong?" He sat on the bed and patted his mother's arm. "Please. What's happened?"

Pearl turned to face Virgil and for a moment her eyes were clear and her expression was intense. "Here. Bad. Woman. No."

"Sylvia's not a bad woman. She's very nice."

"Here. Was." Pearl's eyes moved around the room.

Virgil looked over his shoulder and shrugged. "A bad woman was here?" He asked as he turned to his mother.

"Bad. Yes. Afurd."

"Did you mean afraid, Mama? She made you afraid?"

Pearl nodded and frowned.

"When, Mama?" He motioned toward Sylvia. "This isn't a bad woman."

"No. Blonde. Bad."

Virgil turned the chintz chair to face the bed and motioned to Sylvia to sit down.

"Mama, this is Sylvia. A friend. You can see she's not blonde."

Pearl shifted her gaze to Sylvia. "No. Not bad. Not blonde."

"What's happened?" Sylvia whispered. "Who was here?"

"No idea. I'll be right back." Virgil hurried to the nurse's station. "Sorry to bother you Nancy, but did Mama have another visitor in the past few days?"

"Not that I recall." Nancy cocked her head in thought.

"Yes, she did." The other nurse nodded. "Yesterday afternoon. You'd gone to lunch. I was here alone."

"Is there a problem?" Nancy asked.

"No, no. Mama was trying to mention someone, but she has difficulty speaking. I'm sure it's someone I know, but she can't tell me who. Can you describe her?"

"She was maybe thirty, thirty-five, and on the heavyset side," the nurse said. "She had shoulder-length blonde hair. And she wore the cutest purple-framed glasses. I especially remember those."

Tammy. What in the hell was she doing here? "Thanks. I do know her. I'm sure it was nice of her to stop by." He turned before either nurse could say anything else and almost ran back to his mother's room.

Sylvia looked up as soon as he entered. "I was telling your mother that I was going to landscape your yard." Then she mouthed, "Well?"

"That's nice. Yes, Mama, that's how Sylvia and I met." He sat on the bed. "She's an excellent landscaper. I'll bet you've seen some of the yards she's done." He leaned close to Sylvia. "It was Tammy."

"Oh no!" Sylvia mouthed.

"Nishe." Mrs. Harris's voice was slurred.

"Yes, it's very nice, Mama. Sylvia isn't just good with plants. She's my girlfriend. I like her a lot."

"Not bad. Not blonde. Not her." Pearl turned her head and stared at Sylvia.

"No, Mama, she's not bad at all. That's why I wanted you to meet her. She means a lot to me."

Sylvia leaned over and gently squeezed the older woman's hand. "I care deeply for your son, Mrs. Harris. You did such a fine job. He's a wonderful man."

Pearl Harris smiled.

Virgil sighed. "It's nice to see you smile, Mama. I haven't seen that in such a long time."

Pearl mumbled several words. Both Virgil and Sylvia leaned in until they bumped heads. Sylvia erupted in giggles.

"I'm sorry, Mrs. Harris. I sound like a schoolgirl. I am happy, though."

"Happy."

"Yes, Mama, we're both happy." Virgil looked at Sylvia and smiled.

Pearl slid her arm back and forth, opening and closing her hand. Finally, Virgil reached out and took it. His mother squeezed his hand and turned to look at him.

"Pertect."

"Yes, Mama, I'll protect her. And you."

"Morfit."

Virgil cocked his head. "Did you mean motif?"

"Yes. Motif. Protect."

He wasn't sure who she meant he should protect. He answered as if she meant herself. "I will Mama. I promise. I won't let the blonde come here anymore."

"Bad. Bad blonde."

He'd never find out what Tammy had said or done to his mother, but it had upset her enough she was making the difficult effort to tell him about it.

"Yes, Mama. I'm afraid she is a bad woman. I didn't use to think so. But now I know. I won't let her come back."

Mrs. Harris waved toward Sylvia. "Love?"

"Yes, Mama." He glanced at Sylvia and smiled. "I love her."

"Tell her."

"Tell her what, Mama?"

"Gift."

"He did, Mrs. Harris." Sylvia smiled. "After I found your jour—"

"After I hired her for the job as my landscaper," Virgil loudly interrupted before Sylvia could say *journal*. He shot a brief warning glance her way. "But our relationship quickly became more than that. So I told her. Is that how it happened with Daddy?"

Pearl nodded. "Trust. Must trust."

"Yes, Mama, I do trust Sylvia."

Sylvia put her hand on Virgil's arm. "And I trust him. I'd trust him with my life."

"Life. Blonde. Bad. Protect."

"I will protect everyone, Mama." Virgil stroked her hair. "Promise."

Pearl Harris sighed and her whole body relaxed. She nodded, then closed her eyes.

"Good. Good." Her voice was barely audible as she said the two final words before drifting into sleep.

Virgil released his mother's hand. "I've rarely seen her this animated. She obviously wanted badly to communicate."

"What do you suppose happened with Tammy? And what was she doing here in the first place?"

"Both good questions. And we'll likely never find out."

"What are you going to do?"

"First, I'm going to tell the nurses that Tammy isn't allowed here again."

"I'd suggest telling them no one but you is allowed," Sylvia said.

"Good idea." Virgil nodded. "The Truth Seekers could send someone else. Let's go. I need to do something before Friday night."

"Can I help?"

"Maybe. If helping me catalog Mama's motif supplies won't freak you out."

"Actually, I'd find it fascinating." Sylvia pointed to Mrs. Harris. "Look at your mother sleeping. She's almost angelic."

"She hasn't been like this in a long time. First she was animated and agitated. Now she looks calm and happy."

"Guess she trusts you to take care of whatever happened."

"And I will. If I had any doubts before, I don't now. That town-wide motif is the right thing to do." Virgil stroked his mother's hair then stood. "We're going, Mama. You rest now."

Virgil stopped at the nursing station on the way out. "For now I'd ask that no one else be allowed to visit my mother."

"What's wrong?" Nancy asked. "Did something happen?"

"Don't think so." Virgil made a dismissive wave of his hand. "But she was agitated. It could be nothing. But until I can talk to Tammy Carter, I'd prefer she not visit here. No one else, either."

"You got it." Nancy nodded and picked up a pen. "I'll add it to your mother's computer file and put a note on our white board, so all the nurses will know."

☙❧☙❧☙❧

"Virgil, what is going on?" Sylvia slammed the car door and crossed her arms.

"No idea." Virgil frowned. "Tammy visited AFTER the Truth Seekers knew I met with Marshall and Emma. Were they trying to get information from Mama? Were they trying to intimidate me? Regardless, they've crossed a line. Following me around is one thing. But they have no right to upset her."

"Wonder what Tammy said?"

"Whatever it was, it was enough for Mama to decide Tammy's a bad person. And my mother was never judgmental. Granted, I don't know what's inside her head these days, but I doubt who she is has changed that much."

"I'm a little scared."

"Me too. And really, really pissed off." Virgil wheeled out of the lot. "Let's go home. I want to organize Mama's motif supplies. Maybe it'll calm me down."

Sylvia put her hand on Virgil's arm. "I'm in this with you now. Don't forget that."

"That's the only thing keeping me together."

(36)

Life isn't fair. It's just fairer than death, that's all.
~William Goldman, The Princess Bride

Stan ran from across the street as soon as Virgil pulled into the driveway.

"Oh no. What now?" Virgil's shoulders slumped.

"Probably not good news, but let's see." Sylvia opened her door and stepped out. "Hello, Stan. It's nice to see you again."

"What's up, Stan?" Virgil did his best not to sound annoyed.

"Not outside." Stan's gaze darted back and forth. "Can we go in?"

"Sure." Virgil slammed his car door. "Come on."

Virgil unlocked the front door, and the other two followed him to the living room. Sylvia joined him on the sofa. Stan perched nervously on a nearby chair. They sat in silence for nearly a minute.

Finally, Sylvia asked, "Stan what's wrong? You look troubled."

"It's all right, Stan." Virgil smiled. "I told her. You can talk in front of her."

"Oh, okay. I guess." Stan shifted in his chair. "I gotta quit, but I'm scared to."

"You mean quit the Truth Seekers?" Sylvia asked.

Stan nodded.

"Why do you have to quit?" Virgil cocked his head. "Did they ask you to do something else?"

Stan looked down and chewed his lip. "Cotton wants me to move your fountain. He wants to see what's really buried there. He doesn't believe what you told me about it being stuff from when you was a kid."

Sylvia and Virgil exchanged a quick glance.

"You've seen the fountain." Virgil laughed. "You know it can't *just be moved*. It would take the same Bobcat and other equipment the installers used putting it in. And it was all in pieces. They sealed them all together. It can't come apart without destroying it."

"Tried to tell him. He said maybe I was *in it* with you. Don't have a clue what he thinks YOU'RE into. And I sure ain't in it with you!" Stan's face crumpled, on the verge of tears.

Virgil shook his head. "The Truth Seekers are getting carried away, or at least Cotton is. Becoming dangerous."

"I'd bet Cotton had something to do with Tammy visiting your mother, too," Sylvia said.

"Probably." Virgil nodded.

Stan looked from Virgil to Sylvia and back. "I don't know nuthin' about Tammy, but Cotton scares me."

Sylvia reached over and took the younger man's hands. "It's okay. Virgil will do his best to keep anything from happening to you. But you need to stop having anything to do with them."

"I can't just quit!" Panic crossed the young man's face.

"What do you think will happen?" Virgil asked.

"I'll end up like Dan!"

"Dan who?" Sylvia asked.

Stan grimaced. "Dan Baxter!"

"Local locksmith." Virgil frowned. "Or at least he was until last Saturday. He was accidentally electrocuted on a job."

"Weren't no accident." Stan hugged himself. He started shaking all over.

"Take it easy, Stan. It's okay," Virgil said. "Tell me what you mean."

"Dan was a Truth Seeker. 'Cept he quit. That's why he wasn't there last Thursday with us."

"Are you sure he quit?" Virgil raised his eyebrows.

"Maybe he just had a reason to miss a meeting," Sylvia added.

Stan looked up. "No. He quit. He told me. Sometimes he'd let me help him with jobs." Stan flashed a brief smile. "You know, like you do."

Virgil nodded. "Sure. So tell us what happened."

"We was on a job a couple weeks ago. Changing all the locks at the day care center after those older kids broke in. Anyway, I'd just gone to my first meeting. I told him I was excited I'd seen him there. I didn't think I'd know anybody."

"I'd never have guessed. Dan seemed so…normal." Virgil shook his head. "Sorry Stan, go on."

"That's when he told me he was quitting. I guess they'd asked him to use his locksmithing to spy for them. He was really mad."

"I imagine so," Sylvia said. "He could get arrested. Or lose his license. Or both."

Stan nodded. "Yeah, he said that. Now he's dead. Just a few days later."

"It could be a coincidence." Virgil shrugged. "You can't be sure."

"But I AM sure!" Stan jumped up. "Ya gotta believe me."

"It's not that we don't believe you." Sylvia patted Stan's chair. "Come on, sit down. Tell us what makes you so sure. Something must have convinced you."

"Cotton. When I said I didn't want to move your fountain, he said to think about it real hard. Then he said to remember that accidents happen. Like car accidents or getting crushed on a job site or electrocutions. Then he laughed. HE SAID ELECTROCUTIONS!" Stan slapped his hand on the table, causing both Sylvia and Virgil to jump.

"It's all right, Stan." Virgil leaned over and gripped Stan's shoulder. "Calm down. We'll take care of it."

Stan sighed and chewed his lip. "Thanks, Virg. I'll trust you. You've always done good by me. But I sure can't figure out what you're gonna do."

"I'm not letting any more of my friends get hurt." Virgil's face was grim. "Including you. You go on home. I'll keep in touch."

"Can you stay home for a few days?" Sylvia asked. "Not go out anywhere?"

Stan nodded and wrung his hands. "Sure. Sure, I can do that. Guess I'll be safe there, right?"

"Yes, Stan. As safe as can be."

Sylvia walked Stan to the door. When she returned, she was ashen. "Do you think he's right? Do you think Cotton murdered Dan?"

"Honestly don't know, but I can believe it's possible. When I met him last Thursday there was something really off about him. He smiled when he introduced himself, but it was forced. His eyes sure weren't smiling. They were cold. Hard."

"I wonder what made him so hateful?" Sylvia shook her head.

"No idea, but it must've been big. He seems filled with hate."

Sylvia leaned on the kitchen door frame and hugged herself. "This group is too much. What about Iggy? I'm scared for him. I'm worried he's either going to become like them, or he'll rebel and something will happen to him, too."

"Hopefully after Friday night, Iggy, and everyone else, will be safe." Virgil stood and gathered Sylvia into his arms. "Let's go through Mama's motif items. I want to be sure whatever we do Friday night is as close to perfect as possible. This bullshit has to stop. And I don't want us to make any mistakes."

For the next two hours they circled the dining room table, opening and emptying boxes. Virgil carted everything in from the guest room and added it to the piles. He pulled items out while Sylvia created an inventory list.

❧❧❧❧❧

"That's it." Virgil stretched and rubbed his lower back. "Mama had more things than I remembered."

Sylvia scanned the list. "Half of these items are probably in my pantry or medicine cabinet. Who knew they had more...creative uses."

Virgil laughed. "My ancestors used what they had. I guess those skills were passed down. But we use modern things, too. I used a toy car once. And I've used Barbie and Ken dolls."

"I really don't want to know any specific details. I have to trust you're making the right choices." She paused. "Except for Lisa."

Virgil winced. "Yeah. That was the worst mistake I've ever made. And it will never happen again. Any motifs I do in the future are going to be very carefully planned and reviewed. No more rush jobs."

Sylvia put her arms around him and kissed him hard. "That's what I needed to hear."

Virgil leaned into her embrace. "I'm exhausted. Will you stay?"

"I'd like that."

As tired as he was, Virgil found himself aroused as soon as they crawled into bed. He pulled her to him and smothered her face and neck with kisses. "Can't imagine life without you anymore. I realize it's moved fast. But it feels so right."

Sylvia stroked his cheek and kissed his chest. "It feels that way to me, too. I don't care what Oscar wants. I'm filing for divorce. Want to move on with my life."

"I hate to be the cause of your divorce."

"You are and you're not. There are no guarantees we'll be together long term, but if nothing else, you've helped me see that I don't want to go back. And I like the idea of going forward with you." She snuggled in and put her head on his chest. "Nice." Her voice was sleepy.

"I could get used to this," he whispered into her hair as he drifted off.

They were in deep sleep, in a tangle of arms and legs, when the phone rang, jarring them awake.

Virgil glanced at the clock as he sat up. "Who could be calling at 6:30 in the morning? Hello? Oh. Oh, no. Yes, I'll be right there."

He hung up the phone and slumped against the headboard. His face was pale and drawn.

"What's wrong? What's happened? Is it Stan?" Sylvia sat up and put her hand on his cheek.

"No." He began to cry. "It's Mama. She's dead."

(37)

Some think it's holding on that makes one strong;
sometimes it's letting go. ~Sylvia Robinson

Virgil sped through the early dawn toward Oak Creek. He gripped the steering wheel so hard his knuckles were white.

Sylvia leaned toward Virgil as he drove, her left hand on his leg. "I'm so sorry. Did they say what happened?"

Virgil shook his head. "The aide found her at six when she went in to clean Mama up and change her bed."

"Don't the night nurses check on patients? How long was your mother...before someone found her?"

"The night aides only eyeball the rooms. They don't actually check to see if everyone is breathing. They look in to make sure people are in their beds and haven't fallen out, and that no one is moaning or in obvious distress. But that's it."

"I'm sorry, Virgil. I'm afraid I've no idea what else to say."

"Just having you here is enough."

"So they don't know what caused her death?"

"No. The night nurse called the resident doctor and also Nancy, since she's the director of nursing. They're both on their way, too."

"I'm glad Nancy is coming in. I liked her."

"Me, too." Virgil sighed. "Maybe Mama simply let go. She realized I have someone else to help. To be with. Maybe that was the one thing she was waiting for."

Sylvia nodded. "Hadn't thought of that. I could see it, though. Hanging on because she was all you had. Mothers always put their children first. No matter what. But you said she wasn't happy. That smiles from her were rare."

"Until she met you." Virgil pulled into the dimly-lit parking lot and braked hard, flinging Sylvia forward. "Oh. Sorry."

"Don't worry about it." She squeezed his hand. "Want me to wait here for a bit?"

"NO!" Virgil looked pained. "I need you with me."

"I love you. Remember that."

"I love you, too." Virgil leaned over and kissed her. "Okay. Guess I'm as ready as I'll ever be."

The nurses station was a sea of light surrounded by dim hallways. Virgil approached the desk and stopped. He wished Nancy were here already. He didn't recognize either of the nurses on duty.

"May I help you?" one nurse asked.

The second nurse hurried over. "You must be Mr. Harris."

Virgil nodded.

"I'm so sorry. I'm the one who called you. My name is Dana." She extended her hand.

Virgil shook it automatically. "Thank you, Dana. This is my friend Sylvia. And please, call me Virgil."

"All right, Virgil. It's nice to meet you, Sylvia." Dana inclined her head then gestured down the hall. "I'll follow you."

As Virgil walked to his mother's room he felt like he was moving through quicksand. Each step seemed to drag him down. He must have slowed his pace, because Sylvia put her arm around his waist and gently squeezed.

"I'm here. It'll be okay," she said.

"Yeah."

Virgil froze at the door to his mother's room. Dana bumped into him, clearly not expecting him to stop.

"Oh! I'm sorry." She patted him on the shoulder, then stepped back.

"It's fine." Virgil took a deep breath and entered the room. He was surprised to see his mother looked the same as when he visited. Like she was sleeping. *What did I expect?*

Slowly approaching the foot of the bed, he stared at the body, now nothing more than a shell where his mother had been. His stomach felt sucker-punched and his throat clenched.

Goodbye, Mama. I'll miss you. "She's always been there for me. Now she never will be again." He broke into tears.

Sylvia put her arm around his waist, and he leaned his head onto her shoulder. After a minute, he sighed and lifted his head. He wiped his eyes and turned to the nurse, who stood quietly in the doorway.

"I have no idea how to proceed."

"Nancy, Nurse Williams, will be here soon. So should Doctor Collins."

"Thank you." Virgil turned to the bed. He couldn't take his eyes off what had been his mother only a few hours earlier. But he also couldn't bring himself to go any closer.

Dana walked farther into the room, but remained behind Virgil and Sylvia. "Do you have a funeral home in mind? Did she have any pre-arrangements or plans?"

"Plans?" Virgil shook his head. His voice hitched. "No. No plans. She wanted… Cremated. Don't know…what do…about that."

"We can contact the company we generally recommend, if you like."

"Yeah." Virgil nodded. "Yes, please."

"I'll give them a call, then bring you the forms they'll want." Dana's shoes made soft squeaking sounds as she left.

"What now?" Sylvia asked. "What can I do?"

"Honestly, no idea. I…so young…father died. This is…"Virgil took a deep breath and exhaled slowly. When he continued, he was calmer. "This is the first death I've ever experienced. I'm completely lost."

"I was in my twenties when my grandmother died. But my grandfather wanted an elaborate funeral, not a quiet cremation. So I'm afraid I can't help much."

Dana returned, followed by a middle-aged man in grey slacks and a wrinkled, short-sleeved shirt.

"Mr. Harris, Virgil, this is Dr. Collins," Dana said.

The slightly unkempt man crossed the room, hand extended. "Mr. Harris I'm sorry for your loss. I'm here to confirm death and write a death certificate."

"Thank you for coming." Virgil shook the man's hand. The doctor's grip was firm, his skin soft and meaty. "Met you when we first brought my mother here, but she was pretty healthy, except for her mind. I don't believe I've seen you since."

"No, but I saw her on a regular basis. And you're right. Except for the brain damage, she was healthy. I do apologize for my appearance. I was on an emergency call at a nursing home in San Antonio until four."

Dr. Collins motioned toward Pearl Harris. "Do you want to leave the room while I check on her?"

Virgil nodded, then turned to Dana. "Is there a lounge or waiting area? I've never needed it before, so I don't even know if there is one."

Dana waved toward the door. "Come on, I'll show you."

She led them past the nurses station and into another long hall. Halfway down she pointed to the right. "In here. Would you like me to make a pot of coffee? During the day we keep a fresh pot on all the time, but no one's made any yet today since it's still so early. There's a cooler in there if you want a cup of water."

"Coffee would be nice." Sylvia said when Virgil didn't respond.

"I'll leave the cremation authorization form here on the table. I forgot a pen. I'll bring one when I come back."

When Dana had gone, Sylvia took Virgil's hand and led him to a row of heavily padded chairs.

Virgil sagged into one. "These aren't as comfortable as they look."

Sylvia smiled and sat beside him. "No. I suspect they don't want folks hanging out here all day." She stroked his cheek. "Do you know what you'll do with your mother's ashes? She never said what she wanted?"

"We never talked about it. Guess I'll scatter them somewhere. No idea where. I don't want her ashes as a keepsake." Virgil shook his head. "That's not her anymore. She felt the same way about death. All I can say for sure is that she didn't want a big funeral. I don't know any other wishes she might've had. And now I can't ask her." He dropped his head into his hands.

Sylvia patted his shoulder. "Want some water while waiting for the coffee?"

"No. I'll be all right in a minute." He didn't look up as he spoke.

Dana returned and handed Sylvia a pen. "Here," she whispered as she glanced at Virgil. "I'll make the coffee."

"Thank you," Sylvia mouthed. "Virgil would you like me to fill out as much of this form as I can?"

He nodded.

Sylvia got them each a cup of coffee.

"Thanks." Virgil took the cup and held it to his face. "Nothing like the smell of fresh-brewed coffee to calm the soul." He sipped and sighed.

Sylvia moved to a small table near the water cooler to fill out the cremation form. She was finishing the form when Dr. Collins entered and sat across from Virgil. She joined the two men.

"Mr. and Mrs. Harris, I've finished my examination."

"I'm not Mrs. Harris, just a friend," Sylvia said.

The doctor nodded, then turned his attention to Virgil. "Looks like it was probably a heart attack. I never did a full work-up on her for heart disease. Saw no need. And there's nothing in her chart here to indicate that was a problem. Are you aware of any previous heart issues before she was admitted here?"

"I… Not that I know of. And they didn't say anything when she was in the hospital."

"Had she shown any signs of distress? When did you last see her?"

Virgil shook his head. "No. We were here yesterday afternoon. She was more animated than usual. Almost talkative. Perhaps that wore her out more than we realized."

"That's possible. She was in her seventies. I realize that's not that old these days, but she'd been bed-ridden for several years. That ages and weakens a body, especially one that's…compromised. Even a small thing can be the tipping point." He stood. "I'll prepare the death certificate. Would you like a copy mailed to you?"

"Yes, please." Virgil nodded.

"I'll get your address from the nurses station."

"Thank you."

The doctor reached the door just as Nancy arrived. They exchanged a brief whisper, then the doctor left and Nancy took the chair he'd occupied.

"Hello, Virgil. Ma'am. How are you doing?"

"I'm okay, Nancy. A little shocked."

"I understand. Checked on her yesterday before I left. She seemed tired, but not in any discomfort. And she was smiling. I was happy to see that." The nurse frowned. "But didn't you say she had another episode yesterday?"

"No, not really. She did mention that blonde woman I asked about. Maybe Mama was more agitated than she showed."

"Asked Becky, the other nurse, about it after you left. She said the blonde seemed quite nice. She saw no reason to worry. I'm sorry if her visit had anything to do with your mother's death."

"No need to apologize. Even if Tammy did say something that upset my mother, it's not your fault."

Dana poked her head around the corner. "They're here."

Nancy stood. "The staff from the crematorium are here. You'll need to identify the body for them, then you can go if you like. They don't let you watch their preparations, anyway."

"Why? What do they do?" Sylvia asked.

"It's nothing to worry about. They're very respectful. But the process of draping and removing the body can be stressful on the family."

"I understand." Virgil nodded.

"I can take that form for you," Nancy said. "They'll deliver your mother's ashes to you by courier. Perhaps a week or two, depending on how busy they are."

"Okay." Virgil followed Nancy to his mother's room. Two men were already there, standing beside the bed. They introduced themselves, then one said, "Please identify who this is for us."

"This is my mother, Pearl Harris."

"Thank you. Do you have the form?" one of the men asked.

"I have it," Nancy said from the doorway.

Both men nodded then the same one spoke again. "Would you like another minute before we remove her?"

Virgil didn't, but felt it was the right thing to do. The others probably expected it. "Okay."

Everyone but Sylvia filed out of the room.

Virgil crossed to his mother's bed. Her lips looked bruised, but otherwise she could have been sleeping peacefully. He reached out one last time to brush her hair off her forehead. His hand froze.

"What's wrong?" Sylvia came up beside him. "Virgil?"

"This." He picked something off Pearl's pillow and held it up. "A white hair. I only know one person with cotton-white hair."

(38)

Never doubt that a small group of thoughtful, committed
citizens can change the world. Indeed, it is the only thing
that ever has. ~Margaret Mead (1901-1978)

"Who are you talking about?" Sylvia asked as soon as they were outside.

"Cotton. No idea of his last name." Virgil's face was grim.

"The same man Stan was talking about earlier? The head of the Truth Seekers?"

Virgil nodded.

"And he was here? Why? Do you think he did something to your mother?"

"Probably not directly, or the doctor would have noticed. But, yes, I believe he was responsible for her death." His eyes flashed fire when he turned them to Sylvia. "That's the last straw. We need to specify the Truth Seekers when we do the motif tonight. By name. I'll take my chances on karmic backlash."

"What was that again?"

"When the universe causes something to happen to you because you did a motif against another."

"That sounds bad." Sylvia frowned.

A shadow crossed Virgil's face, but he quickly shook it off and forced a smile. "I've never had anything happen that wasn't worth it for having solved a problem."

"Like what? What's happened to you in the past?"

Virgil held out his wrist so Sylvia could see the angry red welt. "I got this acid burn when I did the motif on Joe."

"Joe who? What motif?"

Virgil grimaced. *I forgot she didn't know.* "A local bad man who frequently sideswiped parked cars, killed animals, and even ran over a child."

"Oh. I think I remember reading about him in the paper. That was your doing?"

Virgil nodded.

"And the acid burn was your karmic backlash? Is that all that happened?"

"Well... I also blew a tire a couple days later."

"I guess those aren't so bad. But does what happens...this karmic backlash, depend on how powerful or direct the motif is?"

"Yeah, pretty much." His stomach lurched thinking about what might be headed his way after the Lisa/Tammy motif screw-up.

"And you three are doing a big motif about the whole town? No. I don't want you taking the chance of mentioning the Truth Seekers by name. I'm afraid your payback could be bad. I don't want to lose you!" She gripped his arm. "Please. Promise me. I love you."

Virgil didn't speak for a full minute, then he uttered a deep sigh. "All right. I promise. We won't mention the Truth Seekers. We'll keep it focused on the broad picture. On just protecting the town."

"Thank you." Sylvia took his hand and kissed next to the burn. "It surprises me how much you already mean to me. Maybe it should scare me a little, too, but it doesn't."

"Same for me."

"You're sure you didn't do one of your motif things on me?"

"I'd never do a love spell on someone. Wouldn't be right. The relationship would be contrived. I couldn't…" He glanced at Sylvia, who was grinning. "You were teasing."

"Of course I was, but I appreciate your sincere answer."

"You got me good." He turned into his driveway. "I realize it's been a long morning, can't believe it's already after nine, but come in for a while?"

"For a few minutes, if you aren't ready to be alone. I'm sure you're exhausted. I certainly am. And I suspect you'll want to rest before tonight."

"All true. But I'm pretty wired up from this morning. A few minutes with you will help calm me down."

They sat side by side on the sofa. They talked little. Sylvia leaned into Virgil and laid her head on his shoulder. He tipped his head onto hers.

"I don't mean to sound dramatic, but you're all I have now." He turned enough that he could kiss the top of her head.

"That's not dramatic. It's sad if it's true."

"I don't want to lose you, too." He paused and took a deep breath. "Move in with me. I can keep you safe if you're here."

Sylvia shook her head. "I'll be fine. I'm not the kind of person the Truth Seekers are after."

"Maybe not, but they could go after you to get to me." Virgil cleared his throat. "Like it seems they did with Mama. And I can't help worrying about you being in the same house as Iggy. I know he's your son, but—"

"You really think my own son would do something to me?" Sylvia sat up, clearly agitated.

"No, not really." Virgil's shoulders slumped. "But Cotton could pump him for information without Iggy realizing it. It sure seems like Cotton is getting dangerous."

"I'll give you that."

Virgil kissed her hand. "That's not the only reason I want you here. I love you. I like being around you."

"You're a confirmed bachelor. I'd drive you crazy after just a couple weeks.

"Or I'd drive you crazy." Virgil grinned. "But if there's a chance we might one day make this permanent, wouldn't a test run make sense?"

"Test run?" Sylvia raised her eyebrow. "Is that what you call it? So I'm like driving a car before you buy it?"

"Aw, I didn't mean it like that."

Sylvia laughed. "No, it's all right. I know what you mean. And I actually agree."

"So will you? You can tell Iggy to move into a house or apartment with friends. Then you can put your house on the market. You said you wanted to sell it. Houses sell faster if they're unoccupied. And it'll be easier to stage it and keep it clean."

Sylvia laughed again. "Listen to you being all practical with real estate logistics and facts. I'll do it because I want to. But I'm not going to put my house on the market right away, in case we discover we can't stand living together. I'll bring enough things that I can stay here most of the time, but not so many they take up too much room."

Virgil gathered her into his arms and kissed her. He stroked her hair. "Bring whatever you want. I'll always make room."

They held their embrace for several minutes, then Sylvia gently wiggled from Virgil's arms.

"Guess I'd better go tell Iggy the good news. Although I bet he won't think it's so good."

Virgil grinned. "If he didn't like me much before, I can only imagine how he'll feel after today."

"It's time he got his own life together. And it's time for me to move on with mine." She kissed him again. "Please be careful tonight. And remember your promise."

"I remember. And we'll be careful."

After Sylvia left, Virgil got his mother's journal and sat at the breakfast table. He stroked the felt tree on the cover. *How old was she when she made it? Was it something else before she turned it into her journal? I'll never find out now.*

Pearl had been in her twenties when she logged her first motif, at least in this journal. Virgil wondered if there'd been others when she was younger. If so, they seemed to be gone now. He'd not found any when he cleaned her house before putting it on the market.

For the next three hours, he read every detail of every motif in the book. There were four hundred sixteen. She'd done about eight a year since before he was born. Some made him smile. The ones encouraging him to improve his grades made him laugh. Only the one against the Truth Seekers, the last one she'd done—or would ever do—was negative toward someone. It made his heart hurt.

She sacrificed her freedom and her very mind for me. Now those bastards have taken her life. They'll pay. I'll find a way without breaking my promise to Sylvia.

Virgil looked at the clock. It was only an hour after noon, but felt like midnight. He was emotionally drained and exhausted and decided to rest before Marshall and Emma arrived for the motif.

He set his alarm for five and closed his eyes. When the alarm went off he'd have sworn only a few minutes had passed. But the clock glowed five.

Time to get this evening started. Virgil climbed out of bed and headed to the shower. He showered, dressed in slacks and a polo shirt, and ate a light dinner. It was still only 5:45.

He took the time to move all of his mother's motif supplies into his own chancel. Instead of simply adding her things to his, he emptied each shelf and dusted, then put everything back in neat rows. He was tucking her journal onto a bottom shelf when the doorbell rang.

Both Marshall and Emma stood on his front porch, each holding a cloth shopping bag. "Hello, you two. Come on in, unless you want to give the spies something to do. In which case, I'll come outside and we can dance in a circle or something."

Emma laughed so hard she doubled over, holding her stomach.

Marshall raised his eyebrows as he studied Virgil's face. "Something's changed."

"A lot." Virgil nodded. The three settled in the living room. "Let me fill you in." Virgil first told them about Stan's visit.

"Those bastards." Marshall shook his head. "Part of me didn't want to believe they were spying on me, but of course I saw it with my own eyes. Sorry you've been added."

"I knew right away. My spies weren't very good." Emma laughed, then scowled. "Plus, after my car was broken into, I got really watchful. Spotted 'em easily. Just to piss them off, I waved every time I went in or out the front door. Even found excuses to go outside, so I could annoy them. Bummer on you, though, Virg."

"There's more." Virgil next told them about Tammy's visit to his mother.

"You're sure it was Tammy?" Marshall asked.

"That blonde chick from the cafe?" Emma cocked her head.

"Yeah, her." Virgil nodded. "And I'm sure. Purple glasses and all."

"What the hell?" Marshall frowned. "Why'd she go there?"

"No idea, but it must have been too much. Mama died sometime last night. I got the call at 6:30 this morning." *They don't need to know about Cotton. I have other plans for him.*

"Your mother died? Holy shit." Emma put her hand on Virgil's arm. "I'm really sorry."

"You still want to do this?" Marshall asked. "It's okay if you don't."

Virgil nodded. "Now more than ever. I'd go after those damn Truth Seekers by name, but I promised Sylvia I wouldn't. So let's be sure we protect the town so well this group decides to find a new home, or disband altogether."

For the next hour, the three pored over every word Emma had written.

"This is good." Marshall rubbed his eyes. "I'm impressed."

"Thanks." Emma pointed about halfway down the page. "Is this part okay? Where I talk about an invisible wall of protection around the town?"

"I think it's great." Virgil smiled. "Your idea how to set up the motif sounds perfect. I like the imagery."

"I agree," Marshall said. "Great job."

Emma grinned from ear to ear.

"One last chance to back out." Virgil held up his hands. "Is this the right thing to do? Are we all sure? Any doubts or concerns about karmic backlash?"

"Not from me." Marshall shook his head.

"Let's do this." Emma stood. "I need to change first."

"You can change in my office or the bathroom."

"Bathroom's fine. No potty breaks during a charm."

"Marshall, you want to change in the guest room?"

The three reconvened in the hallway a few minutes later. Virgil wore his black cotton cassock. Marshall wore a white cassock of similar design. Emma wore a royal blue velour robe with a satin-lined hood.

In response to Virgil's grin, she said, "Got it at a renaissance fair. I wanted something nicer than an ugly Catholic priest's robe."

Virgil led the way into his chancel. Marshall and Emma stood by the table while Virgil lit the corner candles and turned off the overhead light. He directed the others to various cabinets and soon they had the supplies they needed on the table.

"Marshall, you put the UPS directories and the map in the center."

Marshall nodded and laid the small stack of papers down.

Virgil arranged a circle of seven white candles around the papers. "May these candles protect all of the names on the lists, all the residents of Lichen." He motioned to Emma.

Emma sprinkled a ring of sage around the inside of the circle. "May this sage create an invisible wall of protection as a barrier. May it purge anger and hate, and prevent intentional harm."

Marshall set up a second ring of thirteen black candles a foot out from the white ones. "May these drive away the evil that is here now, sending it from the city and those who live here."

Emma sprinkled a line of insecticide powder in a circle outside the white candles. "May this powder repel evil and hate from entering Lichen. Anyone with evil intentions toward our town or residents will find they change their mind and do not enter here."

Virgil sprinkled a second line of sugar outside the black candles. "May the evil be lured away, attracted to new areas and new tasks."

The motif looked like an odd bullseye, made of the papers, a ring of sage, a circle of white candles, a ring of insecticide, a circle of black candles, and finally a ring of sugar.

Virgil handed Marshall and Emma each a long fireplace match and took one for himself. He lighted them and then they took turns lighting candles and saying two lines from the chant.

They lit the white candles clockwise and finished counterclockwise with the black. They repeated the last lines of the chant together.

The town of Lichen is safe

The people of Lichen are safe

Lichen is free from those with evil plans

Those who would harm Lichen citizens are gone

Leave Lichen now. Leave us alone. Leave us in peace.

Emma laid the parchment on top of the UPS pages in the center of the circle. "And it shall be done."

"So mote it be," Virgil said.

"Be thou complete," Marshall said.

Virgil opened the door and Emma and Marshall stepped into the hallway.

"Forgot to extinguish the candles in the corners of the room," Virgil said. "You two relax. I'll be right out. We can have a glass of wine."

As soon as they left, Virgil hurried to the motif. From a pocket, he extracted the white hair Cotton had left on Pearl's pillow.

I didn't promise Sylvia not to personally deal with you. I promised we wouldn't mention the truth Seekers. Virgil held up the hair. He leaned over and lit it from one of the black candles, then dropped the strand on the table, where it quickly vanished, leaving nothing but a thin line of smoke.

May death find you as you

brought it to my mother

Is féidir bás a fhaigheann tú mar

a thug tú é le mo mháthair

Virgil's jaw muscles clenched as he extinguished the corner candles and left the room, closing and locking the door behind him. He forced a smile as he rounded the corner into the kitchen where Marshall and Emma sat.

"How about some wine," Virgil said. "Let's celebrate our pending success."

(39)

Between the wish and the thing, life lies waiting. ~Unknown

The three agreed to not speak or meet again until the last candle burned out. Virgil started his Saturday by organizing his bedroom in preparation for Sylvia's moving in. He rarely bought clothes and even less often discarded worn out items.

It was a task he normally hated, but the anticipation of Sylvia's arrival enthused him and he spent Saturday morning trying on every shirt and pair of pants he owned and sorting all his socks and underwear. Before long, he had three empty dresser drawers and over half an empty closet.

Guess I need a few new things. He stared at the large discard pile on the bed. A few showed their age, but most were too tight. *Guess I need to lose a few pounds, too.*

Sylvia called mid-morning when he was struggling out of tuxedo pants he'd not worn in twenty years.

"Good morning, love!" Her voice was bright and bubbly.

Virgil smiled and sat on the bed, pants stuck mid-thigh. "Hello! How's your morning?"

"Awesome. I'm sorting out old clothes."

"Me, too." Virgil laughed. "Didn't realize how many had shrunk over the years."

"I think there's something in the stuffy air of a closet. Causes clothes to shrink. I have that same problem." Her voice grew serious. "How'd it go last night? Everything okay?"

"Everything went fine. Emma wrote a great chant all about happiness, joy, and being protected from those with evil intentions. You'd like it."

"You kept your promise?"

"Sure did. Not one mention of the Truth Seekers by anyone." *Please don't ask me about Cotton.*

"When will you know it worked? When will something happen? WHAT will happen?"

Virgil could hear the stress in her voice. "*When* is the easy part. Within a day or so after the last candle burns out. *What* is tougher. Sometimes the universe sends a tidal wave, sometimes barely a ripple."

"I don't really understand."

"When I did the motif on the guys who'd beaten Mama, the house where they'd been hiding burned down. They were caught while escaping the fire. They also got the maximum sentence of twenty years."

"Okay. That all could have happened without a motif."

"Exactly, it wasn't really that much out of the ordinary. But another motif I did had more serious results. A repeat drunk driver, a man named Adam Smirnoff, had permanently maimed a small boy, then Smirnoff hired a hotshot lawyer to get him off. The lawyer claimed the parents were at fault because the boy wasn't wearing a helmet. Didn't matter that he was on the sidewalk and Smirnoff jumped the curb. I worked hard on that motif. Thanks to his car meeting a tree, the drunk ended up with severe brain damage. Far as I know, he's still living in Oak Creek, where Mama is…was."

"Oh my. I thought you said you didn't harm people."

"The brain damage wasn't my intention. I did the motif to stop him from driving drunk again. I didn't specify how the universe should do that." *Unlike Joe. I wanted him to crash and be crippled.* "If it makes you feel better, this was the guy's fifth arrest for driving drunk. And it wasn't the first time he'd hit another person, although it was the first child." Virgil's voice turned harsh. "He'd gotten off each time."

"Actually, it does help. I'd hate to think I was moving in with someone who secretly has an evil heart."

"You don't think that, do you!"

"No, of course not. I think you're very caring." Sylvia laughed. "It was your caring about me that led to our meeting in the first place."

"Glad to hear that." *I do care, sometimes too much.* "Want to come over or meet for lunch?" Virgil asked.

"How about dinner? I want to finish sorting clothes."

Virgil sighed. "Don't remind me. I still have to get out of these damn tuxedo pants."

Sylvia laughed so loud Virgil had to pull the phone away from his ear. When she caught her breath, she said, "I'm sorry. I'm picturing what you look like right now."

"Gah! Please don't. See you later." Virgil disconnected, then struggled out of the pants. He tossed them on the discard pile. *Enough of this.*

He retrieved a couple of garbage bags, stuffed his old clothes into them, and loaded them into the SUV. He'd take them to the donation drop-off center tomorrow or Monday. He was closing the back door of his car when he heard a car door slam, then someone calling his name.

"Yoo-hoo! Mr. Harris?"

Virgil stepped from behind his vehicle to see a taxi pulling away from the curb. A handicapped woman wobbled up his driveway on cuff-style crutches. He hurried to her. It took a minute for him to remember it was Stan's mother. She didn't get out often. She wasn't much older than Virgil, but cerebral palsy had crippled her body.

"Mrs. Walker, let me help you. Please be careful."

"Thank you, Mr. Harris." She paused to catch her breath. "I need to talk to you."

"Of course. Want to come in?"

"No, thanks." Mrs. Walker frowned. "I wanted to tell you about Stan. He insisted."

"Stan? Is something wrong?"

"He's in the hospital." Mrs. Walker shook her head. "Bad accident. Just got back. I had the taxi drop me off at your driveway."

"Oh no! I'm so sorry. What happened?"

"He headed out early this morning to help on some construction job. You know he loves to work, and he always does his best."

"He's a good hand." Virgil nodded. "Sometimes he helps with my woodworking."

Mrs. Walker smiled. "He loves helping you. Says you're always nice."

Virgil steered the conversation back on track. "So what happened this morning?"

"Stan's a little confused, but it seems when he got to the job site there were a couple of other people there. They went for supplies, and he was left alone. When the others got back, they found my boy." Mrs. Walker shook her head. A tear slid down one cheek.

"What was wrong?" A chill ran through Virgil. *I told Stan to say home for a few days. Why didn't he listen to me?*

"Construction materials fell on him. Crushed his legs and groin."

"I'm so sorry. What hospital is he in? I'd like to go see him." *I need to find out what happened.*

"Mercy Hospital in San Antonio." Mrs. Walker smiled. "He asked for you. Thank you for going to see him. He'll like that."

"He asked for me?" *I'll do whatever I can to help him.*

Mrs. Walked nodded. "He sure did. He insisted I come tell you what happened. He said…now let me remember exactly…he said to tell you at least he wasn't electrocuted. I have no idea what he meant. He seemed to think you would."

"I'll ask him when I see him." Virgil touched Mrs. Walker's back, in a gentle urging toward home. "Can I help you across the street? Do you need anything while Stan's in the hospital? I know you're there alone now."

"I can make it home. And I'll be okay. My sister's coming down from Denver."

"That's good. Well, please call me if I can help in any way."

"Thanks, I will." Mrs. Walker hobbled down the driveway, then glanced back. "He told the police it was done on purpose, but they don't believe him. If you find out anything, please call me."

"I'll do that. I promise."

As soon as Mrs. Walker was safely on her front porch, Virgil hurried in and called Sylvia.

"Hi! What's up?"

He told her what he'd learned.

"Oh no! I'm coming over right now. I'm going with you to see Stan. Do you think the Truth Seekers had something to do with this?"

"I suppose it could be a coincidence."

"But you don't think so."

"No. I don't."

"I'll be there in ten minutes."

(40)

There is no meeting of minds, no point of understanding
with such terror. Just a choice: Defeat it or be defeated
by it. And defeat it we must. ~Tony Blair

Virgil's face was grim as he sped north. Sylvia sat silent beside him, although her mouth moved as if she was talking to herself. After several minutes, she turned to Virgil.

"Why didn't the motif stop this? Or is that not how it works?"

"The motif doesn't work until after all the candles burn out."

"That hasn't happened yet?"

Virgil hit his hand on the steering wheel. "Dammit, I don't know. I got sidetracked after I heard about Stan and forgot to check."

"I almost wish you'd done something directly to the Truth Seekers."

"Me, too."

"But I didn't want you to get any of that...what did you call it?"

"Karmic backlash." Virgil glanced at Sylvia and smiled. "I know. I understand. And it probably wouldn't have been a good idea to target the group. What if it fell apart and all the members became vigilantes on their own?"

"Kind of like you?"

Virgil flinched. "Ouch!"

"Oh, I didn't mean it the way it came out," Sylvia said. "I only meant that you seek justice on your own. You don't have some group telling you what to do."

"Which could be good or bad, I guess. Depending on what the group instructs its people to do."

"Do you think this was a group thing?" Sylvia cocked her head.

"Not for a minute. I think this was Cotton."

"Another reason not to target the whole group, no matter how tempted you were. What if only a few members of the group are bad? Or it's just Cotton? The motif would have targeted all the members, wouldn't it?"

"Yeah. It would have. Stan's a member, and he's not a bad guy. Confused, or maybe brainwashed."

"Tammy, too," Sylvia said. "She may have acted standoffish with you, but I can't see her doing bad things to you. Or to anyone."

"What about Mama?"

"Do you really think she did something to your mother?"

Virgil sighed. "No, I don't. I think she was probably there on Cotton's orders. And whatever she was supposed to learn or do didn't happen."

"So Cotton went back on his own."

"Yeah. And while Tammy probably didn't do anything, I can't say the same thing about Cotton. I think he's gone rogue."

"It wouldn't be the first time one member of a group went rogue." Sylvia frowned.

"Sure wouldn't."

"What can you do? Will your peace-bringing motif stop the corruption? Will it stop Cotton?"

"It will now." *Oh hell. I shouldn't have said that.*

"What's that mean?" Sylvia frowned. "What aren't you telling me?"

Virgil sighed. *Don't lie to her. You love her and want this to work out.* "Remember that hair I found on Mama's pillow?"

"The white one that you said belonged to Cotton?" Sylvia hesitated. "What about it?"

"I added it to the motif. I didn't tell the others. Any karmic backlash is strictly on me."

"Oh, Virgil. I don't know what to say." Sylvia sighed and turned her face to the window.

They rode in silence for several minutes. Virgil reached over and touched Sylvia's arm. "I'm sorry. I promised not to mention the Truth Seekers, not Cotton himself."

Sylvia's shoulders stiffened.

"Please understand. I couldn't let him get away with Mama's death. He may not have been the hand that killed her, but his presence most surely did."

Sylvia shifted but said nothing.

"Please. He caused Mama's death. And I'd bet money he's the one who hurt Stan. Maybe tried to kill him. Cotton's an evil man. I had to do something. I'm just sorry it was too late for Stan."

Sylvia sighed and turned to face Virgil. "I guess I do understand. I'm disappointed, but I'm more scared than angry. What's going to happen to you?"

"Maybe nothing. He's definitely earned his karma. I didn't send him anything he didn't have coming."

"What DID you send him?"

"I sent him the justice he deserved for what he did to Mama. Since I've no idea exactly what he did, I couldn't say anything specific." *I sent him death, not justice, but I just can't tell her that.*

Virgil was glad they reached Mercy Hospital before the conversation could go any deeper. They hurried inside and stopped at the information desk to find out where Stan was.

The nurse checked the database. "He's still in ICU."

"Can we see him?" Sylvia asked. "We aren't family."

The nurse nodded. "He's not critical, so he's allowed a few visitors in the afternoon."

Stan was dozing when they approached his bed.

"Stan?" Virgil leaned over and whispered.

"Virg! And...aw, I forgot your name."

"It's Sylvia, Stan."

"Oh, yeah. Hi, Sylvia." Stan's voice was almost a whisper.

"Good to see you, Stan. How are you feeling?" Virgil studied the man. He looked pale and drawn. He had only a thin sheet over him, and heavy bandages from his chest down were clearly visible. Monitors behind the bed blinked and scrolled out his vital signs.

"I'm okay. Nurses give me some pretty good drugs for the pain."

"Do you know what happened?" Virgil waved toward Stan's battered body.

"Doc says my legs are broken in three places. I got five broken ribs. And some gut damage. A perfer...profa... A hole in my insides. I didn't really understand that part, 'cept the doc said he had to scrub me all out."

"That's terrible." Sylvia put her hand to her chest.

Stan nodded. "Yeah. Doc says I might be here for a week." He pointed to two IV bags. "Got the usual bag o' water. But I'm also gettin' food this way. For a few days, at least."

"How'd it happen?" Virgil asked.

"It was him, Virg. I'm sure of it." Stan screwed up his face, looking ready to cry. "I was there alone, sweepin' and cleanin' around the job site. After a while, I sat down to drink some water and wait for the guys to get back from the hardware store." Stan looked at Virgil. "It was hot. I wasn't bein' lazy."

"Sure it was hot." Virgil nodded. "So what happened?"

"Guess I kinda leaned back and fell asleep. I heard a noise and looked up just in time to see this ol' big pallet of limestone blocks fallin' toward me. Happened too fast to roll out of the way."

"Oh, wow." Sylvia shook her head.

"Where'd they fall from?" Virgil asked.

"They was up on the forklift. Keeps folks from stealing 'em."

"Wait a minute." Virgil frowned. "They fell off an elevated forklift?"

Sylvia and Virgil exchanged a glance.

"Yeah. Doc said I was lucky the chicken wire broke apart as the pallet fell. I got landed on by a bunch of loose blocks. If the whole thing woulda landed on me, I'd be dead."

"Stan, this is important." Virgil leaned over and patted the man's arm. "Did you hear the forklift start? Was someone running it?"

Stan's voice dropped to a whisper. "I saw him, Virg. I saw Cotton. He was there."

"Are you sure?" Sylvia's hand shot to her mouth.

"Yeah, I'm sure." Stan nodded. "Right 'fore I passed out, I turned to look. Saw a headful of white hair on a man climbing into a car."

"Lots of older men have white hair," Sylvia said. "Did you see his face?"

"Didn't have to. I know it was him."

"How do you know, Stan?" Virgil asked.

"Only man I know with curly, white hair." Stan started crying. "It's my fault. I shouldn't've fallen asleep. Then he couldn't have snuck up on me."

"It is NOT your fault." Sylvia shook her head. "Cotton is a bad man. You did nothing to deserve this."

"Then you believe me! Thanks, Sylvia." Stan wiped his eyes and nose on the sheet.

Virgil frowned. "I realize he threatened you the other day, but what provoked him to do this? Did you talk to him again?"

"Saw him at the meeting that night, after I told you he said he wanted the fountain moved. Told him I couldn't move it. Said you were a nice guy, and there was no reason to move it, anyway. He got really mad. Called me a *stupid retard.*"

"Oh, Stan, I'm sorry," Sylvia said. "You are a sweet, hard-working young man. And you have a good heart. Violent men view that as a weakness. He's a jerk, nothing's wrong with you."

"Aw, thanks." Stan grinned from ear to ear.

"What happened after he called you that?" Virgil asked.

"Told him my mama said not to take bein' treated like that, and I was gonna quit."

"That's good." Sylvia nodded.

"But he wouldn't let me quit. He said if I quit he'd be sure I couldn't talk to no one about what I knew." Stan tried to hug himself but the IV tubes got tangled. "Told him I was quitting anyway, and to leave me alone."

"Looks like he didn't, though." Virgil frowned.

"And it only took him a couple days, too." Stan's voice shook. "He won't come here, will he? Am I safe here?"

Virgil patted Stan's arm. "You rest. I'll talk to the nurses and let them know that if a white-haired man shows up, they need to call security."

"Thanks, Virg. That makes me feel better."

❧❧❧❧❧❧

"Cotton's gone too far!" Virgil said as soon as they were in the hall.

"Yes, he has." Sylvia grabbed Virgil's arm. "What about Iggy? What if Cotton goes after him? Iggy starts and quits things all the time. What if he tries to quit? He's got a copy of that list! He knows more than Stan about that bunch." Her eyes brimmed with tears.

Virgil hugged her, then took her hand as they walked to the nurse's station. He gave them a description of Cotton and asked they not allow him access to Stan.

"We'll watch for him," one of the nurses said. "Stan's a very nice young man. We won't let anything happen to him while he's here."

Once outside, Virgil paused and turned to Sylvia. "The motif must not have been finished when this happened to Stan. I don't know if it is now. I hope it is, so nothing else like this happens."

"I hope it works. And soon." Tears ran down her cheeks.

"I'm damned glad now that I used that white hair in the motif."

They talked little on the return drive to Lichen.

"Do you want to come in?" Virgil helped Sylvia out of the car.

She opened her mouth to speak, then paused. "I was going to say I want to go talk to Iggy. But I've changed my mind. I'd rather come in. This has really shaken me, and I want to calm down and collect my thoughts before confronting him. Want him to be open with me. Need him to realize how much danger he could be in. Not shut him down or piss him off."

Virgil kissed her. "I love you. If things don't change right away, I'll do another motif, this time to stop Cotton. I promise."

"Thank you." Sylvia smiled and touched Virgil's cheek. "No one's ever loved me that much."

"I do." *I will not let him hurt you or your family. I won't let him hurt anyone else. If that white hair doesn't work, I'll take whatever karmic backlash might come from a stronger motif.*

As soon as Virgil opened the door, he smelled it. "That's smoke!"

(41)

The feeling is less like an ending than just another starting point. ~Chuck Palahniuk, <u>Choke</u>

Virgil bolted for the kitchen. *Nothing here. Where is it?*

"Not in here," Sylvia said from behind him.

His face paled when reality set in. "The chancel!"

He hurried to the door, yanking the key from the back of the picture frame, causing the picture to crash to the floor. He grabbed the knob and immediately jerked his hand away. "Shit, that's hot! Call 911. I'm going for a wet towel."

Sylvia grabbed her phone from her purse. As soon as the dispatcher answered, she yelled, "There's a room on fire in the house. The door is closed, so it hasn't spread, but the knob is hot to the touch."

"Ma'am, please do not open the door. Give me your address, and I'll have the fire department to you as quickly as possible."

She was just hanging up when Virgil returned with a bathroom towel, dripping water down the hall. He shoved it against the bottom of the door. "That should keep the smoke in and fresh air out." A thin line of smoke seeped around the upper edges of the door. "Guess I can't block all of it. Damn."

They paced for what felt like an hour, but it was less than ten minutes before Lichen's firetruck pulled up in front of Virgil's house and three men piled out. By then, smoke had begun to boil out of the AC vents in the ceiling. Virgil and Sylvia hurried onto the porch.

One firefighter ran toward Virgil and Sylvia, while the other two took off to connect the hose to a hydrant several houses down. "The fire is contained in one room?"

"Yes. A back bedroom I use for...crafts. I can show you, it's down the hall."

"No, we'll get it through the window. It's safer." The firefighter barked out orders, sending one of the other firefighters to kill the power at the breaker and the other to drag the hose around the house. "Please stay here on the porch."

In spite of orders to the contrary, Virgil and Sylvia followed the men into the backyard. Virgil saw the flames through the window, the black-out covering had burned away.

Oh damn, what went wrong? What happened?

One of the firefighters smashed the window. Flames roared out. The other two firefighters directed the hose through the opening and began flooding the room. Within a few minutes, the flames had died down.

The two firefighters holding the hose shut it off long enough for the third to break the rest of the glass out of the window. He pulled on his respirator and climbed through.

"Bring the hose!" His voice was muffled by the mask. The other two men scrambled through the window, dragging the hose with them.

The force of the water turning back on sounded to Virgil like a jet engine. The firefighters yelled to one another, but Virgil couldn't understand what they were saying. *I wish I could see.* After a few minutes, the water was shut off. *I hope they don't pay attention to what's in there. Or at least to what's left.*

Leaning out the window and dropping the hose on the ground, one firefighter said, "Can you go around and unlock the door to this room so we don't have to break it?"

"Sure can." Virgil ran toward the front of the house, since the back door was still locked. Sylvia followed. Both ignored the shouted questions from the crowd of neighbors who'd gathered on the sidewalk.

Virgil barreled through the front door, choking on the smoke that had escaped from air vents and around the chancel's door. It wasn't until he saw the picture on the floor that he remembered he had the chancel key in his pocket. He quickly unlocked and opened the door. With the towel at the base of the door pushed aside, water poured into the hall. Virgil stepped back, gagging and coughing on the stench of smoke and burned debris.

The firefighters removed their respirators as they stepped into the hall. "Fire's out. Lots of damage, but at least it's in that one room."

"Except for the smoke and water, of course," another firefighter said. "Sorry you lost all your...craft supplies."

"And your work table," said the third.

"I appreciate your fast response. You kept the fire from spreading to the rest of the house." Virgil shook hands with each of the men.

"Thank you, so much." Sylvia wiped a tear from her eye.

"Just doing our job, ma'am." The firefighters nodded. "We'll pack up and head out. The fire marshal will be around soon to complete a questionnaire with you."

"Fire marshal? Why?" Virgil asked.

"Just a formality," the firefighter said. "To figure out what started the fire. Gotta make sure you didn't start it on purpose. You'll need that report for your insurance."

"Definitely not on purpose." Virgil shook his head. "I left some candles burning."

The firefighters all nodded, then one said, "That can do it. Folks don't realize it doesn't take much to start a fire."

"We'll restore power at the breaker when we leave," another firefighter said.

"And shoo the neighbors away as best we can," said the third.

"Thanks." Virgil smiled. "I sure don't want to deal with them right now."

Shortly after the firefighters left the house, the hall light came on.

"Breaker's back on. Now we can get to work," Sylvia hurried toward the bathroom. "I'll get towels to try to keep the water from spreading any farther."

Virgil slowly entered the room, his feet sloshing through water. His stomach lurched and a lump caught in his throat.

Damn. Virgil shook his head in disbelief. The table, which had been in his family for generations, looked like a total loss. The top was split down the middle. The two halves, both scorched to black, tipped away from each other. Years of regular linseed oil applications had left the table's surface highly flammable, allowing the relatively small fire to do severe damage. *Maybe I can restore it. I'll try, in honor of Mama's memory, if nothing else.*

The firefighters had wrenched open all the storage cabinets and saturated the contents. Everything not in a sealed bottle was ruined. Some of the bottles had fallen on the floor and shattered.

"Oh Virgil, I'm sorry." Sylvia came up behind him and put her arm around his waist.

"Thanks." His voice hitched. "It's my fault."

"Your fault?"

Virgil nodded. "It's my karmic backlash for Cotton. Maybe Tammy and Lisa, too."

"You can't know that. It's probably just an accident."

"No. I know. But if my action stops Cotton, it's worth it." His shoulders slumped. "I don't even know where to begin."

"I've put every towel around the doorway and in the hall. Some water's going to spread, but most will stay contained."

"I've got a shop vac in the garage. It'll suck up the water. I'll go get it." He returned a few minutes later, lugging the heavy vac.

"I'll plug it in." Sylvia unwound the cord and looked around.

"Use the outlet in the living room, to be on the safe side. Cord should be long enough."

Sylvia returned to the doorway after plugging in the vac. "I want to help, but these are the only clothes I have."

"You don't need to. It's my mistake."

"I want to." Sylvia crossed the room and put her hand on Virgil's arm. "Please. Let me help."

Virgil sighed, then smiled. "Thank you. I'll get you something."

Sylvia donned the sweat pants and T-shirt from Virgil, then they both got to work. They spent the next several hours vacuuming water and tossing ruined motif supplies into garbage bags. It was almost midnight when they shut the vac off for the last time.

Virgil looked around. "Still a mess."

"I know." Sylvia hugged him. "But we've done all we can do tonight. I'm exhausted. I can see you are, too."

"Yeah." Virgil's shoulders sagged. "Let's go to bed. I don't think even the stench will keep me from sleeping tonight."

"I know what you mean." Sylvia pushed her damp hair off her forehead. "I haven't been this tired in a long time."

In spite of their fatigue, they made slow, gentle love, then held each other tightly in the dark room. "I'm glad you were here. I love you." Virgil kissed Sylvia and stroked her hair.

"I love you, too. I'm sorry you lost your chancel."

"Let's hope it was worth it and that the motif stops Cotton."

(42)

Property may be destroyed and money may lose its purchasing power; but, character, health, knowledge, and good judgement will always be in demand under all conditions. ~Roger Babson

The phone woke Virgil at 7 Sunday morning. He sat up and rubbed his eyes.

"Who is it?" Sylvia mumbled, still half asleep.

Virgil glanced at the Caller ID. "It's Marshall." He clicked onto the call. "Hey. Sorry. I know I should have called you yesterday. It got complicated."

"Well?" Marshall asked. "What's up? Are the candles out?"

"Oh, they're out all right." Virgil hesitated. It was unlikely the Truth Seekers had any way to monitor his phone, but at this point he wasn't taking any chances. "Something happened. Come over. Bring Emma."

"I'll pick up Emma and donuts. Be there soon."

Virgil opened the door to their knock barely thirty minutes later. Both looked bleary-eyed and grumpy.

"Come on in. Sylvia's in the kitchen. She made strong coffee. I need more than tea this morning." Virgil took the box of donuts Emma held out.

Emma wrinkled her nose as soon as she stepped into the house. "What happened? This place stinks."

"Yeah, it does." Marshall narrowed his eyes. "You had a fire?"

Virgil nodded. "Come meet Sylvia, then I'll fill you in." He led them into the kitchen. "Sylvia, I'd like you to meet my friends, Marshall and Emma."

"It's nice to meet you both." Sylvia smiled and shook their hands. "I know Virgil was surprised and pleased to discover there were others like him."

The four quickly settled around the breakfast table, although no one spoke. They shifted awkwardly in their chairs, sipping hot coffee and nibbling on donuts.

After a couple of minutes, Emma yawned, then cleared her throat. "It takes a lot to get my ass out of bed this early on a weekend. Fill us in. Why's it smell like smoke?"

"My chancel burned up."

"What?" Marshall's mouth fell open.

"Yep. So I guess technically the motif is done and all the candles are out."

"Holy crap!" Emma put her hand to her mouth. "What happened?"

"We don't know," Sylvia said.

Virgil shrugged. "She's right. Maybe one of the candles fell over. Maybe one spat out a piece of burning wick. Maybe it just got too hot in there and the paper combusted."

"Too hot?" Sylvia asked. "Just how many candles did you light?"

"Twenty. That's the most candles I've ever burned at once."

"I wonder if the motif will still work." Marshall frowned.

"I don't know." Virgil shrugged and sighed. "Let's hope so. It sure didn't work in time for Stan."

"What about Stan?" Marshall asked.

"Who's Stan?" Emma asked.

Virgil filled them in on what had happened to the younger man, and Stan's insistence he'd seen Cotton.

Emma shook her head. "Let's hope he's the last."

"I hope so," Sylvia said. "That poor young man."

"So what do we do other than wait?" Marshall asked.

"Lay low, I guess. I have to go to Oak Creek and pick up my mother's chair and personal items. They needed her room, so they've already moved her things to a storage area."

Marshall shook his head. "That still sucks. Hard to believe Tammy would've pushed her that hard or scared her bad enough for her to die."

"What about Cotton?" Sylvia asked.

Virgil dropped his head and stared at his feet.

Emma narrowed her eyes. "What's she talking about, Virgil?"

Marshall eyed Virgil. "Virgil? What about Cotton?"

"I'm sorry." Virgil ran his hand through his hair. "I didn't say anything because I wanted any karmic backlash to be on me alone."

"What did you do?" Emma barked. "Did you mess with the charm?"

Virgil nodded and chewed his lip. "It was Cotton in Mama's case, too. He was there a few hours before she died."

"How can you be sure?" Marshall's voice was hard, accusing.

"One of Cotton's white hairs was on Pearl's pillow," Sylvia said.

Emma glared at Virgil. "And what did you do with this hair?"

"Burned it in the motif. After the two of you left the room. I didn't want either of you paying the price." Virgil looked down at his hands, his voice dropped to a whisper.

"That's why your chantry burned," Marshall said.

Virgil's shoulders sagged. "Probably. I knew there'd be karmic backlash. I was willing to pay the price, but like I said, I wanted to keep you two out of it. Please understand. I did it for Mama."

Silence descended on the table. Emma and Marshall stared at Virgil, frowning. Sylvia shifted nervously in her chair. Virgil closed his eyes. He didn't move.

After several minutes, Emma reached out and squeezed Virgil's arm, causing him to jump. He opened his eyes and looked at her.

"I get it." Emma sighed. "If it was my Mom, I'd probably have done the same thing. Nothing would piss me off more than to find out they'd messed with her."

Marshall sighed, too. "I appreciate you keeping us away from that part of the motif. And I guess I agree with Emma. I'd have been tempted as well."

"I just hope you didn't corrupt the charm." Emma frowned.

"Shouldn't." Virgil shook his head.

"Except for Cotton, since he was a specific target," Marshall said.

Sylvia let out a long breath. "I don't really understand any of this, but I'm glad both of you do."

Virgil smiled at Sylvia then turned to Emma and Marshall. "You've no idea how much that means to me. We've only recently gotten to know each other, but you two are the only people on this planet I've met who are like me. I'd hate to lose your friendship."

"Is there anything left of the diorama?" Marshall asked.

"There's nothing left of my chancel." Virgil waved toward the kitchen door. "The garage is full of garbage bags from our cleanup last night."

Emma stood. "I'd like to see the room."

Marshall stood and stretched. "I'm with Emma. I'd like to see the damage."

"You three go on." Sylvia shook her head. "I spent enough time in there last night. I'll clean up the kitchen."

Emma and Marshall followed Virgil. Everyone paused at the door.

"Holy shit. You're right. Not much left." Marshall stepped cautiously into the room. "Even your table burned."

Emma sighed. "Let's hope the charm still works and the price you paid was worth it. If so, things should happen soon."

"What now?" Marshall looked around the destroyed room. "I get we're in waiting mode, but what about the three of us?"

"Have an idea," Virgil said. "I'd like us to meet Monday morning, let's say seven, at Harold's for breakfast. For two reasons. First, we can see how Tammy behaves and find out how Lisa's doing. Second, if we're still being followed by Truth Seeker spies, it'll drive them crazy for us all to meet so brazenly in public."

"I love it!" Emma laughed. "Count me in."

"Why the hell not." Marshall nodded, then waved his arm around the room. "Something pleasant after all this trauma."

"I don't envy you having to rebuild your chapel," Emma said.

"If I even do." Virgil shrugged. "Not sure I want to right now."

"I'm sure you and Sylvia had an exhausting night. We'll get out of your hair." Marshall moved into the hall, with Emma close behind. They said goodbye to Sylvia, then left.

Virgil hugged Sylvia tight and closed his eyes. "I'm glad you met them, but I'm sorry it was under these circumstances."

"Me, too." Sylvia leaned her head on Virgil's shoulder. "You said something about going to Oak Creek. Do you want me to go?"

"I know you're probably anxious to check on Iggy. I'll be okay. You go on home."

"I do want to talk to Iggy. Thanks for understanding." She kissed him. "I love you. I'll call you later."

After she left, Virgil took a long hot shower, then changed into khaki slacks and a green polo shirt. He drove for the last time to Oak Creek.

He had to catch himself from walking past the nurses station directly to his mother's old room. Someone else might already be living there. He double-stepped, doing a little dance with his dolly, and stopped at the counter. He was glad it was Sunday and he didn't recognize either of the nurses. Maybe he'd stop by some other time and say a final goodbye to Nancy, but he wasn't up to that today.

"Good morning." One of the nurses stood and approached him. "May I help you?"

"My mother was Pearl Harris. I was told you'd moved her personal items into storage. I'd like to collect them."

"Of course." The nursed nodded. "Please follow me. And I'm so sorry for your loss."

"Thank you." Virgil dutifully followed the nurse down a wing on the opposite side from the one where his mother had lived. They stopped at the far end.

The nurse unlocked the door, flipped on the light, and stepped aside. "There's your mother's chair. Her personal items are in the boxes on the seat."

Virgil wheeled the dolly under the chair and strapped it in place. "Thank you again. For all you did for my mother. She wasn't ever able to tell me, but I could tell she was comfortable here."

"Thank you. I'll pass that word to the other nurses."

Virgil loaded the chair and boxes into his SUV and headed home. He unloaded the items, then promptly crawled into bed, where he slept for four hours. When he woke, it was late afternoon. Too late to work in his garden. Instead, he made himself a scotch and water and sat in his mother's chair.

I wish I knew my family. However many or few there are.

So much had changed. He thought about his childhood and all the lessons his mother had taught him about motifs, chants, and theurgy in general.

Her sternest lessons had been about ethics. Maybe he should have heeded her warnings. He smiled, remembering the first time she'd stopped him from doing a motif against a specific person.

He'd been tempted his senior year to create a motif to get even with the football coach, who'd called Virgil a *wimpy toothpick* and wouldn't let him try out for the team. Months of mononucleosis had left Virgil underweight and pale. By the time he was well, his six foot frame weighed only one hundred and forty pounds. He'd hoped playing football would get him back in shape. Instead, the coach had laughed him off the field. After that, everyone at school called him Toothpick.

His mother knew the minute he got home from tryouts that something was wrong. She coerced him into telling her what had happened. She'd talked him out of doing a motif.

"Vee, don't let others make you mad enough to use your gift to hurt someone," she'd said as she stroked his hair. "Don't take on that responsibility. Or danger."

Look at me now. Mama'd hate what I've become. I do motifs against others. I try to hurt them. And now, thanks to my karmic backlash, I've lost the table and all my supplies. Her supplies, too. He shook his head. *Oh hell. I even lost her journal. How would she feel? What would she think of me?*

He didn't want to think about the answers. He wiped a tear from the corner of his eye and threw back the rest of his drink. He moved to the kitchen and rinsed his glass, handling it so roughly he chipped the rim. He tossed it in the trash with a scowl.

I don't send people more than they're due. Cotton deserves whatever's coming his way. I'll take his karmic backlash. He pursed his lips and headed to bed, trying not to think about what he deserved because of what he'd done to Lisa.

(43)

Among mortals, second thoughts are wisest. ~Euripides

Virgil was the first to arrive at Harold's on Monday morning. He took his favorite booth and slid in the side facing the door. He'd barely settled in when Lisa hurried over.

"Virgil! Hi! Look, I'm back." Lisa's face was bright and happy, although a faint bruise still circled her neck just above her T-shirt.

"Lisa!" He slid from the booth and gave her a hug. "I'm glad to see you. I've been worried. How are you?" *I'm so sorry. I'll never be able to tell you how much I wish I could take it back.*

"I'm okay. Dr. Peters said I may never really remember what happened. That's fine with me. I don't think I want to know everything, anyway."

Virgil nodded. "Guess I can understand that. I'm so sorry."

"Thanks. At least I'm alive, and no permanent damage was done." Lisa grinned and returned to clearing tables.

Virgil slipped back into the booth. *I hope she's as okay psychologically as she seems. I don't want to be the cause of any long-term trauma for her.*

"Morning, Virgil." Tammy's words interrupted Virgil's musings, causing him to jump.

"Morning, Tammy. How are you today?"

She quickly glanced around, then slid into the booth across from him. She put her arms on the table and leaned toward Virgil, who subconsciously leaned forward in response. "Don't know who else to talk to. I need help." Her voice was barely audible.

Virgil hesitated then nodded. "What's up? What do you need? I'll help if I can."

"I'm worried about Cotton."

Now I didn't expect that! "What's going on?"

"He's gone nuts. He's giving everyone crazy orders. I think he's lost it."

"Okay, but what makes you say that? What's he ordering?"

"He's telling people to break into houses and search them. He wanted Warren to poison another member's dog after they refused to do what he said. I think he did something to Stan. I heard he's in the hospital. Almost got killed on a job site or something."

How much do I share? Must be careful. "I've heard some rumors, too. Wondered if they might be true." He paused and weighed his next words. "Stan's my neighbor. He was hurt. Badly. I saw him yesterday in the hospital."

Tammy's eyes grew big. "Oh no! What happened?"

Virgil told her about the forklift and blocks.

"It was Cotton, wasn't it?"

Virgil hesitated again, then nodded. "Stan's pretty sure."

"Virgil, what am I going to do? I'm scared to quit. I wish I'd never joined."

Virgil patted her arm. "Don't do anything yet. Hang in there. Please trust me."

Tammy stared at Virgil, lips pursed. "Okay. I'll wait for a bit. But if he asks me to do something like—"

"Don't say no. Answer as vaguely as possible. And let me know." He fished a wood-working card from his wallet and held it out. "Call me. I'll help however I can."

Tammy nodded and slid from the booth. "I will. Thank you. I was hoping I could count on you. In spite of what I said recently, I like you. And I feel like I can trust you."

"Thanks, Tammy. That means a lot. Be sure to—"

Before he could finish, Emma and Marshall walked up. Tammy's head swiveled between the three then stopped on Virgil. When he winked, she raised an eyebrow, but said nothing.

"Morning, Tammy. This is Emma." Marshall slid in opposite Virgil. Emma slid in beside him.

"Hey, Marshall. Hi, Emma." Tammy smiled, but her eyes were full of confusion.

Virgil debated, then signaled for everyone, including Tammy, to lean in. "Don't worry, Tammy. We're on your side. We're doing what we can to help."

Tammy nodded. "I'll get y'all some coffee."

"What was THAT about?" Emma whispered after Tammy left.

"Second thoughts." Virgil filled them in.

"My, my. Things are turning already." Marshall nodded. "That's great."

"He's the lynchpin of that group. If people rebel against him, it'll fall apart fast." Emma grinned.

Tammy returned with cups and a pot of coffee. She passed out menus, then leaned in again. "I know y'all are part of something. You two were already on the list, and Virgil was just added. But if you can help, thanks. I think Cotton is wrong. And he's gotten dangerous."

"We've got your back, Tammy. It's okay." Marshall gave her a thumbs up.

"Thanks, Marshall. Now, what'll y'all have?"

"You two sure she's okay?" Emma frowned in Tammy's direction after the waitress walked away with their orders.

"Yes, she's okay." Virgil nodded. "I've known her for several years. She just got sucked into something she thought was doing good. It happens to kind-hearted people. Look at Stan."

"Yeah, that's true." But Emma didn't look convinced.

Virgil signaled to Lisa, who was busy clearing an adjacent table.

"Lisa, this is my friend Emma. And you know Marshall."

"Hey, Lisa, nice to meet you." Emma smiled and offered her hand.

Lisa wiped hers on her apron, then shook hands. She waggled her fingers at Marshall. "Hi, Marshall."

"I'm sure glad to see you." He grinned and waggled his fingers right back.

As soon as Lisa walked off, Virgil whispered. "She's going to be okay. I can't tell you two how glad I am about that."

"I'll bet. And no more stupid mistakes like that." Emma shook her finger at Virgil.

"Deal. Besides, I have no place to do another motif even if I wanted to."

The three spent the rest of breakfast talking about their childhoods, avoiding mystical topics in case anyone overheard. They were finishing up when Virgil glanced around.

"Wonder if our spies are in here. Doesn't look like any of the tables have the same faces as when I came in."

Emma smirked. "Maybe they're stuck sitting in hot cars outside."

"Would serve 'em right." Marshall stared at his coffee. "Cotton's pawns. They shouldn't have agreed to be spies in the first place."

"People can be easily manipulated when you prey on their fears." Virgil shrugged. "But maybe they're not out there. Maybe they're finally tired of Cotton's demands. Maybe our spies are at home where they belong."

"Hope so." Emma stood and tossed a ten on the table. "Well, I'm off. A bunch of us are going swimming at San Pedro Springs."

"Where's that?" Marshall asked.

"Near San Antonio College. A little north of downtown."

Virgil smiled. "Haven't been there in over thirty years. Mom took me there after we moved to Lichen. But don't you work today?"

"I go in at four. Late shift today." She waved. "See y'all later! Text me if anything happens."

The two older men stared after her, then looked at one another. "Wish I was still that young and free spirited." Marshall grinned.

"Yeah, but I'd rather be retired than working the late shift."

"Shit!" Marshall looked at his watch. "Speaking of late. I should have been on my route an hour ago." He picked up Emma's ten. "We decided when we came in that breakfast is on us. We used your candles and supplies. And now you've lost everything."

"No need for that! And the loss is my own fault."

"Yeah, yeah. Just shut up and say thanks."

Virgil grinned. "Thanks."

As soon as Virgil was alone at the table, Tammy returned to sit opposite him. She pushed the dirty dishes aside and leaned on the table as before. "Are y'all sorcerers?"

"No." Virgil shook his head. "We simply know how to have... influence. That's all I can say for now. You'll just have to trust me."

Tammy studied his face. Virgil didn't move and kept his expression blank. Finally, Tammy's shoulders slumped. "Okay. But I'm not used to trusting blindly."

"Not generally a good idea, I admit." Virgil nodded. "But it's the best I can do."

Tammy sighed and nodded.

"I have to ask you a question." Virgil stared hard at Tammy. "If I don't, it's always going to bother me. And I really want an honest answer."

"Okay." Tammy's voice was hesitant. Nervous.

"Why did you visit my mother? Did Cotton tell you to?"

Tammy caught her breath, and she squeezed her eyes shut. "Yes. He made me. I didn't do anything to her. Honest! I just visited and asked her if she could tell me about you. About what you were up to. About what you could do. To others."

"She wouldn't answer you, even if she could still talk that well."

"I figured that before I even went. She's your mother. I tried to talk Cotton out of it, but he insisted. There were three of us still at the meeting when he gave the order. I volunteered because I knew I wouldn't be mean or do anything to scare or hurt her."

"But you did."

"Did what? Hurt her?" Tammy's hand flew to her mouth. "Please tell me that's not true."

"No, you didn't hurt her. But you did scare her."

Tears welled in Tammy's eyes. "Virgil, I'm so sorry. I didn't even want to scare her. I was just scared myself, scared of Cotton."

Virgil frowned. "I guess Cotton wasn't satisfied with your visit. He went there the next night. "

"Oh no." Tammy shook her head. "He's a terrible man. What happened? How's your mom? He didn't do anything to her, did he?"

"She's dead."

Tammy dropped her head into her hands and began to cry. "Oh God. Oh God. Oh God. I'm so sorry. I'd have lied to him if I thought even for a minute he'd go there on his own. What did he do to her?"

"I doubt we'll ever find out. If he did anything, it wasn't obvious enough for the doctor to notice. And no autopsy was ordered."

"I should've quit already. After I left your mother, I should've called Cotton and told him I quit. Instead I just gave him my report. I told him she couldn't talk and probably didn't know anything anyway. I realize now, even trying to tell him anything was a total waste of time."

"Quitting would have been dangerous to you."

"Yeah. I'm really afraid of him."

"Why'd he start the Truth Seekers? Why does he hate what he calls sorcerers so much?"

"I don't know." Tammy shrugged. "He didn't exactly confide in us members. I do know something happened in his past. Something about his daughter. I don't know what, though exactly."

Virgil nodded. "You can see the level of hate and anger in his eyes. Might explain things if it was family related."

Tammy's phone buzzed in her pocket. She pulled it out and blanched as she read the screen. She held it up for Virgil. "Here's what he wants now. I can't do it. I won't do it."

Virgil read the text message from Cotton:

> Need you to follow Lisa home. Be sure she doesn't know anything about what happened to her. Or remember who she saw.

Virgil sat back. "What's that mean? Did he have something to do with Lisa's attack?"

"I don't know, but it scares me even more than I already was." Tammy bit her lip. "Should I go to the police?"

"Think you should? I remember seeing a local police office at the meeting I attended. I wondered at the time if he was a member or a plant."

"That's right, one Truth Seeker is a police officer! And no, he's not a plant, at least as far as I know."

"Better not go to them, then." Virgil shook his head.

Tammy started crying again. "I always thought Lisa was just at the wrong place at the wrong time, and some asshole took advantage. But after this text from Cotton... I don't like it. Not one bit." Tammy slid from the booth, wiping her eyes as she stood.

"Neither do I." *Let's hope that burnt hair causes a response soon.* "Don't go to the police. And don't quit yet. Trust me. Soon you won't have anything to worry about."

"Okay, Virgil. I'll hang in there. For you. For your mom." She turned to walk away then turned back. "But whatever you're going to do, please do it soon. I can't take much more of this."

"It won't be long," Virgil said. He left Harold's intending to head home, but instead turned toward the liquor store. *I think I need reinforcements. It's been a helluva day.*

(44)

*Happy families are all alike; every unhappy
family is unhappy in its own way.*
~Leo Tolstoy (1828-1910), Anna Karenina

The OPEN light blinked on just as Virgil pulled up to Lichen Liquor. *Good, won't be anyone else here but Frank. Not really feeling chatty after this morning.*

"Morning, Mr. Harris," Frank said when Virgil entered. "Haven't seen you in a while. I have some nice specials on all our wines from Enchanted Rock Winery."

"Morning, Frank." Virgil nodded to the owner. "I need a couple bottles of merlot. And maybe a bottle of pinot noir." He walked to the red wine aisle without further comment. Juggling his three wine selections, he headed for the checkout, then froze. *Cotton. Dammit.*

The white-haired man had just come through the door. Virgil retreated to the back of the store to wait until the other man left. He peeked between the bottles on the top shelf, hoping to keep an eye on Cotton's whereabouts. *Where'd he go? Did he leave? I didn't hear the door.*

"Well, well, well."

Virgil jumped and almost dropped his wine. He wheeled and found himself face to face with Cotton.

"Here for some bottled bravery?" Cotton sneered. "Or do you get some of your sorcerer's supplies here?"

"I'm not a sorcerer." Virgil inwardly grimaced at his defensive response, then something in him snapped. *Enough. Enough of this bullshit.* "Leave me alone. I'm sick of your lies and your bullshit."

Cotton's eyes narrowed. "All of you are alike. You can dish it out, but you can't take it. We have ways of dealing with those who try to harm the good people of Lichen. Or hurt honorable families."

In spite of his anger, Virgil laughed. "That's funny coming from you. Just what the hell is your problem, anyway?" *Let's see if I can get any real answers.*

Cotton's face turned red, and his temples pulsed with rage. "My problem? You. Your kind. Destroying other people's lives with your evil magic."

"What lives? What evil magic?" Virgil shook his head. "What are you talking about?"

"I'll tell you what I'm talking about. You sorcerers are out to destroy good people everywhere."

"I was hoping to figure out what the hell's going on. The Truth Seekers. Your hatred of these supposed sorcerers. But you aren't making any sense."

"You're as bad as that piece of shit Brandon. He said the same thing. But he was evil. He didn't want to hear the truth."

There was no Brandon on the list. "Brandon who?"

"Like you don't know. You all probably keep in touch. Planning your takeover."

"Cotton, I have no idea what you're carrying on about." Virgil shook his head again. *I almost feel sorry for the guy.* "What the hell would sorcerers be taking over? And why?"

"Evil doesn't need a reason other than to destroy good." Cotton's face pinched. "Heather was a good Christian girl. It's Brandon's fault. All his fault."

"Brandon who?" Virgil asked again. "And Heather who? And what do either of them have to do with the Truth Seekers?"

Cotton continued his rant as if he hadn't heard Virgil. "I raised her right. She respected her parents. Went to church. Until she went away to college and met Brandon." Spittle flew from Cotton's mouth when he said the man's name.

Heather is his daughter! Tammy was right. But where've I heard the name Brandon? Why is it familiar? Then he remembered. *Oh hell!* "Are you talking about Brandon Welker?"

"Evil sorcerer. Stole my baby girl. Convinced her to go against me. To give up her faith. Abandon her family. I demanded she obey her father. That she come home. To save her soul. Instead she cut me off. Said she never wanted to see me again."

Virgil laughed and shook his head. "You demanded your adult daughter come home? And you expected her to just do it? You can't blame Brandon for her reaction."

"The hell I can't!" Cotton's eyes bulged. "She was raised to honor her parents. He probably put some spell on her. Turned her against her own family. Against me."

"Brandon and your daughter have their own life now. Just let it go. Or tell her you're sorry you tried to control her. Sounds like you owe her an apology."

"Apology? For what? Trying to save her from evil? From hell?"

"Good grief, Cotton. She married someone you don't like. It happens. Get over it. Stop blaming others. Stop looking for demons, or sorcerers, or whateverthehell, under every rock.

"You bastard. You know nothing. You're evil, too. You're one of them. I'll get you all."

So that's why Cotton chose Lichen. Marshall's here. Wonder where Brandon and Heather live now? Why isn't Cotton there? "Instead of going after Marshall and everyone else you want to blame, why not go to your daughter? It's never too late to make things right."

"You think I haven't tried to contact her? Brandon keeps them on the move. I've never even seen my grandkids. I tried to get the little ones away. To save them. I couldn't save Heather. Brandon's sorcery ruined her. But I still wanted to save their innocent children. Now I can't even find them."

"Look, I'm sorry about your daughter, but that's no reason to try destroying everyone you think might be like your son-in-law. People you've just decided are evil."

"You all ARE evil. The Truth Seekers will prove it."

Virgil shook his head. "Your Truth Seekers are finding out who you really are. Your little group is falling apart. Count on it. And it won't be long now."

Cotton's face turned hard and mean. "You can't hurt the Truth Seekers. I'll never let you damned sorcerers win. I'll do whatever I have to do."

"Like you did with Stan?" Virgil leaned in, almost going nose-to-nose with Cotton. "What'd he do to you other than decide he didn't want to play your games anymore?"

"You shut up. And get the hell away from me." Cotton shoved Virgil hard.

Virgil stumbled and dropped a bottle of wine. It shattered on the floor, spraying red liquid over both men and the nearby shelves.

"What's going on back there?" Frank yelled.

Virgil heard the store owner heading their way.

"You watch yourself. I know where you live." Cotton turned and stormed down the aisle, shoving past Frank, who slipped on the wet floor and nearly fell. Cotton slammed through the door as he left.

"You okay, Mr. Harris?" Frank touched Virgil on the arm, startling him back to his surroundings.

"I'm... I'm fine, Frank." Virgil shook his head to clear it. "I'm sorry about the mess. Please let me help you clean it up."

"Nonsense. Mornings are quiet." Frank glanced toward the door. "At least usually. Cleaning up will give me something to do. Let me get a towel so you can get some of the wine off your clothes and shoes."

"Okay. Thanks."

While Frank retrieved a towel from the back, Virgil took several deep breaths. His heart pounded in his chest. His temples pulsed. He'd stood his ground during the altercation with Cotton, but Virgil wasn't a fighter. He'd always used motifs instead of direct confrontation. As he calmed down, he thought about what he'd learned.

It finally makes sense. Marshall was the first name on the list. Emma said he was the reason Cotton started the list in the first place. Cotton's daughter married Marshall's son. Cotton couldn't find his daughter, but he found where Marshall lived.

Virgil accepted the towel Frank brought and patted the front of his pants and the tops of his shoes. When he held the towel out, Frank shook his head.

"Toss it on the floor. I'll use it to wipe up some of the spilled wine."

Virgil nodded and dropped the towel. "I still want these." He held out the two remaining bottles of wine. "And I need another bottle of merlot. I'll grab it on my way to the front."

"Yes, sir. I'll meet you at the counter." Frank took the two bottles from Virgil. "Guess I won't ever be paid for the jug of bourbon Cotton just left with."

Virgil glanced toward the door. "I'm sorry. I'd be happy to—"

"Don't even think about it. One bottle of booze will be a small price to pay if it keeps him from ever coming back here again."

Virgil moved up the red wine aisle and selected another bottle of merlot. His hand shook when he reached for it. He closed his eyes and again focused on taking several slow breaths. *Cotton got to me more than I realized. I've never met anyone as filled with rage and hate as he his. That makes him one of the most dangerous people I've ever met, too. Hope our motif works soon.*

As an afterthought, Virgil cut across two aisles and grabbed a fifth of scotch. *Think I'm gonna need this, too. And after I tell Sylvia about this morning, she's gonna want to join me. Probably Marshall, too.*

(45)

Look forward rather than backward. A story can
drag on forever. You must put a period at the end of
an experience. You must bring closure to it and experience
when it is over. ~Iyanla Vanzant

Virgil found Sylvia in his backyard when he got home. "Hello there!" He called from the kitchen door. "Thirsty?"

She stood and rolled up her tape measure. "Sure am!"

"Looks like you've gotten started." He stepped aside as she entered the kitchen.

"Not really." She crossed to the sink to wash her hands. "I'm marking the areas with orange landscape paint. You'll be able to see how it looks in the actual space compared to the plans."

As soon as she turned off the water, he put his arms around her and kissed her. "Sounds great. I'm glad you're here. Maybe a pretty yard will distract from how rank the house is right now."

"I'm glad I'm here, too." She patted her wet hands on his shirt, then wrinkled her nose. "But it is pretty stinky."

Virgil nodded. "Yeah. I'll call one of those fire restoration companies. Have them get rid of the smoke and water damage.

Figure I'll also have them repair the fire damage in the chancel, too."

"Good idea. You'd never get it all done by yourself. And it's not a pleasant place to live right now."

"I know." Virgil frowned. "I guess you won't be moving in."

Sylvia shook her head. "You know that's not practical at the moment." She kissed his nose. "It'll work out."

"Sure." Virgil stared out the window at the barren backyard. "It's part of my karmic backlash. Although I hate to think you're caught up in it."

"I'm part of your life now." Sylvia turned Virgil's face back to hers. "Of course things that happen to you are going to affect me."

He hugged her tight, then stepped back to arm's length. "Thanks for not giving up on me."

"Not yet." She winked but almost immediately turned serious. "How'd it go this morning?"

"Let me get us something to drink and I'll fill you in."

"Sounds good. What do you have in mind?"

"Hot tea? Sweet tea? Scotch? Wine?"

"Speaking of wine, why do you smell like it?" She pointed to the bottles on the counter. "And I see you went shopping for it, too, among other things. Obviously, more's happened than breakfast with your new friends. Pour us a glass of the merlot. I don't care what time of day it is. It'll soften whatever news you're getting ready to share."

He poured them each a generous glass of the deep red wine and they sat at the breakfast table. He began by repeating what Tammy said earlier that morning. Sylvia's eyes grew large as he spoke. When he told her about the text message from Cotton, her mouth fell open.

"Good grief! He's behind every damn bad thing that's happened."

"Sure seems like it." He shook his head. "There's more."

"Still?" Sylvia took a large gulp of wine. "Okay, let's have it."

Virgil related his encounter with Cotton at the liquor store.

"Oh my God. His daughter ran off with Marshall's son? So that's why he's so angry. At least he backed off confronting you when he did. He might have really hurt you!"

"I'm not sure he would have backed off if Frank hadn't come to see what the noise was."

Sylvia kissed Virgil. "I love you. I don't want anything to happen to you." She lowered her hand and dropped her eyes. "I'm ashamed to say it, but this actually makes me glad you burned that white hair in the motif."

Virgil wiped a tear from Sylvia's eye. "Don't feel ashamed. Cotton deserves whatever's coming to him. I don't send people karma they don't deserve."

Sylvia looked up into Virgil's eyes. "He does need to be stopped. I guess you stopping him is as good a way as any."

"I'm tired of talking about Cotton and the Truth Seekers." Virgil waved toward the window. "How about you show me your plans!"

"Sounds like a great idea. And I'd love to." She retrieved the roll of papers from the patio table and unrolled the thick bundle on the breakfast table. "Ta-da!"

Virgil smiled at the intricate design. "Hand-drawn. Old school. I like it."

"No choice." Sylvia laughed. "Don't know any of the new high-tech software tools. And I always loved drawing by hand anyway. It made the design more real for me."

"This looks great. I really like how you coiled the plant beds toward the fountain, as if it had spiraled out of them."

Sylvia beamed. "You noticed! I hoped you would."

Virgil kissed her again. "You do seem to have me figured out more than I'd expect so soon. Should I be scared of YOUR powers?"

"Maybe." She winked.

"Think I need a refill." He topped off both their glasses with the last of the bottle.

"I'll be tipsy by lunch."

"Who cares? It's been a helluva week."

"Can't argue with that."

Instead of again sitting at the breakfast table, Sylvia headed to the living room. She curled up on the sofa and patted the cushion beside her. "It's my turn to update you."

"Good news, I hope." Virgil sat close and put his hand on her thigh. "I don't think I can take more of the other kind."

Sylvia nodded. "Iggy's quitting the Truth Seekers. He's tired of playing spy. As far as he could see, his target wasn't doing a damn thing wrong."

"Who's he following?"

"Brent Palmer. Recognize the name?"

"From the list, but I don't know him. I wonder if he's another like me, Marshall, and Emma? I'm not up to finding out at the moment, though. I've got enough strangeness going on in my life."

"Including me?"

Virgil grinned. "You're the only normalcy I seem to have at the moment."

"Normalcy?" Sylvia winked. "But I thought I was special."

"More than I can describe. And you're also the one constant in what's recently been a pretty chaotic life."

"I knew what you meant, but it was nice of you to clarify."

"You're terrible!" Virgil laughed. "Anyway, that's good news about Iggy." They clinked glasses in a toast, then Virgil continued, "I hope Cotton doesn't give him any trouble. Tammy was worried Cotton would go after everyone who quit."

"I don't think Cotton will. Iggy told me half a dozen members all said they're quitting. Cotton can't possibly go after everyone."

"I hope not. And the universe should make its move soon, anyway."

"There's more." Sylvia stared at her wine as she swirled her glass.

"Oh?" Virgil couldn't read the tone of her voice.

"Iggy called his dad. Oscar may be a bastard, but he actually agreed to help Iggy go back to school. He's gonna become a licensed electrician."

"That's great! A good future for him, and you won't have to worry anymore."

She looked up and smiled. "I was going to put the house on the market, since I was moving in here, but I guess I'll postpone that for now. I did call an attorney this morning. I'm filing for divorce. No matter what happens with us, I want to move forward."

In one quick move, Virgil set both their glasses on the coffee table and swept Sylvia into his arms. "I love you."

Sylvia's laugh was bubbly and light. "And I love you, too."

Virgil stood and led her down the hall. They made fierce love, opening up and sharing their deepest desires. Afterward, they napped, and didn't stir until the sun was perched on the horizon, painting the sky in shades of pink, orange, and gold.

Sylvia rolled over and stretched. "This isn't helping me get your yard done. It's still a disaster."

Virgil stroked the curve of her side and hip. He gently touched the scar on her breast, a permanent reminder of the cancer she'd fought. "No, but you're healing other areas. Even parts of me I had no clue were damaged. I've kept a lot of things locked in dark places since Mama was attacked. Now that she's gone, I guess it's time to open up and release them to the universe."

"I'm glad I'm a part of that."

Sylvia scooted into a sitting position and leaned against the headboard. "Why don't you move in with me?"

Virgil sat up and leaned on the headboard beside her. "Are you sure? What about Iggy?"

"I'm sure." Sylvia rested her head on Virgil's shoulder. "Come over tomorrow, and you can help me make room for your things. And as for Iggy, it's my house. He can either accept it or get an apartment again."

"That's sweet of you." Virgil kissed the top of Sylvia's head. "How about if I plan on bringing only a few things, just to see how it works out."

"It's either going to work or it's not, no matter where your things are located. Let's plan on you bringing everything. Let's assume the best."

Virgil grinned. "I'm afraid you don't know what you're getting yourself into. You've seen the amount of stuff I have. You could be going to a lot of effort to squeeze me in, only to throw me out a few months from now."

"Don't think like that. Too many people wait for things to be perfect, or the time to be just right. Most of the time that never happens. Let's start our next phase now, instead of putting it off."

Virgil smiled. "Okay. Why not?"

Sylvia climbed out of bed. "Come on, let's shower, then I'll describe in agonizing detail what I'm going to do to your yard."

They spent an hour looking over the plans Sylvia had drawn. She insisted on explaining her reasons for each plant selection. "You realize I'm not going to let you pay me now that we're lovers."

"Out of the question." Virgil shook his head. "You'll still need your own money. I never want you to feel beholden. I want you with me because it's your choice."

"Fair enough." Sylvia smiled. "I hadn't thought of it like that. I just don't want you to—"

The ringing of the phone interrupted. "Hello? That's good news." Virgil gave Sylvia a thumbs up. "Yes, I'll accept. Let me know what else you need from me."

Sylvia raised her eyebrows. "And?"

"The realtor got an offer on Mama's house. Only a couple thousand less than asking price."

"That's wonderful! But I'm also sort of sorry. It's another closure for you."

"A big one." Virgil nodded and silently stared out the window for a minute. "I grew up in that house. At least since I was eight." He put his arms around Sylvia and kissed her forehead. "But it's okay. I'm trying to look down the road. At a new future. This is one more burden released."

Sylvia wiggled out of his arms. "I'm going home tonight. I want to talk to Iggy before you come over. How about you come around ten in the morning? Iggy'll be as ready as he's going to be."

"I'll miss you, but I understand. I'll stop on the way for donuts, as a peace offering, or a bribe, or whatever." Virgil laughed. "What's Iggy's favorite? What's yours?"

"Why not? Can't hurt." Sylvia smiled and nodded. "Maple iced for him. Cinnamon twist for me."

After she was gone Virgil poured a glass of scotch, hoping it would help him relax and sleep. He sat in his mother's chintz chair and stared out at the front yard. The outlines of his roses were skeletons in the darkness.

His mother was gone. Her house was sold. Probably in the next few days her ashes would be delivered. The big motif with Marshall and Emma seemed to be working. Iggy was coming around. Tammy was, too. Stan was alive and safe in the hospital. Lisa was recovering and had no painful memories of what had happened. The Truth Seekers were mutinying against Cotton. The loss of his chancel seemed a small price to pay.

Where do I go from here? My house isn't livable right now. But is moving in with Sylvia the right next step? I love Sylvia. We're happy together.

How long had he and Sylvia known each other? Only a few weeks. Their relationship had moved like lightning. He knew that sometimes things happened that way. Maybe he should be worried, but he wasn't. Not really. Being with Sylvia felt right.

What's the worst that can happen? It doesn't work out. We're adults. We aren't going to be having any babies. Our decisions are ours alone. If it doesn't work out, we'll simply go our separate ways.

Still, something felt off. It was as if his life was moving down the road in the right direction, but he was in the wrong lane. He closed his eyes to concentrate.

What's bothering me? Is it, after all, how fast things have moved with Sylvia? Or is it just so much loss and guilt in my own life?

His eyes snapped open.

Of course! The motif. I'm caught in my own motif. I've been one of the causes recently of pain and suffering in this town. I was worried about karmic backlash. Never occurred to me that the motif would work directly on me, that I'd be one of the direct targets.

An idea slowly formed in his mind. He turned it over, examining it. It felt like the right way to get back in the proper lane of his life. To balance his own karma. Would Sylvia agree? Would he abandon his plan if she said no? He hoped she'd say yes. He wanted her with him as he took the next step in his own life.

I'll ask her tomorrow.

(46)

I have enjoyed greatly the second blooming...suddenly you find—at the age of 50, say—that a whole new life has opened before you. ~Agatha Christie (1890-1976)

Virgil didn't awaken until after eight Tuesday morning. He stared at the ceiling, thinking about how much had changed in such a short time. Some good. Some bad. He now walked a new, uncharted path.

Big day today. Best get started. Already stayed in bed too long. Besides, I'm starving. I don't remember eating anything after breakfast yesterday.

He showered and dressed quickly, then sat at the breakfast table with his morning tea and a breakfast of eggs, toast, and sausage, looking over the landscape plans once again. No matter how Sylvia responded to his idea, or where they ultimately ended up, the house would still need a nice backyard.

The phone rang as he was chewing the last bite. "Hello?"

"It's Marshall. You won't believe what's happened."

"Well, don't make me guess." Virgil tapped his foot.

"Cotton's dead."

Virgil retrieved the phone after dropping it on the floor. He held it to his ear with a shaking hand. "What? When? How?"

Marshall barked a harsh laugh. "Figured that'd get you going. I stopped by Harold's at six for a cup of coffee. Lots of packages today, so figured I'd get an early start. Tammy practically tackled me as I walked in."

"What'd she say?"

"The fire department's calling it an accident. He—"

"Fire department?"

"Yeah. His house burned down last night."

"Holy cow!" Virgil sat down heavily at the table. "How's that an accident?"

"Tammy says he'd been drinking. Pissed at so many people quitting on him."

"How would she know?"

"He made several drunk calls, including to her. Threatening. Pleading. Trying to strike bargains. No one took the bait. She said he was sloppy drunk when he called her around ten last night."

"Okay, but still. How'd the fire start? Why didn't he get out?"

"No solid answers yet, but the neighbors saw it happen. Or at least the tail end of it. Fire started somewhere in the main part of the house, trapping Cotton in his bedroom."

"Wait. Slow down. How'd the neighbors get involved?"

"Let me start over. All this is from Tammy, but I'll tell it to you like she told it to me."

"Good, because I'm confused as hell."

Marshall's voice was raspy and tired. "Neighbors heard screaming around midnight. They rushed over and found Cotton trying to break his bedroom window, yelling that he was trapped. That his bedroom doorknob was red hot, so he couldn't get out."

"*Trying* to break? How hard could it be? I don't understand."

"Paranoid freak Cotton had installed wire mesh glass windows, so he was only able to break out small bits here and there."

"Wire mess glass? What the hell is that?"

"You know, that glass that looks like it has chicken wire embedded in it."

"Oh shit, like we had in school windows when I was a kid," Virgil said. "Nothing breaks that."

"Exactly. And to top it off, he'd put burglar bars on all the windows, too. The permanent kind, not the kind removes easily. So the neighbors couldn't get to the glass to help break it out."

Virgil shook his head. "Figures. Caught in his own trap."

"Yeah. Anyway, the neighbors tried to get the bars off. One of them ran home for a hacksaw. But before he came back, Cotton collapsed from smoke inhalation. Not long after, the bedroom door gave way. The flashover consumed the room in seconds."

"Oh no."

"I know. The fire department got there, but it was too late."

"At least Cotton was out when the fire reached the room." Virgil closed his eyes. *Not much of a blessing. He's still dead.*

"Yeah. Neighbors said right before he collapsed he started screaming that it was the sorcerers' fault."

Virgil put his head in his hands. *It was the sorcerers. In a way. It was me. I killed him as surely as if I'd lit that fire myself.*

"You there?" Marshall sounded worried.

"Yeah." Virgil cleared his throat. "Yes. I'm here. Sorry. Just a little shocked. And feeling guilty."

"Shocked is right. But don't feel guilty. I might not have agreed at the time, but I do think you did the right thing with that hair. The universe decides exactly how to carry out a diorama's intent."

"Yeah, I guess. Thanks." Virgil paused. "Tammy okay?"

"She was freaking out. Alternating between crazy relief and paranoia that someone might be after all of them. Took a while to calm her down. Come to think of it, I never did get my coffee."

"Want to stop by for a cup? Do you have time?"

"Nah, but thanks. I need to call Emma, too. But since you were the one who burned his hair, I figured you'd want to hear it first."

"I really didn't intend for him to die in a fire. Though I did say he deserved justice for pushing Mama over the edge to her own death." *If I'm honest with myself, I can't say I'm sorry, but I also can't admit that to Marshall.*

"I'm not pointing fingers. I really do think you did the right thing. Hopefully your chantry burning down is all the karmic backlash you're going to get."

"Yeah, let's hope." Virgil shook his head. "Oh, I almost forgot. I learned what Cotton's problem was. Or at least what started his original hatred of the so-called sorcerers."

"No shit! So what was it? Someone do a diorama on him?"

"Close, but no cigar. A sorcerer stole his daughter away from him. Led her astray."

"What do you mean *stole*? Like, kidnapped?"

"No. Like, love. She went away to college and fell in love with a young man who had our same ability. When Cotton ordered her home, she told him instead she never wanted to see him again."

"Guess that'd make any parent mad. But seems it sent Cotton off the deep end."

"Yep. Want to know who this evil young man was?"

"Doesn't really matter, does it?"

"Oh, I think it does." Virgil chuckled. "His name's Brandon."

When there was no response for almost a minute, Virgil continued. "Marshall? You there? You okay?"

"Yeah." Marshall's voice was strained. "My son? You're telling me all this started because my son married Heather?"

"Something like that. You didn't know she was Cotton's daughter?"

Marshall's laugh was harsh. "Not a damn clue. She refused to talk about her family. Especially her father. And I never knew Cotton's last name anyway."

"Sounds like your son did a good thing, getting her away from Cotton. And keeping your grandkids away from him. He didn't just suddenly turn mean and hateful. I'll bet he had it in him all along."

"Probably." Marshall blew out a ragged breath. "Thanks for telling me. I guess. Hard to believe I'm even related to Cotton, even if just through our kids' marriage. Wow. Gonna have to think on this for a while."

"Take care. Call if you want."

"Later." Marshall clicked off, leaving Virgil staring at his phone. He noticed it was after 9:30. *Gotta hurry!*

He cleaned up the kitchen and headed for Sylvia's.

Iggy answered the door and smiled. "Hey man. Come on in. Mom's goin' crazy in her bathroom."

"Hi, Iggy. I hear you're going back to school. Congratulations!" Virgil held out his hand.

This time, Iggy gave a firm, but not crushing, shake. "Thanks. Always liked electrical stuff. Seems it's time to move on, ya know?"

"I do, indeed." Virgil grinned. "Moving on can be the best thing in the world."

"Mom seems happy." Iggy's grin morphed into a straight, grim line. "She told me about you moving in here. That's cool, but you don't hurt her. You hear me?"

Virgil grew serious. "I promise you that. I hope we're the happiest couple on earth for the rest of our lives. But if it doesn't work out, if she wants to return to living on her own, I won't be an asshole. I'll pack up and move out."

"That's cool." Iggy's grin returned. "But I'm holdin' ya to it."

Virgil nodded. "Any good son would." *Looks like the motif is working on Iggy, too. He's a changed young man.*

"I thought I heard your voice!" Sylvia entered the room with an armful of bath towels. She dropped them on the sofa then gave Virgil a quick hug.

He wanted to kiss her, but held off in front of her son.

She turned to Iggy. "I sure don't need fifteen bath towels. Take what you want. But these were expensive. Promise you won't use them to scrub your car."

Both Iggy and Virgil laughed. "Deal, Mom. I'll go through them later. I gotta run some errands right now." Iggy glanced at his mother and then Virgil before heading for the door.

As soon as Iggy was gone, Sylvia gave Virgil a long kiss.

Virgil cleared his throat. "Got any scotch?"

"What?"

"Kidding. Mostly."

Sylvia studied his face. "Come sit down. Tell me what's happened this time."

Virgil told her about his phone call from Marshall.

"Oh my." She shook her head. "Oh my," she said again.

"I guess I'm responsible." Virgil sighed.

"You are not!" Sylvia's voice was so sharp it made Virgil jump. "No matter what you did with that hair, he made his own bed. You said you only wished for justice, right?"

Virgil nodded. *What did I say that night? What did I really wish for? Oh yes, 'May death find you as you brought it to my mother.'*

He hadn't just wished for justice. He'd wished for Cotton's death. It was the first time he'd ever wished for someone to die. He hadn't even done that to the men who'd beaten his mother.

But I can't tell that to Sylvia. She means too much to me. I don't want her to hate me. And I swear I'll never do it again. No wonder the motif is working on me, compelling me to leave Lichen. I've become a killer.

Sylvia took his hand. "It's all right. He was an evil man. Now he can't hurt anyone again. Whether you had anything to do with that or not, justice has been done. And I still love you."

Virgil's heart melted. Sylvia looked at him with the most love he'd ever seen from anyone but his mother. "I love you, too."

No time like the present, Virgil. Go on. Do it. He cleared his throat. "I'd like to propose a change of plans."

Sylvia frowned. "Are you… Do you not…"

"No, no! I'm not trying to tell you I don't want to move in. Well, I am sort of, but not really." He edged closer to her on the sofa until their thighs were touching. "I want you to go with me."

"With you?" Sylvia cocked her head. "Where? What are you talking about?"

"Too much has happened here," Virgil said. "Mama's death. Finding out there are others like me. The group motif we did together. The Truth Seekers rise and fall. Mama's house selling. My screw-up with Lisa. My chancel burning down. And especially Cotton's death. I need to get away from here, at least for a while. I need to do some serious soul searching. But I want you with me."

"Where do you want to go?" Sylvia touched Virgil's cheek. He leaned into her touch and closed his eyes.

"I want to go back to Alpine. To where I was born. I lived there with my parents until Dad died. That's where my grandmother lived until she died."

"Alpine? You mean out in West Texas?" Sylvia put her hand to her chest. "Wow."

"Yeah, West Texas. I want to scatter Mama's ashes in the desert there."

Sylvia smiled. "That sounds like a wonderful thing to do. How long do you want to stay?"

Virgil sat back in his chair. "Several months."

"Months?" Sylvia's eyes widened. "Why so long?"

"I want to look for my roots. If I have any other relatives, that's the place to start. I need to get back on a good path. I've fallen away from the lessons Mama taught me about how to use, or more important, how NOT to use, my ability. I don't like what I've become. Neither would she. I need a fresh start."

"I guess I can see that. Nothing like returning to the source to cleanse the soul." Sylvia stared into Virgil's eyes. "What aren't you telling me? This new idea sure came up fast."

"I decided…it's just that…" Virgil sighed. "I think I'm caught by the motif Marshall, Emma, and I did. I've become one of the bad influences the motif was designed to remove from Lichen. Pretty sure that's why I have an overwhelming drive to leave, at least for a while."

Sylvia laughed, then sobered. "Sorry. I know it's not funny. But for someone new to all this, the irony is almost too much."

"Irony is right." Virgil shook his head. "It never occurred to me that when we did a motif on the whole town, I'd end up one of the targets."

"Target sounds so harsh." Sylvia kissed Virgil's cheek. "I shouldn't have laughed. I'm sorry."

"It's okay. My leaving is appropriate. And I should've expected it. The chant included the line *those who would harm Lichen citizens are gone*. I have harmed people here. I need to make amends for that. And Lichen doesn't need me here while it gets its fresh start."

"The idea that you've been part of the problem makes me sad, but I'm glad you want to fix that."

Virgil nodded. "I thought about moving to Alpine, but there're good reasons to come back here. I just met Marshall and Emma, and I want to get to know them better. I want to come back."

"I don't blame you. For the first time you have people who understand a part of you that's always been secret and that you thought was unique to your family." Sylvia leaned over and kissed Virgil. "Besides, if your motif is successful, Lichen's going to be a great place to live."

"That, too." Virgil grinned. "I know that going with me to Alpine is a lot to ask, since we haven't been together very long. But please say yes. If it doesn't work out for you, I swear that we'll come back here. Or I'll send you back alone if that's what you want."

Sylvia didn't move for several minutes. She alternated between watching Virgil's face and staring over his shoulder into space.

"I've always loved West Texas." She eased onto his lap. "Yes. I'll go with you."

"You just made me a very happy man." He kissed her.

Sylvia stroked his cheek. "I'm not sure how Iggy and Donna will take it, but I'm a big girl. When do you want to leave?"

"As soon as Mama's ashes arrive. Maybe a week. I can close my house up for a few months without any concerns. I don't want to think about the chancel right now. And you can install the new landscape when we get back."

"What about the smoke and water damage? Your house might be ruined by the time we get back."

"I'll remove the few valuables I own, then give keys to a remediation company. By the time we return, the house'll be good as new. Marshall can check on it, to be sure the company is actually working on it."

"Is the motif why you're so eager to leave? Any other reason?"

Virgil shook his head. "I'm tired of who I've become, but it's probably a lot of the motif's doing, too."

"We have a whole new life ahead of us. I guess Alpine's as good a place as any to start."

"I'm glad you feel that way. I need to clear up my own life, and my childhood home feels like the right place to do it. There's too much darkness and damage here for me right now."

"I get it." Sylvia kissed Virgil's cheek. "It's definitely been a whirlwind month. For both of us."

"I might even discover I have relatives I never knew, or forgot about in the last forty years. Maybe my aunt is still alive. She was younger than my mother. And who knows, maybe somewhere deep in my family tree, Emma, Marshall, and I have a common ancestor. I like to think we're distant cousins or something."

"That'd be pretty cool." Sylvia smiled. "When we come back, we won't just be returning to Lichen. You could be returning to a whole new family. You can do motifs together. Lichen could end up the most perfect place on the planet to live."

Virgil blanched. "Right now I don't know if I'll ever do another motif. I don't like how my last few turned out. I don't like why I did them."

"Never say never." Sylvia stroked Virgil's hair. "I get why you want to take a break. It's probably a good idea for a lot of reasons. But it's part of who you are. I can't see you never doing one again."

"Maybe." Virgil shrugged. "But I don't want to be Virgilante anymore. I'd like to be just plain Virgil, local wood-worker, regular ol' guy, at least for a while."

"Well, I love you Just Plain Virgil." Sylvia stood and held out her hand. "Come on. Let's start celebrating that new life."

"New life." Virgil grinned as he followed her down the hall. "Can't wait."

The End

www.ingramcontent.com/pod-product-compliance
Lightning Source LLC
Chambersburg PA
CBHW020230180626
46810CB00006B/2120